Aether

Hearts of Heroes 3

Also by Molly J. Bragg

Mail Order Bride

Blood of the Basilisk

Hearts of Heroes

Scatter

Transistor

The War of Souls

The Master of Puppets

Aether

Hearts of Heroes 3

Molly J. Bragg

Aether
(Heart of Heroes – Book 3)

By Molly J. Bragg

ISBN (book) 9781954213692
ISBN (epub) 9781954213708

Desert Palm Press
1961 Main Street, Suite 220
Watsonville, California 95076
www.desertpalmpress.com

Editor: Kaycee Hawn
Cover Design: Jeanette Eileen Widjaja

Printed in the United States of America
First Edition June 2023

Acknowledgements

I would like to acknowledge Beck Use and Kelly Fitzsimons. Without them, this book might never have gotten finished. I'd also like to thank my wonderful editor Kaycee Hawn for not only editing with a light hand, but having a turn around time that boggles the mind, and Lee Fitzsimmons for giving me a chance to share my work with the world.

Chapter One

MAGGIE LEANED HEAVILY ON her cane as she limped into the third-floor break room at One Park Place. Every step sent pain shooting through her hip, and resentment boiled up inside her as she looked around the dingy little room. She didn't want to be there, but the change in pressure as a huge storm moved up the coast was making her bones ache everywhere they'd ever been broken. That meant that her entire right side from just below her breast to halfway down her leg felt like it was being squeezed in a vice, and every step she took felt like she had ground glass where her hip joint should be.

She'd considered taking something for the pain. Despite the rampant paranoia most doctors had developed in recent years regarding opioids, her doctor was rather generous in prescribing them for her. Not that she ever took them. During the week, she didn't take them because Nth dimensional vector spaces and mind-altering substances didn't really go together, and she had work to do. On the weekends, she didn't take them because pot brownies from the local dispensary got rid of the pain without making her worry about turning into an addict.

She lowered herself into one of the folding chairs at the table and breathed a sigh of relief as the pain dropped to an almost tolerable level. She hooked her cane on the edge of the table so it stayed within easy reach and looked around the little space that was decorated in a particularly sad flavor of 1970s ugly. The linoleum floor was yellow with age and peeling in the corners. The refrigerator was a bit newer, but it was still a relic from the Reagan administration. The folding chairs and table pre-dated Nixon's resignation. The microwave might have been a bit newer, but the only thing remotely modern in the room was the off-brand k-cup coffee maker that sat side by side with a Mr. Coffee that was old enough to qualify for a senior citizen's discount. The worst part was the poster of Red Coat, which Maggie had always assumed had been put up before he and the rest of the Sun City Sentries had died stopping the Gacrux invasion eleven years earlier.

Maggie had a love-hate relationship with the grubby little space. She hated it because she only ever set foot in it when her hip chose to remind her of just how disabled that same invasion had left her—not that the cane or the burn scars ever really let her forget. The love part was complicated, to say the least.

"Hey," the complicated part said as she walked into the room carrying a bag from Rosa's and a tray with two large drinks. Maggie, despite the pain and the resentment bubbling inside her, couldn't stop herself from smiling. Sierra always made her smile. The two of them had started grad school at the same time, and Sierra had taken one look at the sad, shy, lonely girl hobbling into the physics department's grad student lounge, leaning on a cane, hair draped so it covered half her face, with a perpetual scowl, and decided they were going to be friends, whether Maggie liked it or not.

Maggie had been prepared to ignore Sierra until she went away, but there had been a huge flaw in that plan. Sierra was Sierra. Beautiful, kind, funny, smarter than most of the professors in the department put together. Maggie had lasted all of a month before she committed the cardinal sin of gay girls everywhere and fell head over heels in love with her straight best friend.

"My knight in shining armor," Maggie said.

Sierra snorted as she set the drink tray on the table. "More like your post-doc in Old Navy," she said as she reached into the bag and started taking out food. She set a foil wrapped sub and a Styrofoam container full of chili cheese fries in front of Maggie, then handed her one of the drinks.

"You say 6,562.8 Angstroms, I say 656.28 nanometers..." Maggie said as she started unwrapping the cheesesteak she'd been daydreaming about all morning. Her mouth was watering just from the smell.

"Did they get your sandwich right?" Sierra asked as she opened a Styrofoam container with a big slab of Rosa's vegetable alfredo lasagna in it.

"Yeah," Maggie said.

"I brought extra peppers, just in case."

"Gimmie!" Maggie said as she reached over to snatch the bag. Sierra laughed and shook her head.

"Think I could get my garlic bread?"

"I don't know," Maggie said. "What's it worth to you?"

"Wanna off-tank the Soul Archive tomorrow night?"

Maggie nearly fell out of her chair. She looked up at Sierra, trying to gauge if the offer was genuine. She'd been begging for a chance to fill one of the tank slots in their weekly raid for months, and Sierra had kept putting her off.

"Seriously?" she asked.

"Yeah," Sierra said. "Your gear's good enough, and you've been doing a great job main-tanking the Sky Palace alt runs."

"What about Garrett?" Maggie asked. Not because she particularly cared about what happened to the man who had been the bane of her existence for the last six years, but because she didn't want to get her hopes up again taking the slot she wanted in the raid if it was just going to get yanked out from under her at the last minute.

"I benched him," Sierra said as she picked up her fork and attacked her lasagna.

"Ouch," Maggie said. "I'm betting he didn't like that."

"No," Sierra said. "There may have been some yelling."

Maggie bit her tongue, trying not to ask why Sierra put up with Garrett in the first place. It was an old struggle. She thought Garrett was a piece of shit, both as a boyfriend and as a human being in general. She'd hated him from the day she'd met him. She'd also gone out of her way to be completely neutral when it came to Sierra and Garrett because she did not want to be blamed for the breakup she considered inevitable. Even if she was planning on throwing a party when it happened.

She fished the foil-wrapped garlic bread out of the bag and passed it over to Sierra, then took out the two small tubs of sliced pepperoncini and dumped them on top of her sub.

"So, I need to ask you a favor," Sierra said. Maggie looked up from her sandwich, suspecting she was about to find out what price she was going to be asked to pay in order to get better video game privileges.

"You need a favor from me?" Maggie asked.

"Yeah," Sierra said, and Maggie could tell from the slightly nervous look on Sierra's face that it was going to be a big one. "You know membership on the Safety and Ethics Committee rotates on Monday, right?"

"I do," Maggie said, wondering what that had to do with either of them.

"They announced the committee roster this morning."

Maggie leaned back in her chair, knowing from Sierra's tone exactly what this had to do with them, and exactly where the conversation was headed.

"Hastings got the physics seat, didn't he?"

"Got it in one," Sierra said.

"Shit. I'm sorry," Maggie said, knowing exactly how much of a disaster the news was for Sierra. Sierra's research into quantum field modeling and imaging was brilliant. Way above the level of work a lot of full professors were doing, much less other second year post docs. Hastings' work on quantum teleportation was good stuff, but nothing particularly original. There were other research teams doing a lot of similar work. Which was why this was a disaster for Sierra. She and Hastings were competing for the same grant, and it was a foregone conclusion that Sierra was going to get it, *if* she could get approval for human trials from the Safety and Ethics Committee.

Approval she'd gotten earlier in the week. That should have been the end of it, but it was standard practice for the incoming committee to review all ongoing projects and reaffirm all clearances. Normally, that was just a formality, but Hastings had been making noises for months, pretty much since the day he found out that Sierra had applied for the same grant as him, that her work was still experimental, and that it was far too early to begin human trials of her quantum field imager.

"How can I help?" Maggie asked.

"Well," Sierra said. "The issue is safety, right?"

"Right..."

"So, it will be a lot harder for that asshat to claim that the quantum field imager is unsafe if I have the results of a human test subject in hand," Sierra said.

Maggie nodded. "Okay. That makes sense, but where do I...Oh. Oh, no. Sierra—"

"Come on!" Sierra said, giving a little huff and a foot stomp that made her sound like an eight-year-old who'd just been told she'd have to finish her homework before she could destroy her nine-year-old brother at Mario Kart.

"You seriously want to put me in your little quantum toaster?"

"It's not a toaster! It's perfectly safe."

"Says you."

"Please? Come on, Mags. I don't have time to find anyone else," she pleaded, complete with what Maggie always thought of as the 'dreaded Sierra Gomez puppy dog eyes.' Maggie didn't think the devil himself could resist those eyes. In fact, she was sure if Sierra added the little lip quiver, Hades himself would throw open the gates of the underworld for her.

"Fine," Maggie said. "When do you want to run the test?"

"Tomorrow," she said. "No one else will be here, so there's no chance of Hastings hearing about it and shutting us down." She smiled at Maggie as she said it, and any trace of reluctance Maggie felt disappeared. Maggie honestly wasn't sure why she even tried to fight. She knew it was a bad choice, but she never made good choices when Sierra was involved.

* * * *

"She's not going to fuck you, you know."

Maggie jumped a little in shock at the unexpected sound of Garrett's voice. The move sent pain shooting through her hip, and she looked up from her computer to see him standing in the door of the closet she called an office, glaring at her.

"What?" she asked, trying to get her head around what he just said.

"Sierra," Garrett said. "She's not going to fuck you." The anger in his voice sent a chill down Maggie's spine. She turned her chair so she was facing him. As she did, she wrapped her hand around the heavy steel shaft of her cane.

"What are you talking about?" Maggie asked, not really needing an answer. There was only one person he could be talking about, because there was only one place where their circle of friends overlapped. She didn't know what brought this on.

Garrett took two steps into her office, and Maggie tightened her grip on her cane. She swallowed her pride and pushed back a bit from her desk. As much as she wanted to pretend like he didn't scare her, the truth was, she'd always thought he was a little scary, and she'd never wanted to be anywhere near him if she could help it. It didn't hurt that having the extra room gave her more space if she needed to use her cane. She wasn't under any sort of delusion that she could win a fight if he actually attacked her, but there were plenty of other offices close by. If she screamed for help, it would come, and a couple of good, solid whacks with the cane might keep him from hurting her too badly before it arrived.

"You think I don't know that this was your idea?"

"I have no idea what you're talking about," Maggie said.

"Bullshit!" Garrett said. "Sierra and I've been together for six years. Girls don't just dump you after that long."

"Sierra dumped you?" Maggie asked, fear suddenly replaced by shock. Sierra hadn't said anything about dumping Garrett at lunch.

"Right," Garrett said. "Like you didn't know."

"Honestly, I didn't."

Garrett snorted and took two more steps forward. He put his hands on her desk and leaned over it.

"She's never going to fuck you," Garrett said. "You think I'm stupid, that I don't know about your little dyke crush on her, but I do. It's pathetic. You're just embarrassing yourself. You're nothing but a charity case. A fucking diversity hire. A hideous, crippled freak. People get sick just looking at your face. And when Sierra realizes the only thing you care about is getting in her pants, she's going to drop you and come running back to me."

For a moment, Maggie's tiny little office was dead silent as she stared at Garrett in shock. Not shock at what he thought about her, but shock that he'd said it out loud. It felt like he'd broken some unspoken rule they'd agreed to, where they both just quietly hated each other but never actually said all the horrible things they thought about each other.

It took longer than Maggie would have liked for it to completely sink in, but when it did, anger replaced shock and fear both as Maggie's temper flared, and she got a reminder of all the reasons she worked so hard to keep her temper in check. As the anger flowed through her, it shut down the part of her brain responsible for thinking and the part responsible for good judgment and the part responsible for self-preservation. She stopped caring that Garrett was built like a linebacker, that he had a good eighty pounds on her, and that half her body was held together with titanium screws and hope rather than solid, reliable bone.

She slid her hand up, grabbed the handle of her cane, and drove the cane down onto the floor of her office. The small click as the top part of the cane caught against the spring-loaded pin that locked the telescoping foot in place sounded a bit like a sword being drawn as Maggie used the cane to force her way up to her feet. The pain shooting through her hip was bad enough that at any other moment, it probably would have dropped her, but between the anger and the adrenaline, she barely noticed it. She leaned forward, getting right in Garrett's face.

"In the six years you and Sierra have been dating, I have never spoken a word against you," Maggie said. "Not once. Not when you acted like an asshole. Not when she had to apologize to a member of the guild because you were a giant dickwad to them in game. Not when you threw a hissy fit because she finished her degree while you were stuck trying to find a new advisor who would put up with your shit. Not even when Sierra was sitting on my couch, bitching up a storm about all the different ways you were a shitty boyfriend.

"If she dumped you, it didn't have a damn thing to do with me. It was entirely because you are a whiney, pathetic, self-righteous, entitled piece of shit with overblown delusions of adequacy."

He was going to hit her. Maggie could see it in his eyes. He hadn't quite made the decision yet, but she could see him psyching himself up for it. She could almost see all the excuses running through his head. She was so focused on him that she almost missed Jamal stepping into the room.

"Is there a problem here?" Jamal asked.

Garrett turned around, ready for a fight right up until he realized who was standing there. Jamal was a thin, wiry man who was a good four inches shorter and probably fifty pounds lighter than Garrett. He had also spent twelve years as a marine before going back to school to get his PhD. Garrett just sort of withered as Jamal stared at him. Something that left Maggie feeling torn. On the one hand, she knew it was for the best. On the other hand, she really, really wanted to see Garrett get the ass kicking he had coming his whole life.

"No problem. I was just leaving." Garrett headed out the door

Jamal moved, letting him pass. Jamal waited a minute before turning to Maggie. "You okay?"

"Yeah," Maggie said. She sat back down as the pain started to hit her. She took a deep breath and looked at Jamal. "How much of that did you hear?"

"Enough," Jamal said. "You want me to go get Doctor Miller so you can file a complaint?"

"No," Maggie said.

"You sure?" Jamal asked.

"Yeah," Maggie said.

"You know, you let him get away with shit like that, sooner or later, he's going to hurt someone."

"Maybe," Maggie said. "But I...don't want to get mixed up in the middle of that."

Jamal rolled his eyes.

"Sierra's my friend," Maggie said.

"If she were your friend, she wouldn't ask you to put up with Garrett's bullshit," he said. "You deserve better than that. You should choose to do what's best for yourself once in a while."

"It's not that easy," Maggie said.

"Sure it is," Jamal said. "He threatens you, and instead of worrying about what Sierra will think, you choose to protect yourself, and file a complaint with Doctor Miller."

"I said no."

"Fine." Jamal sighed. "But if you change your mind, you know where to find me."

"I do," Maggie said.

* * * *

Maggie stared out the passenger's side window of Sierra's minivan as they drove down the interstate. Normally, she would have just walked to the monorail station, but with her hip acting up, she'd accepted Sierra's offer to drive her home. Sierra offered every night, but Maggie normally turned her down. There were a lot of reasons for that. One was her enormous crush on Sierra, which probably would have been enough on its own, but there was also her fear of cars. On her best day, she hated them. With the pain in her hip reminding her of how her parents and her brother died, and the confrontation with Garrett still bouncing around in her head, she was having a hard time not feeling like she should have stuck to her routine, even with the pain.

"Are you okay?" Sierra asked as she moved them into the exit lane that led to Maggie's neighborhood.

"Rough day," Maggie said.

"Aww...Hard time figuring out how to violate the fundamental laws of physics?" Sierra asked. It was hardly a new question, and normally, it would have provoked a cheerful argument over whether the project Maggie was working on violated the law of conservation of momentum or not, but in that moment, the humor was lost on Maggie.

"Did you break up with Garrett?" she asked, looking over at Sierra. The smile on Sierra's face faded as she glanced over at Maggie before looking back at the road.

"How'd you guess?" Sierra asked.

"He came into my office," Maggie said.

"He what?" Sierra asked, and Maggie could hear the anger in her voice.

"He thinks I talked you into dumping his ass."

"Jesus fucking Christ," Sierra said. "I'm sorry. If I'd known he was going to pull something like that, I would have brought my laptop up to your office and worked there all day."

Maggie made a noncommittal noise and went back to staring out the window.

"I should have warned you," Sierra said.

"Is that why you're letting me take the off-tank slot in Soul

Archive?" Maggie asked.

"No," Sierra said. "More like me letting you take the slot is why I finally dumped his ass."

Maggie turned to look at Sierra. "What?"

"I told him I was going to let you have the off-tank slot this week, and he pitched a fit. He said the slot belonged to him because he'd been doing it for six months. When I told him that was why it was time to give someone else a shot, he just started pouting like a baby the way he always does when he doesn't get his way, and I don't know...I just realized that I'd been putting off a lot of shit because I didn't want to deal with his reaction. I sat there, watching him going on this rant about something, I don't even know what it was, and all I could think was that I'd spent the last few years planning my life around what I needed to do to avoid one of his tantrums, and I was tired of it. I was sick to death of missing out on shit I want because my boyfriend is a whiny little manbaby. So I told him to take his shit, get out, and to not come back."

"Really?"

"Really," Sierra said.

"How did he take it?"

"About as well as you'd expect," Sierra said. "I had to write my landlord a check this morning to pay for patching a hole in the wall and putting a new lock on the door."

"Fuck," Maggie said. "I'm sorry."

"It's my fault," Sierra said. "I should have dumped his ass years ago."

Maggie bit her tongue to keep herself from agreeing. She really, really wanted to, but there was a tiny little voice in the back of her head reminding her of all the times in the past when she'd gotten her hopes up because Sierra and Garrett had a fight. She hoped this was different, but she'd give it some time before she ended her policy of not trashing Garrett in front of Sierra. But try as she might, there was one thing she couldn't keep to herself, because not knowing, one way or the other, had been driving her crazy.

"Did you tell Garrett about what happened at the hospital?" Maggie asked.

"What?" Sierra asked, sounding genuinely horrified at the thought. "No, of course not."

"He seemed pretty convinced that I talked you into dumping him because I've got a crush on you."

"He must have figured that out on his own," Sierra said. "I swear, I never said a word. Not to anyone."

"Okay," Maggie said, relief flooding through her. She hadn't realized how much the thought that Sierra had told Garrett about her drug-addled confession had bothered her. The whole thing was more than a little humiliating. She'd broken her hip again, and Sierra was there when she'd woken up from surgery. Not unusual in and of itself. Sierra took Maggie to all her doctor's appointments and had been there for every surgery Maggie had over the six years they'd known each other.

What had been unusual was that somewhere around the time the nurse hung the third or fourth bag of Dilaudid, Maggie had decided to confess her undying love to Sierra. She still wasn't sure why she thought it was a good idea. Maybe a mixture of being high as a kite, and the fact that it was the first surgery she'd had since the invasion where her grandparents weren't there for her recovery.

Whatever made her do it, the whole thing had been humiliating once she'd sobered up. Maggie wasn't sure which part was worse. Having to sit through Sierra's painfully earnest explanation that she was heterosexual or having to deal with her own embarrassment over the fact that she'd recited Emily Dickenson to a straight girl. Maggie had tried to play the whole thing off as just the drugs talking, but Sierra had seen through that right away. She'd sworn that she would never tell a soul, and then she'd proceeded to refuse to let Maggie hide from her, which was probably the only reason their friendship survived.

The thought that Sierra might have broken her promise and told Garrett had been eating at her all day. She hadn't wanted to believe it was true, but she had spent the last six years convinced Garrett didn't know she had feelings for Sierra. The fact that he threw her feelings in her face meant she'd either misjudged how perceptive Garrett was, or that Sierra had told him.

Now that she knew Sierra hadn't broken her promise, Maggie felt a little better about the whole thing, even if the confrontation in her office was a bit scary.

"I'm sorry he accused you of that," Sierra said.

"Don't worry about it. It's not a big deal."

"It is," Sierra said. "It was a shitty thing for him to do."

Maggie shrugged, regretting having brought the subject up at all, and they spent the last few minutes of the trip in silence. When they reached Maggie's house, Sierra pulled into the driveway and put the van in park.

"You want me to come in and help you get changed?" Sierra asked.

Maggie looked out of the windshield of the van and stared at her house as she thought about it. She knew that getting ready for bed when she was hurting like this would be a foretaste of hell. It was bad enough on a regular day. Most of her outfits consisted of stretch waist skirts, button up shirts, and slip-on shoes. Things that let her avoid bending down to get dressed or undressed. In the shape she was in, lifting her arms over her head was a no go, which meant she was either going to leave her clothes in a pile on the floor and sleep in a bathrobe, or reduce herself to tears trying to put on a nightgown.

It would hardly be the first time Sierra had seen her undressed. Maggie had had surgery three times in the last six years, and all three times, Sierra had stayed with her while she recovered. She'd helped Maggie change, helped her get to and from the bathroom, even helped her shower. It shouldn't have been a big deal, just a friend helping a friend, but Garrett's words were still ringing in her ears, calling her a charity case and a hideous freak. Words that would have been a whole lot easier to shrug off if she didn't believe them herself. If that wasn't exactly what she saw every time she looked in the mirror.

"I've got it," Maggie said as she opened the door. It was the wrong choice, but it was the only one her pride would let her make.

"Are you sure?" Sierra asked. Maggie could hear the worry in her voice, and it was almost enough to change her mind, but then she heard Garrett saying, 'She's never going to fuck you,' and it was too much to deal with.

"I'm fine," Maggie said. She swung her legs out of the van and hopped out, ignoring the jolt of pain that shot through her hip. She grabbed her purse and slung it over her shoulder, then grabbed her cane.

"If you're sure," Sierra said.

Maggie looked at Sierra and forced herself to smile. "See you in the morning."

"Okay."

Maggie closed the van door and hobbled to the front door of her apartment. She punched the security code into her door's keypad and opened the door. Once she was inside, she gave the deadbolt a quick twist to lock it, then headed for the kitchen. She grabbed one of the beers she wasn't supposed to drink out of the refrigerator, then headed into her bedroom. She hooked the end of her cane on her desk, kicked off the clogs she was wearing, then pushed her peasant skirt down past her hips and let it fall to the floor before unbuttoning her shirt and letting it drop on top of the skirt.

She sat down at her desk in nothing but a pair of panties and reached for the thousand count bottle of ibuprofen that lived next to her monitor. She popped two of the little orange pills into her mouth and chased it with a swig of beer. Something her doctors assured her was tantamount to suicide, as if that wasn't encouragement to do it more often. She considered going back to the kitchen and getting one of the brownies from the dispensary but decided against it since she had Sierra's experiment in the morning.

She logged into her desktop and spent a good five minutes staring at the Black Sky icon. She considered logging into the game. She knew she should. If she was off-tanking the guild's raid the following night, she should spend a bit of time farming just to make sure she had all the consumables she would need. Maybe tank a couple of dungeons, just to get into the groove. Instead, after five minutes of staring at the icon, she admitted she wasn't feeling it.

She looked down at herself. At the burns that covered the right side of her body. The melted wax look of the skin covering her right arm and leg. The breast that was more silicone implant than living tissue because the original had been so badly burned. She looked and she wondered if Red Coat had really done her a favor when he'd ripped the door off her parents' car and pulled her out of the fire.

She knew her mood was spiraling, but she honestly wished Red Coat had just minded his own fucking business. That he'd just gone and fought the aliens that day instead of trying to save someone who was already past saving.

She took another swallow of her beer and tried to remind herself of all the reasons that wasn't true. She had a great job, she had a wonderful best friend, she had even, the year before, managed to have a girlfriend for a little while. The reminders usually helped, but they weren't working that night. Probably because she was already too far down the spiral.

She took another pull off her beer and reached for something she knew would work. Instead of clicking on the Black Sky icon, she clicked on the one for Digilife, and logged in.

Black Sky was a massive multiplayer online roleplaying game. It had a shared game world full of enemies to kill, dungeons to run, raids, player versus player battlegrounds, and all the usual bells and whistles. It wasn't the most popular one out there, but she and Sierra both preferred the sci-fi theme to the fantasy theme of the larger games. Maggie had spent more hours in Black Sky than she cared to admit, and she loved it, but it wasn't what she needed that night.

Digilife was about as different as you could get from Black Sky. It was a third-generation virtual world. There were games inside the world, but there were also entire cities with parks, schools, office buildings, houses, sewers, warehouses, docks, bars, night clubs, strip clubs, red light districts, hotels, and brothels. There were kingdoms with keeps, castles, towers, labyrinths, caves, dragons' lairs, and fairy groves. There were space stations and star ships and submarines. Anything anyone could dream up; they could build and upload to the grid.

Maggie loved it because it let her escape. When she logged in, she wasn't Maggie anymore. She was Bobbie, and Bobbie was everything Maggie wanted to be but wasn't. Bobbie was confident, bold, and beautiful. She wore leather pants and flannel shirts and strutted around in biker boots. She wore evening gowns and high heels, cocktail dresses, and three-piece suits. She rode horses and motorcycles and flew star fighters and took pretty girls back to her house without having a panic attack when they started unbuttoning her shirt.

It took about two minutes for her Digilife client to finish connecting to the grid, and Bobbie to show up on screen in all her tanned, purple-haired glory, and Maggie could feel her mood picking up the whole time. She didn't even have time to check her contact list to see who was online before a message popped up from Kelly, who, despite not knowing Maggie's real name, was probably her closest friend in the world besides Sierra.

Maggie smiled and started typing.

Chapter Two

SIERRA TEXTED MAGGIE EARLY, letting her know that she was buying breakfast. Maggie knew Sierra well enough to know it was an attempt to make up for the guilt she felt for asking Maggie to be her guinea pig. She also had no qualms about using Sierra's guilt to her advantage, and insisted they go to Rampaging Burrito. Sierra made grumbling noises, but Maggie just smiled and insisted that if she was letting Sierra cook her brains with her quantum field imager, it was only fair that Maggie get to pick her last meal. A full pound of eggs, chorizo, hash browns, cheese, pico de gallo, sour cream, guacamole, black olives, and hot sauce later, Maggie told Sierra that if Sierra did cook her brains, then at least she would be in the midst of a blissful food coma.

Maggie's teasing mood lasted until they reached the Science Annex. The building was a block from One Park Place and housed most of Sun City University's on-campus research science labs. That would change once the new Unified Science Research Complex was finished, but until that happened, all the physicists who were doing applied science rather than just theoretical research worked in the 'basement.' Maggie didn't have a lab there because most of the practical side of her work took place at the Alternative Propulsion Lab up the road at Kennedy Space Center, or across the country at the JPL in Pasadena.

Maggie and Sierra held their breath as they walked past the semiconductor lab, because the place always smelled strongly of burning cinderblock and latex wall paint. One of the grad students had left a CO2 laser on over the weekend a couple of years earlier, and for reasons no one understood, the stench had never gone away.

Once they were past the semiconductor lab, they were in what Maggie thought of as the labyrinth. The Science Annex 'basement' was huge; the building took up nearly half a city block, and it wasn't really a basement. Buildings in Florida didn't have basements as a rule, because the high-water table tended to turn them into indoor swimming pools, but the 'basement' was sunk four feet into the ground, and you entered the building on the floor above, so the nickname had stuck.

Maggie hated the place. It housed nearly two dozen labs doing all sorts of research, but the corridors were all identical white cinderblock walls, dingy white linoleum floors, and completely unmarked. The only way to figure out where you were was to check the numbers on the doors, and if you hadn't memorized the numbering scheme, that didn't help much. Her first time down in the basement, she had gotten lost for twenty minutes and had a panic attack.

Sierra's lab was all the way in the back, next to the machine shop where a lot of the physics and astronomy department's custom equipment was made. It was also right next to Doctor Hastings' lab. The placement, while ironic, wasn't by accident. The machine shop and the five labs along the back wall were all on separate circuits from the rest of the building. The labs were designated as high-power requirement labs, and numbered HPRL 1 through 5.

HPRL 5 was the radiology lab where they kept the various x-ray machines and the CT scanner. Lab HPRL 4 held the Nuclear Magnetic Resonance Imager, or MRI machine. Doctor Chow, the head of the high-energy physics team, was the current occupant of HPRL 3. He had an honest-to-God fusion reactor in the lab. It was a net loss reactor, but Maggie still geeked out over it every time she ventured down into the basement. Doctor Hastings' quantum teleportation rig was in HPRL 2, which always confused Maggie a bit. Quantum teleportation wasn't really her area, but from what she knew, it wasn't particularly power intensive. On the occasions when she gave it any thought, mostly when Sierra was bitching about Hastings trying to get her project shut down, Maggie just assumed Hastings wanted an HPRL lab out of vanity, rather than actual need.

Sierra, being the most junior researcher to be assigned to one of the coveted HPRL labs, got HPRL 1, which was tucked in right next to the machine shop. Most people would have resented that. It was a bit like being assigned a broom closet. Sierra, on the other hand, loved it. She said it made it easier to get her custom parts from the machine shop to her lab. Maggie knew that had more to do with the fact that the guy who ran the machine shop had a sweet tooth and Sierra baked a mean chocolate chip cookie than the lab's proximity, but she never corrected Sierra on the topic.

Sierra swiped her badge, then keyed in her personal access code. The light on the lock turned green, and she opened the door and led the way into the lab. Maggie stopped just inside the door, looking at the device she'd spent the whole morning calling 'The Quantum Brain Toaster.' It sat off center in the room, which had been subdivided by a lead-lined steel wall between the machine itself and the operator's station. Sierra insisted the wall wasn't necessary, but her graduate advisor had been worried about stray x-ray emissions, considering the power levels involved. Safety and Ethics had refused to let her turn the imager on for the first time unless the wall was in place, and once it was there, it was easier and cheaper to leave it than remove it.

"Welcome to my lab-or-atory," Sierra said in a really bad fake accent, which made Maggie laugh as she stared at the imager. It had taken Sierra nearly a year to build it after she'd gotten the initial grant, and she'd been running it for two years. First as part of her dissertation research, then as part of her post-doc work. In that time, she'd imaged rats, cats, dogs, and even a monkey. The theory was a bit out of Maggie's wheelhouse, but she understood enough of it to know that it was an incredible piece of technology and had the potential to be one of the most valuable scientific instruments ever invented.

Maggie jumped slightly when Sierra touched her shoulder. She turned to look at Sierra and gave her a smile.

"Sorry. Little nervous, I guess."

"It's safe, Mags. I promise. No way I'd put you in there if I had even the slightest doubt."

Maggie nodded. "I know. It just reminds me of going for x-rays on my hip."

Sierra slid her hand down to the small of Maggie's back and curled her fingers in, scratching Maggie's back through her shirt. Maggie closed her eyes and did her best not to embarrass herself by purring. The gesture was oddly comforting, and Maggie always wondered where Sierra had picked it up. She never asked, because she was afraid if she did, Sierra would think she didn't like it and would stop doing it, which was the last thing Maggie wanted. She didn't get nearly as much physical contact as she wanted, mostly because she shied away from contact with other people as much as she could, but that was because of her insecurities over her burn and surgical scars, not because she didn't miss the contact, and not because she didn't enjoy the contact when she did get it.

"Come on," Sierra said. "We'll get an hour of footage, and then we can go see a movie."

"Okay," Maggie said. "As long as there are no superheroes in it."

"I promise," Sierra said, grinning as she stepped over to the imager. She held out her hand and Maggie took it, letting Sierra help her up onto the bed of the imager. Once Maggie was laying down on the bed, Sierra helped her get into the right position. She took a minute to make sure Maggie's skirt was arranged for maximum modesty. No burn scars showing below the hem line.

The simple gesture brought a smile to Maggie's face. One that stayed there as Sierra took her hand and just held it for a minute. Sierra didn't say anything, but Maggie understood what she was doing. Checking in to make sure Maggie was still okay with what was happening. Maggie gave her a small nod and let go of her hand. Sierra replied by giving a small salute, and headed around behind the steel wall, taking Maggie's cane and purse with her so they'd be out of the way.

A couple of minutes later, the room filled with a loud whirring sound, like a cooling fan in overdrive. Maggie had seen the imager in action enough to know it was the stirrers in the liquid helium tanks that fed the cooling system. The whirring went on for a couple of minutes before it stopped, only to be replaced by the low thumping of the pumps that pushed the liquid helium through the system.

"It will take about ten minutes for the superconductors to reach operating temperature," Sierra said.

"So, I might die of boredom before this cooks my brain," Maggie said. "Good to know."

Sierra giggled as Maggie watched her through the leaded glass window in the partition. She did something on the control terminal, and a moment later, Norah Jones' voice filled the room. Maggie immediately closed her eyes and let herself be carried away by the low, sultry voice. Norah managed to get through Be Here to Love Me, You've Ruined Me, and Light as a Feather, and was just starting a duet with Willy Nelson when Sierra spoke again.

"I'm starting the entanglement scan. Try to stay as still as possible for the next five minutes."

"'Kay," Maggie said. She closed her eyes and took a couple of deep breaths to center herself, trying to focus on Norah and Willie's voices as the imager came to life. The actual scanners in the imager started moving, sounding a lot like the scan heads of a photocopier. It took Maggie a bit of effort not to laugh at that thought, but by the time Norah and Willie were done, and Norah had followed the duet with a live version of Don't Know Why, the scan was finished.

"You can look now," Sierra said.

Maggie opened her eyes and there, floating about a foot above her face, was a perfect image of her brain painted in rainbow colors. The colors shifted and danced as Maggie watched, rippling and flowing around each other. She'd never seen the imager do anything like this before.

"What am I seeing?" Maggie asked.

"Your soul," Sierra said. "Or at least, a chromatic intensity map of the quantum field generated by your brain's neuroelectric activity. I mapped seven hundred nanometers to 'alive, but inactive' and four hundred nanometers to 'your hormones when you look at a picture of Kristin Stewart'."

Maggie laughed, but it wasn't as long or as intense as it would have been any other time Sierra poked fun at one of Maggie's most enduring celebrity crushes. She was too fascinated by what she was seeing to focus on anything else, and the changes to the image as she started to laugh only deepened that fascination. She was watching herself think in real time.

"Tell me you're recording this," Maggie said.

"Of course I'm recording this," Sierra said. "It's not science unless you write it down. I can't record the field itself, not without a few petabytes worth of storage to house it, but I'm getting a really good recording of the intensity map. Once we're ready for full scale testing, we'll run cognitive exercises on the subjects while we're recording the intensity map. That will let the cognition team over in neuroscience start to build models. And hopefully get us the money for the data cluster so we can start recording the field."

"Sierra," Maggie said.

"Yeah?"

"I know I've said this before, but you're going to change the world with this."

"Always the romantic," Sierra said.

Maggie didn't reply because she knew Sierra was right. She was a romantic. She was watching one of the most amazing scientific breakthroughs of her life unfold in real time right in front of her, and all she could think was that she wanted to congratulate Sierra. And by congratulate, she meant she wanted to kiss Sierra silly. She wanted to make a grand gesture of it, complete with the dip her damaged bones would never let her do.

She turned her head to look at Sierra. Sierra smiled at her, and Maggie smiled back, and that was how Maggie died. Looking at her best friend, grinning like an idiot, and dreaming of kissing her.

Chapter Three

THERE ARE THINGS IN every person's life that they will never forget. Maggie was firmly of the opinion that dying should not be one of them. It wasn't an uninformed opinion, given that she'd died twice, and remembered both times perfectly.

The first time, an alien railgun projectile slammed into her family's car. Her parents had been vaporized, and what was left of the car had been knocked thirty feet sideways by the force of the impact and slammed into the side of a building.

Her brother had been sitting in the passenger's side back seat and was crushed by the impact with the building. Maggie's pelvis and right hip were shattered, her femur was broken in three places, along with her shin, her back, and multiple ribs. She'd broken a total of forty-three bones on impact and punctured her right lung in two places. Then the car caught fire.

Red Coat, a British expat who was a tier three metahuman, member of the Olympus Six, and the leader of the Sun City Sentries, had heard her screams as the fire melted her skin. He'd torn the door off the car and carried her to the nearest ambulance, which rushed her to the hospital.

Her heart had stopped on the way. The doctors had said it was shock, and she had no reason to doubt them, but the why was never as important to her as the fact that she remembered every moment of it. The way the ribs jammed through her lung tore at her with every chest compression as the EMT gave her CPR. The feel of the tube being forced down her throat. The way the defibrillator burned when they shocked her heart back to life.

The second time she died was somehow much less traumatic. She was laying on the quantum field imager, looking at Sierra, then she was filled with pain, but it was over almost instantly. She barely had time to register what was happening. She was just left with the memory of being engulfed in searing pain, like every part of her had brushed against a hot oven rack. Time slowed down to a crawl, and she was aware of everything. She could feel the electric current moving through the quantum field imager, she could feel the displacement of air as Sierra exhaled, she could feel the motes of dust in the lab as they drifted through the room, stirred up by the cooling fans on the imager and the computers.

She could feel the moment a small lump of carbon, less than a nanogram of it, blinked into existence, then blinked back out again as the entire mass turned into energy. Energy that exploded outward, hitting the wall behind her.

It was like she was watching the whole thing in slow motion. The first break in the wall was small, a hole less than half a millimeter in diameter, but enough for fire to pour through like water through a fire hose. The entire cinderblock shattered less than a hundredth of a second later, and that hole spread as other blocks broke free of the wall and were hurled forward. The heat bloom seared the left side of her body, doing to it what the car fire eleven years earlier had done to the right side.

It was the overpressure that killed her. It picked her up and hurled her against the steel, lead, and glass partition with enough force to shatter every bone in her body. She died on impact, just like her brother had.

The imager she had been laying on survived better than anything else in the room. It was built solidly enough that the steel housing took hits from the cinderblock and just shrugged them off. The sapphire imaging windows were dirty but intact, and the cooling loop and power lines were protected by heavy steel conduit. It kept running like nothing had happened, dutifully projecting the chromatic replica of Maggie's soul into the space above where she'd been without a care in the world for the destruction that filled the rest of the lab.

The partition was built just as solidly as the imager, but not so solidly anchored to the floor. For day-to-day use, it was fine, but it had been designed to stop a few stray x-rays. Not an explosion. The anchor bolts ripped out of the concrete floor and the partition tipped and slid, crushing Maggie's body between it and the side of the imager. The ramp created by the knocked over partition drove the explosion up through the acoustic tiles and into the drop ceiling.

Sierra was knocked unconscious when the partition hit her and knocked her to the ground. Maggie watched and felt more relief than she should as dead person. Sierra might have a concussion when she woke up, but the partition had done its job. The radiation wave front had passed, and Sierra had barely gotten dosed. Nothing more than she'd get from an afternoon in Doctor Chow's lab.

Garrett, who shouldn't have been in the building on a Saturday, was next door in Doctor Hastings' lab when the explosion started. He wasn't nearly as lucky as Sierra. He had no protection from the radiation or the heat bloom or the overpressure. He took a lethal dose of hard gamma, but before that could kill him, the heat bloom burned him to ash. Then the overpressure scattered the ashes as it destroyed everything in the lab.

The explosion didn't stop there. It blew into other labs, shattering walls and puncturing storage tanks. Liquid helium and liquid nitrogen spilled and flash boiled in several labs before the blast broke through to the chemical vapor deposition lab. Methane, propane, and liquid oxygen tanks went off like bombs. Then the blast cut the natural gas supply lines that fed the chemistry and biolabs on the first and second floors. The gas in the lines sparked, carrying the explosion into the upstairs labs, setting off chain reactions even as the original explosion tore upwards through the floor.

It felt like hours passed as Maggie watched, but she knew it was less than fifteen seconds from the first flash of pain she'd felt until the entire building collapsed. Not counting her and Garrett, five people died. Two security guards who'd been sitting at their desk, talking about whether the Sun City Mantas had a chance against the Red Sox that night, the supply coordinator, who'd been prepping a load of spent chemical drums for the disposal center, and a grad student who was working in a biolab up on the second floor. The fifth person was a homeless man who was sitting under the awning by the loading dock eating lunch when the outer wall of the building came down on top of him.

Fifteen seconds for the explosion to tear through the building. Another twenty seconds for the building to finish its collapse. Maggie watched it all in silent horror, taking in details she couldn't possibly know as the whole thing played out in slow motion.

When it was finally over, she was just there, watching from outside of her body as the dust began to settle, but she didn't understand why. She could see her body crushed between the partition and the imager. She knew she was dead, and she didn't understand why she lingered. She wasn't sure where she expected to go, or even if she expected to go anywhere. She wasn't religious, wasn't sure she believed in an afterlife at all, so she didn't know if she expected heaven or hell or simply to cease to exist, but she did know she didn't expect to just float there at the spot where she'd died while time seemed to drag at a snail's pace.

It wasn't that she wanted to leave. Not while Sierra was trapped, hurt, and unconscious. She wanted to help her. She was desperate for someone to help her. She just didn't know how to get someone to help her when she was lying on the floor, dead.

She wasn't worried about Sierra's oxygen running out. The explosion had breached the machine shop and blown open the freight elevator shaft, so there was a huge path for fresh air to reach Sierra. Maggie was more worried about fire. There were still dozens of small fires burning. And there was the imager. That scared her more than the fires. By some miracle, the liquid helium tanks in the lab hadn't been punctured and the cooling loop was still working, but if someone didn't shut down the imager before the liquid helium ran out, the superconductors in the imager would hit transition temperature in a matter of minutes, and when that happened, the entire imager would explode. And there wasn't a thing Maggie could do about it.

Seconds crawled by like hours. Minutes felt like days. It was barely ten minutes from the time the explosion had started until the Sun City High Guard, the local Tier Two Metahuman Emergency Response Team, arrived, but it felt like weeks to Maggie.

Delta V was the first one there, running fast enough that most people wouldn't see anything but a blue and hot pink blur, surrounded by streaks of lightning. To Maggie, it looked like she was taking a leisurely Saturday morning jog as she ran up to the building and started circling it, checking people nearby for injuries.

The flyers arrived next. Industry in her power armor, Element riding a current of air, Hoplite on a pair of wings forged by Daedalus himself back before the Trojan War, and Nexus carried on the power of her own mind. Maker, Cinderella, and Mafic, the last three members of the field team, pulled up moments later in a flying car.

To their credit, they only hesitated long enough for Delta V to run up to them and give a report, but even that felt like hours to Maggie as she watched, though she wasn't really paying that much attention to them until she heard what Nexus said.

"Someone's alive down there. One, maybe two people. I can feel someone down there, unconscious but alive, but there's a second presence. It's strange, like there's some sort of echo. She...yeah, it's definitely a she...she's worried about the unconscious person. There's some sort of danger. Not the building collapse. Something else that's still a threat. I can't make it out clearly though. The echo is making it all a jumble."

"Where are they?" Element asked.

Nexus frowned. "Hard to say. The unconscious one is in the building, near the back left corner. The other one...I can't localize it. It feels like she's close to the unconscious one, but it feels like she's right here beside us as well."

"Astral projection, maybe?" Cinderella asked.

"We'll figure it out later," Industry said. "Right now, we've got people to dig out of this mess."

They didn't say much after that. They just went to work, and Maggie was filled with relief as she watched them. She didn't really know a lot about the High Guard. She knew some, because it was impossible to live in Sun City and not know about the High Guard. Sun City had a total of seven Metahuman Emergency Response Teams. Five of those were Champions franchise teams that dealt with small time issues like fires and traffic accidents, and Tier One threats like low level supervillains. Tier One teams were more of a superpowered neighborhood watch than anything else, and no one would have paid them much attention if it weren't for the city's superhero drama.

It was the two Tier Two teams in the city that caused all the drama. After the Sentries died fighting the Gacrux eleven years earlier, City Hall had put together a replacement team called the Sun City Protectors. They'd gotten a few heavy hitters in, led by a former captain from the Marines who had developed powers during a chemical weapons attack. Six years ago, the Department of Metahuman Affairs arrested two thirds of the Protectors membership on corruption charges. When the man the city brought in as the new leader of the Protectors following the arrests got into a very public argument with Industry over her role in reporting the corruption among the Protectors to the DMA, Industry had quit the team and formed the High Guard.

Technically, the Protectors were still the official Tier Two MERT team responsible for Sun City, but since the US Marshals and the DMA had jurisdiction over dispatch for MERT Teams in the US, the High Guard got all the important calls, even though they were independent contractors.

Maggie understood why after watching them work. They moved quickly and efficiently. Element, Nexus, Mafic, and Hoplite cleared the rubble. Maker and Delta V moved around the outside, triaging the injured and helping the paramedics once they showed up. Cinderella turned large pieces of debris into steel I beams, which Industry used to brace unstable sections of the rubble and keep more of the building from collapsing while they worked.

Anyone else would have found the whole thing fascinating, and Maggie might have too, despite her general aversion to anything superhero related, if she wasn't feeling so impatient. Sierra was still unconscious, and Maggie was still worried, and time was still running at a snail's pace for her. She split her attention between watching the High Guard and watching the liquid helium supply. The needle was moving slowly, but it was a race between how quickly the coolant would run out and how quickly the High Guard could get to Sierra.

It was a race the High Guard won. The needle had just hit a quarter tank when Nexus lifted away a section of the floor that had fallen onto the lab. Industry flew in a moment later and dropped a steel brace into place, holding the section of floor away from the collapsed wall of the lab. Once it was braced, Nexus and Delta V dropped into the hole and Delta V ran into the lab.

Maggie watched as Delta V found her body and stopped, looking back at Nexus.

"Are we too late?" Delta V asked.

"No," Nexus said. She pointed to where Sierra lay. "Other side of the wall."

Delta V zipped around the partition. She had to crawl under it, but Maggie felt relief as Delta V found Sierra. She watched as Delta V checked Sierra's pulse before she backed out and ran up to one of the ambulances to grab a backboard and a neck brace, then walked over to Element, who followed her back down to the lab. Element used her powers to lift the partition out of the way, and Industry stepped in to brace it in its new position. Once the partition was out of the way, Delta V fitted the brace around Sierra's neck, then loaded her on the backboard and eased her out from under the collapsed partition, before rushing her out of the lab and up to one of the waiting ambulances. While she was working, Nexus, Industry, and Element looked over Maggie's body.

"I guess we were too late for the second one," Element said.

"I'm not so sure," Nexus said as she approached the imager, which was still cheerfully displaying the chromatic intensity map of Maggie's neural activity. Something she didn't understand, because she was dead and didn't have any neural activity. Industry and Element both gathered around the imager as well.

"Here," Nexus said. "I feel a mind here, but it's weird. It almost feels like there are two minds, or like one mind is occupying two places at once."

"But there's no one here," Industry said. "Just the body."

Element closed her eyes for a moment. When she opened them, her eyes were glowing brightly, and Maggie felt something in the room shift. It was like Element was suddenly taking up a lot more space.

"She's right," Element said. "There's something here."

"A spirit?" Industry asked.

Delta V ran back into the room carrying a large black bag. Maggie was confused by it for a moment, until Delta V spread it out next to her body, and Maggie realized it was a body bag.

"What about a spirit?" Delta V asked as she unzipped the bag.

"No," Element said. "It's not a spirit. It's something else. It feels human. Not a ghost. I've dealt with ghosts before. This feels more vital."

Delta V stood up and looked at the imager. "Could it have something to do with this?"

"I think so," Element said. "It feels like there's a connection, somehow." She turned to Industry. "Any idea what the machine is?"

"No," Industry said as she looked at it. She started to circle around it, then she spotted the liquid helium feed lines and followed them over to the tanks. "We need to find out how to turn it off, though."

"Why?" Element asked.

"I think this is a superconductor cooling loop," Industry said. "The coolant supply is running low. If it runs out, the superconductors will heat up, and if that happens, the machine explodes."

"Can't we just cut the power?" Nexus asked.

"No!" Industry and Delta V said.

"If you cut the power, the coolant feed stops, which causes the same problem as running out of coolant. We have to find a way to discharge the superconductors first."

"There's a computer still running over there," Delta V said, pointing to where she had found Sierra. "I think it's the control system for this."

"Then the girl you took out of here was probably operating the machine," Industry said. "Has the ambulance left?"

"Let me check," Delta V said. She turned the side of her head. "Maker, has the ambulance with the girl I brought up left yet?"

"No," came the response.

"Can you see if she's awake?"

There was a couple of minutes of silence, but while they waited, Nexus used her telekinesis to lift Maggie's body into the body bag, and Delta V zipped it up.

"Not yet," Maker said over the radio. "I asked the paramedic if they could wake her, but they're worried about intracranial bleeding. They want to transport her."

"Tell them to go," Industry said. "Fractal, are you getting all of this?"

"Yes," a voice Maggie hadn't heard before responded over the radio.

"I need you here," Industry said.

"I'm already warming up the second air car," Fractal replied. "I'll be there in ten."

"Thanks," Industry said. She turned to Delta V. "Is the body ready?"

"Yeah," Delta V said. "I'm moving it now." Delta V scooped Maggie's body and disappeared in a burst of speed. Once she was gone, Industry walked over to the area that had been behind the partition and started righting tables and getting the computer and monitors back into place. Once that was done, she opened the faceplate of her power armor, revealing a beautiful Japanese woman.

Maggie watched as she started fiddling with the computer. She wanted to tell her to stop, that she was messing with Sierra's life's work, but she knew that Industry was right. They needed to shut the system down. She watched for what seemed like forever before Delta V came back, holding a black woman in a half mask and a dark gray jumpsuit with a Mandelbrot Cardioid pattern embroidered on the chest in a bridal carry. She set the girl, who Maggie assumed was Fractal, down.

"Okay," Fractal said as she walked over to stand next to Industry. "I thought we had an agreement. I don't play with your power armor, robot, and mechs, and you don't play with horrifically dangerous computer systems."

Industry rolled her eyes and stepped away from the computer.

"You do remember I have a PhD in computer science, right?"

Fractal just chuckled and shook her head.

"Yeah. I also remember half the assholes in DC who are running our country into the ground have degrees in law and political science. A piece of paper doesn't mean a damn thing." She pulled a cable out of her pocket and plugged one end into a USB port on the computer, then plugged the other end into a port on the back of her head. Her eyes glazed over for a minute, then refocused.

"Okay," she said. "The good news is whoever built this thing was paranoid as fuck. If we cut the power, the internal battery backup will take over and the machine will start an automatic spin down of the superconductors."

"I sense a 'but' coming," Element said.

"Yeah," Fractal said. "That's because you've been doing this long enough to know there's always a 'but' coming. And in this case, it's a pretty big one. I'm pretty sure there's a living mind caught in the machine."

"What?" Delta V asked.

"The machine is...well, it's brilliant. That's the only word I have for it. It uses quantum entanglement to replicate a quantum field and image it. It was in use when the explosion happened. I'm assuming the body Vee took out of here was the person being imaged. The imaging field was entangled with the quantum field generated by her brain. When the explosion destroyed her body, her consciousness persisted because it was entangled with the machine."

"So, if we turn off the machine..." Industry said.

"She, whoever she was, dies," Fractal said.

Everyone in the room looked over at the imager and the rainbow-colored image of Maggie's soul still floating there in the space between the top and bottom halves. Maggie ignored them while they gawked and turned what Fractal had said over in her mind. It made a lot of sense. She was still there because she was tied to the machine. It didn't explain everything. It definitely didn't explain how she was seeing and hearing everything going on around her, or why time seemed to have slowed to a crawl. It didn't explain how she was able to watch the explosion as it happened while her body was still alive, but it was a start. And probably an end because they were going to have to turn off the machine.

"Can we move the machine back to the Shiro without turning it off?" Delta V asked.

"I don't think so," Fractal said. "Besides, even if we did, what then?"

"So, you just want to let her die?" Delta V asked.

"She's already dead," Fractal said. "Her body is, at least. Her mind...God knows what she's going through in there. Without a body, she's got no sensory input. Do you know what kind of hell prolonged sensory deprivation is? She may want to die."

"I don't sense any distress," Nexus said. "A little worry, but that seems to be directed towards the woman we took out."

Delta V turned to Nexus. "Can you reach her? Talk to her?"

"I can try," Nexus said.

"Do it," Fractal said. "Ask her what she wants."

Nexus gave a little nod and closed her eyes. Maggie could see the effort on her face, and a moment later, she felt the touch of Nexus's mind on hers. It surprised her how physical the sensation was. It felt like being wrapped in a warm hug after coming into the house on a cold day. Maggie felt herself relaxing more than she had since the explosion. The more she relaxed, the less aware of her surroundings she was, until all that remained was her and Nexus.

<Hello,> Nexus said.

<Hi,> Maggie said.

<I'm Nexus.>

<Yeah. I got that part. I heard everything you guys said.>

<How?>

<No fucking clue,> Maggie said. <Honestly, I don't know what to make of any of this.>

<If you heard the conversation, you know what I'm here to ask you,> Nexus said.

<Yeah,> Maggie said. <Just do me a favor, okay?>

<If I can.>

<Sierra, the woman who was in here with me...don't tell her about this. Tell her I died in the explosion. Tell her it was quick, and I didn't suffer.>

<I can do that.>

<Good. You're not going to find a body, but there was someone else down here when it happened. His name was Garrett Whitehall. He was working in the lab next door. I think his experiment was what caused the explosion.>

<What happened?> Nexus asked.

<I don't know exactly. The lab is supposed to be set up for quantum teleportation research, but I think they were really working on macroscopic teleportation. The teleport failed, and the test object was converted to energy. Not all of it, or the entire block would be gone, but enough. Don't let Sierra get blamed. The person who runs that lab has a grudge against her, and if his research is responsible, he'll try to pin this on her. And don't let her blame herself, either.>

<What's your name?>

<Magdalene Evangeline Bennett, but my friends call me Maggie.>

<Okay, Maggie. I'm sorry we couldn't save you.>

<Don't be,> Maggie said. <I'm okay with this. Just, please take care of Sierra for me. Garrett was her boyfriend up until a couple of days ago. A real piece of shit, but still.>

<I understand.>

<And thanks for giving me a choice this time.>

<This time?>

<Yeah. Look me up. You'll understand.>

<Okay.>

<Oh, and one more thing!>

<Yeah?>

<Clear a girl's browser history? Some things my grandparents don't need to know about me.>

Nexus laughed a little at that, and Maggie could feel her smile, even if she couldn't see it. The mental hug seemed to tighten for a moment.

<I'll get Fractal to take care of it,> Nexus said. <Goodbye, Maggie.>

The psychic hug ended, and Maggie found herself alone for a moment before the world around her came back into focus.

"She wants us to turn it off," Nexus said. "She also gave me a pretty good idea of what caused the explosion."

"Really?" Element asked.

"Yeah," Nexus said. "Someone else died down here. Doesn't sound like we'll find the body, but they were messing around with teleportation and the experiment went boom."

"That's almost a relief," Industry said. "No supervillain, no terrorist."

"Just a lot of bodies," Delta V said.

"But only these bodies," Fractal said as she unplugged the cable from the back of her head. "Supervillains usually leave a trail of them."

"Vee, are you okay disconnecting the power?" Element asked. Maggie could tell from the look on her face that Delta V had expected the question, and wasn't happy about it, but she nodded.

"Yeah," she said. "Probably safest I do it in case the failsafe doesn't hold."

"Okay, let's clear out," Element said. "Nexus, you grab Fractal."

"Got it," Nexus said.

Maggie watched as everyone but Delta V left. Nexus lifted herself and Fractal out telekinetically, while Element and Industry both flew out under their own power. All of the High Guard began moving people back, working with the police to create a safe zone around the building in case there was another blast. It took a few minutes to get everything set up, then Element radioed Delta V.

"We're ready," Element said.

Delta V walked over to the lab's breaker box, took a deep breath, and pulled the main breaker.

Time, which had already been moving at a snail's pace, stopped completely.

Chapter Four

IF MAGGIE HAD KNOWN what would happen after Delta V turned off the imager, she would have begged her not to. It was something she would always look back on as a foretaste of hell. She lost all connection to physical reality, existing only as a disembodied mind no longer attached to the world that had created it in any meaningful way. She had no idea why she continued to exist. She only knew that once she was untethered from any sort of physical form, she perceived time as it truly was, quantized step by quantized step.

Those steps had always just been a theory to her. Planck seconds. The smallest units allowable by the laws of physics as humanity understood them. The universe's fundamental unit of time was merely a thought exercise until she could feel them ticking by, one by one, as the rest of the universe sat idle. With time moving at that scale, for the first time in her life, Maggie didn't just feel isolated by all the things that made her different; she was truly, utterly alone.

It took her what felt like days to even work out that much of what was happening to her, but that was just the beginning of it. Months, maybe years of subjective time passed while Maggie floated there in the wreckage of Sierra's lab. With nothing else to do, she thought about what happened to her. She went over what she knew about Sierra's imager and what she knew about the explosion and came up with what she thought was a working theory. Somehow, the teleportation equipment in Doctor Hastings' lab had interacted with Sierra's quantum field imager and burned Maggie's mind into the quantum membrane. She'd become a defect in the very fabric of space time.

She kept thinking that maybe the membrane would right itself, stretch out the wrinkles and she'd pop out of existence, but nothing happened. Then things got worse, because nothing just kept on happening. The longer she waited, the more she needed something to occupy herself.

Eventually, she turned her mind to work and the reactionless drive she and the team she'd been working with had been researching. She turned over the details in her head. She did countless equations, worked through model after model, working out details. She was surprised to find that dying had done wonders for her memory, but there were moments where she would have killed for a whiteboard. It was easier for her to think in dry erase marker. She eventually worked out all the details, but she was convinced that she would have solved it in half the time if she could just have gotten ahold of a whiteboard.

When she was done, she looked around. Delta V still stood there, her hand on the lever for the main breaker. The same dust motes hung in the same spots in the air. Almost no time had passed at all, but it felt like years. She wanted to scream, but she didn't have a mouth or a voice to scream with. All she could really do was think, so that's what she did.

She thought about everything that had brought her to that moment. About the letter accepting her to a NASA summer program, about wanting to celebrate at her favorite restaurant downtown, about the alien portals opening around the car, and the pain that followed. She thought about all the choices she'd made after she realized the horrific injuries she'd suffered meant she'd never be an astronaut. The choice to become a physicist, to apply for the Alternative Propulsion research team. She thought about the better post-doc placements she'd turned down because she wanted to stay close to Sierra. She thought about staying in Sun City when Sandra had asked her to move to California, about letting Sierra talk her into laying down on that scanner, about not reporting Garrett for what he'd done the day before.

She turned all the decisions, good and bad, over in her mind. How each one had brought her to where she was, and how things might have been different if she'd made different choices. Better choices. What if she'd gone with Sandra? What if she'd refused to be a test subject for Sierra? What if she'd filed that complaint with Dr. Miller?

The possibilities seemed endless and exhausting and all Maggie could think of was that she wanted to be home, in her bed.

No sooner had she had the thought, than that's where she was.

* * * *

At first, she thought she'd just woken up from a nightmare. A bizarre, insanely detailed nightmare. That thought only lasted as long as it took her to sit up, because as soon as she did, she noticed three things. First, she was naked. She could count on the fingers of one hand the number of times she'd slept naked. Second, she wasn't in pain. Something which had not happened to her in eleven years. That led very quickly to the third thing. Her scars were gone.

She got out of bed, surprised at how easy it was to just stand up, and reached for her cane. It wasn't there, which stopped her in her tracks. She hadn't been able to walk without her cane since the day of the invasion, and her first reaction to it not being where she left it was dangerously close to full blown panic. She looked around the room for one of her old canes and spotted one leaning in the corner.

It was close enough that she thought she could make it, so she started to hobble over to it, and nearly fell on her ass when her right leg swung forward without any of the usual resistance. Her right hip was normally stiff and hard to move at the best of times, so when she took the first step, she ended up over-extending and found herself stumbling. She managed to catch herself on the wall, and after taking a moment to steady herself, she tried again, taking care to move slowly and watch her foot placement this time. Two more steps, and she was in the corner where her old cane was, coming to the realization that she didn't need it.

She left it and went to the bathroom. She flipped on the lights and looked in the mirror, which gave her another shock. The face staring back at her wasn't hers. Or it was a version of hers. It took her a moment to realize that she looked like Bobbie, her Digilife avatar. Complete with purple hair and tattoos.

When she'd created Bobbie, she'd modeled the face on her own, but made it look younger, less worn down and sickly. She'd gone for 'beautiful and sexy' instead of her usual 'I've spent the last week in an intensive care unit' chic. No sunken eyes or hollow cheeks or scar lines where the skin grafts were.

It made her wonder if she was still dreaming. It would hardly be the first time she'd dreamed of being Bobbie. That was kind of the whole point of Bobbie's existence. Bobbie was the woman Maggie had always imagined she'd have become if the invasion had never happened. A woman who wasn't ashamed of her own body and wracked with guilt over getting her family killed.

She didn't wonder for very long, though. In the dreams, she never questioned it. Dreams always made sense while she was in them, but none of what was going on made sense to her. This was like having her fondest wish granted by an explosion that killed seven people. Everything about it was wrong.

She went back to her bedroom and grabbed a top and skirt out of the closet and tossed them on the bed. Then added panties and a bra from the chest of drawers before looking around for her grabber before it occurred to her that she could probably get a pair of shoes without it. She went back to the closet and bent down, grabbing a pair of ballet flats like it wasn't a miracle she could do it at all. She got dressed as quickly as she could, then sat down in front of her computer and fired it up.

She wasn't sure what was going on, but she knew one thing. She needed help. She needed it for a lot of reasons. Because she had no idea what was happening to her, because she looked nothing like the woman on her IDs, because her IDs were still in the wreckage of Sierra's lab, along with her keys and her phone, and because her body was currently on the way to the morgue.

She could only think of two people who might believe she was who she said she was. Sierra was still unconscious, which only left Nexus. Since she didn't exactly have the Sun City High Guard in her contacts list, she pulled up Google. A quick search provided her with the emergency reporting numbers for the High Guard. She pulled up Skype, which was thankfully already linked to her credit card, pulled on her headset, and made the call.

"High Guard Emergency Line, this is Bill speaking. What's the nature of your emergency?" the voice on the other end of the line asked.

"I need to talk to Nexus," Maggie said.

"I'm sorry, she's—"

"No, stop," Maggie said, cutting him off. "I know you must get a dozen crank calls a day asking to speak with the team and you're doing your job but put me on hold and do whatever you've got to do to talk with her. Tell her that her friend Maggie from Sun City State University is on the phone. Say it just like that. 'Her friend Maggie from Sun City State University.'"

"Ma'am, I'm sorry, the team—"

"The team is currently trying to stop a device in one of the basement labs at the Sun City State University Science Annex building from exploding, and if you don't get Nexus on the phone with me right now, they may fail."

"Hold, please."

She waited for about a minute and a half before Nexus came on the line.

"Who is this?" she asked.

"It's Maggie. We just talked in the basement of the Science Annex. I said, 'thank you for giving me a choice this time.' You asked me what it meant, and I told you to look me up, and you'd understand. I also asked you to clear a girl's browsing history, because there are some things my grandparents don't need to know about me, and you promised to have Fractal take care of it."

"Fuck," Nexus said. "How are you on the phone with me? We just put your body in the coroner's van."

"I have no fucking clue," Maggie said. "Delta V pulled that lever, and time seemed to stop for a while, but then I just...woke up in my bed."

"Are you at home now?" Nexus asked.

"Yeah."

"Okay. I'm going to send someone to come get you. Stay put."

"Thanks. If it's not too much trouble, my purse was in the lab where you found my body. It has all my ID and my phone in it. Could you..."

"I'll have Delta V get it before she comes to meet you."

"You're sending Delta V?" Maggie asked.

"Who else would I send?"

"I just figured you'd send a cop or something."

"We don't really get along with the cops," Nexus said. "The Marshals are okay, and I am going to send one to get you, but it will take a while for them to get there. I want someone with you right now, so I'm sending Delta V. What's your address?"

"338 Pennsylvania Avenue, Brine Water, FL 32949."

"Okay. Go unlock your front door and turn on your porch light. Then stand clear of the door. Vee is on her way."

The call disconnected. Maggie got up and headed for the front door. She flipped on the porch light, unlocked the deadbolt and knob, and just barely had time to get clear before the front door opened and closed in a blue and hot pink blur, leaving Delta V standing in front of her.

"Maggie?" she asked.

"Hey," Maggie said as she gave a little wave.

The two of them stood there, staring at each other for a moment, which quickly turned into an awkward moment as it started to drag out, but it gave Maggie a moment to look at Delta V. She was Indian. That much was obvious from her skin tone and the costume that was styled to look like a hot pink sari with gold trim worn over blue pants and a top. Whoever had designed the outfit had done a fantastic job using the pattern to suggest a sari, considering it was a form fitting one-piece jumpsuit with no draped bits. The cowl even added to the effect, making it look like the sari was draped over her head and she was wearing a blue mask under it. There was a red stone set in the mask where the bindi would normally be worn, and the emblem on her chest was simple. The Greek letter delta followed by a lowercase v, both written in gold, set into the hot pink fabric.

"Um...oh! Oh! Your purse!" Delta V said, holding up a large blue bag that looked like it was made from the same material as her suit. She unzipped it and took out Maggie's purse. "Sorry," she said. "I was just distracted because you looked different. Well, I mean, of course you look different, because when I saw you before you were...um..."

"Dead?"

"No! Well, yes, but that's not...I mean..."

Maggie smiled when she noticed the slight blush coloring Delta V's cheeks. Maggie was a little surprised, because Delta V had been so confident and sure of herself at the lab, but she honestly found the stammering adorable.

"It's okay," Maggie said. "I'm honestly just as surprised at how different I look as you are."

"I imagine all of this is a bit of a surprise," Delta V said.

"Now that is an understatement," Maggie said. "Um, would you like something to drink? I've got lemonade, orange juice, cranberry juice, diet coke, and water."

"Orange juice would be great," Delta V said.

"I'd offer food, but all I have in the house are cereal bars, energy bars, and ice cream."

"Any of those would be amazing," Delta V said with more enthusiasm than Maggie expected.

"Um, okay," Maggie said. She pointed at the pantry as she headed for the refrigerator. "Help yourself."

Delta V walked over to the pantry, opened the door, and started rifling through Maggie's collection of uneaten breakfast food.

"Oh! Pop tarts! Do you mind?"

"Check the date. If they were made this century, they're all yours," Maggie said as she grabbed a couple of glasses out of the cabinet next to the fridge.

Delta V flipped the box over and let out a disappointed sigh. "How do you have two-year-old Pop Tarts? That's got to be a crime."

"I have this weird thing where I'll decide to start trying to save money by having breakfast at home and order a bunch of breakfast food when I have my groceries delivered. Then I'll remember I hate cold food in the morning and I'm a lazy bitch, so I end up going by the dining hall at work and getting a hot breakfast there."

"They deliver groceries? That's actually a thing?"

"Yeah," Maggie said as she poured them both a glass of juice. "It used to be pretty expensive, but the price dropped a lot over the last five years or so." She put the juice away and headed for the table. Delta V followed, carrying two boxes of cereal bars and a box of protein bars.

"Is this okay?"

"Yeah."

"Industry hates it when people offer us food," Delta V said.

"Why is that?"

"When I'm hungry, I get carried away," Delta V said. "My body burns about ten thousand calories a day when I'm just resting. When I'm out in the field, that number gets a lot higher. People offer me food, and then Industry ends up getting complaints about how much I eat."

"What does she expect you to do, starve?" Maggie asked.

"No," Delta V said. "She always has food out for me at the Shiro, and she buys these ultra-high calorie energy bars for me. There's even a guy whose only job is to keep everyone's field bag stocked with energy bars. It's just, anything that causes bad publicity is a pain, because we already get so much bad press because of the whole gay thing. Wait, you do know about the whole gay thing, right?"

"Yeah," Maggie said. "I'm pretty sure everyone in the city knows about that. It's not like the giant pride flag on the side of the building is subtle."

Delta V smiled. "When Industry wants to make a statement, she makes a statement."

"Do people really complain when you eat too much?" Maggie asked.

"It's happened a few times," Delta V said. "Mostly just stuff on Twitter. There's actually an entire Twitter account that's just pictures of me at various restaurants around town, getting snacks."

"That's rude," Maggie said.

"Right?" Delta V tore open a cereal bar. "You'd think after you saved someone's life, they'd be a little bit grateful, but you'd be wrong. This one time, I pulled this family of eight out of a burning house. The next day, there was a video of me eating a couple of protein bars on Fox news. Turns out the dad shot it."

"What an asshole!"

Delta V took a bite out of the cereal bar in her hand and made a noise that belonged in a porn movie. Maggie watched, more than a little amused, as she ate the whole thing in two bites, then tore open and devoured a second one.

"How can you not eat these?" she asked.

"I live on pizza rolls and take out," Maggie said.

"Oh, I love pizza rolls," Delta V said. "I'm just never patient enough to wait for our cook to make them."

"Seriously? They take about five minutes. Which I'm realizing would seem like forever to you and I'll shut up now."

Delta V grinned as she tore open another bar.

"It's okay. The cook usually just makes a huge plate of subs in the morning for me to snack on. When I'm hungry, I just grab one and pop it in the steamer. Thirty seconds later, hot food. He also makes bigger meals at set times. I also eat lots of cut fruit so I don't die of scurvy, which is a bigger risk for me than is really fair. Cakes, brownies. Also, donuts. So many donuts. I'm pretty sure the cops in the tenth precinct actually took up a collection so they could pay Runaway Donut to open a new store right next to the Shiro so they weren't competing with me for key lime pie donuts and apple fritters anymore."

Maggie laughed at that image. Poor, donut starved cops taking up a collection to keep superheroes away from their sugar fix. She laughed so hard she ended up putting her head on the table and taking deep breaths to get it under control. When she sat back up and looked at Delta V again, the box of Cinnamon Toast Crunch cereal bars was empty, and Delta V was giving her a self-satisfied smirk.

"You did that on purpose."

Delta V nodded. "Yeah. You've had a really bad morning. Laughing helps. So will the debrief with Nexus."

"What about you?" Maggie asked. "I saw you at the Annex. It didn't look like you were having a good time of it either."

"Today wasn't too bad," Delta V said. "And you...no offense, but *if* you are who you say you are, the worst part of my day just goes away."

"Oh, God. I'm sorry. I didn't even think about that."

"It's okay. I can't speak from personal experience, but I've been told that coming back from the dead is just a bit distracting."

"Well, having done it twice now, I can say this time was a lot weirder than the first time," Maggie said.

"First time?" Delta V asked.

"During the invasion," Maggie said. "I died on the way to the hospital, but they brought me back. I remember it all."

"That sounds awful."

"It was, but there was an ambulance, paramedics, a defibrillator, doctors, and a hospital. It sucked, but it made sense. Today was just strange."

"Strange is kind of par for the course with the High Guard," Delta V said. "I honestly don't remember what normal feels like, but there could be an easy answer for all of this. You could have a meta gene that gives your body duplication powers, like Multiplex from the San Francisco Gatekeepers."

"I don't know who that is," Maggie said. "I don't keep up with superheroes."

"Really?" Delta V asked.

"Yeah," Maggie said. "Bad memories."

"Oh," Delta V said. Maggie kicked herself when the smile disappeared from Delta V's face. "I'm sorry."

"Not your fault."

"Still, we're supposed to help people."

"Maybe we could pick a different topic," Maggie said.

"Yeah," Delta V said. She blushed again and looked around the house. "Um...what kind of work do you do? I mean, I know it's got something to do with quantum fields, but I'm a chemist, not a physicist."

"That's actually Sierra's work," Maggie said. "The woman you carried out on the backboard. She's a friend, and she conned me into being her test subject. I work with NASA's Alternative Propulsion Laboratory."

"You work for NASA?" Delta V asked. Maggie smiled at the excitement in her voice.

"Sort of," Maggie said. "I'm a second-year post-doc researcher at SCSU. I have a PhD in physics, and I'm ABD in math and engineering."

"ABD?"

"All but dissertation. I've done all the graduate level coursework for a PhD in math and engineering, which isn't as impressive as it sounds when you consider how much overlap there is between those fields and physics. I did my dissertation on warp drive theory. That's why I went to SCSU in the first place. They're one of the only schools in the country with a warp drive physics group."

"So, you're working on a warp drive?"

"No. I got pulled onto another project. It's still a new type of engine. It's just not a Faster Than Light one, and shit, I just realized I'm probably going to miss the Monday morning conference call with JPL."

Delta V laughed, and Maggie felt butterflies flutter in her stomach. The laugh was positively musical, the smile that went with it was beyond radiant, and Maggie couldn't help but wonder what she looked like under the mask. She immediately gave herself a mental kick because it really wasn't the time to be thinking about anything like that.

The whole situation was beyond bizarre. She'd died alongside six other people less than an hour ago. One of the people she'd known and spent a huge amount of time with over the last six years, even if she'd hated his guts. Sierra was hurt and on her way to the hospital. She shouldn't be sitting there thinking about how cute one of the local superheroes was, but she felt oddly detached from what had happened that morning.

It felt like something that had happened a long time ago. Months, maybe years ago. She could remember every detail of what had happened from moments before the explosion right up to the present with perfect clarity, like it was still happening, but the time she'd spent moving in Planck time distorted her perception. Made it feel more time had passed than actually did.

Delta V stopped laughing and reached up, touching a spot on the side of her cowl.

"Got it. We'll be out in five." She looked up at Maggie. "Ride is here."

"Okay," Maggie said. She downed the rest of her orange juice, then took the empty glasses over to the sink and washed them out while Delta V cleaned up the food wrappers.

"Best way to do this and stay incognito is for you to open the door. I'll speed by you and be in the van before anyone can see me. You lock up, then walk out and get into the van like it's just another day."

"If we're going to go incognito, give me a minute." Maggie said. She went into her room and opened her desk drawer and pulled out one of her folding canes. She didn't use them much, but she kept them around when she traveled. It was a lot easier to take a fold up aluminum cane on a plane with her than a heavy steel one. Once she had the folder, she grabbed a couple of scarves. She wrapped one around her head, so it hid the purple hair, then tied another around her neck, the way she normally would to hide her scars. She added a pair of oversized sunglasses that covered a huge portion of her face, then headed back into the living room.

Delta V took one look at her and bit her lip for a moment, like she was trying to figure out how to politely tell Maggie she was being an idiot.

"Um...the idea is not to draw attention," Delta V said.

"My neighbors are used to me having frumpy brown hair and dressing like a nun. If I walk out of here with purple hair and no scars on my face, someone will notice, but this...this is a fairly normal look for me."

"Okay," Delta V said. "Sorry."

"It's fine," Maggie said. She slung her purse over one shoulder, then dug out her keys before she finally unfolded the cane.

"Ready?" she asked.

"Ready," Delta V said.

Maggie opened the door, and Delta V vanished. Maggie stepped out and spotted a minivan with dark tinted windows sitting in the driveway with the driver's side sliding door open. She locked the front door, then walked to the van, making sure to lean heavily on the cane, and take extra care when climbing in. Delta V was sitting in the third-row driver's side seat, out of sight of anyone looking at the van from any angle other than the front porch of Maggie's house. As soon as Maggie was inside, the driver closed the sliding door. Maggie took a minute to put on her seatbelt, while Delta V moved to the seat beside her and buckled in.

"We'll be at the Shiro in about fifteen minutes," the man in the driver's seat said.

"Thanks, Pete," Delta V replied.

Maggie folded up her cane and slipped it into her purse, then settled in for the ride.

Chapter Five

EVERY CITY HAS A handful of buildings that everyone just knows. Some cities have more than others, but there are always landmarks. Sometimes it's an office building, sometimes it's the courthouse or city hall. In Sun City, one of the most prominent landmarks was the Shiro.

Most MERT teams worked out of a US Marshal's building. The reasons for that were simple and practical. The US Marshals handled dispatch for the MERT teams, and they arrested and contained the supervillains MERT teams dealt with. Even the Champions teams, which were privately owned and funded franchises that worked as independent contractors, usually worked out of the local Marshal's office if there was room for them.

Sun City was a bit different. After a series of high-profile supervillain attacks back in the mid-90s, the city decided that they needed a Tier Two MERT team and had funded one out of city resources. No one was going to argue the need, given that for some reason, it seemed like the moment anyone south of the Mason Dixon line and east of the Mississippi developed supervillain tendencies, they made straight for Sun City to start some shit. So the city council had recruited Red Coat, the second most powerful of the Olympus Six, built him a headquarters building called the Citadel, and gave him enough funding to recruit whoever he liked. For more than a decade, his team, the Sun City Sentries, had been one of the most popular and most celebrated superhero teams in the country. Then all seven members had disappeared through one of the alien portals during the Gacrux invasion. No one knew what happened to them, but they knew whatever happened, the Sentries were responsible for stopping the invasion cold.

Sun City had mourned its heroes, then tried to replicate its success with the Protectors. That hadn't gone well at all. Half the Protectors had ended up going to jail after Industry had turned them in for working with the mob, and Praetorian, the man who had been recruited to rebuild the team afterward, had gotten into a very public pissing match with Industry over the fact that she'd reported the corruption on the team. There were also allegations of sexism, homophobia, and racism directed towards Praetorian.

In the end, the city had sided with Praetorian, while the Marshals and the Department of Metahuman Affairs had sided with Industry. The

DMA had given Industry a charter for a privately operated MERT team, and Industry had made a point of going out of her way to recruit openly queer and ethnically diverse heroes for her new team.

She had also built what was pretty much universally acknowledged as the single coolest superhero headquarters in the country. The Shiro was modeled after Nagoya Castle in Japan. The lower ten stories of the building were a stacked stone façade that angled up at seventy degrees. The upper five levels were a series of tiers, strong white walls, green tiled roofs with upturned eaves, and massive gables. The main building was connected to a shorter secondary building by an honest-to-God drawbridge.

The secondary building was a visitor's center. It had its own ten story base, but only two tiers on the upper level. It included a souvenir shop, a museum dedicated to both the High Guard and the Sentries, and administrative offices for all the charity programs the High Guard sponsored.

Maggie had been to the Shiro once before. Early in their friendship, before Maggie had told Sierra about her history with superheroes, Sierra had dragged her along when she took the tour. This time, though, instead of the visitor's center, Maggie was headed for the main building. One of the massive doors in the base of the main building stood open as the van approached, with a pair of twelve-foot-tall battle mechs standing guard on either side of the door.

"They do know we're coming, right?" Maggie asked as she stared at the huge guns the two mechs carried. The question prompted a laugh from Delta V.

"Yeah," she said. "I know they're a little scary, but don't worry. They haven't blown anyone up yet."

Maggie gave her a weak smile but kept her eyes on the mechs. They were an upgraded version of the model the National Guard had used during the invasion. Juggernaut Mark III's. They'd been developed for police and military personnel to use against superpowered individuals when there were no MERTs available. They didn't see a lot of use, because they were expensive as hell to buy, even more expensive to maintain, and couldn't keep up with most supervillains anyway. They didn't even come close to something like Industry's power armor, but they were supposed to be easier to learn to use, and unlike Industry's armor, they didn't have to be custom built for the wearer, so they could be mass produced.

The van took them through a door that looked like it belonged out at the Cheyenne Mountain complex in Colorado, where they kept NORAD. The walls of the building were a lot thicker than Maggie had expected, too, nearly three car lengths thick, but once they were past the wall, they ended up in a massive garage. There were more of the Juggernaut suits, six of the flying cars like the team had used that morning, and an assortment of regular cars and motorcycles. Part of the floor was marked off as a repair area, and off to one side was a huge freight elevator that looked like you could fit two of the air cars in it.

The van came to a stop near the back of the garage, close to a set of double doors. Both the sliding doors on the van started to open before the van was even in park, and Delta V zipped around before Maggie had finished unfastening her seatbelt. She offered Maggie her hand, and Maggie took it, more out of habit than because she needed it.

Delta V led Maggie inside the double doors to a security station, where a pair of guards with US Marshal badges on their belts put her through a screening that would have put any airport to shame. When it was done and Maggie had been cleared, Delta V led her to a bank of elevators.

"There's a lot more people here than I expected," Maggie said as they rode up to the fifth floor.

"Yeah," Delta V said. "I had the same thought my first time here, but it takes a lot more than just a few metas to actually make a superhero team work. You need maintenance, medical, housekeeping, security ironically enough, food services, drivers, a good forensics lab, dispatch, containment. In addition to the actual team, we've got about a hundred and fifty people on staff here, and maybe another hundred marshals in the building at any given time. And that doesn't include the people in the second building who run all the charity, public outreach, and public relations stuff."

"Wow," Maggie said.

"For a Tier Two team, that's actually a bit on the small side," Delta V said with a shrug. "Since we're officially sponsored by Hashimoto Enterprises, we're able to outsource a lot of legal and admin functions to them."

Maggie had tons of questions she wanted to ask, but the elevator dinged, announcing their arrival on the fifth floor. Delta V made a small gesture, indicating that Maggie should follow her, then led the way down a short corridor and through a pair of double doors into what looked like an emergency room.

A tall, thin woman with tanned skin and brown eyes stood off to one side wearing a white doctor's coat over a pair of green scrubs. She smiled at Delta V.

"Hey, Doc," Delta V said.

"Hey, Vee," the doctor said. "I take it this is Miss Bennett?"

"It's Doctor Bennett, but please, call me Maggie." She glanced over at Delta V. "Why do I get the feeling I'm about to be poked and prodded?"

"Probably because Doctor Sanchez here is about to run every medical test known to man on you. Twice," Delta V said.

"Oh. Well, that would explain it." Maggie turned and looked at the doctor.

"It's true," Doctor Sanchez said, giving Maggie a smile and a shrug. "We handle weird pretty well around here, but there's weird, and there's growing a whole new body ten miles from where you apparently died."

"I don't suppose I can argue with that," Maggie said.

"Well, you could, but it wouldn't be very productive," Doctor Sanchez said. She gestured to a curtained off area with a bed in it. "There's a gown on the bed. Why don't you get changed, and we'll get started?"

Maggie stepped into the curtained off area, and Doctor Sanchez pulled the curtain closed behind her. She changed a lot faster than she normally would have been able to without help, then climbed up onto the bed, which was already propped in a sitting position, and pulled the sheets over her legs.

"Ready," she called out.

A black man in a pair of scrubs pulled the curtain aside, carrying a phlebotomist kit.

"Hey. I'm Alfonzo, and I'll be your vampire today," he said with a big smile on his face.

"Oh, goody," Maggie said. "It must have been two months since I've had any bloodwork done. I was starting to forget what a pincushion feels like."

Alfonzo laughed. "Frequent flyer?"

"Lots of orthopedic hardware," Maggie said. "I've had to have a couple of plates replaced due to infections. My doctor likes to keep a close eye on my numbers."

"Then you know the drill. Anything you want to tell me before we start?"

"The veins in my left arm are easier to find because there..."

Maggie stopped and looked down at her right arm, which was completely devoid of scar tissue. “Okay, that’s going to take some getting used to.”

“Should I not ask?”

Maggie shrugged. “Up until about an hour ago, I had extensive burn scars over about forty percent of my body. The people at the lab I went to always took from my left arm because the scars on my right made it hard to find my veins.”

“Well, why don’t we stick to the left side anyway, since that’s what you’re used to?”

“That works, but I’ll tell you right now, if you ever say the words ‘arterial blood gas’ to me, I’m going to hit you with your own tray and make a break for it.”

“Sweetheart, I wouldn’t even blame you. Those are rough. Fortunately, that’s not on the list for today.”

He set his kit down on a rolling tray and pulled up a stool, then went through the usual setup. He wrapped a tourniquet around Maggie’s arm, cleaned the site with alcohol swabs, inserted a needle with an attached hose, taped it in place, attached the Vacutainer holder, then connected the first Vacutainer tube and opened the valve on the hose.

Maggie watched the whole process with her usual level of boredom during blood draws, right up until Alfonzo twisted the valve to stop the flow of blood into the first vial, and the blood in the vial immediately vanished. He looked up at Maggie, then down at the vial, then back up at Maggie.

“I’ll be right back.”

* * * *

They drew two more vials of blood before giving up. The first time, Doctor Sanchez and Delta V had stood there and watched as the blood in the vial disappeared the moment the valve was turned. The second time, they put the vial on a scale and watched as the weight increased as the vial filled up, then dropped back to its empty weight the moment the valve cut off the flow of blood. The same thing happened to the hair sample, saliva sample, and nail clippings. They tried to get Maggie to give a urine sample, but she couldn’t pass anything, so they finally gave up on that and took her to radiology.

The x-rays and CT scans went a lot better, though what they showed was as impossible as everything else Maggie had seen that day.

There wasn't a single screw or plate in her body. All the bones were in perfect shape. There was no scar tissue or sign that she'd ever broken a bone.

Somewhere between the second and third set of films, Maggie noticed the nails they'd cut had grown back. Doctor Sanchez had cut them again and watched as they returned to their original state the moment Maggie looked away. Doctor Sanchez did a quick check and noticed the hair that had been cut had grown back, and that the blood draw site was completely healed too.

In the end, Maggie spent more than five hours getting poked and prodded, only to discover that she was in better than perfect health. Better than 20/20 vision, better than normal hearing, heightened sense of smell, taste, and touch. Nerve conduction was excellent. Lung capacity was slightly ridiculous. At one point, Delta V showed Maggie a series of yoga poses, and Maggie matched her pose for pose, even though she'd never done yoga before in her life.

Sanchez finally decided she was done, though Maggie was pretty sure the decision had more to do with how frustrated Sanchez was than because she'd actually learned anything from the various tests. Maggie, on the other hand, was just happy to get out of the hospital-like medical area.

Delta V led her down two floors to what was obviously an interrogation room, complete with the huge two-way mirror set into one wall and cameras in every corner of the room. Once Maggie sat down, Delta V asked what she'd like for dinner. Maggie told her, and Delta V disappeared. She returned fifteen minutes later with a cheesesteak with extra cheese and peppers, a plate of chili cheese fries, and lemonade. Maggie was a little surprised when Delta V sat down with her, and while Maggie ate her food, Delta V plowed through two chicken parmigiana subs, a huge slab of lasagna, and a salad. They even split a cheesecake, though it was an uneven split. Maggie had a slice, and Delta V ate the other seven.

They ate in silence, though Maggie figured that was more her fault than Delta V's. She was exhausted and not really in the mood to talk, and Delta V seemed to pick up on that and just kept her company instead of pressing her. When they were both done eating, Delta V cleared away the dishes, and came back with a fresh cup of lemonade, then left again after promising to come back soon.

Maggie, as she often did when left to her own devices, began to worry. She wasn't sure what she had expected when she called the High

Guard in the first place. She'd known she couldn't just turn up to work on Monday when her body was in the morgue. Especially not when Sierra had been with her when she died. She'd also known that the radical change in her appearance would raise all sorts of questions. Calling the High Guard had seemed like the only option at the time, but after five hours of tests and being locked in an interrogation room, she was beginning to wonder if she was a prisoner, rather than someone they were trying to help.

The door opened before Maggie could get too far down her worry spiral, and she felt relief wash over her as Nexus walked into the room carrying a folder and a pen. She was still in her costume. A gray jumpsuit, boots, and gloves with her emblem on the upper left part of her chest and a mask that covered her face from the hairline down past her cheeks, leaving just her mouth, chin, jaw, and the lower part of her nose exposed. She took the seat across from Maggie where Delta V had been sitting, laid the folder and the pen on the table, and gave her a smile. "Hello."

"Hey," Maggie said. "Thank you."

"For what?"

"For believing me when I called. For not trying to save me when I was stuck in the machine. For promising to help Sierra."

"Ah. All of that." Nexus shrugged. "No thanks necessary. That's all part of the job, but you're welcome."

"So, what happens now?"

"Well, that depends."

"On?"

"Whether or not you're willing to submit to a telepathic and magical examination," Nexus said. "We had the body diverted here, and our on-staff medical examiner, who's licensed by the state as a subcontractor specializing in metahumans for the state medical examiner's office, is currently conducting the autopsy. What we know so far is that Maggie Bennett died in the explosion, and that she was not a carrier of either the M1 or M2 meta gene complexes. That means, if you are Maggie Bennett, you're now qualified as a Type Uniform Non-Magical Aberration. Which is Department of Metahuman Affairs speak for 'We don't know what the fuck you are, but we're mostly certain there was no magic involved.' Which just leaves the question of whether or not you are actually Maggie Bennett."

"You think I'm not?"

"I don't know. You look vaguely like her, but again, we have her body in the morgue. She had extensive scarring and numerous internal orthopedic devices, as well as extensive dental work, and a breast implant on the right side. She was also two inches taller than you. All of those are strikes against you. We've matched the serial numbers of the breast implant, the titanium plates holding the body's pelvis together, the dental implants, and the plastic lining in her hip socket to Maggie Bennett's medical and dental records, which are more strikes against you, but what you said to me over the phone matched what someone I assumed was Maggie said to me at the site of the explosion.

"Normally, we could sort this sort of thing out with a DNA test, but we can't take samples for testing, and I can't be certain the entity I touched minds with this morning is the woman known as Maggie Bennett."

"But you could if I submitted to a telepathic exam?"

"Most likely, yes," Nexus said.

"Okay," Maggie said. "How do we start?"

Nexus opened the folder she'd brought into the room with her and took out a sheet of paper. She slid it across the table, then set the pen on top of it.

"Sign this," Nexus said. Maggie looked down at the paper. It was a release form for a telepathic and magical examination. She gave it a quick read through, then signed it and handed it back to Nexus.

"What now?"

"Just take a few deep breaths and relax," Nexus said.

Maggie leaned back in the chair and closed her eyes, then took a couple of long, slow breaths. As she was inhaling for the third time, she felt the same sensation she'd felt that morning. Like being wrapped in a warm hug, only it was her and Nexus's minds being pressed together instead of their bodies.

<Hello,> Maggie said.

<Hello again,> Nexus said.

<What now?>

<Show me lunch yesterday,> Nexus said.

Maggie frowned, wondering why Nexus wanted to see that particular memory. She thought about it for a moment, focusing on everything she remembered. The way her hip had burned the whole time, the peeling linoleum in the breakroom, the taste of her food, the way it felt when Sierra smiled at her. The whole time, she could feel Nexus watching, but oddly, she felt a sense of recognition coming from her. Nexus had seen this before.

The connection broke suddenly, and Maggie opened her eyes to find Nexus looking at her with shock and fear clearly written on her face.

"How did you do that?" Nexus asked.

"Do what?"

"Follow the link back into my mind."

"I didn't," Maggie said, but when she thought about it, she realized she must have been reading Nexus's mind at least a little bit to pick up the feeling of recognition. "Did I? I mean, I could tell you'd seen the memory before, but—"

"Because you were reading my mind!"

"Oh. Um...I'm sorry?"

Nexus held up a hand, and Maggie was surprised to see it trembling.

"Just stay here," Nexus said. She got up like she couldn't get away from Maggie fast enough and rushed through the door.

Maggie sat back in the chair and stared at the mirror. She assumed that Nexus was in there with the rest of the High Guard, talking about her, and she was starting to get more than a little annoyed by the idea. She'd called the High Guard for help figuring out what happened to her. So far, they'd treated her like a lab animal and a suspect. She could understand them being confused, since she was confused herself, but it was starting to feel like they thought she was some kind of criminal.

She thought back to that morning. It felt like months or years had passed since the explosion, but the thought that a bunch of people were on the other side of that mirror talking about her, made her think back to the way her senses had expanded during and after the explosion. She'd been able to see everything in the entire building, and even a bit of the street outside. She wished knew how it happened, wished she could do it again, and just like when she wished she was home in bed, as soon as she wished for it, it happened.

She could sense everything happening in the Shiro. The mechanic in the garage replacing a thermocouple in one of the battle mechs, the cook cleaning the grill in the kitchen, the tour guide leading a group of kids through the visitor's center. It was busy, crowded, and not what she really wanted. She wanted to see the room on the other side of the mirror. Just that room, so she could focus on it.

And for the third time, as soon as she wished for it, it happened. It was like the wall and the mirror vanished, and she could see everyone in the other room. Nexus, Element, Industry, Cinderella, Delta V, Fractal,

Maker, Doctor Sanchez, and Sierra. She supposed Sierra's presence explained where and how Nexus had seen the memory of Maggie and Sierra having lunch together the day before.

"I don't know," Sierra said. "Maggie didn't have superpowers. She doesn't even like superheroes. She won't really talk about it, but I always got the impression that she blamed Red Coat for not saving her family during the Gacrux invasion."

"You're sure?" Industry asked.

"Yes," Sierra said. "She could barely walk some days. Even on her good days, she had trouble getting around. The face is mostly the same. It's what I imagined she'd have looked like if it weren't for her injuries. The voice is close too, like if her vocal cords hadn't been damaged by the fire. But Maggie had brown hair, and she always wore it down to cover the scars on the right side of her face."

"Burn scars, right?" Doctor Sanchez asked.

"Yeah," Sierra said. "She got caught in a burning car during the invasion. Red Coat got to her in time to save her, but not before the fire reached her."

Everyone looked at Doctor Sanchez, who shook her head.

"No scar tissue anywhere on her body."

"She's listening in," Cinderella said.

"What?" Element asked.

Cinderella turned and looked right at Maggie through the mirror.

"She's listening to us."

For a moment, Maggie felt panic. The same sort you feel when you get caught staring at someone, or listening to a conversation you shouldn't be hearing. She thought about trying to figure out how to pull her senses back in, but before she could even try, the panic turned to anger. They were talking about her, trying to decide if she was telling the truth, treating her like a criminal after she'd come to them for help. She hadn't done anything wrong, so why shouldn't she listen to what they were saying?

She took a deep breath, and instead of drawing her senses in, she reached up and touched two fingers of her right hand to her brow and gave Cinderella a little mocking salute. Cinderella grinned.

"I'm going in there," Cinderella said.

"What?" Nexus asked.

"I'm going in there," Cinderella repeated. She headed towards the door, and Maggie imagined her senses expanding out into the hall so she could follow Cinderella's progress. It worked, and she was able to follow her from the observation room into the hall and then into the interrogation room, where she took the chair Nexus had been sitting in.

"Hello," she said. The first thing Maggie noticed was that Cinderella didn't meet her eyes. She looked right at Maggie, but it felt like she was focused on Maggie's forehead, instead of her eyes.

"Hello," Maggie said.

"You know who I am?"

"Sort of," Maggie said. "I know you go by Cinderella. Not sure why. It's not really your typical superhero name. I know you're supposed to be a witch, or something."

"I'm an alchemist," Cinderella said. "Though I have been called a sorceress by a handful of higher powers, so I'm a bit flexible on that one. Witch doesn't really fit, though. Witches are a bit more instinctual in their craft. What I do is closer to what you do than what a witch does."

"So, you sit around all day and do math?" Maggie asked, and immediately winced at the sarcasm dripping from her voice. She probably needed to dial that down a bit.

"Some days. Have you ever read any of the stuff the Hermetic Dawn wrote? I swear every one of those bastards had a hard on for Isaac Newton."

Maggie couldn't stop herself from laughing at the deadpan delivery and the utter loathing in the way she said Isaac Newton's name. It took her nearly a minute to stop laughing, but when she did, she took a good look at Cinderella. She lived up to the name she'd chosen for herself. Tall, blonde, beautiful in a very classical way. Her hair was fixed in a complicated updo with a black Alice band in it, and her costume was a light blue, white trimmed open front robe over a royal blue jumpsuit clearly meant to evoke memories of a certain animated movie. There was a symbol on the upper right chest area of the robe, a ballet flat inside of a circle inside of a square inside of a triangle inside of another circle. Maggie could see the same symbol on the back of her robe in the mirror. She was also wearing a gold chain around her neck with a large gold pendant set with a blood red stone.

Maggie still didn't understand why she'd picked the name she did. Most of the other members of the High Guard had names that made sense. On the other hand, there were more than a few heroes with nonsensical names. Focus and Scatter came to mind.

"I know you already agreed to the magical examination, but I wanted to make sure you understand what that means," Cinderella said.

"Is it something I should worry about?" Maggie asked.

"Yes," Cinderella said. "The thing is, Nexus can't tell, one way or the other, if you're really Maggie. She's sure you are who she spoke to in the lab, and the memory you showed her seems to match up close enough to what Sierra showed her, but when she felt you reading her, she cut the telepathic link for her own protection. You shouldn't have been able to read her at all. Not with all the psychic defenses she's got in place."

"I scared her," Maggie said.

"You terrified her," Cinderella said. "And right now, she's probably glaring daggers at me for telling you that."

Maggie looked up through the mirror at Nexus.

"You're not wrong," she said.

"Well, most people don't like it when other people know they're scared. Me, I've always been up front about the fact that I'm a coward, so I'll tell you to your face that you're scarier than the devil himself."

"Me? Scary?"

"Absolutely," Cinderella said. "People always fear what they don't understand. The less they understand, the more they fear, and no one here understands what you are. It's only made worse by the fact that you're dripping with power."

"I don't want it," Maggie said. "I just want to make sure Sierra is okay, and then go home."

"I can understand that, but want it or not, you do have it, and as the people who are responsible for keeping this city safe, we want to make sure you're not a danger. So, I'm going to ask you to do something dangerous."

"Why?"

"Because it will tell me, one way or the other, if you are who you claim to be."

"What do you want me to do?"

"First, pull in your senses."

Maggie took one last 'look' at the people in the other room. Mostly, she focused on Sierra, who looked like hell. She had a line of stitches in her forehead and a nasty looking goose egg on her cheek. Maggie really wanted to get up and go to her, but she had to deal with whatever this was first, so she wished her senses back to normal. As soon as she did, she couldn't see anything outside of the room.

"Good. Now, what I want to do is called a soul gaze."

"Right," Maggie said. She must not have kept the skepticism out of her voice, because Cinderella rolled her eyes.

"I get it. You're a scientist. You don't believe in the mumbo jumbo."

Maggie shrugged. "I get that what most people call magic is real. Doesn't mean it's actually magic. Just means that there are bits of the universe we haven't figured out yet."

"Fair enough," Cinderella said. "And you're probably right, but while I might not have peer reviewed theory backing me up, I do have an empirical understanding of what I am doing. What I'm asking you to do is let me look at your soul, to see your true self."

"Okay. How is that dangerous?"

"Lots of reasons. More for me, normally, than for the person I'm soul gazing. The thing is, a soul gaze is a two-way street. I see you, but you also see me. It's dangerous for me because I have no idea what I'll see when I look into your soul. People have been driven mad when they think they're looking at a person and accidentally soul gaze some sort of demon, eldritch being, or someone who's been tainted. I know what's in my soul, at least, well enough to know what you see won't hurt you."

"You said it wouldn't normally be dangerous for me, but 'normally' is a pretty big qualifier."

"You're right," Cinderella said. "A soul gaze can tell me what kind of person you are, but not normally who you are. The thing is, you cannot lie to someone doing a soul gaze. You can refuse to answer, but you cannot lie."

"So, you're going to ask me who I am while we do this," Maggie said.

"Yes," she said. "Which is why it's dangerous. If you answer, you're going to tell me your name."

Maggie leaned back in her chair and took in what she'd just heard. She might not believe in magic as something which could violate the laws of the universe, but she was a huge geek. She'd devoured science fiction and fantasy books her whole life, and in every system of magic she'd ever heard of, names had power. Specifically, true names had power. And if she was compelled to tell the truth, then she would be giving Cinderella power over her.

"You're saying if I answer, you'll know my true name?" Maggie asked, just to be sure.

"Yes. 'Your true name, spoken from your own lips' as the saying goes. It's not as powerful a thing as most practitioners would have you believe. We remake ourselves all the time. The magic I could work with your name will become useless soon. For a normal person, if I learned their true name, I could work it for a year or two. More or less depending on what stage of life they're in. The older someone becomes, the less often they remake themselves. With you, I doubt I could work your name in a week. Maybe not even in a day."

"Why?"

"If you'd told me your name this morning, before the explosion, I wouldn't be able to conjure it now. You're not the same person you were. You've been through something that changed you drastically. I expect the next few weeks will bring more changes as you learn who you are with the new abilities you have. Names are magic things. You tell me today you're Magdalene Evangeline Bennett, and you tell me a week from now you are Magdalene Evangeline Bennett, to the average person, they sound the same, but to those of us who know how to listen, there will be a world of difference."

Maggie sat for a moment, considering what Cinderella was telling her. She might not believe in a lot of the trappings of magic, but she wasn't an idiot. She knew people like Cinderella could do things that science had yet to explain. The mysticism surrounding it might be garbage, but Cinderella did have power, which meant Maggie needed to take what she was saying seriously.

In the end, she didn't have a lot of choice. She needed to prove who she was if she wanted to go back to her life.

"Do it," Maggie said.

Cinderella held up her index finger, looking at Maggie without meeting her gaze again.

"There is one more thing. This is...intimate. Not physically, but we're going to see each other completely exposed. You'll see who I am, and that image will never go away. You will remember what you see with perfect clarity until the day you die."

Cinderella's words made Maggie hesitate for a moment. She knew from experience that one of the primary ways people dealt with pain was to forget. Things hurt less because time wore away the edges of memory. That was what separated pain from trauma. Pain faded. Trauma burned itself into a person's mind and made it impossible to forget the moment. Maggie already had a memory like that. A moment that she could remember with perfect, unfading clarity eleven years later. Signing up for another one didn't sound like fun.

Of course, that assumed it was a bad memory. Cinderella was warning her, but she didn't seem to think that what she was proposing would be something that would scar Maggie. Still, that did make Maggie wonder if Cinderella would be scarred by what she saw.

"You've done this before?" Maggie asked.

"A handful of times. It's not always the most pleasant experience."

"What about the people who've seen you?"

"None of them have ever seemed to mind what they saw, but I am serious when I say you will never forget it."

"There are some pretty awful things in my past."

"I won't see your memories," Cinderella said. "I will see your soul. You might not like that word, but I don't know any other way to describe it. I'll see the core of yourself. The good, the bad, the ugly."

Maggie sat and thought about it for a couple of minutes. She didn't like the idea at all. Being that exposed sounded horrible. There were parts of herself she wasn't proud of. Parts she wished she could make go away. If the circumstances had been different, she might have told the entire High Guard to go fuck themselves and just left. Her grandparents would recognize her. She was sure of that. She could find another job. She loved her work, but she wasn't so attached to it that she was willing to risk her sanity to keep doing it.

The more she thought about it, the more it felt like walking away would be the best choice, but Sierra was there, and Sierra wasn't sure she was actually Maggie. Taking the risk was the only way she could get her best friend back, and Maggie always made bad choices when Sierra was involved.

"Let's do it."

"All right. Take a deep breath. The feeling is a bit intense."

Maggie sat up a little straighter and took a deep breath. Just as she finished inhaling, Cinderella shifted her gaze and their eyes finally made contact, and as they did, Cinderella spoke a word. Maggie didn't know what the word was, but it hit her like a gust of wind, and as it passed, it carried the world away.

There was no description that would ever do justice to what happened next. Cinderella stood before her, naked and bare, and Maggie saw her. Not just the color of her eyes, the curve of her hip, or the swell of her breast. She saw all of that, but she saw past it. If someone had asked her before that moment if souls existed, she would have said she wasn't sure, but she doubted it. After that moment, the answer would forever and always be yes, because she'd seen one with her own eyes, and she would never forget it. It would be impossible to forget something so overwhelmingly beautiful. She could see all the places filled with joy and happiness, the places filled with fury and rage, the places filled with shame and fear, and the places which cried out for justice and longed for a world filled with compassion and hope. Maggie couldn't read Cinderella's mind, but she knew without a doubt that the woman before her was a good and kind woman, driven by love, compassion, and a deep, deep well of pain.

"Who are you?" Cinderella asked.

The question struck Maggie with more force than the word Cinderella had spoken to start the soul gaze. Or maybe it only felt that way because in the place where she was, there was no shield against it. Either way, the question filled her and consumed her. Lying was unthinkable. Impossible.

"Magdalene Evangeline Bennett," she said.

The name filled the space between them, a physical, tangible thing. Maggie thought she should be afraid, but she wasn't. She knew without a doubt that she trusted the woman in front of her.

Cinderella smiled and nodded in acknowledgement, and then it was over, and they were back in the interrogation room.

"Hey, Maggie," Cinderella said. "I'm Ashley. It's nice to meet you."

Maggie smiled.

"It's nice to meet you, too."

Chapter Six

THE DOOR TO THE interrogation room flew open, and Sierra rushed in. Maggie barely had enough time to stand up before Sierra pulled her into a crushingly tight hug.

"I'm so glad you're okay," Sierra said.

"I'm glad you're okay too," Maggie said. "When the explosion started, I was terrified you'd get hurt."

"It happened so fast, I don't even remember it," Sierra said. "I just woke up, and they told me there'd been an explosion and the building had collapsed."

"I remember all of it," Maggie said. "Trust me when I say you got the better deal. Whatever happened to me that let me stick around without a body happened at the same time as the explosion. I think it actually tore my mind loose from my body before I died."

"What makes you say that?" Industry asked as she stepped into the room. Maggie looked at her and reluctantly let go of Sierra.

"My perception of time shifted when it happened. It was like the whole world just slowed down while my senses expanded. I didn't see the start of what happened exactly, but I could see into the other labs in the building before the actual explosion. I didn't see it disappear, but I did see the object Garrett was trying to teleport reappear, and I saw it decay into energy."

"Garrett?" Sierra asked.

Maggie turned to Sierra, and she felt the blood draining from her face as Sierra looked at her in confusion.

"What does Garrett have to do with this?" Sierra asked. Maggie looked around, desperate for help, when Nexus's voice came over a PA system.

"I haven't had a chance to tell her," Nexus said. "We had her brought over from the hospital as soon as she woke up."

"Fuck," Maggie said. "A little warning would have been nice."

"Maggie?"

Maggie looked at Sierra. She could see the confusion being replaced with understanding and pain, and she hated it. She reached down and took Sierra's hands in hers. She glanced over at Ashley, who gave a small nod.

"We'll give you two the room," Ashley said. She walked over and shoved Industry towards the door, and then closed it behind them.

Maggie turned back to Sierra.

"I asked Nexus to tell you while I was stuck in the machine. I thought I was going to die when they turned it off, and I wanted someone to be there with you when you found out. Garrett was in Hastings' lab when it happened."

"When what happened?"

"It was an accident," Maggie said. "I'm not sure if Hastings has been lying about what he and his team have been working on, or if Garrett was off-book, but the experiment he was running wasn't quantum teleportation."

That last part was a lie, and she knew it. There was no way Garrett was off-book. He didn't have the chops for it. On his best day, Garrett was a mildly competent bottle washer. It was one of the reasons she hated him so much. He always acted like he was on Sierra's level when he wasn't. Maggie knew her limits. She was a decent theorist, and a good experimental scientist, but her real strength was applied science and engineering. She was extremely good at taking theory and turning it into working hardware. Sierra, on the other hand, was one of those rare, wonderful individuals who could do all three with equal levels of competence. She was a brilliant theorist, her experimental design was top shelf, and she was amazing at applied science as well. The best Maggie could say about Garrett was you could trust him not to fuck up an experiment if he had good, step by step instructions.

"What was he doing?" Sierra asked.

"Macroscopic teleportation," Maggie said. "I didn't see the moment of transmission, but I saw the test object reappear, and something went really, really wrong, and it immediately decayed into energy. That's what caused the explosion."

"But if he was in the lab where the explosion went off..."

Maggie watched as the realization set in. She hated it. She didn't want to be the one to tell Sierra this for so many reasons, but there wasn't anyone else. She was Sierra's best friend, and she was there. She owed it to her, so she squeezed Sierra's hands and offered what little comfort she could.

"It was quick," Maggie said. "He couldn't have felt anything."

"No," Sierra said, shaking her head. "No, please."

Maggie pulled Sierra into her arms and held her as she started to cry.

"I'm sorry."

"I...oh, God. We...we fought, and I know I was mad, but I didn't want that to be the last thing I ever said to him."

"I know," Maggie said. She squeezed Sierra tightly, rocking her back and forth the way Maggie's mother used to do when Maggie was upset. "I know."

"If I hadn't taken him off the raid—"

"No," Maggie said. "Don't do that. It's not your fault."

"But—"

"It's not your fault," Maggie said, glad, for once, for all the hours she'd spent on a therapist's couch over the years. "I blamed myself for what happened to my family. I'm pretty sure you figured that much out, but I never told you why. The day of the invasion, we were going into town to celebrate. I'd gotten an acceptance letter for one of NASA's summer programs, and when they asked me where I wanted to go to celebrate, I asked if we could go to my favorite Mexican place downtown.

"I spent years thinking that if I'd just agreed to get pizza like my dad suggested, that they'd all be alive. That I wouldn't be scarred and broken. But there's no way to know if it would have changed anything. We could have gone for pizza and still died. There's no way to know. Just like there's no way to know what would have happened with Garrett. He might still have gone into the lab today, or he might have done the experiment on Monday, when the Annex was full of people, and instead of killing six people, he might have killed six hundred. There's no way to know, but I promise you, this is not your fault."

Sierra nodded and leaned forward, resting her head on Maggie's shoulder. Maggie just stood there, holding her while she cried.

* * * *

"Thank you," Maggie said to Nexus as she closed the door to the guest room where Sierra had fallen asleep.

"It's the least we could do," Nexus said as they started walking towards the elevator. "I wanted to apologize. I should have told her before we brought her over from the hospital."

"I'm glad you didn't," Maggie said. "I mean, I'm not going to lie. In the moment, it sucked, and I hated you for it, but all things being equal, it's better this way. I was there to comfort her when she heard, and she really needed someone who would understand and tell her that it wasn't her fault. She's still going to be eaten up by the guilt, but the earlier and the more often people tell her not to blame herself, the better."

"Sounds like you're speaking from experience," Nexus said.

"You weren't listening in on what I said after Ashley and Industry left?"

There was a flash of something on Nexus's face when Maggie said Ashley's name. At least, Maggie thought there was. It was so brief she wondered for a moment if she'd imagined it, but then Nexus shook her head and started talking, and Maggie put it aside for later.

"We wanted to give you some privacy. You're not criminals, just people who've gotten caught in a really shitty situation."

"Well, no offense, but you guys really need to go back and reread the 'how to not treat someone like a criminal' section of the superhero manual."

"Yeah," Nexus said. "That's probably fair. In our defense, it's really easy for this job to make you a bit paranoid. Especially in Sun City. Sometimes, I really wish we were someplace like Pontian or Del Leon."

Maggie laughed. "I'm sure your desire to go to Pontian has nothing at all to do with the unbelievably hot resident hero there."

"Which one?" Nexus asked.

"Focus," Maggie said.

"Funny. I figured you more for the Scatter type," Nexus said.

"I honestly forget she's back most of the time. I try not to pay attention to any of the superhero news. The only reason I know the stuff I do about the Sun City teams is you can't live in this city without hearing about the drama."

"I wish you were wrong about that, but to answer your question, no. I mean, don't get me wrong, Focus is gorgeous, but the woman puts peanut butter on her spaghetti."

"What? Like, with the tomato sauce?"

"No. It's not that bad. She just does this thing with some sort of peanut butter, ginger, and sesame oil dressing and puts that on the noodles instead of tomato sauce. And that's probably the least weird thing about her. There's also the fact that she and Scatter are so disgustingly in love I get cavities every time we're in the same room."

"The horror."

"She also hangs around with that fucking dragon."

"Ice Dragon?"

"No," Nexus said. "Ice Dragon can be a bit much, but she means well. I'm talking about...well, if you spend much time around Ashley, you're going to meet Eurion."

There was so much bitterness in the last bit of what Nexus said,

Maggie could actually taste it, and she immediately understood the look Nexus had given her earlier when she'd used Ashley's real name instead of calling her Cinderella. Nexus was jealous. Of her a little bit, and of this Eurion a whole lot.

"Not a fan?"

"No," Nexus said.

Maggie didn't say anything else the rest of the way to the elevator. Instead, she spent the time wondering what sort of high school level drama she'd gotten herself mixed up with where one of the superheroes who was supposed to be helping her out was jealous because she used another one's name, and because that other superhero liked to hang out with a dragon.

When they reached the elevator, Nexus hit the call button and they waited a moment for the elevator to arrive, then stepped inside.

"You know," Maggie said as Nexus hit the button for the tenth floor. "Most people would probably be wondering if Sierra and I were behind the explosions, and I was using Garrett as a cover."

"Most people couldn't feel the pain radiating off both of you. She's been confused, terrified, and devastated by turns since she woke up."

"And me?"

"Calmer than I would have expected. When it comes to the explosion, it's as if you're talking about something that happened months or years ago. Normally, that would make me worry that you're having a dissociative episode, but you definitely feel the immediacy of your situation and Sierra's distress. There's a bit of guilt, but that's entirely directed at the fact that you feel no remorse over this Garrett's death."

Maggie shrugged.

"I'd lie and say I did, but you'd know it was a lie, and the truth is the guy was a schmuck. I didn't want him dead, I definitely didn't want to watch him die, but considering that he blamed me for his and Sierra's breakup and came within a hair's breadth of beating the shit out of me yesterday, I can't say I'm all that broken up about his passing."

"He what?"

"Sierra dumped him the night before last," Maggie said. "He walked into my office yesterday and started ranting about me. If a coworker hadn't stepped in, I'm pretty sure he would have physically attacked me."

"Fuck. And Sierra dated this guy?"

"For six years," Maggie said. "I know I should be sad he's gone, but in my best moments, I can muster up some indifference. Most of the time, I just feel relief that I'll never have to see him again."

"Sometimes you can't help how you feel," Nexus said. The elevator stopped, and Maggie felt a bit of relief as the doors slid open. Instead of replying to what Nexus had just said, she followed her down a couple of long hallways, around a couple of corners, and through a door marked 'Lab 6'.

Based on the label on the door, Maggie had expected something like one of the labs at work. Instead, she got something out of a fantasy horror movie. Lots of wood paneling. Tables covered with modern chemistry equipment next to actual cauldrons. Shelves of heavy, leather-bound books. What she assumed was an actual summoning circle, complete with pentacle and runes set into the floor in what looked like pure silver. Lots of candle stands. Industry, Element, Ashley, Doctor Sanchez, and a Japanese man Maggie hadn't met before were all sitting at a heavy wooden table, waiting for them.

Industry had shed her power armor and was wearing a flight suit done in a black, maroon, red, and brass art deco diesel punk aesthetic. Element was in jeans and a tank top. Ashley was in a sharp royal blue pant suit with white pinstripes and a pair of ballet flats. Sanchez was still in her scrubs, and the new guy was in a dark suit that might as well have had 'federal agent' written on the lapels.

None of them were wearing masks, which wasn't that much of a surprise. Genuine secret identities were a rarity in the superhero world. There *were* a few, but they were the exception, rather than the rule. A lot of them wore masks to make it harder for people to recognize them out of costume, but in the age of YouTube, facial recognition software, and constant surveillance, most superheroes who did manage to keep their real names hidden were some sort of shapeshifter.

"How's your friend?" Element asked.

"Asleep, finally," Maggie said as she sat down. "Bad day for her for a lot of reasons."

Nexus took the seat next to her and touched a bracelet on her left wrist that Maggie hadn't noticed before. Her costume vanished, replaced by a pair of loose-fitting jeans, a t-shirt with an image of Spock giving the Vulcan salute with the caption 'Live Long and Prosper,' and a pair of sandals. The bracelet seemed to vanish as soon as Nexus stopped touching it.

"I can imagine," Element said. She nodded toward the Japanese man in the suit. "This is Special Agent Junichi Hasikawa. He's our in-house Department of Metahuman Affairs liaison."

"Nice to meet you," Maggie said. It was a lie, but her mother had raised her to be polite.

"No, it isn't," Junichi said. "It's okay, though. I get it. I don't get to meet most people under the best of circumstances. Most incidents which result in the manifestation of metahuman abilities really suck. Even spontaneous manifestations can be rough. Despite what you may have heard, a DMA liaison's job is to help people. Once we've figured out what has happened to you, we can help you learn how to manage your abilities so you don't hurt yourself or anyone else, and get you signed up for any sort of assistance or accommodations you need."

"Yeah," Maggie said. "Sounds great, but having been on the receiving end of one government assistance program already, I think I'll pass."

"Well, I'll be here if you change your mind," he said.

Maggie ignored him and turned to Ashley.

"Nice lab. Yours, I'm guessing?"

"How ever did you tell?" Ashley asked with a grin. "I'm sure you'd rather stick to what science could tell you about your situation, but I think today has demonstrated that science doesn't currently have the capacity to quantify what has happened to you. At least not yet. If Sierra had been a few more years along in her research, that might be different, but for now, I think I can do a better job of studying and defining what's happened to you."

"Hey, you've already changed my worldview once today. If you can give me an answer I can work with, I'll take it."

Ashley nodded. "If it's okay with you, I'd like to try something and see what happens."

Maggie couldn't stop a grin from spreading across her face. "I'm not sure about how it goes with magic, but in science, that usually leads to having to recharge the fire extinguisher and fill out a lot of paperwork."

Element burst out laughing and looked over at Industry. "She's seen you work."

Industry glared at Element, but the effect was spoiled by the obvious blush on her cheeks and the way everyone in the room laughed.

"I promise this is safe," Ashley said. "Or at least, safer than what we did earlier."

"Okay," Maggie said. "What do you have in mind?"

"Stand up," Ashley said. Maggie and Ashley both stood up. Then

Ashley walked around the table and placed her hand between Maggie's breasts and pushed. The push, as intense as it was, wasn't physical. Maggie felt it everywhere, from all directions, not just where Ashley was touching her. After a moment of being squeezed like she was in a vice, there was a release of pressure like the cork in a bottle of champagne coming out, and Maggie suddenly found herself floating above the spot where she'd been standing. Ashley was floating in front of her, hand still on her chest, but Maggie could still see Ashley standing below in the same space where she'd been. The Ashley below her still had her hand pressed against the front of Maggie's shirt, but the shirt and the rest of Maggie's clothes were empty. Maggie didn't see her body anywhere.

"Okay," the Ashley floating in front of Maggie said, "I probably should have expected this."

"Expected what?" Maggie asked. Ashley just nodded towards her. Maggie looked down and let out a yelp of surprise when she realized she was naked.

"Sorry," Ashley said.

"Um...it's okay, I guess." Maggie looked back up at Ashley. "Any particular reason you're still copping a feel?"

"It keeps our time scale synched. If I let go, I'm pretty sure you'll drop into that hyper-accelerated time you described to us earlier. My link to my physical body creates a limit on how fast my perceptions can occur. As long as our astral selves are in contact, you'll be held to my time scale. The moment I stop touching you, you'll exist without any sort of physical connection again and the universe will slow to a crawl."

"Okay," Maggie said. "That sort of makes sense, but what the hell happened to my body?"

"It doesn't exist right now," Ashley said. "In the strictest sense, it never existed. It's an illusion created by your desire for a physical form."

"It's a pretty solid illusion."

"Well, I could have said that it was just something you conjured up because you wanted a body, but I was trying to stick to language you're comfortable with. But yes, it's solid, but only because you want it to be. And when I let go, you should be able to recreate it the same way you did this morning, by wishing to have a body again."

"Except I'll be naked in a room full of strangers."

"Wish yourself back into your clothes."

"Will that work?"

"Only one way to find out," Ashley said. "I'm going to let go now."

Ashley pulled her hand away, and the instant she broke contact, the whole world froze as Maggie returned to Planck scale time. She looked down at her clothes and did what Ashley suggested. She wished she was back in her body, standing where she had been, still wearing her clothes. As soon as she wished it, it happened, and time started moving again. Ashley smiled at her and took her hand away.

"Okay, that was exciting," Maggie said.

"What?" Junichi asked. "Nothing happened."

"Something did," Ashley said. "It just happened too quickly for you to see it. I used a technique that some magic users use to help them teach their students astral projection. Normally, it would push the person's astral body out of their physical body. In this case, when I did it, Maggie's body ceased to exist until she recreated it. You didn't see it because while we were out of our bodies, our time scale accelerated, so she was only gone for a split second."

"She didn't go anywhere," Junichi said.

"She did," Ashley said. "I can run the footage from the high-speed security camera back for you if you like, but for right now, take my word for it. For a fraction of a heartbeat, Maggie didn't have a body again. Which tells me that my working hypothesis is correct."

"Thank you for not saying theory," Maggie said.

Ashley smiled and nodded her head slightly.

"I thought you would appreciate that."

"What was the hypothesis?" Industry asked.

"The way I would describe it, Maggie's soul was torn from her body, but the machine held it in our world after she died. Without a body to draw quintessence from, and unable to move beyond the veil, Maggie somehow learned to tap the Aether directly to draw in quintessence. By doing so, she learned to sustain herself on this side of the veil without a body. Her connection to the Aether allows her to conjure a physical form, but it has no true substance. It's a projection, created and sustained entirely by her will and fueled by the Aetheric energies from which she's drawing her life force."

Maggie, and everyone else in the room, stared at Ashley for a moment. Maggie couldn't help but think Ashley was showing off somehow, but she didn't understand for whom, until Industry broke the silence.

"You're saying her cognitive quantum field was entangled with the field in the machine when she died, and that she somehow learned to tap into the cosmic foam and draw on the zero point energy of the universe to sustain her mind as a disembodied cognitive field, and that the body is actually made of virtual matter she's assembled and is controlling?"

Junichi looked confused. Element looked at Industry like she was going to throw her onto the table and have her way with her right there in front of them. Doctor Sanchez looked annoyed, and Nexus looked at Industry and Ashley like she wanted to smack them both. Maggie got the feeling the whole thing was some sort of inside joke and ongoing friendly pissing competition at the same time.

"I like her explanation better," Maggie said to Ashley.

"I'm not surprised," Ashley said. "We said the same thing, but Industry framed it in terms you're more comfortable with. The important thing is, you're tapping into the Aether, and if you can conjure a body for yourself, I don't see any reason you shouldn't be able to conjure other things, like clothes. Once you learn how to let go of the body you've conjured, you'll be able to travel anywhere with a thought, or stop time and assess the situation. You'll also be able to heal any injury you receive just by wishing it away. And of course, you've got your expanded senses. So the ability to teleport, to regenerate, to manipulate your own perception of time, to create at least temporary objects at will, and to sense things around you beyond normal human limits."

Ashley smiled as she leaned back in her chair and looked Maggie in the eyes.

"Congratulations, Maggie. You've got superpowers."

"Thanks," Maggie said. "Can I get a refund?"

Chapter Seven

IT WAS LATE BY the time Ashley finally showed Maggie to the guest room they had assigned her. She was relieved that it turned out to be the one right next to Sierra's, because it meant she was able to check in on Sierra with her new senses without having to work too hard to do it. Once she was sure Sierra was still sleeping soundly, she sat down and tried to figure out what to do next. She wasn't tired at all. She knew she should be. It felt like years had passed since the last time she slept, but all she felt was restless.

It was the first time in eleven years she wasn't in pain, and she felt like she should be doing all the things she used to love. She wanted to ride a bike and go for a run, or maybe go swimming. Swimming sounded amazing. Her parents' house hadn't been right on the beach because they didn't want to live on the barrier islands, but she'd spent tons of time there growing up, and loved swimming in the ocean. She hadn't been swimming since the invasion. She didn't even own a suit.

She put swimming on the top of her to do list once all this business with the High Guard was over and started digging in her purse, intending to spend some quality time digging through her favorite tags on Archive of Our Own. She thought maybe a nice fake dating fic would keep her busy until morning, but before she could find her phone, someone knocked on her door. She stared at it for a moment, wondering who it could be and hoping whoever it was didn't have more bad news.

She decided to try one of her new tricks and extended her senses out beyond the door. A thin, athletic Indian girl was standing there, holding a cooler. It only took Maggie a second to realize it had to be Delta V. She set her purse aside and opened the door.

"Hey," Delta V said, sounding oddly hesitant. It surprised Maggie a little.

"Hey." Maggie immediately wanted to kick herself for saying it, but she was a little out of practice with talking to cute girls. At least, face to face.

"Mind if I come in?" Delta V asked.

"Uh...sure, come on in," Maggie said. She stepped back, making room for Delta V to slip past her into the room. Delta V walked over to the table in the corner and set the cooler on it.

"I brought kulfi," she said as she opened the cooler. "I'm not sure if you've ever had it, but I like it better than ice cream, but I also brought a few pints of Haagen-Dazs Cookies and Cream, just in case. I figured even if you like kulfi, you might need some comfort food. I know I did. Which is why I brought kulfi. It's one of my comfort foods. But I also brought the Haagen-Dazs, because I saw an empty pint in your trash when I threw away the wrappers for the cereal bars, so I figured that was probably your comfort food. I just figured, the night I got my powers, I went through about three gallons of mango kulfi before I calmed down, and I thought it might help."

"Hey," Maggie said as she rested a hand on Delta V's shoulder. "Slow down a bit."

Delta V smiled, and it was hard to tell, but Maggie was pretty sure she blushed.

"Sorry," she said. "I talk a lot when I get nervous, and I've never really done this before."

Maggie smiled and gestured towards one of the chairs at the table as she sat down.

"Maybe have a seat and tell me what this is."

Delta V dropped into the other seat and took a deep breath.

"I thought you might want to talk, or want some company, even if you didn't want to talk. Nexus usually does the 'comforting people after weird shit happens' thing, but she's a little scared of you, and honestly, I don't think she'd be good at it in your case anyway. I'm not sure any of the others would be. They don't really get what it's like. Industry and Element both chose this life. Same with Maker, Fractal, and Hoplite. Cinderella did too, in a way. She's been trained from birth as an alchemist, but she didn't really need to join a MERT team. She could have just spent her life turning lead into gold and living on the proceeds. Sometimes I feel like Nexus and Mafic should get it, but Nexus got her powers really young, and Mafic's had his powers longer than I've been alive, so I don't think he remembers what it was like at the beginning. So I thought maybe you could use someone who does remember and who understands what it's like to suddenly have your whole world turned upside down when all you wanted to do was finish a bit of work, then go home and play video games, and I'm talking too much, aren't I?"

"No," Maggie said. Someone else might have thought so, but she thought it was adorable. Though not nearly as adorable as the smile Delta V gave her. The smile lit up the room, and Maggie felt her heart skip a beat. She had to remind herself to not make an idiot of herself just because a cute girl smiled at her. Delta V was famous. She probably had women throwing themselves at her all the time. Maggie didn't even know her real name.

"What do I call you?" Maggie asked.

"Oh! I'm sorry. I forgot. I don't meet new people that often. Well, no, I do, I mean, I meet new people every day, but that's in costume and...I need to stop and take a breath." At which point, she did just that. She closed her eyes, and took several deep, slow breaths, and Maggie forced herself to look at Delta V's face and not watch the way her breasts rose and fell. She opened her eyes and looked at Maggie again.

"Hi. I'm Varsha," she said. "Varsha Patel, but everyone here just calls me Vee, since it works in and out of costume."

"Do you prefer being called Vee?"

Varsha shrugged.

"I don't mind."

"Varsha's a beautiful name. Be a shame not to use it." Maggie wanted to high five herself at how smooth that sounded. Like a line she'd use when she was talking to someone as Bobbie in Digilife. She was even prouder of herself when Varsha gave her another one of those megawatt smiles, and she had to fight not to grin like an idiot.

"So, what's kulfi?" Maggie asked.

"Oh! Right, sorry. Most people call it Indian ice cream. It's not really the same, though. It's thicker and richer. The milk is simmered until it reduces by half, and it's not whipped either. It's more like a frozen custard. I like mango best, but I brought mango, pistachio, vanilla, and rose."

Maggie was pretty sure she would have tried candied spiders if Varsha had offered them to her in that moment. Turning her down would have been too much like kicking a puppy. Luckily, mango frozen custard sounded delicious.

"I'll try the mango if you're willing to share," Maggie said.

"Of course," Varsha said. She opened the cooler and took out a couple of stoneware pots and a pair of spoons, sliding one of each over to Maggie. Maggie lifted the lid off the pot and looked inside. The kulfi was a light orange color with chunks of mango clearly visible. She picked up her spoon.

"Thank you for this," she said.

"No problem," Varsha said. She took a bite of her kulfi and Maggie did the same, and immediately embarrassed herself by moaning at how good it was.

"I nearly died when it happened," Varsha said. "I was at school. College. Fourth year pre-med with a dual major in chemistry. My parents wanted me to be a doctor. I wanted to be a chemical engineer. I was working in the Organic Chemistry Lab, and I heard one of the other students say, 'Oh shit' and slam the front of the hood closed. I looked up just in time to see them hit the alarm. I don't know how well you know your chemistry, but the last thing you want to hear in a chemistry lab is someone saying, 'oh shit.' It never ends well."

She took another bite of kulfi. Maggie just waited for her to go on.

"The explosion happened before I could even start to run, and I should have died. Everyone in that building should have died. But the world just stopped. I've never been so scared in my life. I didn't understand what was happening, and I stood there for a minute, just staring at this frozen explosion, before I decided to run. I got two steps before I realized I couldn't just leave everyone else there. So, I grabbed the kid who had started the explosion, and I carried him out of the building. Then, I went back in. I went back again and again, and somewhere along the way I realized the explosion wasn't completely frozen, but that didn't stop me. I got every single person out of that building.

"When I was done, I just collapsed on the ground. I was so tired and hungry, I'm not sure I had another trip in me, but I would have tried. As soon as I sat down, time started moving again. I watched as the wall of the lab I'd been in blew out. The fume hood the kid had been working in landed half a block away. Within a couple of minutes, the whole building was on fire."

"How many people did you save?"

"A hundred and ninety-three," she said. "When my metagene kicked in that day, I got speed, strength, I got a lot tougher, I can see farther."

"You're a true speedster then? Not a time stall?"

"I'm surprised you know the difference," Varsha said. "Not a lot of people do."

Maggie took another bite of the kulfi, enjoying the taste as she stalled for time.

"I used to be really into the whole superhero thing," she said. "I loved them. Science fiction. Fantasy. Superheroes. I could tell you code names and power sets and origin stories. I still remember most of it, even if I tried my best to forget."

"What changed your mind?" Varsha asked.

"You weren't here during the Gacrux invasion, were you?"

"No," Varsha said. "My family lives in Orlando. It wasn't one of the cities that got hit. I came to Sun City for college. Stuck around because the High Guard gave me a place."

"I grew up here. Red Coat was one of my heroes, and he was amazing. I mean, he had a ridiculous accent, and I realized later that basing his costume off a colonial era British army uniform was probably not the most culturally sensitive thing he could have done, but for the most part, he was the real deal. Always one of the first to arrive at a disaster scene. Always one of the last to leave. Stepped into fights that would send most heroes running."

"Bit of a crush?" Varsha asked, which made Maggie laugh and shake her head.

"Nooo. No, no, no, no, no," Maggie said. She blushed a bit as she started into the kulfi pot. "I had a huge crush on Airheart."

Varsha let out a squeal of joy, and when Maggie looked up, she saw her smiling from ear to ear and bouncing in her seat.

"Did you have the poster?" she asked. "Tell me you had the poster."

"I had the poster," Maggie said. She didn't need to ask which one. When it came to Airheart, 'The Poster' only meant one thing. The cover shot for the issue of Rolling Stone magazine where they'd interviewed her right after she and Ice Dragon went public about their relationship. The image was burned into the mind of every queer girl in America. Airheart, wearing nothing but a bomber jacket and a smile, lounging on the coils of a blue Asian dragon.

"You know, she's even hotter in person," Varsha said.

"I'm not sure that's possible," Maggie replied.

"Oh, it is. I got to meet her a couple of years back, and I've seen her a few times since. Ashley goes to brunch with her, Ice Dragon, Eurion, Focus, Scatter, and a couple of others in Pontian a couple times a month, and Element keeps trying to recruit her. Element and Airheart used to be teammates. Element was a reserve Irregular for a while. But Ice Dragon won't leave Boston, and Airheart won't go anywhere without Ice Dragon."

"I didn't realize the High Guard were actively recruiting," Maggie said.

"We're trying to keep it quiet, but we've got a couple of holes in the line-up. Mafic is the only real brick we have. Industry and Hoplite are tough in their armor, but neither of them can really soak damage the way someone like Mafic or Airheart does. Aside from Industry, none of our flyers can even come close to supersonic flight, and we don't have any serious airlift capacity. On top of that, Hoplite's pushing fifty, and has been making noises about retiring for a while. So we're looking."

"But Airheart is fifty if she's a day."

"Fifty-six, and not aging," Varsha said. "None of the Olympus Six are. Or if they are aging, it's too slow to detect."

"I hadn't realized that," Maggie said. The mood in the room shifted as Varsha looked down at her kulfi and dug her spoon in a bit more forcefully than before.

"It happens with certain power sets," Varsha said. "Ones that come with regenerative abilities or high damage resistance tend to slow down aging or stop it completely."

It only took a second for Maggie to understand the sudden shift in mood. Varsha had a powerset that came with regenerative abilities and high damage resistance.

"You?" she asked.

Varsha shrugged.

"We don't really talk about it, you know," Varsha said. "Most people think it's this gift. Stay young, live forever, but after a while, you start to figure out what it really means, and when you look at the ones who've been around for a while, you can see it in their eyes."

Maggie sat there for a moment, trying to find words, but she couldn't.

"I don't...I don't know what to say."

Varsha shrugged and waved it away.

"You were talking about Red Coat," she said.

"Oh. Yeah. Red Coat. Um...no crush, but I thought he was cool. I had all the sentries action figures and the trading cards."

"What happened?"

"He saved my life," Maggie said. "For a long time, I wished he hadn't. I'm honestly not sure if I ever really stopped wishing that. My family was in the car when the invasion happened. We were on our way downtown to celebrate my getting into a NASA summer program when the portals opened up. One of the Gacrux shot our car. My parents and my brother died, and by the time Red Coat got to me and pulled me out of the car, I had full thickness burns over forty percent of my body, and so many broken bones the doctors had to put me back together with titanium screws and plates."

Maggie looked down at the kulfi and dug out another spoonful to avoid the pity she expected to see on Varsha's face.

"I had a hard time after that. I know he saved my life. I know the Sentries died stopping the invasion, but I was sixteen years old, disfigured, crippled for life, eaten up by guilt because I had to pick a restaurant downtown for the celebration dinner instead of just going for pizza. I spent a lot of time hating Red Coat for pulling me out of that car."

Varsha took Maggie's hand, and Maggie looked up in surprise.

"I've been in that place," Varsha said. "I'm glad you made it out."

Maggie smiled at her and squeezed her hand.

"Can I ask?"

"My parents are immigrants," Varsha said. "They both came over to study medicine and ended up staying, but they're still very traditional. Their parents even arranged their marriage. When I came home from my first year of college, they started talking about finding me a husband. I decided the easiest way to put a stop to that was to tell them I'm gay."

"Didn't go over well?" Maggie asked, already knowing the answer.

"No," Varsha said. "There was a lot of screaming, a lot of yelling, a lot of threats. They took away my car and phone, and eventually kicked me out of the house. I packed my bags, bought a prepaid phone at the gas station, and called a friend in Sun City to come pick me up. I was lucky enough to have a full ride at school, so once the fall semester started, I was okay, but that summer got really bad."

"Did they ever come round?"

"Eventually," Varsha said. "After I almost died in a very public way. About a year after I joined the High Guard, I had a bad fight with a speedster named Octane."

"I remember that," Maggie said. It had been impossible to avoid the news stories about him. Superpowered serial killers were ratings gold for the news. "He liked to douse people with gasoline and set them on fire."

"Women," Varsha said. "He liked to douse women with gasoline and set them on fire. Specifically women who had insulted him. I managed to take him down, but even with my powers, the doctors weren't sure I'd live, so they called my next of kin.

"When I woke up, there was a lot of crying and apologizing. Eventually, there was a lot more yelling and screaming, but we worked it out. I even go home sometimes on my days off. My brother and both my sisters are good about it. One of my brothers-in-laws was a dick about it for a while, but I gave him a little demonstration of my powers once, and he mostly keeps his mouth shut about me these days."

"That's good," Maggie said, wondering what, exactly, that demonstration had involved.

"What about you?" Varsha asked.

"When I was twelve, my mom pulled me aside and told me that she wanted me to know if I liked girls, it was okay. That her and dad would be fine with it. I came out about a year after that. When they died, my dad's parents took me in, and they were great about it. Grandma's younger brother is gay, and they're super close. When he came out, his parents disowned him, so Grandma told them to get bent and took him in. I don't think she or Uncle Toby ever spoke to them again. Grandpa and Toby's husband are still business partners. They restore classic cars."

"What about your mom's parents?"

"I pretend they don't exist and they never come near me. We're all happier that way."

"Ah."

Maggie went for another spoonful of the kulfi and frowned when she realized the pot was empty.

"More?" Varsha asked.

"Yeah," Maggie said. "What's left?"

"You like pistachio?

"Who doesn't?"

"Praetorian."

"The asshole who kicked Industry out of the Protectors?" Maggie asked.

"Yep. He has a tree nut allergy. Ask me how I know."

"How do you know?"

"Industry sends him a box of chocolate-covered almonds every year for Christmas."

Chapter Eight

MAGGIE NEVER MADE IT to sleep that night. After she finished the pistachio kulfi, which was delicious, she had mentioned to Varsha that D.E.B.S. was her favorite movie. Varsha had admitted she'd never seen it. Maggie had declared that a travesty, and insisted they had to correct the situation immediately. She'd dragged Varsha over to the bed, and after logging into one of her streaming accounts, they'd watched D.E.B.S., then moved on to I Can't Think Straight.

Varsha had begged off watching Better Than Chocolate and left at about two in the morning, saying she had an early patrol and would be really cranky if she didn't get her full four hours of sleep. Apparently not needing as much sleep was another benefit of being a speedster. Once she was gone, Maggie had turned off the lights, crawled into bed, and spent a good thirty minutes staring up at the ceiling, wondering if she even needed sleep before she gave it up as a bad job.

She wasn't even sure if she could sleep anymore. If she tried, she might end up throwing herself back into Planck scale time or lock herself into a never-ending dream state since there wouldn't be any sort of biological wakeup call. She made a note to talk to Ashley and Industry about it the next day, then grabbed her purse and took out her phone, fully intending to spend the rest of the night on that nice fake dating fic she'd been craving before Varsha had shown up, but there was a message notification for Digilife on her lock screen.

She frowned. She had message notifications turned off for Digilife. At least, she thought she did. She tapped the notification and entered her PIN to unlock her phone, then waited while the Digilife app opened. The app wasn't as full featured as the desktop version, but it did let her pop in-world if she wanted to, but she had been sure she'd turned off messaging. The last thing she wanted was someone at work to find out her avatar name. She had never even told anyone at work that she used Digilife.

When the app finished opening, her chat window popped up with Kelly's name. That made a little bit of sense. Maybe she'd set things up so she'd get an alert if Kelly messaged her. She tapped the name.

Kelly: Are you okay?

Kelly: Bobbie, tell me you're okay.

Kelly: I'm not fucking around here. It's all over the news. The science building at your school blew up with a bunch of people inside.

Kelly: You better be okay.

Kelly: If you're not okay, I'm going to get both my girlfriends to kick your ass.

Kelly: I'm not even kidding. They're tough. One of them was in the army.

Kelly: Please be okay.

Maggie kicked herself. She hadn't even thought about the fact that Kelly knew where she worked and might be worried. She tapped in the chat box and started typing.

Bobbie: I'm okay. It wasn't the building I work in.

She hit send, and a moment later, she got a notification telling her Kelly was online.

Kelly: Thank God!

Kelly: No, I take that back. Don't thank God. I've met God, and God is an asshole.

Kelly: But I'm glad you're okay.

Bobbie: Yeah. I'm sorry you were worried.

Kelly: I know you were probably busy all day, but I was really scared.

Bobbie: I'm sorry. I didn't have my phone with me for most of the day.

Kelly: Why not?

Bobbie: I spent most of the day with the people investigating the explosion.

Kelly: I thought you said it wasn't the building you work in.

Bobbie: It's not, but I was on campus when it happened. I'm not really sure how much I'm allowed to talk about, but for the record, the building I work in is One Park Place. The building that blew up was the Science Annex. They're about a block apart.

Kelly: Noted. Are you sure you're okay?

Bobbie: Honestly? No.

Kelly: Can you tell me?

Bobbie: You remember straight BFF?

Kelly: Yeah. Stupidhead. What about her?

Kelly: Oh, shit! Was she in the building that got blown up?

Bobbie: She's fine.

Bobbie: Her boyfriend was in the building.

Kelly: Fuck.

Bobbie: What makes it worse is he was her ex-boyfriend. They broke up a couple of days ago.

Kelly: Jesus. It never rains but it pours.

Bobbie: Yeah.

Kelly: How is she holding up?

Bobbie: About as well as you'd expect. Blames herself for him being in the office on a Saturday.

Kelly: I'm sorry, girl. That's got to suck.

Bobbie: Yeah. The whole day has been weird.

Kelly: I'm sorry, hun. I wish I could be there for you.

Bobbie: Thanks. That means a lot.

Bobbie: You want to hear the weirdest part?

Kelly: You know me. I'm all about the weird.

Bobbie: Well, it's not as weird as your 'The Devil is secretly funding dozens of civil rights organizations' theory, but it's definitely odd.

Kelly: Girl, that is not a theory, that is straight up fact.

Bobbie: Right. Sure it is.

Bobbie: Seriously though, I kind of...went on a date with one of the rescue workers.

Kelly: What?

Kelly: You mean I've been sitting here worrying my electronic ass off, and you were out getting your freak on?

Bobbie: No! It wasn't like that.

Kelly: I am both pissed off and impressed.

Kelly: Was she a firefighter? I'll bet she was. A really buff firefighter.

Bobbie: No. Not a firefighter.

Kelly: EMT? Oh, I'll be jealous if it was an EMT. All the EMTs I work with are big sweaty men. Not attractive.

Bobbie: Don't you have two girlfriends?

Kelly: I do. Doesn't mean I can't enjoy looking.

Bobbie: Fair enough. She wasn't an EMT either. It's a long story, but she thought I could use someone to talk to, so she got some kulfi and we sat and talked for a while, and ended up watching a couple of movies together. It was nice.

Kelly: Kulfi?

Bobbie: It's kind of like frozen custard. It's an Indian desert. She had mango, pistachio, vanilla, and rose. I tried the mango and the pistachio. They were really good.

Kelly: I'm totally jealous. That sounds amazing.

Bobbie: It was.

Kelly: So...

Kelly: Did you kiss her?

Bobbie: No.

Kelly: Why not?

Bobbie: Um...because we just met.

Kelly: This is why you're single.

Bobbie: I'd tell you I'm logging off, but honestly, I've got nothing better to do than sit here and get insulted.

Kelly: You should get some sleep.

Bobbie: I'm honestly too worked up right now.

Kelly: Yeah. I get that. Sometimes it's hard to get to sleep when something crazy happens at work.

Bobbie: Are you ever going to tell me what you actually do?

Kelly: Probably not.

Bobbie: Well, I know that there are EMTs involved now.

Kelly: You know too much!

Bobbie: I know you're an IT specialist and you work with EMTs. It's not that much.

Kelly: Too late. The black helicopters are on their way. I'm sorry it's come to this.

Bobbie: You work in a hospital, don't you? You work in a hospital and you bang your hot nurse girlfriend in the on-call room while other people are trying to sleep.

Kelly: Oh, please. As if Nurse Hotness would ever agree to a quickie at work.

Bobbie: No?

Kelly: Don't think C Cup and I haven't tried.

Bobbie: Do your girlfriends know the nicknames you have for them?

Kelly: You say that like I don't call them C Cup and Nurse Hotness to their faces.

Bobbie: ...

Bobbie: You know, I actually believe you on that.

Kelly: Why does that feel like an insult?

Bobbie: No reason.

Bobbie: But while we're on the subject, why aren't you currently the filling in a C Cup/Nurse Hotness sandwich?

Kelly: They're asleep.

Bobbie: Kind of my point. It's the middle of the night in Atlanta.

Kelly: It's the middle of the night in Sun City, too.

Bobbie: Yeah, and She Who Brought Me Kulfi only left about

twenty minutes ago, because she needed to sleep so she could go to work tomorrow. Why aren't you tucked between your two gorgeous girlfriends getting some of that hot, hot sleeping in a cuddle pile action?

Kelly: Insomnia. I don't really sleep that much.

Bobbie: Oh. That sucks.

Kelly: It's not so bad. Between Digilife and fanfic, I keep busy.

Bobbie: You write fanfic?

Kelly: Yes.

Bobbie: How did I not know this about you?

Kelly: We've only known each other for about nine months. A girl needs to keep a few secrets. Otherwise, you'd lose interest.

Bobbie: Not likely. So, out with it. What's your username on AO3?

Kelly: Why should I tell you?

Bobbie: Because I promise to comment on every chapter.

Kelly: Wow. Going straight for my weak spot. I see how it is.

Bobbie: It worked, didn't it?

Kelly: *sigh* Yes.

Bobbie: So...

Kelly: BestMistakeEver

Bobbie: Not what I expected, but hang on one second.

Kelly: Hanging on.

Bobbie: Holy shit! That's a lot of fic.

Kelly: I have a lot of free time.

Bobbie: How? You've got a job and two girlfriends.

Kelly: The job doesn't keep me that busy.

Bobbie: Apparently not. Jesus. How has this all been posted in the last year?

Kelly: Did I mention the job doesn't keep me busy?

Bobbie: Yeah, but still.

Kelly: See anything you like?

Bobbie: Lots. How the hell did you have time to do three complete series rewrites of Supergirl?

Bobbie: No, don't answer that. Just tell me which one I should start with.

Kelly: That depends. Do you prefer Cat/Kara, Kara/Lucy, or Kara/Nia?

Bobbie: Ask the hard questions, why don't you?

Kelly: Okay, let's try it this way. One is a nice slow burn age gap ice queen romance where it takes them four seasons to finally kiss. One is a messy, sloppy, angsty dumpster fire about a repressed lesbian from a tradition-bound homophobic culture falling in love with a closeted gender fluid queer person who is dealing with living in the shadow of a famous sister and a bigoted, unreasonable, overbearing father. One is a nice, tender love story about a woman dealing with the ethics of falling in love with the person she's mentoring, while both of them lead a double life as high-profile figures in a civil rights movement fighting against anti-alien bigotry.

Bobbie: You had me at 'messy, sloppy, angsty dumpster fire.'

Kelly: I kind of figured you'd say that, but if you really want to bleed for my art, you should start with my Mass Effect series. Nothing hurts quite so good as FemShep/Liara.

Bobbie: Okay, seriously, how have C Cup and Nurse Hotness not married you yet?

Kelly: Polygamy is still illegal in Georgia.

Bobbie: You know what, come marry me.

Kelly: You just want me for my fanfic.

Bobbie: Woman, you wrote ten full seasons of Batwoman. Of course I want you for your fanfic.

Kelly: No one ever wants me for cheap, tawdry sex. I don't know what the world is coming to.

Bobbie: I figured you were getting all the cheap, tawdry sex you could take from C Cup and Nurse Hotness.

Kelly: Well, yes, but that's not the point.

Bobbie: I'm going to go blow through some of this fic. Talk to you later?

Kelly: Any time. I've got my notifications set to tell me if you message me. Unless I'm fighting a supervillain or having cheap, tawdry sex, I'll be on to answer you within about five minutes.

Bobbie: I appreciate it. Good night.

Kelly: Good night. Glad you didn't die.

Maggie closed out of Digilife and picked one of Kelly's stories, then started reading.

* * * *

Maggie headed down to the cafeteria early the next morning. She wasn't really hungry, but she figured she should eat if Ashley was going to try to teach her how to control her powers. When she got there, it wasn't what she'd expected. The place looked more like a ballroom set for a formal dinner than a cafeteria. Instead of a food line off to one side and long tables, there were a lot of large round tables with linen table clothes that seated twelve, plus a handful of two tops along the wall. There was no food line or even a coffee station. The only thing that looked even remotely like a food service station was a small buffet table with a stack of plates and a massive silver tray covered with a domed lid sitting on it, and a sign with Delta V's emblem above it on the wall.

Element and Industry sat at one of the two tops, holding hands across the table as they nursed huge mugs of coffee. Maggie couldn't see Industry's face from the doorway, but Element's expression promised a slow, painful death to anyone who approached. A muscular Latino man sat at another of the two tops, reading an actual newspaper while eating what looked like an enormous piece of sushi. Two men sat at a third two top, talking animatedly over a breakfast of bread, fruit, and spreads.

For a moment, Maggie was at a loss, but then she spotted Ashley, who was already waving her over to the table where she was sitting with Nexus, Sierra, a muscular black man that Maggie assumed was Maker, and a black girl who was pretty obviously Fractal, given the cable plugged into the back of her head and the laptop in front of her.

Maggie took the seat next to Sierra and placed a hand on her back, rubbing gently.

"How are you doing?" she asked.

Sierra looked up from the mug she'd been staring into, and Maggie could see the misery on her face. Sierra forced a smile.

"I'm okay," she said. The lie was obvious, but Maggie decided not to call her out on it. At least, not while they were sitting at a table of relative strangers. Instead, she scratched Sierra's back in imitation of the way Sierra scratched hers when trying to comfort her. Sierra gave her a look of gratitude, and Maggie smiled at her. She was so focused on checking in with Sierra, she didn't even notice the waiter arrive until he spoke.

"What can I get you this morning, ma'am?"

"Uh...is there a menu?"

A soft metallic rattle filled the room, and Maggie felt a gust of wind. She turned her head to find Varsha sitting on her other side, with two subs on a plate in front of her.

"Just order anything you want," Varsha said. "I mean, don't get too crazy, like ordering some really exotic sourdough bread that takes a week to make or something because they need warning for things like that, but within reason. I'll have my usual, Rob. Do you like pancakes?"

Maggie stared for a moment, then looked back at Rob the waiter.

"Just bring two of whatever she's having," Maggie said.

Ashley, Nexus, and Maker all snorted.

"How would you like your steak cooked, ma'am?" Rob asked.

"Medium rare," Maggie said.

"And to drink?" he asked.

"Mocha latte, triple shot of chocolate syrup, and a large orange juice."

Rob the waiter nodded and headed off to the kitchen while Maggie wondered what she'd gotten herself into. Varsha was already halfway through one of her subs, presumably eating it as a snack to hold her over until breakfast arrived. She wasn't too worried about it, because Sierra didn't have a plate in front of her. She hoped she could use whatever ridiculous amount of food Rob brought her as a way to convince Sierra to eat.

"You're going to regret that," Maker said.

Maggie glanced over at him and watched as he added a splash of hot sauce to his waffles.

"Not as much as I'd regret chicken and waffles for breakfast," Maggie said. "Wait, I didn't order chicken and waffles for breakfast, did I?"

Varsha laughed and shook her head.

"No. Well, yes. No. Sort of. Twenty-four-ounce porterhouse steak. Three egg omelet stuffed with mushrooms, green peppers, onions, and chicken with fajita seasoning, topped with cheddar and jack cheese, then smothered in sour cream, salsa, and guacamole. Six strips of bacon. Six large blueberry pancakes with maple syrup, and a large waffle. So, there's chicken and there's waffles, and there's even hot sauce if you want it, but it's not chicken and waffles like Garnell is eating."

"Remember to breathe, Vee," Ashley said.

Varsha rolled her eyes and took another bite out of her sandwich. Maggie glanced over at Industry and Element.

"They don't eat with the rest of you?"

"Not breakfast," Fractal said. "Trust me, we all prefer it that way."

"They're not that bad," Garnell said, which prompted Nexus to shake her head.

"Yes, they are." She turned and looked at Maggie. "Do not ever speak to them before they've had their coffee. Industry especially."

"Industry?" Ashley asked. "Really? Element's the one who set my costume on fire."

"Yeah. I remember," Nexus said. "Element is surly in the moment, but Industry is vindictive. I tried to ask her about a press release one morning. She glared at me until I went away. I thought that was the end of it, but later that afternoon, I found out she ordered the kitchen staff not to serve me chocolate for a month."

"Okay, that's harsh," Garnell said.

Fractal picked up a piece of her toast and waved it at Nexus.

"People have gone full-on supervillain for less than that," she said before taking a bite of the toast.

Maggie laughed a little at that.

"Speaking of things that will drive people to supervillainy, I need to get my laptop and the wifi password. I have some stuff I want to write up and toss in the drop box for my research team."

"You should probably hold off on that," Ashley said.

"Why?" Maggie asked. Ashley straightened up in her chair, and Maggie could tell from the look on her face she was getting ready to deliver bad news.

"Officially, you are currently in a medically induced coma because the explosion aggravated your prior injuries. The High Guard and Department of Metahuman Affairs is providing you with lifesaving non-standard medical intervention because you are a material witness to an event which may have involved a metahuman."

"What?" Maggie asked, a little stunned by what she'd just heard. "Why would you do that?"

"A couple of reasons. First, a metahuman was involved. I mean, technically you're a Type Uniform Non-Magical Aberration, but legally that still falls under the metahuman blanket. Also, legally, it doesn't matter if you were a metahuman when the incident started. The law covers incidents where superhuman abilities manifest, which leads us to the second reason. Potential metahuman involvement allows the DMA to claim jurisdiction, which allows us to seize Sierra's quantum field imager as evidence."

Sierra looked up from her coffee, her expression going from miserable to horrified so quickly Maggie was a little worried she'd pull a facial muscle.

"No!" Sierra said. "You can't take my imager. It took me—"

"Easy," Ashley said, cutting Sierra off. "Take it easy. We didn't make the decision. It came down from Washington. They've asked Industry, Fractal, and Maker to strip it down and figure out how it did what it did to Maggie so we can make sure it doesn't happen again.

Frankly, the DMA doesn't give a shit that they're putting you out of a job, but Industry is a better engineer than a physicist, and Fractal's specialties are computer science, cybersecurity, and artificial intelligence. Maker's not bad with a soldering iron and a microcontroller, but he's mostly a blacksmith and a machinist. The truth is, they're in over their heads with your machine. Once Industry has had enough coffee to be more coherent than an extra in a zombie movie, she's going to come over here and offer you a job as a 'consultant' on the 'figuring out how the heck your machine gave Maggie superpowers' project."

Maggie still had her hand resting lightly on Sierra's back. When Sierra slumped in response to what Ashley had just said, she reached up and scratched lightly between Sierra's shoulder blades, just to remind Sierra she was there. Sierra turned and looked at her.

"All my research," Sierra said, tears welling up in her eyes. Maggie understood. The imager had been the focus of Sierra's work, her whole life really, for years. If anyone even suspected it had been responsible for the accident, she'd never get a grant to rebuild it. She'd be lucky to get another post-doc position at all, much less a tenure track teaching position. Her career as a scientist would be over before it really started.

"Everything is still backed up in your office in One Park Place," Maggie said. "You can pull down copies of all the digital files, and the lab notebooks are yours. It will slow down the cognitive modeling project, but once the DMA has their answer, we can get the imager released back to the college and find you a new grant."

It was a lie, and Maggie knew it. University politics, especially when grant funding was involved, was brutal. Unfortunately, Sierra knew it too.

"You know it won't be that easy," Sierra said. "The fact that the DMA confiscated it at all...Hastings will have a field day with this. I'll lose my post-doc slot."

"You're assuming Hastings survives the fallout once word gets out that he was working on experiments that hadn't been approved by Safety and Ethics. Illegal experiments. Research on macroscopic teleportation has been banned for more than a decade. He's going to lose his tenure. He might even go to jail."

"And we'll work something out," Ashley said. "Industry's a good person. At least once she's properly caffeinated. She's not going to let someone as brilliant as you get your career tanked by office politics."

Maggie gave Ashley a grateful smile as she felt some of the tension ease out of Sierra. Sierra leaned against Maggie, and Maggie slipped an arm around her and gave her a squeeze.

"I don't know what to do, Mags," she said.

"Well," Maggie said. "First, help me eat the huge breakfast I ordered. Then, talk to Industry once she's caffeinated enough to stop craving brains. We'll go from there, but Ashley's right. This isn't going to be the end of your career. We'll figure something out. I promise."

Sierra didn't say anything, but she did give a small nod, and when the food arrived a few minutes later, Maggie convinced her to eat the pancakes, and pretended not to notice when Sierra stole the bacon.

Chapter Nine

THE TRAINING ROOM REMINDED Maggie of a high school gym. It was large enough to hold a couple of basketball courts, and the ceiling had to be at least thirty feet high. That was where the similarities ended, though. The floor and the walls were covered in a thin layer of rubber, but the bank vault-like doors made her think they were probably heavily armored. Something Ashley confirmed as they walked across the open space to the center of the room.

"This is the hard room," Ashley said. "Though, honestly, most of the team just calls it the box. It's designed for serious heavy hitters to be able to train in. The walls are fifteen-inch-thick hardened steel plate. Someone like Red Coat or Airheart could bust their way out, but it would take some work. I don't expect you to be able to punch in their weight class right away, but I think you might get there eventually."

"Are you kidding?" Maggie asked.

"No," Ashley said. "Industry could probably put it in terms you'd be more comfortable with, but you're tapped into the Aether itself, drawing raw quintessence from the very fabric of the universe. You've conjured a body for yourself out of pure will. If you are what I think you are, the only limits on your power are the limits you place on yourself."

"So, 'do or do not. There is no try,' is what you're saying."

Ashley stopped and turned around, giving Maggie an annoyed look. Then she struck so fast, Maggie never had a chance to react. She punched Maggie right in the chest, knocking her clean out of her body. Maggie stared down at where Ashley's astral fist was still pressed against the sternum of her astral form for what felt like a good minute before she looked back up at Ashley.

"Rule number one," Ashley said. "I am not Yoda. Rule number two. This is not a joke."

"Sorry," Maggie said.

"Sorry doesn't cut it in here. You've been given a gift, but that gift is like a loaded gun. Used carefully, it can be an invaluable tool. Used carelessly, it can end countless lives. What I'm going to teach you here will keep you from hurting someone the first time you lose control of your temper. Someone like Sierra or your grandparents. You can take what I teach you and use it to live something close to a normal life. Get up, go to work, fall in love, get married, if that's what you want to do."

"What else would I do?"

Ashley shook her head and pulled her fist back. The instant the connection between Maggie and Ashley was broken, Maggie found herself dropped back into Planck scale time. She could still see Ashley's astral form in front of her, her empty clothes unmoved from where they were when Ashley knocked her out of her body, and the empty room just sitting there, waiting for them. Maggie sat there for a long time, thinking about what Ashley had said, what she'd implied, and what she hadn't said.

Go to work. Fall in love. Get married. Something close to a normal life, but not actually a normal life. There was no mention of having kids or growing old, and Maggie knew why. Her body was an illusion, a projection of her will, given substance by twisting the raw energy that made up the fabric of the universe into a shape she desired. The form existed only as long as she willed it to exist, and the moment she let go, the universe snapped back into its natural shape, and her body simply vanished. She wasn't going to grow old. She could change her body, maybe, make it look like she was growing old, but true age would never come. She would never have a normal life.

Did that mean she should put on a costume, become a hero, help people, fight supervillains? Was that what she was supposed to want? Did having the power she did mean she had a responsibility?

There was a time when she would have jumped at the idea. She'd loved superheroes. She'd dreamed of being one, of going into battle alongside Red Coat, Airheart, Focus, The Gentleman, Ice Dragon, and the rest. Facing down monsters like Aerosol, Demos, or Chernobog.

At fifteen, she'd have jumped at the chance. At sixteen, she'd gotten a brutal lesson in what happened when a superhero wasn't good enough, or fast enough, or strong enough, or in the right place at the right time. She'd had to live with that lesson for eleven years, with the pain and the scars. Even if the marks weren't on her body anymore, she still had to live with the fact that she would never see her parents or her brother again.

She didn't want to be that person. The one who wasn't good enough, fast enough, strong enough, in the right place at the right time. She didn't want to leave the scars that superheroes left behind when they failed.

She looked down at her clothes again, hanging there empty in the middle of the room, and willed herself back into them. She reappeared just in time to get the wind knocked out of her as Ashley's fist slammed into her chest. She staggered back, gasping for air while Ashley just stood there, a neutral expression on her face.

"Ouch," Maggie said.

Ashley didn't say anything. She just took a step back and lowered herself to the floor with more grace than should be possible for someone dressed in jeans and a t-shirt. She looked up at Maggie, then gestured at the spot on the floor in front of her.

"Sit," she said, then started taking off her shoes.

Maggie lowered herself to the floor. It was awkward. She hadn't sat on the floor in over a decade, and she wasn't sure she'd ever done it in a skirt.

"I hurt you," Ashley said.

"Yeah." Maggie said.

"Good. That's your first lesson. In this room, I am not your friend. In this room, you have no friends. Only teachers and enemies. I will be both, but there will be others."

Maggie watched as Ashley folded her legs into a perfect lotus pose.

"This isn't off to a promising start," Maggie said.

"It's starting off better than you realize," Ashley said. "No matter how much you've changed, at the end of the day, you're still alive. Some people never make it this far. You also haven't killed anyone. That's not something a lot of metahumans can say when they start their training. Due to the nature of your abilities, I don't think we have to worry too much about the first, so your training will focus on making sure the second remains true.

"I have spent my entire life working towards achieving a small fraction of what you have been given by chance. I don't say that out of resentment or to make you feel guilty, only as a statement of fact. You have power. You have ability. You currently lack knowledge and skill. I can teach you. What I cannot do is translate for you. I learned to harness my powers within a certain conceptual framework, and I will teach you within that framework, because I do not know enough about science to put my understanding into terms you will be comfortable with. It will be up to you to recontextualize what I teach you into a conceptual framework you're comfortable with. Do you understand?"

"Yes."

"And are you comfortable with that?"

"Do I have a choice?"

"Of course. You can choose not to learn. You can choose to be a danger to those around you. But if you make that choice, I will be forced to bind you, or to find a way to sever your connection to the Aether and destroy you. You can choose not to learn, but you will not be allowed to choose to hurt anyone through deliberate ignorance."

"So, no choice then," Maggie said. "How do we start?"

"Have you ever meditated before?"

"Yes," Maggie said. "I had a physical therapist who suggested I try it to help deal with the pain."

"Did it work?"

"Not as well as Dilaudid, but well enough to get me through to my next dose when it wore off early."

"Well, that's a start," Ashley said. "Put yourself in lotus, and we'll get started."

Maggie stared at Ashley for a moment in disbelief, before remembering that she probably could get into lotus position with her new body. She took her shoes off, and sure enough, it was easy to fold herself into the lotus position. She took a moment to rearrange her skirt, then looked at Ashley.

Ashley waved her hand and the room went dark. A moment later, five torches lit, surrounding them in firelight. Maggie glanced down and saw the mat they were sitting on was now inscribed with a pentacle set in a circle, with runes filling the space between the points. The base of the torches were on the ground outside of the circle, one at each point of the pentacle.

"A little protection. The entire building is heavily warded against malicious spirits, but I prefer to err on the side of caution." Ashley waved her hand again, and the sound of chanting filled the room. It was low and soft, but loud enough for Maggie to make out the rhythm of the chants.

"We're going to start with a guided meditation. Then I'll lead you through a few exercises that should teach you how to exit your body at will. Normally, that's a difficult skill to master. In most people, the body and the spirit want to be whole. For you, the situation is reversed. The spirit wants to be free and unbound, but you're holding it within a body. We simply have to teach you how to release that hold."

"Sounds easy enough," Maggie said. Ashley gave a small laugh that made it pretty clear she didn't agree.

"We'll start with your breathing. Take a deep breath and let it out slowly."

* * * *

Three hours later, Ashley shook Maggie awake.

"Sorry," Maggie said.

"It's okay," Ashley said. "It's actually a good sign. I wasn't sure you were still capable of sleep."

"Neither was I," Maggie said. "I suppose that means we accomplished something today."

"What put you under?" Ashley asked.

"I'm not really sure I'm prepared to admit the answer to that," Maggie said.

"Okay, now you have to tell me."

Maggie could feel the blush rising in her cheeks. She didn't think that was even remotely fair, given that her body was supposed to be an illusion. She glanced at Ashley, who was sitting there, a patient look on her face, and decided to just get it over with.

"I was reciting the first hundred prime numbers," Maggie said.

"I'm not sure if I'm impressed that you have them memorized, or empathetically embarrassed that you're that big of a nerd."

"Both is good," Maggie said. "Should we try again?"

"Yes," Ashley said. "Start reciting the primes, but this time, I want you to pay attention to how you feel as you do. We need to find that place where the outside world falls away, but before you fall asleep."

"Right," Maggie said. "Sounds easy." She took a deep breath and started running the primes again. Two, three, five, seven, eleven, thirteen... She'd gone through the list about four times when she realized it had happened. She was awake, but the outside world had slipped away, and all she was aware of was herself. She was so surprised by the realization that she opened her eyes, and the rest of the world slammed back into her awareness.

"Damn it!"

"What happened?" Ashley asked.

"I had it for a moment, but as soon as I realized it, I shocked myself out of it."

Ashley laughed.

"Everyone does that their first time," she said. "Try again."

Maggie closed her eyes and started counting again. She expected it to be hard to get back to that place, but she focused on what it had felt like, and after a couple of breaths, she found herself sliding right back into that space. She waited a while, wanting to make sure she could hold on to it, but she felt it start slipping away. She took a couple of quick breaths, reciting the primes as she did, and slipped right back into the place where she wanted to be.

She stopped and started a few times, finding that in between space, then deliberately pushing herself out of it by focusing on something physical. It took some practice, but before long, she could find and enter that place at will. It wasn't a lot different from the trick she'd learned with expanding her senses, but it worked in reverse.

"Okay, what's next?" Maggie asked, once she was sure she could make it back to that space whenever she wanted.

"Inside you, there's tension. A place where it feels like you're holding on to something. You need to find that place."

"Okay," Maggie said, feeling more than a little dubious. It wasn't that she didn't think she could find a place inside herself where she was holding on to something; it was that she knew she was holding on to a lot of things. Her guilt, her shame, her crush on Sierra, her resentment of Garrett, her feelings for Sandra. It was a mess in there.

She started reciting the primes, determined to try and find what Ashley was looking for. It was easy enough to slip back into that liminal space where the world went away. Turning her eye inward was harder, mostly because she knew what she would find. It was every bit as messy as she expected, and she was self-aware enough to admit that maybe she should go back to therapy soon. For all the mess, she found what she was looking for a lot sooner than she expected. It wasn't quick, but it didn't take days, either.

She wasn't sure tension was the right word for it, though she supposed it fit. Sort of. It felt more like letting her arms hang down at her side, while keeping her hands balled into fists. It wasn't like the migraine-inducing tension she was used to when she'd been working too hard, or when she had a doctor's visit coming up, or like she used to get before her therapy sessions.

"I've found it," Maggie said.

"Good," Ashley said. "Now, let it go."

"I'm not sure how," Maggie said.

"Try visualizing the tension flowing out, like a muscle relaxing."

Maggie didn't want to argue about whether it was tension or not. Besides, Ashley's advice gave her an idea. She pictured a fist slowly opening and closing. She kept running the image through her head as she concentrated on that place inside her. It happened slowly, but as she worked through the visualization, she started to feel a difference. More effort when she pictured the fist closing, and less at rest when she pictured the fist relaxing. Back and forth, until one time, when she imagined the fist opening, she found herself floating above where her body should have been, staring down at Ashley and her empty clothes. She floated there for a while, feeling amazed that she'd worked it out this quickly. When she decided to return to her body, instead of just wishing herself back into her clothes like she had before, she imagined closing the fist.

She opened her eyes and looked at Ashley sitting across from her.

"I think that worked," she said.

"What happened?"

"I managed to slip out of my body for a moment."

"Good," Ashley said. "That's good. Now, the next question is, how modest are you?"

"What?" Maggie asked, wondering where Ashley was going with a question like that, and not at all sure she wanted to find out.

Chapter Ten

"HEY. WHERE IS EVERYBODY?" Maggie asked as she dropped into the chair next to Sierra. The cafeteria was mostly empty. Just her and Sierra at the same table as they had sat at that morning, and a couple of grease monkeys from the garage over in a far corner. Sierra looked up from the drink she'd been staring into and glanced around the room.

"I'm not sure," she said. "It was like this when I got here."

Maggie reached over and rubbed Sierra's back.

"How you holding up?" she asked.

"I've been better," Sierra said. "I'm wondering if I should go see Garrett's family."

"Have they been notified?" Maggie asked.

"Yeah," Sierra said. "Nomi told me a cop went to see them this afternoon."

"Nomi?"

"Oh, um, that's Industry's name. Nomi Hashimoto. She's nice. I spent a lot of today filling out new hire paperwork while you were training. Nomi had my imager brought over and put in one of the empty labs. We're going to start pulling it apart tomorrow, looking for damage. Once we've stripped it down and made sure everything's in working order, we'll put it back together and see if we can figure out how it did whatever it was it did to you."

"How long do you think that will take?" Maggie asked. Sierra just shrugged.

"Stripping it down will take at least a week, because we'll have to organize and label all of the parts. Two weeks or more to put everything on the bench and make sure it's still working according to spec. If we don't have to replace anything, another two weeks to reassemble and test in place before I can fire the imager up. If I have to replace anything, it will slow things down. They have a circuit board fab on site, but I'll probably have to order components, and it can take weeks to get specialty components shipped. And then I'll have to do surface mount work. I hate surface mount work."

"I remember you bitching about that the first time around. Then you flashed those gorgeous brown eyes of yours at that poor kid from Doctor Chen's digital instrumentation team, and he fell all over himself to volunteer for your assembly team."

"You make me sound terrible," Sierra said.

"What? No! I'm totally jealous. I wish I had your power. Just bat my eyelashes and have cute first year grad students fall all over themselves to do my bidding."

"That's not what happened!"

"It totally is," Maggie said. "Poor...oh, what was his name?"

"Cedric."

"Yes! Poor Cedric. He had such a crush on you."

Sierra was about to say something, and Maggie was sure it would have been biting, but Rob the waiter chose that moment to appear.

"Can I get you anything, ma'am?"

"You ever been to Rosa's down by SCSU?" Maggie asked.

"Yes, ma'am," Rob said.

"Can you guys do a cheese steak and chili cheese fries like they do?"

Rob scoffed. "I think you'll find we can do a good bit better than that, ma'am."

"That's a big claim," Maggie said. "Steak with grilled onions and bell peppers, topped with double sliced pepperoncini and splashed with the brine. White American. Extra cheese. Rub the bun in the beef tallow and steam the whole thing once it's assembled."

"Chili with or without beans?" Rob asked.

"Without," Maggie said. "And melted cheese, not the sauce out of the can. Sour cream and Cholula on top. Grilled onions, peppers, and pepperoncini."

"Very well," Rob said, then turned to Sierra. "Would you like to order food now, ma'am?"

Sierra shook her head.

"Can I get two large pieces of spanakopita as well?" Maggie asked.

"Of course," Rob said. "The spanakopita will take about twenty minutes. Would you like your sandwich and fries first?"

"I'll wait, but I would like some lemonade now," Maggie said. Rob nodded and headed off to the kitchen.

"You didn't have to do that," Sierra said.

"You're not eating on your own," Maggie said. "But I know you. No chance in hell you'll pass up a piece of spanakopita."

"I'm just not hungry," Sierra said.

"Which is the depression talking," Maggie said. "Trust me. I know."

Sierra leaned against Maggie's side, and Maggie gave her a squeeze.

"I feel like shit," Sierra said.

"I know. It will get better. I promise. In fact, sit up for a minute. I might be able to help with that."

"Oh?" Sierra asked as she straightened up.

"Yeah," Maggie said. "Want to see something cool?"

"Sure."

"Just watch me," Maggie said. She waited until Sierra was watching, then reached down into that place she'd found with Ashley's guidance and eased her grip. Her body and clothes vanished, dropping her into the frozen world of Planck time. She moved across the table and tightened her grip, reappearing in the chair on the other side of Sierra as she conjured herself and her clothes back into existence. Then she tapped Sierra on the shoulder.

"Hello," she said.

Sierra jumped and yelped, spinning around to face Maggie.

"What? How?" She looked back and forth between where Maggie had been sitting and where she currently was. Maggie smiled and waited until Sierra turned to look at her without looking away.

"You didn't get any of the details last night, and we didn't have a lot of time to talk at breakfast before Ashley dragged me away to training, but whatever happened yesterday had some pretty strange side effects."

"You mean aside from giving you a new body?" Sierra asked. "Because that's not strange at all."

"Point taken," Maggie said. "But this is pretty much the same side effect. The new body is apparently temporary. According to Ashley and Nomi, I'm borrowing energy from the cosmic foam to build it, but it only exists as long as I'm actively holding it together."

"What happens when you get tired?" Sierra asked.

"Nothing," Maggie said. "I mean, I fell asleep earlier today and nothing happened. It actually took a lot of work to teach myself to let go so the body would vanish. That's what Ashley was teaching me today. How to stop holding the body together."

"Why?" Sierra asked, fear in her voice. "If you let go, you might not be able to put it back together."

"No chance of that," Maggie said. She disappeared and reappeared back in her original seat. "I can put it back together whenever I want."

Sierra jumped again and turned to face Maggie.

"Don't do that!"

"Sorry," Maggie said, even though she really wasn't. "I don't get to show off very often, and this is really exciting."

"Yeah," Sierra said. "I'll bet. How does it work?"

"How does what work?" a voice said, and this time, Maggie was the one to jump. She turned to see Varsha sitting next to her, with a curious look on her face. She had two subs on a plate in front of her and looked like a puppy that was expecting a treat. Maggie smiled at her, then turned back to Sierra.

"Fair warning this time," she said. Sierra nodded.

Maggie disappeared, then reappeared on the other side of Varsha and tapped her on the shoulder. She was a little disappointed when Varsha didn't jump in surprise.

"Oh! Teleportation! Nice. What method are you using? I've seen dragon portals, which are basically like wormholes, and I've seen psionic teleportation, which is what Focus and Scatter use. Not sure of the physics behind that, though I've heard people suggest it's Akashic record editing, which would sort of make sense. There are supposedly monks who can do that, but it's supposed to take decades or even centuries of study. Dimension shifting? No, that's never instantaneous because you still have to travel the distance in the other dimension, and there's always an optical tesseract effect."

"It's not actually teleporting," Maggie said. "The new body is a sort of projection. Something I'm creating by gathering up a bit of the fabric of the universe. When I want to move, I just let go, and the body disappears, then I recreate it at the new location."

"That is cool!" Varsha said. "But if your body is a construct that you're taking apart and putting back together, how are you taking clothes with you?"

"I'm not," Maggie said.

"What? You are! You totally are! Believe me, I'd notice if you were suddenly naked," Varsha said. Maggie watched as Varsha realized what she'd just said. Her eyes went wide, and her face, normally a lovely, warm shade of brown, turned a bright reddish-brown color as she blushed. Maggie just grinned at her.

"At least buy me dinner first," Maggie said, making Varsha blush even harder. "But look at what I'm wearing." Maggie scooted back from the table a bit so both of them could see the pink cami top, knee length peasant skirt and sandals she was wearing. She looked over at Sierra.

"Fair warning," she said. Then she disappeared and reappeared sitting between Sierra and Varsha. This time, she appeared wearing a purple babydoll t-shirt, white capris, and yellow sneakers. She added purple lipstick too, just for effect.

"Wow!" Varsha said when she turned and saw Maggie. "You're creating clothes too."

"Yeah," Maggie said. "Which is kind of awesome, because my entire wardrobe is long sleeves, ankle length skirts and ballet flats. You can't imagine how amazing it feels to be able to wear short sleeves again."

"You're happy," Sierra said. Maggie turned at her, and a wave of guilt flooded through her as she realized how she must be coming across.

"I...um..."

"No," Sierra said. "No, I didn't mean it that way. I'm just surprised. I don't get to see you happy that often."

Maggie frowned.

"I'm happy a lot," she said.

"No," Sierra said. "Not really. You fake it really well when you're excited, curious, interested in a problem, or caught up in a project, but you're not really happy that often. I don't think I've seen you happy since Sandra left."

"Sandra?" Varsha asked, and then it was Maggie's turn to blush.

"Sandra was her girlfriend," Sierra said.

"Oh," Varsha said, some of the curiosity gone from her voice. "I didn't know you were seeing someone."

"I'm not," Maggie said. "Sandra works at JPL out in California. She spent a few months here last year working with the Alternative Propulsion Laboratory at Kennedy Space Center. That's the research team I work with. We kind of hit it off."

"Hit it off is an understatement," Sierra said. "She came down from Kennedy for a beach party a couple weeks into her stay. About two hours in, she and Maggie disappeared. They didn't come up for air until Monday. Then, every weekend after that the whole time she was at Kennedy, she'd pop down for a booty call."

"It wasn't like that!" Maggie said.

"It was totally like that. God, what was it you said? 'I could integrate those curves all night'."

Varsha started laughing, while Maggie just glared at Sierra.

"I hate you," she said.

Sierra reached out and took Maggie's hand, giving it a squeeze.

"I'm too cute to hate," she said.

"No, I'm pretty sure I hate you," Maggie said. "Are you okay?"

"Yeah," Sierra said. "Believe it or not, this helped. I still don't feel like eating, and I'll probably have a breakdown at some point, but I'm happy for you. I worried a lot, after Sandra went back to California."

Maggie squeezed Sierra's hand before turning back to Varsha, who had only just managed to stop laughing.

"You done?" she asked.

"I don't know," Varsha said. "Are there more sleazy science-based come-ons in your past I should know about?"

"You think you're made of copper and tellurium, don't you?" Maggie asked.

Varsha gave her a confused look, but Sierra groaned.

"Now you've done it," Sierra said. Maggie just let out a dramatic sigh.

"I told a chemistry joke, but there was no reaction."

The confusion disappeared off Varsha's face, and she burst out laughing.

"Cute," she said. "Copper and tellurium. God, that's awful."

"Well," Maggie said, "that's the problem with chemistry jokes. All the good ones argon."

Varsha groaned and looked to Sierra for help. "Is there any way to make her stop?"

"No," Sierra said. "You just have to ride it out."

"How long does that take?"

"Going on six years, so far."

Chapter Eleven

NOMI, ELEMENT, AND JUNICHI met with the Sun City University administration about the explosion first thing Monday morning. Maggie and Sierra both wanted to go to the meeting, but Nomi had refused to let them. She'd pointed out that Maggie was still officially in a coma, and that Sierra was the only official witness to what happened, and the DMA didn't want her in the same room as Hastings. Sierra and Maggie both hated being left out, but they didn't really have a lot of choice, so they stayed behind at the Shiro.

Maggie took one look at them when they got back and knew something was wrong. She didn't have to wait long to find out what it was, either. Nomi led them, along with Element and Junichi, into a conference room. Maggie grabbed a seat next to Sierra and smiled a little when Varsha sat down next to her.

"I'm afraid that most of what I have to say is going to be bad news," Nomi said. "The meeting didn't go well at all."

"Who all was in the meeting?" Maggie asked.

"A lot of people," Nomi said. She looked over at Junichi, who had a notebook in front of him.

"Doctor Chris Roth, Dean of the College of Arts and Sciences; Doctor Abigail Larsen, Associate Dean for Research, Innovation, and Graduate Studies; Doctor Amie Massey, Assistant Dean for Post-Doc Programs; Doctor Saul Cabrera, Chair of the Department of Physics and Astronomy; Doctor Sabrina Morales, Associate Chair for Physics; Doctor Yahya Chavez, Director of Post-Doc Physics Research; Doctor Muhammad Black, Lab Facilities Manager; Doctor Alistair Hastings, Assistant Chair of the Department of Physics and Astronomy, also acting in his capacity as the physics representative for the Experimental Science Safety and Ethics Committee; Doctor Elle MacDonald, acting in her capacity as Sierra Gomez's post-doc advisor, and Doctor Jerry Robinson, acting in his capacity as Maggie Bennett's post-doc advisor."

"Holy shit," Maggie said.

"They've already made up their minds," Sierra said.

Maggie looked over at Sierra. She could hear the defeat in her voice, but she couldn't bring herself to say anything. She'd had the same thought as she listened to the list of people present.

"Pretty much," Nomi said. "This meeting was supposed to be a quick meeting with Doctor Roth and Doctor Cabrera to update them on the status of the investigation, but Doctor Roth began the meeting by asking what information we had about what unauthorized experiments Sierra was performing. We explained that all evidence we had showed that all you had been doing that morning was a test run of your quantum field imager, and that nothing suggested you were connected to the explosion at all, other than happening to be in the building when it happened.

"At that point, they started asking why we took the imager if it didn't have anything to do with the explosion. I told them that we took it because it was considered a piece of evidence in an ongoing investigation, and we couldn't release any more details than that, but that the evidence we did have pointed to the explosion originating in a different lab. They asked what lab. We asked if we could speak with Doctor Roth and Doctor Cabrera privately, but they said that since the investigation had a serious impact on the University, all relevant parties had to be present."

Nomi gestured to Element.

"I had Elisa step out at that point. She went ahead and called the warrant team, and sent them to Doctor Hastings' office, while I explained that we had evidence suggesting that Doctor Hastings' lab was the origin of the blast, and that he was involved in illegal research into macroscopic teleportation. At which point, the entire thing turned into a screaming match.

"Hastings accused us of lying and covering up for you. MacDonald called Hastings a reckless asshole who didn't give a fuck whose research he destroyed in order to get grant money. I believe Hastings may have called MacDonald a useless cunt, but I'm not sure. Too many people were yelling by that point. Doctor Roth managed to get everyone to shut up long enough for me to tell them that we were executing a warrant on Doctor Hastings' office and home at that moment, which started another screaming match. Doctor Roth decided to inform me that the university would be conducting its own investigation. I told them that was fine, as long as they didn't expect access to the evidence or the site until the DMA investigation was done.

"It got a little ugly after that, and when it was over, Doctor Cabrera pulled me aside and asked if I could pass a message on to the two of you. I told him I could pass one on to Sierra immediately and to Maggie as soon as she woke from her coma. He asked me to inform you that the university has terminated your post-doc contracts, effective immediately. He said not to come in to get your things. That your offices would be packed up and your personal affects would be mailed to you. I told him that wouldn't be necessary, and I had Elisa tell the warrant team to pack up your offices as well. Doctor Cabrera and Doctor Roth both tried to object, but I told them the warrant was written broadly enough that I could seize everything in One Park Place if I deemed it necessary, and if they gave me any reason to think they might attempt to destroy evidence, then I'd lock down the whole building until my investigation was finished."

"Well, damn," Maggie said. "I've never been fired before."

"I'm sorry," Sierra said. Maggie looked over at her.

"Don't be. Mark has been trying to get me to cut my post-doc short and take a permanent position up at the Alternate Propulsion Lab anyway. I was just riding out the contract so I could keep hanging out with you."

"But if you get fired, Mark might change his mind," Sierra said.

"Mark isn't an idiot, but even if he was, I'm not exactly hurting for money. I can afford a few months while I job hunt," Maggie said. It was true enough. Her grandparents had bought her the house she lived in when she started college. It had been easier than trying to find a rental that had all the accessibility features Maggie needed. On top of that, she still had the money from the sale of her parents' house, and the life insurance policies on her mom, her dad, and her brother. Her grandparents had put the payouts for the policies in a trust fund for her that had opened on her twenty-fifth birthday.

What Maggie didn't say was that if the investigation went badly, she might be stripped of her security clearance. If that happened, the NASA job would go away. Mostly because Sierra didn't know Maggie had a security clearance. As far as she was aware, only Mark and the other members of the Alternative Propulsion Lab knew.

"I wouldn't worry too much about it, Sierra," Nomi said. "I've seen enough of your work to know that I'll want to keep you on, even after we've finished figuring out what your imager did to Maggie. In fact, I might just set up a new division at Hashimoto Enterprises to develop the tech."

"What about Maggie?" Sierra asked.

"I'm sure we can find something for her if she needs it."

"If worse comes to worst, there's always the Metahuman Incident Displacement Fund," Junichi said.

"Yeah," Maggie said. "Having already been the recipient once, I'll pass."

Junichi looked a little stunned by that, but Maggie didn't much care. If she wanted to die under an avalanche of paperwork, she'd take a job that involved applying for grants.

* * * *

The rest of that week was in turns amazing and boring. Maggie got up every morning and had breakfast with Varsha, Sierra, Ashley, Garnell, and Fractal before Varsha went on patrol, Fractal and Garnell went off to do whatever it was they did with their days, Sierra went to work on tearing down the imager, and she and Ashley went to the training room. She and Ashley spent most of their time working on figuring out how to control Maggie's new abilities. Sometimes, Ashley would get called away to help the team deal with some situation.

Once the day was over, Maggie would have dinner with Varsha, Sierra, and most of the High Guard. She finally got Nexus's proper name, which was Hannah, and met Mafic and Hoplite, whose names were Juan and Kevin, along with Kevin's husband Xander, who was the most adorably swishy gay man Maggie had met in years.

After dinner, Maggie would spend some time on work. Varsha had run to her apartment and retrieved her laptop for her after she promised not to let anyone know she was awake. Work frequently got sidelined when Varsha showed up for a late night kulfi and movie break. They made their way through several of Maggie's favorite lesbian movies, while Varsha introduced her to Indian lesbian cinema. Once Varsha left, Maggie would do more work, or spend time chatting with Kelly. She technically wasn't supposed to be doing that last bit, but she figured since Kelly didn't know who she was, it didn't count, and she needed someone to gush to about Varsha's visits.

Junichi became her personal nemesis during the week. Every time she saw him, he had some form for her to fill out. She decided that whoever ran the DMA had a documentation fetish. Every time she displayed a new ability, there was a stack of paperwork to be filled out. Given the flexibility of her powers, that was about four times a day.

Around lunch on Thursday, she asked if anyone had ever become a supervillain just to avoid filling out DMA paperwork. He said she'd have to file a freedom of information act request if she wanted the answer to that. It had taken her an hour to realize he'd been joking.

She'd almost forgiven him for laughing at her expense when he turned up with a form for something called "Safety Training Assistance Funds." It turned out that, in a rare and honestly stunning moment of good sense, the government had realized it was cheaper to pay someone's salary for four to six months than to clean up the buildings they knocked down because they couldn't afford to take time off to learn how to use their newfound superpowers. There were limits, but the DMA would pay up to six months of a new metahuman's salary at the same rate of pay they were making prior to the manifestation of their abilities. They even filed a short-term disability claim with your job, so it was protected when you were done with your training.

Maggie was a bit hesitant to take the money. She'd dealt with government assistance programs before – the Metahuman Incident Displacement Fund had paid every medical bill she'd had since the invasion – and they were usually all up in your business. If she hadn't just been fired, she might have refused. She immediately regretted agreeing to it once she started filling out the paperwork, but she knew her bank accounts would thank her.

Training was amazing. By the end of the day on Monday, Maggie could conjure perfect replicas of any simple object she'd examined with her expanded senses. No moving parts. A three-piece suit was easy, but she couldn't manage Industry's power armor. Knives but not guns. Eyeglasses but not hearing aids. Ashley was convinced that she'd be able to manage more complex things with time and practice, and Maggie suspected she was right.

By the end of the day on Tuesday, she'd learned to copy people. Their bodies and their voices. She couldn't read their minds, despite what had happened with Hannah, and she honestly preferred it that way.

Wednesday was a bit scary at first, but by the end of the day, Maggie felt indestructible. Ashley had started by getting her to do the opposite of what she did when she teleported. She went to that place inside her where it felt like she was making a fist, and instead of opening the hand, she gripped tighter than normal, so the body was held more rigidly in shape.

Once she'd figured out how to do that, Ashley had started throwing things at her. At first, it was small things, like racquetballs. By the end of the day, Ashley was hurling bowling balls at Maggie at a hundred miles per hour, and Maggie was laughing as they shattered.

Thursday, two superheroes named Stutter and Barker showed up for breakfast. Barker was the leader of the Crater Bay Champions, one of the Tier One MERT teams that worked the various wards of Sun City. His powers were sound based, but he wasn't there to train Maggie, so much as to be moral support for Stutter. Stutter was a speedster, but her powers worked differently than Varsha's. She was what was called a time stall. Where Varsha simply moved incredibly fast, Stutter actually sped up how quickly time moved in a localized pocket around her.

Stutter was painfully shy around Maggie at first, but she and Varsha were friends, and between Barker, Varsha, and Ashley, they were able to help Stutter and Maggie get through the initial awkwardness. Once it was passed, Maggie quickly decided Stutter was amazing. By the time Varsha got back from her patrol, Stutter had managed to teach Maggie how to shift her perception of time without leaving her body. By lunch, Maggie could speed up until she was moving about twenty times faster than the rest of the world.

She wasn't as fast as Stutter, and definitely wasn't as fast as Varsha, but Stutter and Varsha were both inordinately pleased that Maggie could beat someone they called Finish Line. The real surprise though was that Stutter could drop into Planck scale time and carry people into that space with her. She took Maggie there and began teaching her how to manipulate her perception of time in that space. By dinner time, Maggie could move around without a body without dropping into the frozen world of Planck time.

Friday morning started with fast teleportation drills. A target would light up, Maggie would teleport to it and hit it. She had five seconds to do so, but as soon as she hit the target, it would trigger another one, and Maggie had to stick to normal time, even while incorporeal. By that point, Maggie had so much practice dropping in and out of existence she could do it at will, so it was easy. Pop out, smack the target, and disappear.

She'd been at it about ten minutes when the distractions started. At first, it was just loud noises, but then guns in the ceiling would shoot rubber balls at her. After a while, Ashley started throwing spells. It made it a lot harder at first, and Maggie started missing the timer. It wouldn't have been a problem if she was allowed to adjust the flow of time but having to work in normal time made it hard.

She eventually got it, though. She learned to focus until she could pop out, tag the target, and vanish before Ashley or the computers controlling the sensors in the ceiling even knew she was there. Then she'd wait in her incorporeal form while the next target lit up.

Once Ashley figured out what she was doing, she congratulated Maggie on a clever solution, then banned her from using it. A few minutes later, Elisa showed up, and started battering Maggie with hurricane force winds, fireballs, lightning strikes, and rain so hard it would have left bruises if Maggie could still bruise.

By the time lunch rolled around on Friday, Maggie was pretty sure she would have had no problem teleporting around the beaches of Normandy on D-Day, if D-Day had taken place in the middle of a hurricane.

Chapter Twelve

"WHAT ARE THESE?" MAGGIE asked, looking at the two five-gallon buckets in the middle of the training room. She'd come back from lunch expecting more of the fast teleport drills they'd been doing that morning, but Elisa was out on patrol with Nomi, and Hannah was there instead.

"Trash," Ashley said. "I asked Garnell if I could have some wood scraps for your training. He was even nice enough to run a sander over the pieces, so you won't get any splinters."

"Okay," Maggie said. She bent down and picked up a chunk of wood. "What am I supposed to do with them?"

"We're going to see if you can take something with you when you teleport," Ashley said.

Maggie looked down at the chunk of wood in her hand, then back up at Ashley.

"I don't think that's going to work," she said. "I'm not really teleporting. I'm just dispersing an illusion and recreating it in another location."

"I know I'm the one who used it first, but illusion isn't really the right term," Ashley said. "You're conjuring a physical form out of the Aether, and then dispersing it back into the Aether when you let it go. The physical form naturally wants to dissipate and sink back into the Aether because that's where it came from. I'm guessing that you might be able to tease apart...let's call them permanent objects. You might be able to tease apart permanent objects into the Aether that makes them up, and then put them back together on the other side. And since they are permanent objects, they should have a natural tendency to stay whole."

Maggie stared at Ashley for a minute.

"That sounds suspiciously like wishful thinking," Maggie said.

"Well, it won't hurt to try," Ashley said.

"It might," Maggie said. "Remember how all of this started? What if I'm able to tease something apart just enough for the particles to lose coherence and decay into photons the way the matter in Garrett's experiment did?" She held up the chunk of wood. "Let's say this is about a pound and a half of wood. That's roughly fifteen megatons worth of rest mass energy. If it goes boom, that's a thousand times more energy than the bomb dropped on Hiroshima."

"You make an excellent point," Ashley said. "Fortunately, it's one I have already thought of."

Maggie stared at her for a moment. "Really?"

"Yes," Ashley said. She reached over and touched her wrist. The bracelet Maggie could never see unless Ashley was touching it appeared, and instantly, the jeans and t-shirt Ashley'd been wearing were gone, replaced by her field costume. She let go of the bracelet, which vanished again, and took out the wand that was hanging on her belt, pointed it, and said something that sounded Latin.

A pentagram inscribed with runes appeared on the floor.

"That is a teleportation circle. It goes to an underground DMA facility designed to contain up to a fifty-megaton detonation. Stand in the center, and I'll activate it. Hannah will maintain a telepathic link with you so we can talk. When you're done, you can teleport back."

Maggie dropped the chunk of wood into the bucket.

"You can't be serious."

"She's absolutely serious," Hannah said. "The whole point of this is to make sure you're not a danger to yourself or others. Tell us, what would you do if Sierra was trapped on the seventh floor of that building you worked in, and the first six floors were on fire?"

Maggie looked at Hannah, thinking about what she would do in that scenario. After a few seconds, she reached down and picked up the buckets.

"Here's hoping I'm immune to nuclear explosions," Maggie said before walking over to stand in the center of the teleportation circle.

Ashley said something that sounded vaguely Latin again, and Maggie found herself in a massive hemispherical room about the size of a football stadium. The floor looked like it had started out nice and flat, with a steel dome above it, but both floor and dome had seen better days. There were scorch marks everywhere, places where the steel had obviously been melted, dents the size of cars. Gouges. One place that looked like claw marks, if the individual claws had been bigger than Maggie was.

<What is this place?> Maggie asked through the telepathic link. <A guest room for Godzilla?>

She could feel Ashley and Hannah's amusement through the link.

<Not officially,> Ashley said. <But a few MERTs have tossed a Kaiju or three in there for safe keeping for a while. Officially, it's Explosive Ordnance Disposal Facility Nine. There are a dozen of them. Everyone with access has been informed that Facility Nine is in use today, so you

don't have to worry about any of the MERTs tossing a nuke or an antimatter warhead in there with you.>

<Well, that's not as reassuring as you probably think it is,> Maggie said as she set the buckets down. She picked up a chunk of wood. <So, how am I supposed to do this?>

<Visualization seems to work pretty well for you,> Ashley said. <Just teleport but picture the block going with you.>

<Right. I can do that.>

Maggie looked at the chunk of wood and imagined herself ten feet away with the block still in her hand. Then she teleported. She'd just finished rematerializing when she heard the block hit the floor. She looked over and saw it laying next to the spot where she'd been standing and let out a sigh as she thought of how long it took her to be able to leave her body that first day.

<Don't get discouraged,> Ashley said. <It was only your first try. Remember how long it took you to learn to teleport in the first place.>

<Reminding me of that is the opposite of helpful,> Maggie said. She walked over and picked up the block, glaring at it. <Any other suggestions?>

<Try slowing down,> Ashley said. <You need to focus on picturing the block disappearing with you while you're vanishing. You can't do that if you're speed porting.>

<Right.> Maggie looked at the block, and took a deep breath, letting it out slowly as she relaxed the tight spot inside her that held her body in place. As she did, she pictured herself and the wood slowly fading out until there was nothing left. Once she was completely incorporeal, she looked around, and sure enough, the wood block was gone too. She could feel it with her, a spot that wasn't quite a part of her, but wasn't completely separate either.

She reappeared ten feet away, coming back slowly, picturing the wood coming back with her. When she looked down, the block was right there in her hand.

<Holy shit,> Maggie said.

<Nice,> Ashley said. <That was a lot easier than I expected.>

<I know, right?> Maggie said. She tossed the block up in the air, feeling a bit smug, only to watch it vanish the instant it wasn't in contact with her skin anymore. She stared at the empty space where the block had been for a moment and sighed.

<On the plus side, no boom,> Hannah said.

Maggie laughed and reached up to rub her face.

<I don't suppose there's any chance we can just give this up as a bad idea?>

<No,> Ashley said. <You can do this. It's just going to take some time.>

Maggie walked over to the bucket and picked up another piece of wood. She took a deep breath, then teleported again. This time, when she was putting herself back together, she squeezed that place inside of her harder, focusing on the image of the wood in her hand, picturing it as something solid, something real, that would last past her letting it go. She imagined herself setting it down on a table and it staying there.

When she came out of the teleport, the wood was still in her hand. She let go of it, and it fell. It didn't disappear, it just fell, and for a moment, Maggie thought she'd done it. Then the wood hit the floor and crumpled into a pile of sawdust.

<Fuck,> Maggie said.

<At least it's progress,> Ashley said.

* * * *

It was progress, but to Maggie's immense frustration, it was the last progress she made for almost two hours. Ashley actually had to get five more buckets of wood scraps sent down from Garnell's workshop because Maggie kept running out. In the end, Hannah figured out the solution. One that was so obvious, Maggie wanted to slap herself for not thinking of it.

She wasn't reintegrating the wood properly because she was only picturing what they looked like. After Hannah suggested it, she started studying the wood chunks with her enhanced senses, going all the way down to the subatomic level as she took in every detail of the wood before she teleported. Then she used the image in her head to put the wood back together.

It worked the first time she tried it, and after she'd done it once, she spent another hour teleporting chunks of wood around with her. At first, just one or two, but eventually, she was teleporting two entire buckets at a time. When she was satisfied she had it down, she teleported herself and the buckets back to the training room in the Shiro.

She'd barely had time to put the buckets on the ground before Ashley pulled her into a hug.

"I knew you'd get it," Ashley said. Maggie hugged her back, a little surprised by Ashley's enthusiasm.

"That makes one of us," Maggie said. Ashley let go and took a step back.

"You're good at this," Ashley said. "You're learning much faster than I expected."

"Thanks," Maggie said.

"She's right," Hannah said. "You're doing great. Really."

Ashley smiled and turned towards a table she'd set up. It was covered in all sorts of objects that were a lot more complicated than the wooden blocks. There were broken tools, old laptops, smart phones, and a handful of toys.

"Hey, Ash," Hannah said.

"Yeah," Ashley said without looking up from the table.

"If it's okay with you, I'm going to take off. You don't need me for the telepathic link anymore."

Ashley looked up at Hannah, and Maggie could see the way her shoulders dropped.

"Oh," she said. "I...um...sure. Yeah. You must be busy."

"Right," Hannah said. She turned to Maggie. "Keep up the good work." She turned and headed for the door. Maggie watched until she was gone, then turned to Ashley.

"What was that about?" Maggie asked.

"Nothing," Ashley said.

"Sure," Maggie said. "I totally believe that."

Ashley sighed and looked towards the door.

"It's complicated," Ashley said.

"Want to talk about it?" Maggie asked. "Sometimes a fresh pair of eyes on a problem can help."

"Yeah," Ashley said. "I used to think that, which is kind of what got me into trouble."

"What do you mean?"

"A while back, I took a detached assignment. A new meta was dealing with some supernatural shit. Something a bit beyond the edge of my wheelhouse, but close enough that I got pulled in. The DMA agent who tapped me for the job also pulled in Eurion, a local reserve asset. Eurion and I spent a lot of time together during the mission. We got to be friends, and we've been spending some time together."

"And Hannah is jealous," Maggie said.

"Yeah," Ashley said.

"You know, you could just tell her you're into her," Maggie said.

"That's the complicated part," Ashley said.

"What? You're not into her?"

"I am," Ashley said. "It's just..."

"Complicated," Maggie said. "I get it."

"Yeah," Ashley said. "I've seen enough of the way you and Sierra interact to bet you do."

"That's not complicated. That's just bad luck. Falling in love with your straight best friend is bullshit."

"Please," Ashley said. "That girl is about as straight as boiled spaghetti."

"The fact that she spent the last six years dating a guy would suggest you're wrong."

"Bisexual people exist," Ashley said.

"I know," Maggie said. "But Sierra isn't one of them."

"If you say so."

"Don't do that," Maggie said.

"What?"

"Look, it took me a long fucking time to move on from Sierra, okay? I'm not saying I don't still love her, but I moved on, I dated a really great girl. I dealt with the fact that she and I are not going to happen. Don't stir that shit up again, okay?"

"God. Shit, I'm sorry," Ashley said. "That was rude."

"Don't worry about it. I was poking your sore spot. You poked mine."

"Still, I'm sorry."

"And I'm sorry if I made you uncomfortable. I just wanted to help."

"I appreciate it. I just..."

"What?"

"You ever want to tell someone something about you, but you're ashamed to?"

"No," Maggie said. "I mean, I've had to tell people stuff I'm ashamed of, but I never wanted to. But, if you feel like you need to tell Hannah something, I think she'd listen, and I don't think she'd judge."

"Maybe," Ashley said. "The funny part is, I've mostly been spending time with Eurion because she's trying to help me work through all of this so I can talk to Hannah, but it's just made things harder."

"Maybe you just need to rip off the Band-Aid," Maggie said.

"Maybe," Ashley said. "Come on. Enough of my problems. Let's get back to training."

Maggie walked over and looked at the objects on the table. She picked up a cheap looking solar powered calculator, and let her senses wash over it, then teleported to the other side of the room, before punching in a math problem. The calculator gave her the right answer. Maggie smiled and teleported back to the table.

She spent the next hour teleporting with objects on the table. After the teleports, she'd make sure the computers still worked, that they didn't drop off the wifi connections, that the smartphones still had cell signal, that the old power tools still worked.

She got bored of the whole process a lot faster than Ashley did. She'd just finished another practice run, and Ashley was confirming the laser range finder still worked, when Maggie spotted one of the objects she hadn't teleported yet. Mostly because it was so simple. It was just a blue racquetball. She focused on it, letting her senses wash over it as if she was going to teleport it, but instead, she conjured one out of the Aether, the same way she conjured clothes. Only this time, she squeezed harder, like she did when she was teleporting an object with her.

Ashley looked up as the ball appeared in Maggie's hand. She gasped slightly when Maggie tossed the ball up, and instead of vanishing, it rose up and fell back into Maggie's outstretched hand.

"Is that permanent?" Ashley asked.

Maggie shrugged.

"I don't know," she said. She turned and tossed it at the wall, expecting it to bounce back. Instead, it exploded just before it hit.

Chapter Thirteen

"I AM SO SORRY," Maggie said for what must have been the hundredth time. She was honestly getting sick of hearing it, but the guilt wouldn't go away.

It didn't help that Hannah was glaring daggers at her. Except for Kevin, who was out on his evening patrol as Hoplite, the entire High Guard was piled into the emergency room, trying and failing to stay out of Doctor Sanchez's way while she stitched up the cut on Ashley's forehead.

"It was an accident," Ashley said. "And not a bad one. I didn't even get a concussion. Just a little scrape."

"A scrape doesn't require five stitches," Sanchez said.

"You're not helping," Ashley said.

"Well, excuse me," Sanchez said. "Next time someone needs to shove some guts back inside one of you, I'll be sure to send someone who's helpful."

Ashley rolled her eyes and looked at Maggie.

"We'll figure out how to do that in a controlled fashion, but not today. I think we're done for today."

"I think a blanket 'don't do that' will work just fine," Maggie said.

"Are you kidding?" Elisa asked. "With that kind of firepower on top of everything else you can do, there isn't a Tier Two MERT in the country that won't let you write your own ticket. Hell, you could probably get onto one of the Tier Three teams right away if you wanted."

Maggie stared at Elisa in shock for a moment.

"I don't want to be a superhero team," she said. "I just want to learn to control my powers so it's safe for me to go back to work."

She could see confusion and disbelief written all over Elisa's face and braced herself for the response she knew would come.

"But why? Think of what you could do!"

"I am thinking of what I could do," Maggie said, pointing at Ashley's forehead. "I can accidentally blow things up. Accidentally split people's heads open. Accidently kill my friends. I'll pass."

"No, that's not what I meant," Elisa said. Nomi put a hand on Elisa's shoulder, and Elisa turned to her.

"Elisa," she said. "Leave it be."

"No," Elisa said. She turned back to Maggie. "You can't just let all that power go to waste."

"You know what I care about going to waste?" Maggie asked. "My entire life. I worked hard to get my degrees, to get into grad school, to get my post-doc, and to get a spot at the Alternative Propulsion Lab. I'm working on technology that's going to open up the solar system. I'm not going to let some accident make me walk away from the life I want. Not again."

"Okay, enough!" Sanchez shouted. "I only let you lot in here because you were worried about my patient, but if you can't keep quiet and let me finish stitching her head closed, get out."

Maggie didn't argue. She just turned and headed for the elevator. She sped her timeframe up a little, just to get away from Elisa faster, and it worked. She made it to the elevator doors without anyone bothering her. She punched the button and waited a moment for the doors to open. She stepped inside, and hit the button for the residential floor, when Varsha zipped inside next to her.

"You okay?" she asked. Maggie shrugged.

"I'm fine," she said.

"Bullshit," Varsha said. "You need to get out of this place."

"Yeah, except I'm still in a coma."

"Doesn't mean you don't need to get out of here," she said. "I'm sorry about what happened back there. Elisa can be an ass sometimes. No, that's not right. Elisa is kind of wonderful. Element can be an ass sometimes. Unfortunately, Element forgets to be Elisa more and more lately, and honestly, I'm not sure even Elisa would really understand where you're coming from. She means well, but she wanted her powers. Went on some sort of quest to earn them. She forgets that not all of us had a choice."

"You mentioned that before," Maggie said. The door dinged and started sliding open.

"Didn't get any less true," Varsha said. "Come on."

Varsha started leading Maggie down a different corridor than the one where her room was. Maggie was about to argue, but Varsha took her hand and gave it a small squeeze, and whatever she was going to say just kind of poofed out of her brain. She was pretty sure Varsha could have led her to the ninth circle of hell and she would have been too taken by how warm Varsha's hand felt to notice.

Unfortunately for Maggie's heart, Varsha led her somewhere far scarier than hell. She led Maggie to her room. Or rooms, as it turned out. The room Maggie had been assigned was like a hotel room. It had a bed, a desk, a table with a couple of chairs, a bathroom near the front door, and a closet. Varsha's room was a full-blown apartment. There was a huge living room, an office to one side, a full kitchen, and a dining room. It was nearly as big as Maggie's house.

Varsha didn't stop in any of the common areas, though. She led Maggie right through to her bedroom. By the time Varsha let go of her hand, Maggie's heart was hammering in her chest.

"You learn how to make new clothes from examples, right?" Varsha asked as she walked over to her closet. "I know I recognize some of the things you've been wearing from Ashley's wardrobe."

"Yeah," Maggie said, doing her best not to turn into a babbling idiot. "She had a rolling rack of clothes in the gym, and I just copied them. I had to resize, but that's easy enough. Learning to switch colors took a little longer."

Varsha pulled a gray jumpsuit out of the closet and tossed it on the bed, then bent down and grabbed a matching pair of boots and set them next to the jumpsuit. Then she pulled a mask off the shelf and added it to the pile.

"I know you said you don't want to be a hero, but learn those, just in case. It's a DMA training uniform. Anyone who sees you in it will know you're not certified. If a call comes in while we're out, you change into that and come back here immediately while I go deal with whatever's going on."

"We're going out?" Maggie asked.

"Yeah," Varsha said. "I'm off rotation tonight, and you need to be somewhere that isn't the inside of this place." She pointed at the uniform. "Go on."

"Okay," Maggie said. She turned and let her expanded senses take in the uniform, getting every detail, the same as if she were going to carry it through a teleport. She took in the faux leather shell, the anti-ballistic inserts, the mask, the moisture-wicking fabric. All of it, until she was sure she could duplicate it in perfect detail. When she was done, she turned around and found Varsha holding up another outfit.

"Wear this, with the uniform boots, but make the boots black," Varsha said as she laid the outfit on the bed. Maggie took in the outfit, the same way she had the uniform. It was a lot different from what she was wearing. Black leather pants, a black scoop neck T-shirt, with a red leather jacket. She shifted her clothes, changing them to the outfit, then looked at Varsha, who frowned.

"Something's off," Varsha said. "The jacket isn't working."

Maggie turned and looked in the mirror on the inside of the closet door, and immediately spotted the problem. She smiled and turned back to Varsha as she shifted the color of the jacket to the same purple as her hair. Varsha's face lit up when she saw the change.

"That's perfect!" she said. She reached up and tapped her forehead. "Add the mask."

"What?"

"I'm not trying to change your mind," Varsha said, "but you need to get out of here, and I know somewhere we can go where you can wear the mask, and it will help you blend in."

Maggie looked down at the mask. She thought about the first time one of the team had suggested she could become a hero, and how she'd felt in that moment. It was enough to make her refuse, and Varsha must have sensed that, because she took Maggie's hand in hers again and gave it a squeeze.

"Trust me, Maggie," she said. Maggie looked up, and Varsha smiled at her, and any resistance she still felt melted away under those warm brown eyes.

"Okay," Maggie said. "Okay." She took a second, conjuring a copy of the mask on her face in the same purple as the jacket.

"How's this?"

Varsha bit her lip as she looked Maggie up and down. She pointed and twirled her finger. Maggie took it as an order to turn around, so she did a quick spin, letting Varsha see everything.

"Not bad, Bennett," she said in a voice that made Maggie's mouth go dry. "Not bad at all." She reached down and touched the disappearing bracelet on her arm, and suddenly, she was wearing her Delta V costume. She reached into a pouch on her belt and pulled out an earbud, offering it to Maggie.

"Just a precaution," she said. "Make sure you can teleport with it."

Maggie took the earbud and fit it into her ear, then took a moment to let her senses examine it. She memorized it the same way she had the laptops and cell phones she'd carried with her in training. Once she was sure she could teleport with it, she gave Varsha a nod. Varsha gave her a devilish smile in return.

"Try to keep up," she said, as she ran for the door.

* * * *

Varsha took it easy on Maggie. Maggie knew it, and she was thankful for it. Her new body was in really good shape, so she could hit about twenty miles per hour without playing with her clock, and when she did play with her clock, she could hit about four hundred miles per hour. When she was training with Stutter the day before, Stutter had hit four fifty. Then Varsha had climbed on the treadmill and put them both to shame by hitting nine hundred miles per hour, just to prove she could outrun both Maggie and Stutter put together.

That night, she held it down so Maggie could keep her in sight as they ran, but the fact that Varsha was going easy on Maggie didn't stop either of them from showing off. Varsha ran up and over a building while Maggie went around. Maggie responded by teleporting through the next one. Then Varsha ran circles around Maggie, literally. After that, the two of them played a game of superpowered parkour across three wards. Varsha led the way as they left Crater Bay, where the Shiro was located, then ran through Bay View and into the Narrows before they finally came to a stop on the roof of a building across from an old warehouse that had been converted into a nightclub called Cape Town.

When Maggie saw where they were, the mask made sense. Cape Town was the kind of place everyone knew about, even if they'd never dream of going there. It was a superhero bar. Maggie could see the line wrapped around the building. People waiting to get in, hoping to mingle with members of the MERT teams and other metahumans that might choose to hang out there. Paparazzi snapped pictures. Music spilled out into the streets every time one of the bouncers opened the door to let someone in.

Maggie jumped as she felt Varsha's hand take hers, threading their fingers together.

"We don't have to go in," Varsha said. "Not if you don't want to."

"Why did you bring me here?" Maggie asked. Varsha smiled at her.

"It's like I said. You need to see some place that isn't the Shiro." She looked down at the club. "I'm not trying to change your mind, Mags, but superhero or not, when you take that mask off and go out in the world, you're going to have to hide a part of yourself. Down there...that's our place. We don't have to hide. We don't have to pretend. Down there, we're not the outsiders."

Maggie watched as a woman in a two-toned jumpsuit, light blue from the waist up, navy blue from the waist down, walked past the line. The bouncer waved her through after she arced lighting between her hands.

The sight brought a smile to her face as she realized just what it was Varsha was offering her. A choice. On the one hand, she had a chance to experience real freedom, a kind she'd never had before. No parents or grandparents looking over her shoulder, no broken, scarred body holding her back, no rushing home to take some medication on schedule, no best friend playing mother hen. On the other hand, she could go back to the Shiro, and keep doing what she'd been doing. Just letting all of this happen to her.

She knew what she would have done before the explosion. She would have been scared. Terrified at the thought of going down there. She still was, but before the explosion, she would have let that feeling make her turn around and go back to the Shiro. She could see it clear as day, written in all the choices she'd made leading up to the morning she'd walked into Sierra's lab. The question was, what choice would she make now, and there was really only one possible answer.

"Okay," Maggie said. "Last one down buys."

Chapter Fourteen

MAGGIE TELEPORTED DOWN, BUT the bouncer barely had time to flinch before Varsha skidded to a halt next to her.

"Cheater," she said, but Maggie could hear the amusement in her voice. Varsha turned to the bouncer. "Hey, Dutch."

"Hey, Vee," he said. "Good to see you. New friend?"

"Very new," Varsha said. "Still kicking the tires on her mask."

Dutch nodded.

"We'll keep an eye out," he said as he pulled open the door.

Maggie followed Varsha inside, and she was pretty sure her eyes bugged out as she did. Most of Maggie's experience with nightclubs was virtual. She'd spent a good deal of time cruising them in Digilife, but in the real world, she'd only ever set foot in one, and that had been reluctantly. After she'd come out to her, Sierra had dragged Maggie to Girl Bar, a lesbian bar up in Bywater. Maggie had spent the whole time convinced that the girls were staring at her, but not in a good way, and she'd made Sierra take her home after half an hour.

Cape Town was something else entirely. It had to be the size of a football field. There was a massive stage at the far end where a live band was playing. There were cages hanging from the roof with men and women in street clothes dancing inside them. One wall was covered with a mural depicting Red Coat and the rest of the Sentries, Back Beat, Duster, Gale, Running Eagle, Gulnara, and Racer in all their glory. The opposite wall had a mural of the Olympus Six—Airheart, Red Coat, Cavalier, Firebird, Hachiman, and White Tiger.

There were ten raised booths, five along each wall, with an emblem above all but one of them. On the right, the Bywater Champions had the first booth, then the Crater Bay Champions, the third table had the Sentries emblem over it, with the table and the booth draped in black. The fourth table had the Bay View Champions, and the fifth had the Protectors. On the opposite side, the first table was set aside for the Waterside Champions, then the Narrows Champions, then the High Guard. The fourth table just had an old-fashioned Welsh dragon above it. The last table didn't have an emblem over it.

Between the platforms that held the raised booths, there had to be fifty or sixty tables filling the half of the room closest to the door, while the half closest to the stage was taken up by a dance floor and the bar.

Maggie was still trying to take it all in when Varsha grabbed her hand and pulled her over to the High Guard's booth. They'd barely had time to sit down when a waitress appeared carrying a tray loaded with two stacks of steaming naan, several bowls of various dips, and a large pitcher of lemonade.

"Hey, Vee. Know what you want?" she asked as she unloaded the bread, dips, lemonade, two glasses, and a pair of appetizer plates.

"You like samosas?" Varsha asked.

"Who doesn't?"

Varsha turned back to the waitress.

"Samosas party platter and a double order of beef patties."

"Gotcha, hun," the waitress said, then turned to Maggie. "Anything else, sweetie?"

"I'm good, thanks."

"Okay, but if you need anything, my name's Rhonda. Doesn't matter how loud it gets out here, you call me, I'll hear it." Rhonda pointed at Varsha. "You just be good to my girl here, and we'll get along just fine."

Before Maggie could say anything, Rhonda was gone. Not turned and walked away gone. Just gone. Vanished.

"What the hell?"

Varsha laughed.

"That's Rhonda," she said. "She owns the place. No one's sure what her power set is, but she personally smacked down Red Coat once. Between her and Dutch, nobody starts trouble in here."

"The bouncer?" Maggie asked.

"Bouncers," Varsha said. She pointed. Maggie turned and saw Dutch standing by the bar watching the dance floor. Varsha pointed to a different spot, and Dutch was there too, tending bar and waiting tables in three other spots.

"He used to be on a MERT in California. Codename was Century, because he can split into a hundred identical copies of himself."

"That must save them a ton of money," Maggie said as she looked around. The woman she'd seen outside tossing lightning around was sitting in the Narrows Champions booth, nursing a beer. A guy in a gray and black flight suit with a black mask was sitting in the Bay View Champions booth, talking to a girl in a skimpy blue dress. An absolutely gorgeous black woman with short, natural hair wearing a jumpsuit covered in little iridescent squares of holographic fabric sat in the Bywater Champions booth, watching the band as she nibbled on an order of potato skins. A guy in what looked like a baseball outfit and domino mask sat in the Waterside Champions booth, and he wasn't even trying to hide the fact that he was looking at Maggie and Varsha. When Maggie looked at him, he raised his glass with a smile and a nod. Maggie returned the nod before moving on. The Crater Bay table was empty, but there were two guys sitting at the Protectors table, glaring.

"Va...Vee?" Maggie said, forcing herself not to use Varsha's real name in public.

"Yeah?" Varsha asked. Maggie nodded towards the Protectors table.

"What's that about?"

"Don't worry about it," Varsha said. "Some people are just born assholes."

Maggie turned to her.

"I'm trying not to worry, but I haven't seen a glare like that since Billy Carson found out I asked his sister on a date after I turned him down."

"That sounds like a fun story," Varsha said.

"Billy outed me to the whole school, which turned out to be really embarrassing for him when I dated his younger sister for the rest of the school year."

Varsha giggled as she reached for one of the stacks of bread. She took a piece and covered it in a white dip with pomegranate seeds in it.

"Why'd you break up?"

"They moved away," Maggie said. "Atlanta, I think. Is there any raita?"

"These are all raita," Varsha said. She pointed at one particular dish. "That's the one you're looking for, though. Cucumber raita."

"Sorry," Maggie said.

"Don't be," Varsha said. "Most people make that mistake. They think raita is something specific like tzatziki. It's more like saying 'dip'."

Maggie grabbed a piece of naan and pulled the cucumber raita over.

"Well, I do know that chai is just the word for tea, and naan is just the word for bread."

"You're doing better than a lot of people," Varsha said.

Maggie glanced up as the band started a new song. She was shocked to hear what she thought was a cover of a Miracle of Sound song, but sure enough, those were the opening chords of New Black Gold.

"Who's the band?" Maggie asked.

"They're called Anla-shok," Varsha said. "They're pretty good. Rhonda books them pretty regularly because their sets have a lot of superhero-themed stuff in them."

Maggie smiled at the name, not surprised that someone who was a big enough geek to pick it would know a band as obscure as Miracle of Sound. She turned back to Varsha to ask another question about the band, but the mood at the table shifted before she got the question out. She turned, half expecting to find a supervillain standing in front of them.

She wasn't far off. One of the guys who'd been glaring at them from the Protectors booth stood in front of the table. He wasn't especially big, but his costume gave him a bulkier look. It had a pseudo-roman motif. A silver leather Lorica Segmentata chest piece and greaves over a red jumpsuit and brown boots. The costume wasn't that bad, but Maggie could tell immediately that she was going to hate the person wearing it. The way he was standing too close to their table, the sneer on his face. He might as well have been wearing a t-shirt that read 'professional asshole.'

"Who's she?" he asked Varsha.

"Hello, Praetorian," Varsha said, voice dripping with sarcasm and loathing. "Good to see you again. I've so missed our little chats. How have you been? Had any luck with your recruiting?"

His face went red at the last question, and he practically growled at Varsha. "I haven't received anything from dispatch about a new person on your roster," he said.

Varsha sighed and shook her head. "You haven't received notification about an addition to our roster because there hasn't been one. My friend here isn't MERT certified yet. She's just here to blow off some steam."

"If she isn't certified, she should be wearing a training uniform," he said.

Varsha held up both hands, gesturing around the room.

"Does this look like a response scene to you? No? Good. Go bug some cosplayers or something."

He stood there for a moment, looking like he wanted to say something, but a tall woman who bore a striking resemblance to Catherine Zeta-Jones walked up behind him in an expensive, well-tailored suit and heels, and tapped him on the shoulder. He turned around, ready to snap at whoever was bothering him, and turned white as a sheet when he saw the woman. The woman smiled as she raised her hand and made a little shooing motion.

"Shoo," she said. Praetorian didn't quite run, but it was a near thing. The woman turned and gave Varsha and Maggie a huge smile.

"May I join you?" she asked.

"Of course," Varsha said. The woman slid into the booth on the opposite side of Varsha from where Maggie was sitting.

"It's lovely to see you again dear," the woman said. "I don't believe I've met your new friend, though."

"I doubt it," Varsha said. "Eurion, this is Maggie. Maggie, this is Eurion."

Maggie's eyes went wide as she realized who Eurion was.

"You're the dragon," Maggie said.

"Oh!" Eurion said, delight clear in her voice. "You've heard of me."

"Um, yeah," Maggie said. "Just by reputation, I'm afraid."

"Well, I assure you, all the rumors about me eating people who annoy me are completely unfounded. Humans are terrible for the digestion."

"Eurion, behave," Varsha said. "I swear, you've been spending too much time around Ice Dragon. She's starting to rub off on you."

"I see how it is. Jai Li can be as naughty as she wants, and no one cares, but I make a tiny little joke and I get scolded like a puppy." Eurion turned to Maggie. "You would think after two thousand years, I would have earned some respect, but no."

"Two thousand years?" Maggie asked.

"Give or take a century or two," Eurion said. "Human date-keeping is a bit tedious. You lot keep changing your calendars."

"Don't let her fool you," Varsha said. "She knows exactly how old she is, to the day. Probably to the hour. She just doesn't like to admit it."

"Must you give away all my secrets, dear?" Eurion asked.

"Only to keep you from taking advantage of the new girl."

"I would never!" Eurion said. She turned and looked at Maggie, and Maggie suddenly felt a bit on display. "Though she is rather lovely."

"Don't you dare," Varsha asked.

Eurion blew out a puff of smoke in Varsha's direction, and Maggie caught the scent of woodsmoke filling the air.

"She's new, Eurion," Varsha said. "Please, step lightly."

"Oh," Eurion said, her whole demeanor changing instantly. She looked at Maggie. "I apologize if I've made you uncomfortable, my dear."

"You haven't," Maggie said. "I'm a bit confused, more than anything."

"Well, Varsha knows that I enjoy a bit of company now and again," Eurion said. "Us old dragons do get a bit lonely, after all."

"Ashley keeps telling you that you need to find a wife," Varsha said.

"Ashley is right about that, as she is about many things, but alas, it's easier said than done." Eurion raised her hand and waved in the direction of one of the Dutches, who rushed over.

"Hey, Eurion," he said.

"Hello, old friend. Might I get my usual order?"

"Of course," he said. "It's already on the way. I put it in when I saw you at the door."

"Ah, I do love good service. Please bring it to my table, and tell that lovely wife of yours I said hi, would you?"

"I'll pass it on," he said before he walked away.

Eurion turned back to Varsha.

"Tell me, dear. Will Ashley be in this evening?"

"I don't think so," Varsha said. "There was an accident in the training room today. Nothing serious, but Ashley got a bit of a cut on her forehead, and you know how she is about being seen with a facial injury."

"I do," Eurion said. "Though if she was hurt, I don't know why she didn't call me. I could have come over and taken her up to Atlanta. Igeza or Transistor could have dealt with it easily enough."

"I've honestly given up trying to figure out anything Ashley does," Varsha said.

"Probably a wise move. She does seem to be a bit...oh, how do you say it?"

"Determined to make herself miserable?"

"Well, yes, but that describes so many of us. I was going to say 'inscrutable,' but I fear your description is closer to the truth, some days. Now, what was that business with that nasty little man?"

"Oh, that was just Praetorian being Praetorian," Varsha said. She turned to Maggie. "You know the story, don't you?"

"A little bit," Maggie said. "It was hard to miss. Industry was part of the Protectors and turned them in for corruption."

"There's more to it than that," Varsha said. "But Industry and Praetorian have been in a pissing match for years, and Praetorian hasn't won a single round. It's killing him, and he hates everyone even remotely associated with Industry for it."

"Fun," Maggie said.

"Fun to watch," Eurion said. "I'm not sure how fun it is to be a part of. I do worry that Industry is going to get herself in a tight spot one day because of how much she hates that man."

"You're not the only one who worries about that," Varsha said. "On the other hand, Industry's got a lot of people in her corner."

"So she does," Eurion said. "And I have taken enough time away from the two of you, so I shall now retreat to mine."

"You don't have to go," Varsha said.

"My dear, that's very kind of you, but I'm far too old to survive the awkwardness of being a third wheel on a date. Enjoy your evening."

Eurion slipped out of the High Guard booth and moved over to the one with the Welsh dragon above it, and Varsha just shook her head.

"She's just sitting there like she isn't close enough to hear every word we say," Varsha said.

"I didn't say I didn't enjoy being a voyeur, my dear, but there is a difference between that, and the awkwardness created by sitting in the middle of two people trying to connect," Eurion said from her booth.

Varsha laughed, and Maggie couldn't help but laugh with her, but when they were done laughing, an awkwardness settled over the table. Maggie wasn't sure why Varsha was suddenly looking anywhere but at her, but Maggie knew she was wondering if Eurion was right, and this was a date.

Fortunately, the arrival of food saved the day. Rhonda reappeared carrying a tray of samosas. Two Dutches arrived a few moments later. One of them went to Eurion's booth, while the other set down a large platter of fried pastries.

"One samosa party platter, and two orders of beef patties. You going to want seconds, sweetie?" Rhonda asked.

"Not sure," Varsha said. "If I do, I promise I'll order off the menu."

"Honey, you order whatever you want," Rhonda said. She turned to Maggie. "You too, sweetie. Any friend of Vee's is always welcome here."

"Thanks," Maggie said.

Rhonda nodded, then disappeared again as the two Dutches turned and headed back for the kitchen.

"That is going to take some getting used to," Maggie said.

"It does," Varsha said. "Try the patties."

Maggie picked up one of the patties. It was a deep-fried pastry, kind of like the samosas, but it looked more like the empanadas Doctor

Hernandez always brought to the department potluck dinners. Maggie took a bite and moaned at how good it was.

"God, that's good," she said.

"I know, right?" Varsha said. "I dated a girl from Jamaica my sophomore year in college. She got me started on those."

"Why do I get the feeling that the way to your heart was through your stomach long before you got your superpowers?"

Varsha laughed and blushed a little.

"I can't help it," she said. "I went to college on a track and field scholarship. I've always been a runner. I did my first marathon at twelve. It takes a lot of fuel."

Maggie smiled and reached for one of the samosas, and for the next few minutes, the two of them just sat, eating in companionable silence. Maggie kept sneaking peeks at Varsha as they ate and thinking about Eurion's insinuation that the two of them were on a date. It felt a lot like they were. Maggie loved Varsha's company. She had since the moment the two of them had met. That first night, sitting across from each other eating kulfi, had been a large part of what helped her get through all of this. She'd been doing her best to take care of Sierra, but Varsha had been taking care of her, and Maggie didn't really want that to stop, but she couldn't help but wonder how compatible their lives would be if Maggie went back to her day job. Part of her wondered if Varsha was looking for a way out.

"Can I ask you a question?" Maggie asked.

"Sure," Varsha said.

"Why did you join the High Guard?"

She almost took the question back when she saw the look on Varsha's face. The smile disappeared, replaced by something close to misery, and her eyes dropped.

"I didn't have anywhere else to go," she said.

"I'm sorry," Maggie said. "It's not my business."

"No," Varsha said. "It is. Right now, it definitely is." She looked up at Maggie.

"I don't want you to misunderstand. I love what I do. I get to help people, to save lives, and I get to run all the time, but it was hard at first. Most colleges, including SCSU, won't let metas attend without a safety certificate from the DMA stating that they have demonstrated they are capable of controlling their powers.

"When I got my powers, I lost my scholarship, because being a meta disqualifies you from athletics. I lost half a semester's worth of work because I couldn't finish the classes I was in, which pushed back my graduation by a year, because those classes are only offered in the spring. I lost my place at Harvard Medical School. I lost my shot at Valedictorian. I lost my apartment, because the training stipend was based on my salary at my part time job and didn't include my scholarship funds. My family wasn't speaking to me at all.

"And real speedsters are rare. Most of the speedsters are time stalls, like Stutter. Speed Freak was part of the High Guard at the time, but the High Guard had never taken on a trainee before. Quick Step is the next closest, but she's up in Atlanta with the rest of the Patriots, and they're a Tier Three team. They don't do trainees. I thought I was going to have to go to DC or Phoenix, but Elisa, the woman in charge of metahuman recruitment for the Southeast, convinced Industry and Element to let Speed Freak take me on as an apprentice.

"When I walked into the Shiro for the first time, I was fucking miserable, and I was terrified. I didn't want to be there any more than you do."

Varsha took a drink of her lemonade and picked up a patty, taking a bite and chewing slowly, like she was taking her time to organize her thoughts.

"I didn't think I was going to make it. I felt so lost and alone, I just wanted to curl up and die. I might have, too, but one night, a few weeks into training, I met Tux."

"Tux?"

Varsha blushed and looked down at the table.

"Yeah," she said. "You stick around long enough, you'll meet Tux, too. Tux has been around for a long time."

Maggie stared at her for a moment, taking in what she was hearing, the look on Varsha's face, and something clicked.

"You love her?" she said.

Varsha laughed.

"Yeah," she said.

"Oh. I..." Maggie looked down, kicking herself and calling herself a fool for thinking someone like Varsha would be interested in her. "I didn't realize you were seeing someone."

"I'm not," Varsha said. "You don't understand. Everyone's a little in love with Tux. And I have spent the night a few times, but Tux doesn't really do relationships. She's more like a..."

"A booty call?" Maggie asked, teasing a little, and feeling a whole lot of relief at the idea that maybe she hadn't completely misread the situation. Varsha blushed that adorable blush again at Maggie's words.

"I was going to say a cross between the mom friend and a friend with benefits," Varsha said.

"Okay, see, now I have to kink shame you," Maggie said.

Varsha laughed and threw a napkin at Maggie's face.

"It's not like that," she said. "Tux is the reason I stayed with the High Guard. Don't get me wrong, I really like my teammates, but Industry and Element are kind of wrapped up in each other. Hoplite spends most of his free time with his husband. Cinderella and Nexus are wrapped up in whatever the hell is going on between the two of them. Maker and Fractal weren't on the team yet. Speed Freak was my teacher. Clockmaker wasn't really interested in anything besides Speed Freak and her gadgets, and Mafic isn't exactly a people person. It gets lonely in that castle pretty quick.

"Tux was my friend before any of the rest of them were. She was the one who convinced me that it would be okay if I wanted to walk away from this when I got done training. She helped me figure out who I was, and who I wanted to be. She taught me that it was okay to let go of the dreams I'd grown up with, that I was allowed to want something different for myself. She was the first person to make it my choice to stay, or to go back to my life. And she gave me the best piece of advice anyone has ever given me. She told me I should pick the life that would make me happy, because that's the place I can do my best work."

"And that's why you stayed?" Maggie asked.

"Yeah. I could have gone back to school. I did, in fact. Finished premed. Got certified as an EMT, then as a paramedic through courses offered by the DMA, but I didn't go to medical school or become a chemical engineer. If I had, I would have ended up like my parents. My dad's an orthopedic. My mother's a dermatologist. They're good doctors, but it's just a job to them. They get up, they go to work, they collect a paycheck. It's something they do to make money so they can have the life they want.

"Me, I put on this costume, and I save lives. I make the world a better place. That's what I grew up wanting to do. When I was thinking of being a doctor, when I was thinking of being a chemical engineer, all I wanted was to make the world a better place. This isn't how I imagined doing it, but that is what I'm doing. For me, that's worth the tradeoffs."

"Do you think I'm being selfish, wanting to go back?" Maggie asked.

"It doesn't matter what I think," Varsha said. "People will throw that Spider-man crap at you. 'With great power comes great responsibility.' It's bullshit. We don't go tell people 'you're in good shape, it's your duty to become a cop or a firefighter or a soldier.' There are plenty of people out there who would make really good first responders or doctors or whatever, but don't want to do those jobs. And there are people who become cops and firefighters and doctors and EMTs and soldiers and decide that isn't what they want to do with their life and they walk away from it. That doesn't make them bad people.

"Your life is still your life. You don't want to be a superhero, don't be a superhero. Go make rocket engines. Find a pretty girl. Settle down and raise cats. Find something that makes you happy and hold onto it with both hands and to hell with anyone who tells you that isn't what you should do with your life."

Maggie leaned back in the booth and stared at Varsha. She could feel something uncoiling inside her in response to Varsha's words. Tension, dread, resentment. Maybe a mix of it all. Whatever it was, it was melting away, and Maggie felt lighter than she had since the night of the explosion.

"Thank you," Maggie said. "I think I needed to hear that."

"I know you did," Varsha said. She tipped her head towards the tables down on the floor. "That girl at the third table on the right has been checking you out," she said.

"What?" Maggie asked, confused by the non sequitur.

"The girl at the third table on the right. Cute. Blonde. Wearing a pink backless keyhole top over a short white skirt with a floral print and white sandals. She's been checking you out for the last five minutes."

Maggie started to turn and look, but Varsha shook her head.

"Don't look. Use your powers."

Maggie nodded slightly and reached out with her expanded senses. It was easy to spot the girl Varsha was talking about. Maggie had to admit she was cute, and she was definitely sneaking glances at her. Maggie smiled, and Varsha smiled right along with her.

"Well, don't just sit there," Varsha said. "Go ask her to dance."

"What?" Maggie asked, suddenly feeling very confused.

"Mags, if I just wanted to feed you, give you advice, and let you vent, I could have taken you to Decadence out on Crater Bay Pier and ordered the chocolate fountain. I brought you here because I figured you might want to see what that new body can do for you." She raised her hand and made a shooing motion. "Now go ask the pretty girl to dance."

Maggie sat there for a moment, feeling torn. On the one hand, she'd played out scenarios like this in Digilife more than a few times. Walk up to a pretty girl, strike up a conversation, and see where things went. On the other hand, as nice as it was to know a pretty girl was interested in her, she was feeling pretty much no interest in the girl Varsha was pushing her towards. As she turned it over in her head, Varsha's words came back to her. 'Find something that makes you happy and hold onto it with both hands'.

"Ask the pretty girl to dance?"

"Yeah," Varsha said. "It's easy."

Maggie stood up and held her hand out to Varsha.

"Would you like to dance?"

Varsha stared at her for a second, but Maggie saw the moment understanding set in. The smile on Varsha's face changed from cute to breathtaking, and she reached out and took Maggie's hand.

"I'd love to," she said.

Maggie helped her up, and then led her out onto the dance floor. The song the band was playing was heavy on the bass and had a fast tempo, something obviously arranged for a club, and for a moment, Maggie panicked. It had been more than a decade since she'd been able to dance, much less danced with a girl.

She shouldn't have worried. Varsha turned around and took Maggie's hands, placing them on her hips and pressing her back up against Maggie's front, then started moving with the music. It wasn't quite like her dad leading when he taught her how to waltz, but it was easy to keep up with Varsha as she moved. It felt good. It felt great. The feel of Varsha's body, soft and warm, pressed up against her was intoxicating. It was the first time in a long time she'd been touched like that, and it was the first time in a very, very long time she didn't feel shame at being touched.

The song changed to something slower, and Varsha turned around, smiling up at Maggie as she locked her arms around Maggie's neck, looking up into her eyes. The look wasn't remotely innocent, and Maggie felt herself smiling as she slipped her hands up, running them over Varsha's back.

"I thought for sure you'd go for the cape chaser," Varsha said.

"I'd rather have you," Maggie said, a little surprised at her own boldness.

Varsha slipped a thumb up under the hem of Maggie's shirt and brushed the pad of her thumb over Maggie's stomach, right at the top of her panties.

"I think I'd like that," Varsha said. "I think—"

"Alert! Alert! Alert! Multiple explosions reported at Sun City State University. Event still in progress. Mass casualties expected. This is an all-hands response. Repeat. This is an all-hands response."

Varsha closed her eyes and took a deep breath. When she opened her eyes, Varsha was gone, replaced by Delta V.

"I don't have a field bag," she said. "Can you get it and meet me there?"

"Where is it?" Maggie asked.

"The garage," Delta V said. "Ask anyone and they'll show you. Get the one marked Unknown Situation. Wear the training suit."

"See you there," Maggie said, but Delta V was already gone.

Chapter Fifteen

THE GARAGE WAS A madhouse when Maggie arrived. An alarm was sounding, a team was pulling an air car over to one of the elevators, pilots were climbing into battle mechs, and dozens of people were running every which way. The battle mechs made Maggie pause for just a second, but she didn't have time to figure it out. She looked around for someone to ask about Varsha's field pack, but in the end, she didn't need to. There was a rack near the door that had four hot pink backpacks with labels above each one. Patrol, disaster, assault, unknown situation. Maggie teleported over to the rack and took a second to switch to the gray training uniform, then let her senses take in the field pack as she pulled it off the rack. Once she was sure she had it, she stepped into the Aether.

With a thought, she was standing in front of One Park Place, but she wasn't back in the normal world. She stayed in Planck scale time and looked around.

It was like stepping back in time eleven years to the day her family had died. The entire campus looked like a war zone. There was a hole through the seventh, eighth, and ninth floors of One Park Place where the physics and astronomy offices were. The math building was on fire. The sides of the basketball stadium had collapsed. Every window in the main library was shattered. The student center looked like someone had dropped a bomb on it. The parking structure next to the law library was nothing but a pile of rubble. The outer wall of the law library connected to the parking structure had collapsed, leaving the entire library open on that side. Tindal Hall was just gone, nothing left but a crater where it once stood.

Maggie spotted Varsha and dropped out of the Aether half a block ahead of her, which gave her just enough time to spot Maggie and come to a stop. Maggie held out her bag. Varsha took it as she looked around. A moment later, Stutter and Finish Line dropped out of Planck scale time, both sitting on motorcycles. Barker was on the back of Stutter's bike, and Praetorian was on the back of Finish Line's.

Varsha looked at Maggie.

"You know this place better than I do. Where should we start?"

Maggie hadn't expected anyone to ask her that, but she didn't hesitate. The answer was obvious to anyone who knew the school.

"The libraries and the office towers," Maggie said.

"Why are you asking her?" Praetorian asked. "She's not certified."

"No, she's not," Varsha said. "But she worked on campus until a week ago, and we don't have time to argue."

"Vee's right," Barker said.

Maggie turned to Praetorian, deciding that explaining her reasoning would be faster than getting into a pissing match.

"The lecture halls and student labs close at 2:00 PM on Fridays. The libraries don't close until 10:00 PM and a lot of the graduate assistants stay late on Fridays to catch up on grading. The grad student carrels are in the office buildings."

"Dorms?" Barker asked.

"Urban campus," Maggie said. "The dorms are ten blocks north on Plantain Row. I looked. They haven't been hit."

"Right," Barker said. "You heard the lady. Stutter, take the law library. Finish line, take the main library. Vee, the burning building is all yours. Praetorian, fire control."

The speedsters all vanished as Barker gave them orders. Praetorian looked like he was about to argue, but swallowed it and jumped into the air, leaving Maggie alone with Barker.

"Maggie, I need you to search the upper floors of that building with a hole in it. Find out if anyone's trapped and let me know. We'll have fliers on site for evac soon."

"Right," Maggie said. "Search building, report trapped survivors for evac."

Barker nodded, and as soon as Maggie had confirmation, she dropped into the Aether and sailed across campus to One Park Place. Since time was effectively frozen for her, she started at the bottom of the building, expanding her senses so she could take everything in, floor by floor. She worked her way up the building, taking careful note of anyone she found. Once she'd searched the entire building three times, she dropped back out of the Aether next to Barker.

"There are three grad students on the tenth floor," she said. "Everyone else in the building is below the damage and already making their way out."

Barker nodded.

"Barker to inbound fliers. Request ETA."

The air split with the echo of a sonic boom as a man in a two-toned blue jumpsuit arrived on scene. He came to a screeching stop in the air above Barker.

"Blue Bird, onsite," he said. Barker pointed at One Park Place.

"Three civvies, tenth floor. Evac needed. Go."

Blue Bird shot off towards the building, and Barker turned back to Maggie.

"You can search every building on campus in the time it takes me to blink. Go. Find everyone. Report back."

Maggie nodded.

"Recon. Find civvies. Report back." Maggie said.

Barker nodded, and Maggie stepped into the Aether.

The next two hours were like that. Orders given in short sentences. Shorter replies. Frantic work to save lives. The city had something like seventy working metahumans on the MERTs, with another dozen in various support roles and maybe fifteen reserve and retired metas. By the end of the night, there were two hundred metas working the scene. Agents from the local branch of Warne Global Security office worked alongside the MERT teams. Metas from Orlando, De Leon, and Pontian showed up. All one hundred Dutches from Cape Town. Eurion and another dragon named Rachel showed up and spent most of the night moving heavy chunks of debris and holding up buildings that looked like they might collapse.

Most people would think that on a Friday night, a college campus would be practically deserted, and by most standards, they would be right, but the MERTs and other first responders still ended up pulling almost fifteen hundred people out of the various buildings that had been hit. The student center was especially bad. The theater, which wasn't normally a huge draw because it mostly played foreign language and arthouse films, had been showing Princess Bride and was almost full. Two hundred and twenty-four people had been in there. Eight survived. The campus radio station got hit badly as well, but that, mercifully, was only six people. Five survived. The school paper wasn't so lucky. Thirty people had been working there. None survived. And there was the homeless. A lot of homeless people camped on campus, because there were a lot of warm spots, nooks and crannies that stayed dry and were shielded from the wind coming in off the bay. Places cops didn't check. They didn't fare a lot better than the kids in the theater. And there was Tindal Hall. Maggie kept looking at the crater, wondering how many people had been inside when it went away.

Of the fifteen hundred odd people they pulled out of the wreckage, around nine hundred were alive when they were found. A handful of professors, librarians, IT workers, maintenance, janitorial staff, restaurant staff, and undergrads, but mostly grad students. The worst injuries came from the various restaurants, bars, and other hangouts interspersed among the various buildings. Busted windows and flying debris didn't care who you were.

Eventually, the fires were out, the last of the wounded were packed into ambulances, and the cleanup started. Most of it would be handled by regular crews. The MERTs and other metas were clearing debris off the road and securing anything that might be a hazard while the coroners cleared away the last of the bodies, but One Park Place had to be dealt with. The building was twenty stories high, and no longer structurally sound because of the huge hole burned through it. Traffic through the campus couldn't be reopened while the building was still standing.

Element and Breakdown, one of the Protectors, were going to bring the building down while Fuerza, a meta from one of the Orlando MERTs, contained the debris. Maggie volunteered to do a last sweep of the building before they brought it down, double checking for bodies while the three of them conferred with city engineers. Maggie stepped into the Aether, and this time, she started at the top and worked her way down the building, finding nothing. When she reached the ground level, she expanded her senses out beyond the building, checking around the edges in case there were still any homeless people hiding in the area.

As she searched, she let time run a little faster. Not quite real time, but fast enough that she could actually listen for things like movement, breathing, or a heartbeat, and as she searched the alleyway next to One Park Place, she found one. A soft, fast heartbeat.

She focused in on it and spotted a body that she'd tagged earlier that hadn't been collected yet. For a moment, she was horrified, afraid she'd mistaken someone who was still alive for a dead body, but as she focused her senses on it, she realized the heartbeat wasn't coming from the body. It was under it.

She dropped out of the Aether and knelt next to the body. A black man, and from the clothes, pretty obviously homeless. He'd been hit on the head by falling debris and hadn't survived it. Maggie rolled him over, as gently as she could, trying her best to be respectful. The tortoiseshell kitten he'd been shielding when he died looked up at Maggie, let out an absolutely terrified shriek, and took off running. Maggie barely had time to react before it was in the street, and one of the coroner's vans was barreling towards it. But 'barely had time' was not the same as 'didn't have time'.

Maggie stepped into the Aether and time stopped. She focused every sense she had on that kitten. She memorized every hair, every claw, every flake of dandruff. She paid attention to the fur pattern, to the little collar around the kitten's neck with the name tag that read Maxine. She burned every detail into her mind before she dropped out of the Aether, her time still running twenty times faster than the rest of the world. She reached down and lifted the kitten up as gently and carefully as she could and stepped back into the Aether.

She found Ashley, hoping that if she messed this up, Ashley might be able to correct her mistake. Ashley was leaning against the side of the main library, drinking a bottle of water as Varsha bandaged a cut on her arm. Maggie dropped out of the aether, and just like she did when she was carrying something with her, she focused on what she was carrying, a tiny life that was depending on her, and she squeezed that place inside that held her together harder than she'd ever squeezed before. Harder than when she was carrying an object with her. Harder than when she was making her body immune to damage. She squeezed as hard as she could as she focused on the kitten, on imagining it alive and running and playing, on imagining it doing all the things her old cat Sally used to do.

"Are you okay?" Varsha asked.

Maggie looked down at the kitten, which was looking back up at her, alive and well.

"I'm fine," Maggie said.

"Well, I'm not," the kitten said. "You're holding me too tight, and I want Henry back."

Maggie stared at the kitten, then looked up at Varsha for a moment, before both turned to Ashley, who was staring down at the kitten.

"What the actual fuck?" was all Ashley had to say.

Chapter Sixteen

"GOOD MORNING," NOMI SAID as she walked into the room with Elisa trailing a step behind her. The entire team was present in the briefing room. Ashley and Hannah sat together near the head of the table, Garnell and Fractal sat next to them, then Varsha, then Maggie. Kevin sat on the opposite side of the table, leaving an empty seat between him and the head of the table that Elisa dropped into. Juan sat on Kevin's other side, then Junichi. All of them watched as Nomi sat down at the head of the table.

"Last night, as you are all aware, there were a series of explosions at Sun City State University's downtown campus. I'd like to start the meeting here by saying that everyone here performed admirably during our response to the incident. I would also like to extend special thanks to Maggie, who stepped up despite a lack of training or obligation, and whose efforts and knowledge of the SCSU campus saved, by dispatch's most conservative estimates, at least one hundred and seventy lives that would otherwise have been lost by the time we were able to locate them."

Everyone around the table started clapping except for Maggie, who just stared at Nomi, completely stunned by what she'd just heard. She'd known she probably saved a couple of people who would have bled out if she hadn't been there to direct help to them immediately, but a hundred and seventy people seemed like too much. She couldn't quite get her head around it. She glanced over at Varsha, looking for confirmation. Varsha seemed to get it. She smiled, and gave a little nod, as if to say that yes, Maggie had really done that.

The clapping came to a stop when Nomi started speaking again.

"For those not directly involved in the investigation of the prior incident, we had submitted our preliminary site analysis of the explosion to the US Marshals, the DMA, and the SCPD on Wednesday. That analysis concluded, based on the pattern of debris scatter, that the explosion had originated in High Power Requirement Lab Two. Four different independent teams have also conducted their own site analysis, including the Department of Homeland Security, the Bay View Fire Marshal, the US Marshals, and at the request of SCSU Administration, Warne Global Security. All four concur with our findings. In addition, a psychometry reading on the site conducted by a metahuman in the employ of WGS, though not admissible in court, corroborates Maggie's eyewitness account of the explosion.

"The investigation is still ongoing; however, preliminary finding of fact in the case will have to wait several weeks until the full analysis of Doctor Gomez's quantum field imaging device is complete, along with the teleportation device used in Doctor Hastings' lab. Unfortunately, that analysis will be slowed because the teleportation device must be recreated from schematics and notes seized from Doctor Hastings and Garrett Whitehall's offices, and because it is currently unclear as to whether Doctor Gomez will be able to continue consulting on the investigation."

"I'm sorry, what?" Maggie asked.

"The nature of the investigation has changed in light of last night's events," Nomi said. "I'm sorry, Maggie. I know Doctor Gomez is your friend, but as of this moment, she's considered a person of interest in the investigation, and before you ask, I will explain shortly."

Maggie bit her tongue, because she was sure anything she said would get her kicked out of the meeting. Nomi seemed to understand, though, and gave Maggie a small nod of thanks for not saying anything.

"Up until now, we had been working on the assumption that the prior incident was an accident. One possibly caused by illegal experimentation and criminal negligence, but an accident nonetheless. We still believe that to be the case. However, last night's events are clearly the result of criminal activity. Because Maggie has submitted to both telepathic and magical interrogation, and because she technically died during the incident, she's been cleared of suspicion. Doctor Gomez will be offered the chance to submit to telepathic interrogation as well. If she does and is cleared, she will be brought back into the investigation. Until and unless that happens, no details of the investigation will be discussed with her. Is that clear?"

Nomi asked the question while looking straight at Maggie, and Maggie reluctantly nodded. She didn't believe for a second that Sierra was involved, but she did understand compartmentalizing information. She wouldn't have had a security clearance if she didn't.

Nomi touched the surface of the table, and the screen on the opposite wall came to life.

"On the right is an overhead map of the SCSU Campus. On the left is a computer simulation reconstructing the explosion based on traffic, security, and cell phone footage. We're also lucky in that one of Channel Four's hero cams is located on the Sand Dollar FCU building, which is located immediately adjacent to the campus, meaning we have a full recording of the entire event, taken from only a block away."

"Before we begin, Maggie, what can you tell us about this building?" Nomi asked as a marker popped up on Tindal Hall.

"Aside from the fact that it's not there anymore? It's an old building. It used to be a parking structure, but it was closed and turned into a mixture of classrooms, teaching labs, grad student labs, storage rooms, and the campus post office. The school has had plans to close it down, demolish it, and replace it with a newer facility since the initial conversion, but no one expected it to ever actually happen because the school can never open classroom space as fast as it needs, and grad students will practically murder each other in their sleep for lab space."

"Do you know if Doctor Hastings had a lab in the building?" Nomi asked. Maggie frowned as she thought about it.

"Maybe? I think so. I remember some of the graduate students bitching when he moved into HPRL2 because he wasn't releasing his old lab space. I know when I was an undergrad and took his classes, we were in Tindal Hall and his lab was next door. I honestly didn't pay a lot of attention to lab allocation once I started with APL, though."

"Fair enough," Nomi said. "Please watch the screen." She started the simulation, and Tindal Hall exploded. The explosion was off center, though, and took out one of the structural walls of the student center, the one closest to the movie theater, which caused it to collapse in on itself. The second explosion happened ninety-three seconds later on top of the parking deck next to the law library, but it was almost as if it were the muzzle flash for a gun, because the hole was blown through One Park Place from the direction of the parking structure a fraction of a second later. The fire in the math building looked like splash damage from the hit to One Park Place, and the shattered windows in the main library looked like they might be the result of the concussive blast. The third explosion was in the parking lot next to the basketball stadium, and it looked like it triggered the collapse of the stadium wall, along with several secondary explosions all over campus.

"There," Nomi said. "Three primary events, the third of which caused or triggered several secondary events. Now, I'm going to run it again, superimposed with data from the three DHS Nuclear, Biological, and Chemical sensors located closest to the sites of the primary explosions."

She restarted the simulation, and Maggie watched the three graphs running at the bottom. There was a small gamma spike at the moment of the Tindal Hall explosion, and much larger spikes during the parking structure and parking lot events.

"Now, I'm going to run the data from the first event last night side by side with the data recorded from the NBC sensor outside the Science Annex building last week."

She hit play again, but Maggie already knew what she was going to see. The gamma spike was weaker during the Science Annex explosion, so the graph was smaller than the Tindal Hall event, just the same way the Tindal Hall event was weaker than the parking structure and parking lot events, but in all four events, the shape of the graph was identical.

"Motherfucker!" The words were out of Maggie's mouth before she could stop them. She heard a couple of laughs, but she turned to Nomi.

"The next slide is all four events, normalized for magnitude, right?"

Nomi nodded, and hit play again, and sure enough, all four events played out on screen at the same time, and all four graphs showed the exact same waveform. Maggie looked at the numbers. The parking structure event stood out as being a lot more powerful than the other three events, which didn't make sense, because the parking structure didn't collapse for almost three minutes.

It took Maggie a minute to work out why that was, but then she realized that the parking structure event was the one that had punched a hole in One Park Place, which was four blocks away.

Maggie turned to Nomi.

"Do we have a map of the location of the NBC sensors?" she asked.

"Yes," Nomi said. She pulled up the information Maggie had asked for, and Maggie stared at the screen for a moment.

"Show me which ones we took each reading from," she said.

Numbers appeared next to each one, indicating which event it recorded and the intensity of each event. Maggie looked at the NBC sensors for the parking structure and the one, the only one, that recorded the parking structure event was between the parking structure and One Park Place.

Maggie turned around and looked at Nomi.

"Someone's figured out how to weaponize Doctor Hastings' teleporter," she said. "The gamma discharge from that third blast is directional."

"Fractal and I came to the same conclusion when we analyzed the data," Nomi said. "But we found something else while the data was processing. We were running facial recognition on all the security footage we could find, and we got lucky, because it turns out SCSU archives security footage at an off-site data warehousing company. We were able to pull security footage from Tindal Hall, and we found this."

She touched the controls built into the table again. Maggie turned around, and for a moment, she froze. There was a single frame from one of the security cameras in Tindal Hall. Two men were coming in from the street level entrance. Maggie didn't even need to look at the comparisons from the facial recognition software. She'd know both of those faces anywhere. The one on the right was Doctor Alistair Hastings, and the one on the left was Garrett Whitehall.

"Motherfucker!"

This time no one laughed.

"Who is that?" Garnell asked.

"The rat bastard with the bald spot who looks like a ZZ Top impersonator is Doctor Hastings. The younger one who looks like a low rent Brandon Routh is Garrett Whitehall. Who should be dead, because I watched him burn into a pile of ash last Saturday."

"You're sure it was him?" Nomi asked.

"Yes!" Maggie said. "If you could see it..." She shrugged, because she didn't know what else to say. She'd watched Garrett die, but there he was, on screen.

"Could we?" Nomi asked.

"What?" Maggie asked, looking at Nomi.

Nomi gestured towards Hannah. "Could we share the memory?"

Maggie looked over at Hannah, who looked like she might be ill at the thought.

"Would you be okay with that?" she asked. Hannah looked like she definitely wasn't okay with that, but she nodded.

"Just, no piggybacking your way into my brain this time," she said.

"I'll try," Maggie said. "But I didn't mean to do it last time."

"I know," Hannah said. "Which is what makes me so reluctant. You've got no control. I'd hoped we could address that in training at some point."

"Wait," Juan said, "she's telepathic too?"

"Yes. No. Maybe. Sort of. Fuck if I know," Hannah said. "I was doing a telepathic scan of her, and she slipped through my barriers without me feeling it and was doing a surface scan of me. As far as I know, she hasn't been able to form a telepathic connection on her own, though I'll admit, we haven't spent a lot of time trying."

"Interesting," Juan said.

"Terrifying," Hannah said. "My barriers are rock solid. I survived a full force telepathic assault by Mindster and my barriers didn't so much as flex. She went through them like air through a screen door."

Maggie stared at Hannah for a moment, more than a little shocked. She knew Hannah had to be a heavy hitter to be on a Tier Two team, but she hadn't realized she'd fought Mindster. Mindster was one of those supervillains that even people who didn't follow superhero stuff were terrified of. He, or she, no one was really sure, would telepathically possess someone and use their bodies to go on killing sprees. There was a theory that they used the spree kills to cover murder for hire, but no one was sure.

"I'll do my best to stay out of your head," Maggie said. "But I should warn everyone. The memory involves a lot of pain. I was dying while all of this happened, and it wasn't a comfortable death."

"Noted. I'll do my best to filter out the pain," Hannah said. She looked around. "Everyone up for this?"

She got nods and murmurs of agreement from around the table, so she settled back in her chair. Maggie could see the subtle shift in everyone's face as the telepathic connections were made. Then, after everyone else was linked up, she felt the now familiar sensation, like a warm hug, as Hannah touched her mind.

<Are you ready?> Hannah asked.

<Yes,> Maggie said.

<Focus on the memory of the explosion,> Hannah said.

Maggie didn't answer; she just started replaying that morning in her head, from the moment she and Sierra walked into the lab, right through the explosion. Hannah helped her replay the memory of Garrett's death three times, and it was more horrible every time. She could sense the gamma radiation flowing through him. There was no question that the dose was lethal, any more than there was any question that the heat bloom burnt him to ash, or the overpressure scattered the ashes. The rest of the team was satisfied, but something about it bothered Maggie.

<Can you show it again?> Maggie asked.

<I can,> Hannah said. <But why?>

<Something isn't right, but I can't put my finger on it,> Maggie said. <Could we slow it down?>

<Yes,> Hannah said.

It was strange, asking that. The memory already moved at a snail's pace, but Hannah replayed it even slower. It was like watching a movie process at a rate of one frame every five seconds or so. It dragged and dragged and dragged, until Maggie spotted it. It was just a flash, a split second, but it was there. She didn't even have to ask Hannah to back the memory up and slow it down even more.

Everyone watched as the carbon particle started to decay. The moment of brilliant success collapsing into an expanding front of death and devastation. Then it happened, and Maggie could feel the confusion around her. A doorway, or a portal to some place outside the lab, and for an instant, Garrett existed on both ends. He'd been in a state of superposition.

"It happened to him too," Maggie said as she pulled away from the link. Hannah let it drop, and everyone in the room turned to Maggie.

"What happened to him?" Elisa asked.

"Superposition," Maggie said. "When I died, I was in two places at once, but only a part of me. Only my cognitive quantum field. I was anchored to the machine, duplicated, and because one of the fields survived, both survived until Vee cut the power."

"Right," Ashley said. "We know this part."

"But it happened to Garrett too. He was in two places at once. He was in a state of quantum superposition. On both ends of the teleportation path at once, but it doesn't make sense. Why did both persist? The wave function collapsed. There should have only been one Garrett. It doesn't make sense."

"What wave function? What are you—" Elisa started to ask, but Maggie held up her hand to stop her.

"Thinking. Thinking. Quiet."

Maggie could see it, but she couldn't. It was all right there, the math swirled around inside her head, not quite fitting together, but coming closer and closer and for some reason, she kept thinking about cinnamon. It didn't make any sense.

She could feel herself getting deeper and deeper into the problem, but she needed to see it to work it. She needed a marker in her hand, so she teleported across the room to the whiteboard on one of the walls. She snatched up a marker and popped off the cap. She took a deep breath, inhaling the familiar, comforting scent of dry erase maker, then she started writing. She got about three quarters of the way through before she hit a mathematical wall she couldn't work around and stepped back from the board.

"No. No. Doesn't work. H bar is too small. Damn it." She waved her hand, wiping the whiteboard clean and started again. A different approach. A different model. Something was missing. She could feel it.

She wiped the board again.

"Jesus Christ," she muttered. "What the fuck am I missing? It's stupid. It's obvious. I can feel it. I can see around it, but I can't see it. Two points in superposition. H bar is too small. Why the fuck do I smell cinnamon?"

"What is H bar?" someone asked.

"Reduced Planck's constant," Maggie said. "H bar determines the range of uncertainty. The larger the value of H bar, the greater the uncertainty. If you can make H bar large enough, a person could stand on both ends of the wormhole, but H bar is too small, and I'm missing something, and why the ever-loving fuck do I smell cinnamon?"

"What do you need?" someone asked.

"Sierra," Maggie said. "I need Sierra to kick me in the head."

She stared at the equations on the board. She could see where the hole was. She just couldn't see what went in it.

"Mags, are you a math zombie again?" Sierra asked over the intercom.

"Yes," Maggie said. "Kick me in the head?"

"Define the problem."

"Assuming standard values for H bar. Macroscopic superposition. I can't make it work with an Einstein-Rosen bridge. What am I missing? Why do I smell cinnamon?"

"Jesus fuck, Mags, you're not serious, are you?"

"I'm going to feel stupid, aren't I?"

"Yeah. Really fucking stupid. This is high school shit for you."

"Hit me."

"The spice must flow."

"Motherfucker!"

Maggie waved her hand, wiping the whiteboard again and started writing. "Run numbers for me. Rest mass energy for an unwashed male grad student before lunch."

"Math or physics?" Sierra asked.

"Physics. Wannabe gym rat subtype."

"One eighty pounds. Nice round number. Roughly eighty-two kilos. Call it ten to the nineteenth Joules."

"Thanks. Love you.

"Love you too. Try not to eat any undergrad's brains. The paperwork is a bitch."

"I'll try. Have to math now."

"Bye."

She heard the intercom click and she lost herself in the math, working the numbers in dry erase. She wasn't sure how long she was lost in the math, but when she finished, she stepped back and looked at the numbers, and there was only one reaction any sane person could have had.

"No wonder you fuckers are spilling hard gamma all over the place. Hastings, you fucking asshole."

She turned around and looked at Nomi.

"You see it?" she asked.

"Sort of," Nomi said. "Enough to be terrified. Not enough to know where you're getting that much energy."

"Would someone mind explaining for those of us who didn't take advanced squiggles in college?" Elisa asked.

"We were looking at it wrong," Maggie said. "Doctor Hastings' experiments were supposed to be in quantum teleportation. Quantum teleportation is the teleportation of information. Not matter. The principals involved don't scale. I'd assumed he found a way around that. There's plenty of ideas on how you can use quantum teleportation to move matter. Most of them are bullshit, because the energy requirements are insane. On the order of ten to the nineteenth Joules. And none of them would result in anything close to what I saw in that memory.

"My first thought was an Einstein-Rosen bridge, what most people call a wormhole, but the problem there is, we saw Garrett in two places at once, and H bar is too small for that."

"You said that before, but I have no idea what that means," Juan said.

"Right," Maggie said. "Because I am no longer hanging out with a bunch of overworked physics grad students and need to remember that before I scare the cats again. H bar is a number. A universal constant. In this case, it's also a hard constraint. It's hard to explain without the math, and it doesn't really matter in this given situation. Just take it as a given that the value of H bar means that what we saw can't be a wormhole."

"Okay," Juan said. "I might ask you to explain more later, though."

"I'd be happy to," Maggie said. "The thing is, I couldn't figure out how he was in two places at once until I talked to Sierra. Thanks to whoever got her on the intercom, by the way."

Varsha nodded her head, and Maggie couldn't stop from smiling.

"Why is all of this important?" Element asked.

"I wasn't sure it was until Sierra kicked me in the head."

"The spice must flow," Varsha said. "He's folding space."

"Yes!" Maggie said. "Someone has read Dune! I knew it as soon as I saw it, but my brain was stuck on teleportation, so I couldn't wrap my head around it. Because it shouldn't be possible, and because I didn't want to think about what it would mean."

"I'm still not following," Elisa said.

Maggie looked around the room for a moment.

"Does anyone here not know what folding space means?"

Kevin raised his hand.

"Archaeologist. Right," Maggie said. "Someone give me a piece of paper."

Kevin looked down at the notepad he was writing on and tore loose a sheet of paper. Maggie took it and drew two dots on it, then labeled one 'A' and the second one 'B.'

"Pretend this is the universe. I'm here," Maggie said, pointing to 'A.' "I want to be over here." She pointed to 'B.' "Normally, to get from A to B, you have to travel across the surface of the paper, and that's a long trip. But if I do this," she folded the sheet so that 'A' and 'B' were pressed together, "the distance disappears. You can stand in both spots at once."

"So, you're talking about folding the universe in half?" Kevin asked.

"Not necessarily in half. Think of it more like pinching a little bit of your shirt, and pressing two points together, but yeah, that's the idea. It's something that's been bouncing around in science fiction for decades. Not the point, though. The point is, if you fold space, as long as you maintain the fold, you'd be in both spots at once, in a state of superposition."

"I think I follow," Kevin said.

"Right. Good. So, Garrett wasn't experimenting with teleportation. He was experimenting with folding space."

"And that's important?" Elisa asked.

"Yes!"

"Why?" Elisa asked.

"Because it means..." Maggie stopped, horrified as the high of the math problem faded and the implications finally hit her. The dry erase marker fell from her hand and bounced on the table, and she looked at the team who were sitting there, waiting for an answer.

"It means I can't tell you," she said.

Chapter Seventeen

"WHAT DO YOU MEAN, you can't tell us?" Elisa asked.

"I mean, I can't tell you what's going on, and before you ask, no, I can't tell you why I can't tell you."

"It's a security clearance issue, isn't it?" Junichi asked.

"I can't tell you that either," Maggie said.

"Right," Junichi said. "A moment."

He reached forward and tapped on the table, then the display screen showed a DMA seal until a short, older woman sitting in front of a wall decorated with the same seal appeared.

"Madam Secretary," Junichi said.

"Agent Hasikawa," the woman said. "I take it you're calling to tell me why one of my cities has a school shaped hole in it."

"We're working on that question now, ma'am, but we seem to have run into a bit of an issue with what I assume is a security clearance. I have Doctor Maggie Bennett with me. She said she knows what occurred last night, but that she's not able to reveal that information to us or tell us why she can't do so."

"I see. Doctor Bennett, do you know who I am?"

"No, ma'am."

"I'm Lynn Banks. I'm the Secretary of Metahuman Affairs."

"Pleased to meet you, ma'am," Maggie said.

"You know something?"

"I do, ma'am."

"And you're unable to share that information with the class, is that correct?"

"Yes, ma'am."

"How sure are you?" Banks asked.

"Pretty sure, ma'am," Maggie said.

"Very well. Doctor Bennett, it's my understanding that you're able to adjust your appearance at will, is that correct?"

"It is," Maggie said.

"Then, if you intend to keep your identity secret, I suggest you make yourself look a bit more like you used to. I will be back in moments."

The screen went back to the DMA seal, with the words 'Hold Please' superimposed over it. Maggie took a deep breath, and slipped into the Aether, then she focused on her memories of herself, of what she saw when she looked in the mirror. She fixed the image in her mind and dropped back out of the Aether.

Several of the people sitting around the table had a visible reaction when she reappeared. To her surprise, Varsha wasn't one of them. She just smiled at Maggie like nothing had happened.

"Did I get it right?" Maggie asked.

"Pretty close to the pictures I've seen," Varsha said.

Maggie winced at that, wondering where Varsha had seen pictures. Maggie had always avoided the camera like the plague, though she knew there were a few floating around. One on her page on the SCSU Department of Physics and Astronomy website, one on her Facebook page. A handful on Sierra's Facebook. A few ID photos. None of them were particularly flattering.

The screen changed, and Banks came back, but the screen was split, and on the other half was Mark Corrington, the head of the research group Maggie worked with at the APL at NASA.

"Thank you for joining us, Doctor Corrington," Banks said.

"Of course, Madam Secretary. How can I be of assistance?" Mark said.

"Hey, Mark," Maggie said.

"Maggie? Is that you?" Mark asked.

"Yeah," Maggie said. "How you doing?"

"How am I doing? I should be asking you that. They told me you were in a coma. When did you wake up? Are you okay? You look like death warmed over," Mark said.

Varsha reached down and took Maggie's hand under the table, giving it a squeeze, and Maggie squeezed back, doing her best not to break down. She knew Mark hadn't meant anything malicious, but that didn't stop his words from stinging.

"Um, funny story," Maggie said. "No coma. Just..." She waved her free hand around at the other people at the table.

"Doctor Bennett is currently in protective custody as a witness to the events that occurred at the SCSU campus a week ago today," Banks said.

"Damn it, Maggie. You never do anything by halves, do you?"

"No," Maggie said. "Which reminds me. Did you kill my access?"

"I've got your account locked down, but I didn't have it purged. When SCSU told me they were stupid enough to fire you, I decided to offer you a job as soon as you were back on your feet. I don't know what the fuck they were thinking, firing you."

"That's a long story, and I might even be able to tell you about it one day, but right now, we have a problem."

"What kind of problem?" he asked.

"The 'I can't talk about it, or even admit why I can't talk about it' kind." Maggie watched as Mark turned white as a sheet. He just sat there, looking like he was going to throw up for nearly a minute before he spoke again.

"Maggie, the Secretary of the DMA told me she's adding everyone on this call to the compartment for Project G. Please, for the love of all that's holy, tell me we don't have an issue there."

"I'd be lying if I did," Maggie said. Mark took a deep breath and nodded.

"Right. What kind of issue?"

"I think some of the tech is in the wild. Can you pull up the access logs and see if anyone has been in the source tech archives?"

There was silence from everyone for about five minutes while Mark worked, but Maggie knew what he was going to find. When he leaned back and pinched the bridge of his nose, she knew she was right.

"Someone pulled a full dump of the G-Four source technology archive on December 16th of last year."

"It was Elizabeth Fairchild, wasn't it?" Maggie asked.

"How'd you know?"

"Because after she left the team in January, she went to work for Doctor Alistair Hastings at SCSU. A better question is, how did she get that level of access? I thought Doctor Johns and I were the only ones on the Sun City team cleared for Project G."

"You are, and yes, that is a better question."

"Start the forensics on your end. I have a feeling you're going to have a DMA team crawling so far up your ass they will see your teeth in about five minutes."

"I suspect you're right. Any chance you can tell me what the hell is going on?"

Maggie looked over at Banks.

"Your call, ma'am, but it might help them with the forensics if they knew."

"It would be nice if you explained it to the rest of us as well, Doctor Bennett."

"Right," Maggie said. "Okay. The explosion last Saturday was centered in a lab run by Doctor Alistair Hastings. It was the result of a small amount of carbon undergoing total energy conversion. At the time, I believed that the event was the result of a failed attempt at testing macroscopic teleportation technology.

"For those who are unaware, it's believed that experiments in macroscopic teleportation were what first attracted the attention of the aliens known as the Gacrux and prompted their invasion eleven years ago. As a result, there is currently a worldwide embargo into all research into macroscopic teleportation. Metahumans with teleportation powers are exempt from this, because as near as we can tell, it's not the teleportation itself that caught the Gacrux's attention, but the machine which made teleportation possible.

"When the Sun City Sentries stopped the invasion, a lot of Gacrux equipment was left behind. We know that some of it is floating around on the black market, but most of it was collected and turned over to the DMA, which in turn gave it to various research teams, including the Alternative Propulsion Lab at NASA. The project I work on is focused on reverse engineering the reactionless drives used in their assault craft, but it shares a lot of tech with their portal generators. The portal generators function using a process called space-folding.

"Based on a review of the evidence from the incident last night, I now know that the explosion last Saturday was not, in fact, a result of an attempt at macroscopic teleportation, but instead, a result of an attempt at reverse engineering a Gacrux portal generator. That conclusion is based on two facts.

"First, the explosions last night displayed similar gamma spikes to the first event. When normalized for magnitude, the waveforms of the gamma spikes were identical to the explosion in Doctor Hastings' lab. In other words, whatever caused the explosion in Hastings' lab caused the explosion last night.

"Second, Doctor Hastings is the current faculty advisor for Elizabeth Fairchild, who left the Alternative Propulsion Lab in January, after illegally accessing the G-Four Source Technology Repository in the Project G data archive, which held all schematics, research, and information pertaining to the space-fold devices used by the Gacrux during their invasion."

"This is bad," Mark said. "This is really, really bad."

"Aside from the booms, you mean?" Juan asked.

"Yeah," Mark said. "Aside from the booms. The Gacrux, or more formally, Gamma Crusis Sapien, control an irregularly shaped empire of space centered around their home star Gamma Crusis, more commonly known as Gacrux, which is about eighty-eight-point-six light-years from

Earth. They are fanatically xenophobic and determined to wipe out any other lifeforms that might pose a significant threat to them. From what we know from the various aliens living on Earth, or who have visited in the last ten years or so, the Gacrux haven't been very successful with their genocidal tendencies because they're surrounded by significantly more advanced powers. The rest of this region of the galaxy looks at them the same way we look at North Korea.

"The problem is, as crazy as they are, the Gacrux are somewhere between one and two hundred years ahead of us in terms of technology, and we've got no allies in the larger galactic community. If the Gacrux are North Korea, we're the galactic equivalent of Siberian nomads. Yeah, we might have a snowmobile or two and some cast iron stoves, but at the end of the day, we're still a bunch of primitives who can't defend ourselves if push comes to shove.

"This is bad, because we have no idea how the Sun City Sentries stopped the prior invasion. One of the reasons we've kept such a tight lid on research related to the recovered Gacrux technology is we've been afraid that if they detect us using any of their tech, it might trigger another invasion."

"So, this is bad," Elisa said.

"End of the world bad," Maggie said.

"There is something I don't understand, though," Mark said.

"What's that?" Maggie asked.

"Where's he getting the power?"

"That's a damn good question," Maggie said. "I have no fucking clue. We do know there was an energy expenditure on the order of ten to the nineteenth during at least one incident."

Mark frowned. "Well, that's not...Wait. No. Ten to the nineteenth MeV, or TeV?"

"Joules, Mark. Ten to the nineteenth Joules."

"No. That number can't be right. Sun City wouldn't be there anymore."

"If the energy was released, yes. It's on the order of five gigatons. Everything south of Savannah and east of Tallahassee would be on fire, including Grand Bahama. The Keys might survive, though I wouldn't put money on it, but I said the energy was expended. Not released."

"Then where did it go?" Mark asked.

"There was a person caught in the fold when it collapsed. We have good reason to believe the person ended up on both sides of the fold."

Mark stared blankly for a minute, and Maggie was suddenly very aware that every eye in the room was on her.

"Walk me through it," Mark said.

"One of Hastings' grad students tried to open a fold and move a small weight of carbon. Something on the order of a nanogram. The fold failed. The carbon made it across the fold, but immediately decayed into energy. That was the first event. The blast that brought down the Science Annex, but there was a second fold. When it collapsed, the grad student, a man named Garrett Whitehall, was in the fold, and ended up on both sides."

"I'm sorry, I still don't follow," Mark said.

"The fold collapsed, but there was enough energy available for the wave function to collapse in both directions. It created a duplicate of the person caught in the fold. One of the duplicates died in the explosion, but the other one ended up wherever it was the fold led to."

"That can't...you're sure?"

"No," Maggie said. "But the other hypothesis makes even less sense."

"I'm afraid to ask," he said.

"I couldn't tell you anyway," Maggie said.

"Right," Mark said. "I'm going to go start the forensics and see if we can figure out how Fairchild got access to the Project G files. Madam Secretary, if there's nothing else?"

"You can expect that DMA team Doctor Bennett mentioned to crawl up your ass sometime later today, and stay there until we know how badly compromised your security is."

"Of course," Mark said. "Good day."

"Good day."

Mark disconnected, and Banks immediately focused on Maggie.

"What's the hypothesis you didn't want to share with Doctor Corrington?"

"Well, up until now, we've been assuming that I got my powers because I was caught in the quantum field imager," Maggie said. "But there is the possibility, however unlikely, that the imager just held me in place afterwards, but I got my powers from somewhere else, and Garrett was affected by the same thing I was."

"So, there might be someone out there who can do all the things you can do, but is a cold-blooded murderer?" Banks asked.

"Possibly," Maggie said. "Possibly more powerful. I haven't been tossing around hard gamma. But I don't think that's the case."

"Why not?" Banks asked.

"First, because I'm pretty sure whatever happened to me was only able to happen to me because I was connected to the quantum field imager. Garrett wasn't, so whatever happened to him, I think it's something completely different. On the off chance that I'm wrong about that, there's also the matter of figuring out how to use his powers.

"I don't want to sound arrogant, ma'am, but Garrett Whitehall is a bottle washer. He's competent enough to carry out an experiment that someone else has designed, but original work is not really his wheelhouse. Sierra and I started grad school a year behind him, and we're both second year post-docs. He's got at least two more years before he defends his dissertation.

"Given how much help I needed from Ashley to work out how to use my powers, I'm not convinced he would have made anywhere near the level of progress I've made in the same amount of time. If our powers derive from the same source, he might very well have the same ultimate potential as me, but even if that's the case, it's likely I have far better command of my powers and a far better grasp of that potential than he does."

"All right," said Banks. "I'm not going to take that as a given, but you know the man, so I'll take it under advisement. Industry."

"Yes, Madam Secretary?" Nomi replied.

"I'm going to get out of your way now. I know what it's like to have someone else nudging your elbow when you're trying to work. I would, however, like a moment to speak with Doctor Bennett alone."

"Of course," Nomi said. She turned to Maggie. "There's another conference room across the hall. Identical set up. I'll send the call there."

"Right," Maggie said. She let go of Varsha's hand and got up, then stepped into the Aether. She reappeared in the conference room across the hall in her new body and sat back down. The call came through a moment later, and she tapped the flashing red button on the table in front of her to accept it.

"What can I do for you, ma'am?" She asked.

"Getting your head out of your ass would be a good start," Banks said.

"Excuse me?"

"Junichi said you pitched a fit last night. He said you're not going to go through MERT certification."

"I didn't pitch a fit. I told Element I didn't plan on joining a MERT because I don't, and she pitched a fit. I just pointed out that I've already got a job. One I'm good at and worked hard to get. Then I walked away. Do I need to tell you the same thing?"

"Won't do any good. I won't listen. Last night was your first time out, and you saved a hundred and seventy lives. Imagine what you could do fully trained. And before you start on about your job, I'm not saying you have to give up on spaceships. Hell, Industry runs a multinational with a market cap of nearly half a trillion dollars, tinkers with her suit, and still has time to make moon eyes every time Element so much as breathes."

"Look, ma'am—"

"Don't fucking ma'am me, Bennett. Pick a code name and have someone design you a suit. I have a combat instruction team on the way down to start teaching you how to fight."

"You people don't listen very well, do you?"

"I'm listening, but all I'm hearing is bullshit. Project G is my compartment, so I already knew who you were before all this started, and when a new metahuman pops up as powerful as you, I get a file on my desk. A really big god damned file. I know things about you I don't want to know, but one thing that stands out is that you grew up wanting to be a hero."

"I didn't want to be a hero, I wanted to be an astronaut."

"Same damn thing."

"Yeah, well, an alien railgun took that away from me and I had to pick again, and I still don't want to be a hero. I want to be a scientist."

"Bullshit. People who don't want to be heroes don't run into burning buildings, they don't save a hundred and seventy lives, they don't step in front of speeding trucks, and they sure as hell don't run towards explosions. You did all of that last night. If you didn't want to be a hero, you would have gone back to that hideous fucking eyesore the High Guard calls a base when the alarm sounded and waited the whole thing out.

"If you'd done that, we wouldn't be having this conversation. You didn't. You stepped up and got down in the mud and blood with the rest of us. So don't give me that 'I don't want to be a hero' bullshit. Whatever the hell it is that's keeping you from stepping up, get over it, because if you don't, someone is going to die because you could have been there and weren't, and that blood will be on your hands."

The connection cut before Maggie could say anything. She sat and stared at the screen for a moment, trying to decide if she was angry, but she didn't even get that far before something jumped into her lap. She looked down to find Maxine, the kitten from the night before, staring up at her.

"Pet me," Maxine said.

"How did you get in here?" Maggie asked as she petted her.

"I walked. Scratch behind my ear."

Maggie laughed and gave Maxine her scratch. "Demanding much?"

"I'm a cat," Maxine said like that explained everything, which honestly, it kind of did.

"A cat I left in my room," Maggie said.

"Your room sucks," Maxine said. "It's boring. You're not there, and Henry isn't there."

Maggie sighed and picked Maxine up, hugging the tiny kitten against her chest.

"Sweetie, Henry isn't coming back."

Maxine buried her face against Maggie's chest.

"I know," she said, and Maggie could hear the pain in her voice. "I miss him, though."

"I know," Maggie said. She leaned down and kissed Maxine on the head. "I've got to get up."

"You suck," Maxine said. She wiggled out of Maggie's grasp, then hopped down on the floor, and before Maggie could stop her, she walked right through the wall.

"Well, that's new."

Chapter Eighteen

THE BRIEFING ROOM WAS quiet when Maggie walked back in. She dropped into her seat next to Varsha and looked around the table, wishing all eyes weren't so firmly focused on her. Varsha reached out and took her hand, giving it a tight squeeze.

"You okay?" Varsha asked.

"Fine," Maggie said. "Banks just told me I need to pick a code name and step up, whether I want to or not."

"Well, she's not wrong," Elisa said. A second later, her head jerked forward like someone had slapped her on the back of it.

"Ow! Fuck, Vee! Not cool!" Elisa said.

"You were being an ass," Varsha said.

Maggie smiled.

"Well, she's not wrong," Maggie said, earning a glare from Elisa, an eye roll from Nomi, and a chuckle from the rest of the table.

"Moving along to our new visitor," Nomi said.

"Yeah, about that," Maggie said. She looked over at Junichi. "She can walk through walls."

Junichi shrugged.

"There's a form for that. Actually, there's three. It depends on whether a cat door appears, or if it's a rippling water effect, or if it's just straight through."

"Rippling water," Maggie said.

"Any idea how a kitten with superpowers ended up linking up with a homeless man?" Nomi asked.

"I don't think one did," Fractal said. She touched the surface of the table, entering a few commands, and two pictures of a black man appeared on the screen. One of them was of a young marine in uniform. The other was a mugshot dated six months before.

"This is Captain Henry Duncan Cooper. He's a veteran of Desert Storm and Iraqi Freedom. Separated from the Marines in '94. Reenlisted October 1st, 2001. Medically discharged in 2005, though from what I can gather, the medical was a courtesy so he didn't have a psych discharge stapled to every job application he filled out for the rest of his life.

"Severe PTSD. He was captured and held by hostile forces for nearly three weeks. Homeless since 2007. Known to the SCSU campus police, SCPD, and Brevard County Sheriff's Office of Animal Services, but no arrests until six months ago when he was arrested for assault in an altercation over a dog. The State's Attorney declined to press charges against Mr. Cooper. The other man is doing a nickel in the State Pen for animal cruelty.

"Six weeks ago, Henry brought a box of kittens into the Brevard County Sheriff's Office of Animal Services. Not unusual. He apparently dropped off a lot of abandoned puppies and kittens. According to the bloodwork, they were all perfectly healthy, perfectly normal kittens. They don't store samples, so we can't do DNA tests to confirm, but the ages are right and there were two other tortoiseshells in the box, so it's a pretty sure bet our guest is part of the same litter."

"So, you're saying she was a perfectly normal kitten?" Nomi asked.

"Looks that way," Fractal said.

"They why can she talk?" Nomi asked.

"Yeah, um…my bad," Maggie said.

"Really?" Nomi said as she gave Maggie a look usually reserved for a child with chocolate smeared on their face who was telling you she didn't eat the entire pan of brownies while you were moving a load of clothes from the washer to the dryer. "Want to share with the class?"

"I squeezed too hard," Maggie said. Nomi frowned.

"What does that mean?"

"When I come out of the Aether, it's like making a fist. Normal me is a normal fist, like I'm holding my cane or something. I'm not squeezing very hard. When I make myself invulnerable, I squeeze harder, make a tighter fist, like I'm getting ready to punch something. The harder I squeeze, the more solid I become, and other things are less able to change the image I have of myself. When I come out of the Aether carrying an object with me, I have to squeeze harder than I do to just reassemble myself. Not a lot harder, but harder, and I have to have the memory of the object fixed in my mind. The thing is, when I grabbed Maxine, I was panicked. I'd never carried anything living through the Aether before, so I squeezed as hard as I could, while focusing on every mental image I had of a healthy, living cat."

"Know a lot of talking cats?" Garnell asked.

"Sort of," Maggie said. "I grew up watching Sabrina, the Teenage Witch. I used to pretend that my cat Sally could talk the way Salem could. I was a kid, and it was a game, but you know how real kids' games can feel to you at the time. When I was coming out of the Aether, I used those memories as a visualization tool, and I think a bit of my imagination got pressed into Maxine's reality."

"Is this something that's going to happen every time you carry something living through a teleport?" Nomi asked.

"No," Maggie said. "I just need a bit of practice to get it right. I was thinking we could start with plants, maybe."

"We'll avoid Venus fly traps," Ashley said. "No reason to risk turning Little Shop of Horrors into a documentary."

Several people chuckled at that, Maggie included.

"Great," Nomi said. "Now that that's settled, are there any other questions?"

"I've got one," Elisa said.

"What is it?" Nomi asked.

"Where the hell were Focus and Scatter last night?" Elisa asked. "We really could have used them."

"I asked Banks that same question," Nomi said. "Apparently, there was some sort of incident on the moon last night. The DMA doesn't have a lot of assets that can deal with things beyond Earth's atmosphere. Focus and Scatter were tapped to investigate."

"The moon?" Elisa asked. "Seriously?"

"That's what Banks said."

"Any idea what it was?" Ashley asked.

"No," Nomi said. "Just that it happened roughly the same time as the events at SCSU. I believe the timeframe puts it about five minutes after the Tindal Hall event. Investigation was deemed a priority."

"Not surprising," Fractal said. "Ever since the Gacrux invasion, the DMA has been twitchy as hell about anything extraterrestrial."

"Any other questions?" Nomi asked.

"Okay, then. Let's move on to assignments. Hannah, Junichi, speak with Doctor Gomez and see if she'll consent to the telepathic interrogation. Elisa, Juan, I need you two at SCSU. The city has asked for help shoring up any geological instabilities. Fractal, I need everything you can get me on Garrett Whitehall, Alistair Hastings, and Elizabeth Fairchild. Doctor Bennett and Doctor Gomez both knew Whitehall, so feel free to pick their brains about online usernames. The search warrant for Whitehall's residence is being executed right now, so you should have his computers by the end of the day. I'll have legal start the paperwork for the warrants for Fairchild. Vee, I need you on rapid response. If we get any sightings on Whitehall, Hastings, or Fairchild, they will be routed directly to you. Just go, and we'll follow. Garnell, she'll need tracking devices that can stand up to hard gamma and to EMP pulses. Get on it. Kevin, I need you to cover the entire patrol schedule today. Ashley, call Vera, Alan, and Tracy. Tell them we're looking at a full package. Maggie..."

"Yes?"

"Let's take a walk."

* * * *

Nomi led Maggie to the elevator in silence and hit the button for the ninth floor.

"I meant what I said in the meeting," Nomi said as the elevator carried them up. "You did an amazing job last night. I don't think I've ever seen someone who's new to a MERT team deal with their first major crisis that way."

"Training will do that," Maggie said.

"What training?" Nomi asked.

"I worked in the library as an undergrad. We were required to take the Red Cross First Aid, CPR, and AED classes. I had to take them again as a lab instructor, along with hazmat containment and some other emergency preparedness classes."

The elevator opened on the ninth floor, and Nomi stepped out, leading Maggie down a long hallway.

"Ever have to use them?" Nomi asked.

"A couple of times," Maggie said. "College students are dumb. They'll go too long without eating or drinking. The first time you see someone collapse due to a blood sugar crash, it looks an awful lot like a seizure."

"I'll take your word for it," Nomi said. She stopped in front of a door and put her hand on a palm scanner. It took a moment for the scanner to work, but then the light on top turned green as the lock buzzed. Nomi pulled the door open and waved Maggie through.

"How did you react the first time it happened?" Nomi asked.

"I picked another kid in the library and told them to call 911. Then I got down on the floor and rolled the girl on her side and stuffed a sweater under her head. Made sure she was breathing okay and waited for the paramedics."

"You got down on the floor with your hip in the shape it was in?"

"Yeah," Maggie said as she looked around the room they were in. "I paid for it later. I might have smoked a joint or three when I got home to deal with the pain."

The room was some sort of high-tech workshop. Maggie recognized a few of the CNC machines, because she'd seen similar ones in the machine shops at SCSU and NASA. Others were completely unfamiliar. Some looked like they came off a Star Trek set. Others looked like they belonged in a 1920s factory. All of it looked meticulously organized and maintained.

"Do you know my story?" Nomi asked.

"Just the bit about you turning in the Protectors for corruption," Maggie said. "Honestly, before last week, the only reason I knew the High Guard roster was because one of the grad students I work with is a huge cape fan. Loves everything superhero related. I knew bits and pieces about the local superhero drama because it comes up on the news all the time. I knew you and Elisa were a couple and most of the team is some flavor of queer because you guys all do the Pride Parade every year."

Nomi led her past the various CNC machines, and some old-fashioned manual machine tools to the back part of the room, where there were dozens of suits of power armor on display. All of them were visibly variations on the basic Industry design, but it was clear a lot of them were less refined than her current suit. She walked over to one that looked particularly crude compared to the suit Maggie was used to seeing. It was chunkier and less elegant, though the color scheme was the same. Red lacquer, bare copper, maroon enamel, and brown leather. It looked like a cross between the Rocketeer and a set of Samurai armor.

"My parents held seventy-five percent of the voting stock in Hashimoto Enterprises. My father was an amazing businessman, but my mother was the real heart of the company. She was a brilliant engineer and almost eighty percent of our products came off her drafting table. They both taught me everything they knew. I graduated college with a PhD in engineering and an MBA at the age of twenty-four and went to work with Mom.

"The Industry Worker Assistance Exoskeleton was my first project. It was designed to assist workers with manual labor. There were obviously other applications. Providing independence to the disabled and elderly, search and rescue, environmentally sealed units for firefighting, deep sea diving, and space exploration. I knew law enforcement and military would come calling eventually, but I really hated the idea of seeing more work used that way. I made Mom and Dad promise they would turn down any military and law enforcement contracts before I would even show them the designs.

"What I didn't expect was the Unitarium."

"They actually exist?" Maggie asked.

"They exist," Nomi confirmed.

Maggie needed a moment to take that in. The Unitarium was one of those things that everyone had heard of, but no one actually believed in. Like Bigfoot, the Loch Ness monster, Mothman, or the Illuminati. An organized crime ring made up entirely of supervillains. Of course, there were metas mixed up with organized crime. Tony Ragusa was a famous example. The mob boss everyone called 'the little dragon.' But most of the Ragusa crime family were just ordinary human thugs. The idea of an entire crime family of metahumans was the stuff of urban legend. Maggie had been fascinated with the idea back before the invasion, when she was still into superheroes and all the trappings, but after the invasion, she'd dismissed the whole idea as nonsense.

"It's a lot to take in," Nomi said. "I get that. I thought they were bullshit at first too, but they're very real, and however scary you think they are, I promise you, they're scarier. I found that out the hard way. I still don't know how they even found out about the Industry project, but they came calling. They demanded the blueprints. My parents refused. A week later, they died in a car bomb. Once I'd assumed control of the company, they came to me, showed me proof that they were behind the bombing, and gave me four weeks to turn over all the blueprints and research."

"I'm guessing you didn't," Maggie said.

"No," Nomi said. "I agreed. I arranged the exchange. Then I put on this suit." She reached up and ran her hand over the shoulder of the suit in front of them. "When they showed up, I beat them senseless, tied them up, and called the DMA. That's how I met Junichi. He managed to keep me from getting arrested, on the condition that I sign on to one of the MERT for training.

"It was a plea bargain of sorts. Community service. I hated it. Then I joined the Protectors, and found out they were in the Unitarium's pocket, so I helped the DMA clean house. By the time it was over, I realized something."

"What's that?"

"This is what I was meant to do," Nomi said. "I still run Hashimoto, I still design products for them, but this is my true calling. This is what I was born for."

Maggie had to work not to roll her eyes. Not because she didn't respect Nomi or what she'd been through, but because the moral of the story was so obvious.

"That's great," Maggie said. "You made a choice that you're happy with."

"You made your choice last night," Nomi said.

"People keep saying that," Maggie said.

"Because it's true," Nomi said. "Just like it's true that I made my choice the first time I put on this suit. I didn't want to admit it at first either. I didn't want to admit that my life had changed, that it wouldn't be what I planned. I was angry; I wanted to take my life back from the people who destroyed it. To me, that meant putting things back to the way they used to be. It took me a long time to realize that whatever life I was going to have going forward wouldn't look the same as my life before my parents died. Right now, you're in the same boat. It's just harder for you, because it's the second time it's happened to you."

Maggie let out a sigh and shook her head. "I don't want to have this conversation."

"Neither did I," Nomi said. "I know Vee's been telling you that you can walk away, that it's your choice. She's telling you that because she likes you and she knows how hard this life can be. Vee lets her compassion run away with her good sense, sometimes. She wants to believe you can walk away, that you can go back, but she's wrong.

"Some people believe our choices and actions define our character, but the truth is, they reveal our character. They are the outward displays of who we are. The choices made without thinking, doubly so. Character is something fundamental. Something at our core, which drives us to act in those moments when there isn't time to think. Last night, you faced one of those moments. To stay and help, or to come back to the Shiro and wait. You chose to stay, because deep down, that's who you are. Just like you helped that student who collapsed. It hurt you, you knew it would hurt you, but you still did it. You paid the price willingly, without even thinking about it, because it was the right thing to do."

"That's different," Maggie said. "Last night, I was already there. When that student collapsed, I was already there."

"With your powers, you're never more than a thought away from the crisis," Nomi said. "You can teleport anywhere, at any time, and that's what's going to keep happening."

"What do you mean?" Maggie asked.

"You're the kind of person who helps. You run into burning buildings because you hear people crying for help. You step in front of a speeding van to keep a kitten from getting hurt. It's an instinct. You help because you can't stop yourself from helping.

"The truth is, I didn't bring you up here to convince you to be a superhero. I don't need to. That's going to happen. The only question is how long you're going to fight it. I brought you up here to show you this."

Nomi gestured to the rows of machine tools and CNC machines around them.

"This is my workshop. I spend as much time here as I do in my suit. I tinker; I experiment. I design new products for my company. I design new suits for myself. I build equipment for members of other MERT teams in the city.

"I brought you here to show you that you can do both. You can put on a costume and mask and help when we need you, and you can work with NASA and design rocket engines. If you want to be a scientist, be a scientist. Just be this too. You can use the gift you've been given without giving up your dreams."

Maggie turned to look around the shop, taking it all in, trying to buy herself a moment to think.

"What are you offering?" Maggie asked.

"Computers, software, whiteboards, machine tools, lab space. When Maker came on, I bought out his machine shop and moved all of his tools in here, then hired his people on as support staff. I hired private instructors to come in and conduct the DMA paramedic training courses on site for Vee. I set up Ashley's lab and Kevin's library. I converted some of the unused space and built Fractal the fifth most powerful supercomputer in the world. I taped off a corner of the garage so Juan can tinker with classic cars, and I put in a meditation garden for Elisa and an office for Junichi. This building is enormous, and nearly a third of it is unused space. You can have whatever you need, including space and funding for anything Sierra wants to do. You just have to tell me what it is."

"Why?" Maggie asked.

"That's the same offer I've made everyone I recruited," Nomi said.

"But why do you want to recruit me?"

"Ah," Nomi said. "That."

Nomi walked over to a worktable and leaned back against it. It was clear to Maggie from the expression on her face and the way she was chewing her lower lip that she was trying to decide how truthful she wanted to be.

"I'm afraid," Nomi said. "I'm proud of the High Guard, don't get me wrong. We've done some amazing things in the last six years, and we're one of the most effective Tier Two teams in the US. We're also one of the few that handles the investigative side of the job in-house instead of farming it out to the US Marshals. The thing is, Sun City is a magnet for problems. It has been ever since Ubermench blew that crater out there into the Florida coastline back in '42, and it's getting worse. I don't have enough heavy hitters. I've got a team full of glass canons. Juan is great. I mean, it's hard to stop a guy who can turn his whole body into solid rock and turn the ground under you into molten lava, but he's the only one of us who can really soak damage. I've been trying to recruit a couple of good bricks for years, but when someone like Red Coat or Airheart shows up, they get snapped up fast, and the teams will do almost anything to keep them."

"I'm not Red Coat or Airheart," Maggie said.

"No, but Ashley tells me you can probably soak even more damage than them when you turn your powers on, and you can dish out damage at range.

"There's also team chemistry to consider. A lot of people don't realize how big an issue that is. There's a red dragon in town. You want to talk about someone who can soak damage and bring the pain, Eurion is it. That old bitch is hard to kill and could level cities before anyone could stop her. On paper, she's everything we need, but I can't recruit her until Ashley and Hannah sort out their shit, or I will lose Hannah, and we need Hannah. The High Guard doesn't work without Nexus.

"You, on the other hand, are a safe choice from a team chemistry standpoint. You make Hannah a little nervous, but once we get you some training for your mental abilities, that will go away. You're not a threat to whatever the hell is going on between Hannah and Ashley. You're not a threat to any of the other relationships in the team. You seem to get along well with everybody.

"So, you have a powerset that we could really use, and from a team chemistry standpoint, you're a nice, safe choice. Those two alone would make recruiting you a no brainer, but there's another reason too."

"I'm listening."

"Vee," Nomi said. "I know Vee loves her job. I know she gets up every morning, eats breakfast, and runs out into the city to save lives, and that means the world to her, but she's burning out."

"What?" Maggie asked.

"It's not the job that's getting to her. She's lonely here. I've tried. So have Elisa, Ashley, Hannah, Juan, and hell, even Fractal, but Vee keeps all of us at arm's length. She's downright skittish. The only person I know of that she's ever opened up to is Tux, and that isn't healthy. Don't get me wrong, I love Tux. Everyone loves Tux. Sometimes, two of us at once, which is fun, but it's not what Vee needs.

"Then you walk in here, and suddenly, Vee's sharing her mom's homemade ice cream, and she's eating every meal with you, she's taking you to Cape Town. She's holding your freaking hand during team meetings. I don't know why you're different, and I swear, if you break that girl's heart, I will find a way to kill you and make it hurt the whole time you're dying, but at the end of the day, I don't care about the why. I just care that it is.

"So, you want to know the real reason I want to recruit you? It's Vee. We need her, and for whatever reason, she needs you, or someone like you. Someone she can connect with."

"You're playing matchmaker?"

"Are you going to tell me you aren't interested?" Nomi said. "Because if you do, I'll call you a liar to your face."

"No, I'm definitely interested," Maggie said.

"Good. Because she needs someone. Maybe as a friend, maybe as a girlfriend. I'll let you two sort that out. All I know is, you fit the bill. So, tell me, what will it be?"

Maggie stared at Nomi for a minute while she thought about everything. About how she'd felt the night before helping save lives, about what it had felt like, waking up in the hospital and finding out she was the only one who made it out of that car alive and what it would be like to be responsible for that much pain.

The two memories stuck in her mind, warring with each other, and she honestly wasn't sure which one was winning.

"Can I have some time to think about it?" Maggie asked.

"How long do you need?" Nomi asked.

"Can I take the day? No training, no costumes or masks. Just a day for myself?"

Nomi nodded.

"Yeah, I think we can do that. Do you need anything?"

"No," Maggie said. "I've got it covered. I'll give you my answer tonight."

Chapter Nineteen

MAGGIE USED HER EXPANDED senses to make sure no one was looking at the front porch of the house, and that the occupants weren't in a spot where they could see the entryway before she dropped out of the Aether. Then, with a thought, she conjured a duplicate of the house key she'd carried with her for the past eleven years. The deadbolt stuck just a bit, and she smiled. Her grandfather had been promising to fix that since they bought the house and had never gotten around to it. Maggie didn't mind. The lock always gave easily enough.

She opened the door and stepped inside. With her expanded senses, she could feel her grandparents moving in the kitchen. She hurriedly shut and locked the door, then she stepped back into the Aether for just a second, rematerializing with her scars and brown hair in place. She took a moment to glance in the mirror by the door, the one she'd always hated, and saw herself the way she'd looked before she got her powers.

She was surprised at how strange it felt. The person she'd seen in the mirror for the past eleven years felt like a mask.

"Maggie?" her grandmother said. Maggie turned to face her, forcing herself to smile, when all she really wanted to do was cry.

"Hey," she said as her grandmother rushed forward to hug her. "Surprise."

The word sounded weak, even to her ears, but her grandmother didn't seem to care. She just squeezed Maggie tightly, careful as she always was not to put any weight on her.

"I was so worried," her grandmother said. "When the building at your school blew up, they said you were in protective custody, and we couldn't see you. They said to tell anyone who asked that you were in the hospital, in a coma. Are you okay? What happened? Why are you here?"

"Give the girl a chance to speak," her granddad said. Maggie smiled over her grandmother's shoulders at him. Her grandmother gave her another quick squeeze, then stepped back.

"Where's your cane?" she asked. "Come on. Let's get you off your feet."

"Okay," Maggie said.

She followed her grandmother to the living room, feeling the same twinge of guilt she always did when she came home. Her grandparents had spent a fortune having the house built in a rush while Maggie was still in the hospital, because there was no way she would have been able to negotiate the stairs or narrow halls in their old house. They'd spend another fortune making sure every inch of it was wheelchair accessible, because the doctors hadn't been sure at the time if Maggie would ever walk again.

Maggie had always felt guilty about them selling the house they'd lived in for twenty-five years just so she would have a home she could move around in with as little difficulty as possible. She'd felt even more guilt when they'd bought Maggie her own house as a present when she'd started college.

Things hadn't changed much in the six years she'd been gone. The leather living room set was still comfortable but firm, so she wouldn't have any trouble getting up. Everything was spaced wide enough for her to get through with her cane. There were still first aid kits tucked away in every room in the house, and handrails in the hallway.

Maggie sat down in the tilt lift chair they'd bought for her. It was comfortable and familiar and the only reason she'd been able to stand up without help for the first year after she got out of the hospital. Her grandparents sat down on the couch opposite her. Maggie could tell they were worried. It wasn't that surprising, since she was supposed to be five hundred miles away in Sun City.

"Everything's okay," Maggie said, hoping to put their minds at ease. "I'm sorry you were worried, but the DMA wanted to make sure I was safe."

"The DMA?" her grandfather asked. "They said the US Marshals had you in protective custody."

"I know," Maggie said. "I'm honestly a little surprised they didn't give you the same story about me being in a coma that they gave work. They didn't even ask me about that. They just did it."

"Why?" her grandmother asked. "What's going on?"

"That's complicated," Maggie said. "How close have you been following the news?"

"Pretty close," her grandfather said. "Becky called us last weekend and told us your school had blown up. It was Saturday, so we weren't too worried to start with, but when you didn't answer your phone, we started getting a little nervous. Then a marshal showed up and told us you were in protective custody while the investigation into the cause of the explosion was carried out. I set up a few news alerts, just in case. Then last night, everything went crazy."

"That's a good way to describe it," Maggie said. "I'm sorry I worried you."

"It's not your fault, sweetheart," her grandmother said.

"Still," Maggie said. "I know I've caused you a lot of worry over the years."

"You're our granddaughter. Worrying comes with the territory," her grandfather said.

Maggie smiled and shook her head. She'd heard him say that more times than she could count. It was his way of telling her he loved her, though he'd never been shy about saying that, either. She looked at them both and thought of all they'd been through because of her over the years and hated herself for dropping even more worry in their laps, but she needed their advice.

"I need to tell you both something, but I'm not sure how to say it."

"Just get it out, honey. No need to pretty it up for us," her grandfather said.

"Okay," Maggie said. "It's just big and scary, and I need you to hear me out before you ask any questions, because there's a lot to take in, and I really need some advice from someone I trust."

"Sweetheart, we—" her grandmother started, but she stopped when Maggie's grandfather put his hand on her arm.

"Let her talk, love," he said, then turned to Maggie. "We're listening."

Maggie took a deep breath to steady her nerves. She looked down at the floor before she started speaking.

"I was in the building last Saturday when it exploded," she said. She didn't look at their faces, but she could feel the tension in the room increase the moment she said it.

"I was helping Sierra with an experiment. Well, not really helping. I was her test subject for the experiment. It was a new type of medical imaging machine. I was plugged into the machine when the explosion happened, and I...well...I died."

"What?" her grandmother asked, but her grandfather squeezed her arm, and she took a deep breath and settled back onto the couch.

"I died," Maggie said. "My body was thrown against the wall by the explosion, and it killed me. Except something happened to me."

Maggie slipped into the Aether, then came back in her new body. She was back so fast her grandparents wouldn't have even seen her disappear. Just, one second, she would have been the Maggie they knew, then the next, she would be her new self. She let them get a good look at her new body, then she teleported to stand behind the chair.

"I ended up with superpowers," Maggie said before teleporting back into her chair.

* * * *

Maggie spent the next couple of hours filling them in on all the details she could discuss. She didn't hold anything back. She told them about being stuck in Planck scale time, about appearing in her own bed, calling the High Guard, the interrogations, about how broken up Sierra was. She told them about Varsha, blushing through the whole thing while her grandfather smiled and her grandmother gave her a look she didn't quite understand, but that made her a little nervous. Then she'd told them about the night before. The accident in training, the trip to Cape Town, the alarm, the fires and broken buildings and dead bodies. About the lives she saved and the lives she couldn't save. About Henry and Maxine and about the conversation with Banks and the one with Nomi.

Maggie was pretty sure they took all of it better than she had when it was happening. At least, right up until she asked them the big question.

"What do you think I should do?"

"If NASA's offering you a job, I think you should take it," her grandmother said without hesitation. The answer didn't surprise Maggie at all. She loved her grandmother, but she knew she was a worrier, and superpowers or no, she would want Maggie to be safe. Her answer had been a foregone conclusion and wasn't really why Maggie was there.

"Do you want to join the High Guard?" her grandfather asked.

"I think so," Maggie said. The answer surprised her, because up until that moment, she hadn't really been sure.

"I love being a scientist, I do, but last night, I saved a hundred and seventy lives. I'm proud of that. I helped people. And I know a lot of people who have powers don't join the MERTs, but I'm not sure I could live with myself if I walked away from this. Before last night, maybe I could have. When it was all still theoretical. But knowing what I can do, knowing I can save lives, how can I not?"

"Then what's stopping you?" her grandfather asked.

It made Maggie smile, because he'd always had a knack for cutting through the bullshit. She glanced down at the floor, turning it over in her head. She kept thinking about Red Coat pulling her out of the car, of how he was too late to save her parents and her brother.

"I'm afraid I'll fail," she said. "I'm afraid I won't get there in time to save someone."

"I thought it might be something like that," her grandfather said.

She looked up at him as he scooted forward so he was sitting on the edge of the couch. He reached out, and she did the same, taking his hands.

"You're thinking about Red Coat. About how he couldn't get there in time to save your parents and your brother."

"Yes," Maggie said.

"Honey, I've held back saying this, because I didn't think you were ready to hear it, but I think now might be the time. Red Coat didn't fail that day."

"What?"

"Red Coat didn't fail. I know you feel like he did, but you're wrong. Red Coat saved you. If he hadn't been there, you would have died, along with your parents and your brother. I know that sometimes, you think that would have been better. I know you feel like what happened was your fault, but whether you believe it or not, the world is better with you in it, and we are grateful, every day, that he saved you. If you go out there and you become a superhero, every life you save will be one more life than if you weren't there. You won't be able to save everyone, but every life you can save will make the world a better place. And that is all anyone can ask of you."

Maggie looked at her grandfather as tears welled up in her eyes. She didn't really understand what she felt in that moment, but there was an overwhelming feeling of relief. Like a weight had been lifted off her shoulders. One she didn't realize she'd been carrying. She tried to blink away the tears, only to cause them to spill down her cheeks as she turned to look at her grandmother.

"I just want you to be safe," her grandmother said.

"I know," Maggie said.

"I love you, and I'll support you whatever you decide."

"I think I need to do this," Maggie said.

"Okay," her grandmother said.

"You just bring your girl around for a visit," her grandfather said, making Maggie blush.

"She's not my girl," Maggie said.

"Yet," her grandfather said. "You give me a hug, and then you go work on that."

Chapter Twenty

MAGGIE DROPPED OUT OF the Aether in her room at the Shiro and flopped down onto the bed. A moment later, she felt a solid weight slam into her gut. She looked down to see Maxine staring at her as she started milk treading on her sternum and purring. Maggie reached up and started scratching behind her ears.

"Forgive me for this morning?" Maggie asked.

"No," Maxine said firmly. "You still suck, but my ears need scratching."

Maggie smiled.

"Does your head need kisses too?"

"Yes!" Maxine said. She tilted her head down, and Maggie leaned forward and kissed her on the top of her head.

"Nomi wants me to stay here and be a member of the team," Maggie said.

"I like it here. We should stay," Maxine said. Maggie laughed and scratched near the base of Maxine's tail.

"Selfish," Maggie said.

"No," Maxine said. "You like it here too."

"Yeah," Maggie said. "I do."

"Then stay," she said.

"I'm going to." She kissed Maxine on the head again. "And I'm going to find the person who hurt Henry."

"Good," Maxine said.

* * * *

Maggie knocked on Sierra's door, then waited for an answer. It took a couple of minutes before the door opened. When it did, the first thing Maggie noticed was the look on Sierra's face. She looked miserable. Maggie didn't even have to guess why. She immediately wanted to kick herself, thinking she should have stuck around until the interrogation was over. Then she would have been there when Sierra found out that Garrett was alive.

"Hey," Sierra said. The word sounded weak, almost lifeless. Not like Sierra at all.

"Are you okay?" Maggie asked. Sierra shrugged and backed away from the door, making room for Maggie to come in.

"Not really," Sierra said. Maggie stepped inside, and Sierra closed the door behind her, then walked over and sat down on the bed.

"Nomi and Hannah questioned me about Garrett," she said. "I'm guessing you know about him, right?"

"Yeah," Maggie said. "Nomi showed us the pictures in the meeting this morning."

"You couldn't have warned me?" Sierra snapped. Maggie flinched at the anger in her voice. She didn't think she'd ever heard Sierra's angry voice directed at her before.

"No," Maggie said. "I wish I could have, but—"

"I know," Sierra said, cutting her off. "I'm sorry. I'm not okay. None of this is okay, but I shouldn't take it out on you."

"I probably deserve a little bit of it," Maggie said. "You needed me, but I was off dealing with my own shit. I wish I could have been here, but I didn't realize they were going to tell you in the interview. If I had, I would have hung around so I could have been there afterwards."

"That would have been nice," Sierra said. "Where'd you go, anyway?"

"I went to see my grandparents," Maggie said. "I needed some advice."

Sierra frowned.

"You usually come to me for advice," Sierra said.

"Yeah," Maggie said. "I think I needed an outside perspective on this one, though."

"What for?"

"Nomi asked me to join the High Guard when my training is finished."

"Oh," Sierra said. She just sat there, staring at Maggie, not saying anything else. Maggie waited. She could see Sierra thinking about it, processing the implications of what it would mean. She expected questions, or maybe anger, but instead, Sierra just nodded.

"You should do it," she said.

"You think so?"

"Yeah," Sierra said. "I think it suits you. You've been happier this last week than I've ever seen you. I don't think I ever realized how much you hated being confined to a desk."

"Was I really that bad?" Maggie asked.

"Yeah," Sierra said. "There were times it got so bad I was terrified you were going to hurt yourself if there wasn't someone there to keep an eye on you."

"Right after Sandra left?" Maggie asked.

"That was one of them," Sierra said. "Probably the worst."

"That was hard," Maggie said. "I was...I was so surprised that she wanted to be with me when it started, and then she left, and I just...I felt like she was the only one who would ever want me. It got really hard to look in the mirror after that. I felt broken and alone, and mostly, I just felt ashamed."

"Why would you feel ashamed?"

"I didn't want to be someone's pity fuck," Maggie said.

"God, Mags. I wish you would talk to me sometimes." She reached up and wrapped her arm around Maggie's shoulder, pulling Maggie against her side. "I promise you, you were not a pity fuck."

"I don't know," Maggie said. "Sometimes I think you're right. Most of the time, but sometimes that voice in the back of my head asks what else I could be."

"She adored you," Sierra said. "Right from the start. The first time she saw you go math zombie, I thought she was going to come on the spot."

"Okay, no. That didn't happen."

"It did," Sierra said. "That woman thought you were the hottest thing this side of a fusion reaction. I was convinced she was going to stuff you in her luggage and take you back to California with her."

Maggie looked away, avoiding Sierra's eyes. She'd never told Sierra that Sandra had asked Maggie to move to California with her or that the reason things had gotten so bad after Sandra left was because Maggie was kicking herself for not going.

"You're exaggerating," Maggie said.

"No, I'm not," Sierra said. "She had it bad, and honestly, she's not the only one."

"What?"

"You remember that red-headed undergrad who followed you around like a puppy for three semesters?"

"She needed tutoring," Maggie said.

"Right. A nursing student who needed tutoring in modern physics I'd buy, but E&M and Quantum Mechanics?" Sierra said.

"Come on. Knock it off."

"She had a picture of you as wallpaper on her phone. Girl was hot for you."

"Right," Maggie said.

"Fine, don't believe me, but your only problem is self-confidence. If you put half the swagger into getting a girl you put into running a dungeon, you'd have to buy a second house to hold the toaster ovens."

"I never should have explained that joke to you," Maggie said. She reached down and took Sierra's hand. "You know, I'm supposed to be comforting you, but this is the second time this week you ended up turning the conversation around and making it about me."

"You noticed that, huh?"

"Yeah," Maggie said.

"It's easier if I don't think about it," Sierra said. "I feel guilty."

"Why?"

"Lots of reasons," Sierra said. "When I told you about the breakup, I might have glossed over some things. The truth is, Garrett and I hadn't been getting along for a while. We'd been fighting for months. Mostly about you. He was convinced you had a crush on me."

"Well, to be fair, he's not wrong. A few years too late, but not wrong."

"You're terrible," Sierra said. "He was also convinced you hated him."

"Again, not wrong."

"Really?" she asked. "I knew you didn't like him, but I always thought it was because...you know."

"Because I had a huge crush on you?" Maggie asked. "I could have gotten past that if he wasn't a huge asshole, but I honestly never really got what you saw in him."

"I've been asking myself the same thing for months. I mean, when we started dating, he was attentive and sweet, and really good about making me feel special. That changed somewhere along the way."

"Right around the time you scheduled your defense," Maggie said.

"Really?"

"Yeah. You didn't notice, but I don't blame you. Both of us were a little crazy in the run up to our defense."

"You noticed, though."

"Yeah, but I had the advantage of distance," Maggie said.

"I guess," Sierra said. "I just know that somewhere along the line, he got moody and snappish. I couldn't say anything right, and he was always so defensive. He got pushier about everything, and he got really jealous of you. Any time I suggested letting you take a turn tanking the raids in Black Sky, he threw a fit. He'd pout when we hung out together. Towards the end, he was convinced you were trying to get me to break up with him."

"I think you getting your doctorate before him hurt his precious little ego," Maggie said. "He couldn't stand that you're a better scientist."

"Yes," Sierra said. "Exactly. I thought it was just me."

"No."

"Why didn't you say anything?"

"Two reasons. First, I am not an unbiased observer. Don't get me wrong. Dilaudid-fueled confessions aside, I never thought we were going to be anything other than friends, but I'd be lying if I said I didn't have a predisposition towards hating your boyfriends. Sometimes, it's hard to tell if the person dating your huge, hopeless crush is an asshole, or if you're just a jealous bitch who wants them to be an asshole. Second, I didn't want to get splashed with the blame when the relationship crashed and burned."

"You thought I'd do that?" Sierra asked, and Maggie could hear the hurt in her voice.

"Not intentionally," Maggie said. "But people do stupid things when they're hurting. God knows I can be a total bitch when I'm in a bad place. And I'm sorry for all the times I put you through that, by the way."

"You were hurting," Sierra said. "I understood."

"That doesn't make it okay," Maggie said.

"The worst thing you ever did to me was shut me out," Sierra said. "I was more worried than hurt. I wanted to help, and you wouldn't let me."

"It hurt too much, sometimes," Maggie said. "Normally, I was pretty good at dealing with what I felt for you, but when I was feeling sorry for myself, it got a little raw."

"I'm sorry," Sierra said. "I never realized."

"Well, that's because I am a gold medalist when it comes to bottling up my feelings and letting them ferment into something toxic. Part of that was the guilt. I felt like I deserved to suffer. Which was probably another reason I never said anything. I felt like watching you with someone else was some kind of penance, as fucked up as that sounds."

"It sounds pretty fucked up," Sierra said. "God, I knew he wasn't your favorite person, I just misjudged why."

"You really thought it was all jealousy?"

Sierra shrugged.

"Well, all the more reason to stay out of the middle of your relationship," Maggie said.

"You might have a point," she said. "I don't know. I'd been thinking of breaking up with him for a while, if I'm honest. I knew it was over, I was just dreading the actual break up. That last fight was just the final straw, but then he was dead, and I felt so guilty. Now that he's alive, I'm angry, and I wish he'd stayed dead, and I feel guilty about that."

"You shouldn't," Maggie said.

"What?"

"It's okay to be angry," Maggie said. "It's okay to wish that he was the person you thought he was, instead of the monster he turned out to be."

"Is it?" Sierra asked. "I was supposed to be in love with him, but now, all the memories I have of the time we were together are tainted. I feel stupid. I feel used. I feel like I've been lied to."

"It's okay to feel all of that too," Maggie said as she slipped an arm around Sierra's waist and hugged her. "Except the stupid part. You're not allowed to feel stupid. You're brilliant and wonderful and someday, you're going to find someone who appreciates all of that."

"I already did," Sierra said. Maggie looked at her in confusion, wondering what she was talking about. "I found someone, but I was too scared to accept it at the time."

Maggie felt her whole body tense up as she looked at Sierra. She kept telling herself that she was misunderstanding what Sierra was saying, but Sierra seemed determined to prove her wrong. She reached up and cupped Maggie's cheek in her hand.

"You know why I thought you were jealous of Garrett?" Sierra asked.

"Because I was really bad at hiding it?" Maggie asked.

Sierra smiled and shook her head.

"It was because I was jealous of Sandra," Sierra said. "I knew I should be happy for you. I could see how good she was for you. How she made you laugh and smile. But I hated her. Every time she touched you, I wanted to claw her eyes out."

"Sierra, don't," Maggie said.

"Don't what?" Sierra asked. "Don't tell you how I feel? Don't tell you that Garrett was right to be jealous of you? Don't tell you the reason I broke up with him was because I realized that I wanted you more than I wanted him?"

Maggie stared at Sierra, letting the words sink in. Words that she would have given anything to hear, once. Then, she reacted the way any brave, strong, courageous, fearless, newly minted superhero would react when the woman she'd had a crush on for six years was about to lean in and kiss her. She panicked and teleported ten miles away.

Chapter Twenty-One

MAGGIE'S HOUSE WAS PRETTY much how she left it. A little better, in fact. The cleaning lady had paid a visit. The trash had been taken out, the hampers emptied, the laundry washed and put away. There was still no food, but Maggie didn't need to eat so that wasn't a problem. On the other hand, staring indecisively at a refrigerator full of food would have given her something to do other than beat her head against the wall while wondering which god she had pissed off.

She was willing to admit that running away was probably not the best way to deal with the situation, but it was the only solution she could come up with in the moment. That didn't make it a good one, but it was better than the disaster that would have resulted from staying and letting Sierra kiss her.

Yes, she had told Sierra how she felt about her, but it hadn't really been by choice. She'd been stoned out of her mind at the time. She had three bags of Dilaudid running through her, and Dilaudid made her stupid on the best of days. She'd been scared and vulnerable, and Sierra had been there. It had been a nightmare once she'd sobered up. The embarrassment had kept her up at night for months.

Sierra had been kind and understanding about the whole thing, even if Maggie could have done without the painfully earnest 'I'm straight' speech. She'd gone out of her way to keep Maggie from withdrawing from their friendship in abject humiliation, and once Maggie had gotten past ritually shaming herself every night, she had worked on moving on.

She wasn't going to pretend she didn't still have some feelings for Sierra, but she had worked very, very hard to let go of them and get on with her life. Then she'd met Sandra. Nice, safe Sandra. Sandra who came with an expiration date. Sandra who was always going to go back to California.

The two of them had hit it off. Maggie had thought Sandra was gorgeous and wonderful, and maybe she hadn't understood why Sandra wanted to be with her, but she'd been able to accept that she did. They'd dated for nearly nine months while Sandra was on loan to the APL at Kennedy Space Center. Sandra had come down to Sun City every Friday night and gone back to Titusville every Monday morning. She'd been Maggie's first lover, and she'd made Maggie feel things Maggie had never expected to feel.

Then Sandra had to go and break the rules. She had to tell Maggie she loved her, and ask Maggie to go to California with her when her time at APL ended. Maggie had wanted to. God, she'd wanted it so much, but she couldn't do it. She couldn't convince herself to make that choice. The choice that would mean giving up her house and her job and Sierra. The choice that meant taking a chance that someone could love her for who she was.

She told Sandra no, and Sandra had accepted it. They'd parted amicably enough, but as soon as Sandra was gone, Maggie regretted it. She'd spent nights lying awake, trying to work up the courage to call Sandra and ask if it was too late, but the voice in the back of her head that told her she was a horrible, disfigured freak kept telling her no one would ever love her, and she'd believed it, and she'd spiraled hard.

Sierra had been there, and she'd helped Maggie out of one of the worst depressive episodes she'd ever had, but it was different than it had been before. Sierra wasn't a raw, open wound anymore. She wasn't the romantic epicenter of Maggie's life anymore. She was just Maggie's hot best friend, and Maggie's feelings for her were just a sort of pleasant emotional background noise.

Then the explosion had happened, and Maggie had gotten a new body, and she'd met Varsha and Varsha had taken her to Cape Town and they had danced, and Maggie was pretty sure that if the alarm hadn't sounded, they would have ended up back at the Shiro in either her or Varsha's bed.

Maggie threw herself on her bed and stared up at the ceiling.

Why now? Why had Sierra waited until now? If Sierra had leaned over and kissed her in the van the night before the explosion, she would have let her. If she'd done it the morning before the explosion, Maggie would have let her. Six fucking years, they had known each other before the explosion, and Sierra could have kissed her at any point. If she had, Maggie probably would have done something stupid like proposed on the spot, because she always made bad choices when Sierra was involved. Six fucking years when Maggie would have believed it was because Sierra loved her and wanted to be with her.

She stopped herself, because she wasn't far enough gone to even pretend she believed that bullshit. At least, not after Sandra. There would have always been that voice in the back of her head telling her she was nothing more than a fucking charity case. A pity fuck. And this whole mess was like the universe was just confirming she was right.

She lay there, turning a single thought over in her mind. She hadn't been good enough for Sierra when she was scarred and broken. She wasn't good enough until Garrett was a wanted criminal who had been lying to her for God only knew how long. She wasn't good enough until she had the body of an underwear model, the face of a cover girl, and superpowers to boot.

As much as she loved Sierra, in that moment, she hated her. She wanted to yell and scream, because it hurt, because it was humiliating. Because no matter what, no matter how many times Sierra told her she'd been planning to be with her before the explosion, there would always be a part of her that doubted it. A part of her that would be angry that she hadn't been enough for Sierra until she was magically made whole. A part of her that would always believe that Sierra had been lying to her every time she said that if someone really cared about her, they wouldn't give a damn about the scars.

Maggie got up off the bed and marched back into the kitchen. She yanked open the fridge and grabbed the half empty jug of cranberry grape juice and slammed it down on the counter, then opened the freezer and reached for the emergency vodka. She had the bottle in hand and the cap halfway off before she stopped and screamed at the top of her lungs as she realized she couldn't even drown her problems in over-priced alcohol.

She didn't know how alcohol would affect her powers, and as pissed off as she was, she wasn't irresponsible enough to get drunk. Not after what happened to Ashley when she'd been careless with the conjured racquet ball.

She screwed the cap back on the emergency vodka and shoved it back in the freezer, grabbed the juice jug, and did what she always did when she wanted to hide from the entire fucking world. She went to her computer and logged into Digilife.

Her avatar hadn't finished rezzing when she got a message from Kelly.

Kelly: You are alive!

Bobbie: Yes.

Bobbie: Shit, I did it again, didn't I?

Kelly: No.

Kelly: I knew you were safe. I mean, you told me about getting fired, so I knew you weren't on campus, but what the hell is going on in that city of yours?

Bobbie: It's a long story.

Kelly: I'll bet. Want to talk about it?

Bobbie: No.

Kelly: Okay.

Kelly: Are you all right? I'm getting a bit of a vibe.

Bobbie: No. Definitely not all right.

Kelly: Want to talk about it?

Bobbie: No. Yes. Fuck if I know.

Kelly: It sounds like you need to talk about it.

Bobbie: Yeah, I do.

Kelly: Tell me what's going on.

Bobbie: You remember the rescue worker I told you about?

Kelly: The one you haven't stopped gushing about all week? No. I've completely forgotten her.

Bobbie: Point taken. We went on a real date last night. She took me out to a nightclub. We ate, we danced. I'm pretty sure we would have ended up back at her place, or maybe my place. Not sure which.

Kelly: But?

Bobbie: But half the fucking city got blown up, and she's a first responder.

Kelly: Ah. Yeah. Been there.

Bobbie: Seriously?

Kelly: Nurse Hotness, C Cup, and I all work for emergency services.

Bobbie: Ah. I was guessing hospital, but that makes sense.

Kelly: So, you got crotch-blocked by a terrorist attack, and now you're all broody?

Bobbie: No. Remember my friend? The one I have a crush on?

Kelly: Stupidhead.

Bobbie: Right. She tried to kiss me.

Kelly: WHAT?

Kelly: Way to bury the lead.

Kelly: Wait, what do you mean *tried*?

Kelly: Did she trip or something?

Kelly: Is she a horrible kisser?

Kelly: I bet that's it!

Kelly: She's terrible.

Kelly: That's what kissing guys will do to you, you know.

Bobbie: I don't know.

Bobbie: When I realized what she was about to do, I ran away.

Kelly: No fucking way!

Kelly: Seriously?

Kelly: I figured you'd have done her on the spot.

Bobbie: No. Sorry to disappoint. As much fun as it is in Digilife, cops tend to frown on public sex IRL.

Kelly: :P

Bobbie: I know. Totally unreasonable.

Kelly: Absolutely.

Kelly: So, really, why run away? All joking aside, I thought you would have been jumping for joy.

Bobbie: A couple of reasons.

Bobbie: First, there's Rescue Girl.

Kelly: Who you met a week ago.

Bobbie: Who I really, really like.

Bobbie: Maybe more than like. I know it's quick, but we really hit it off. We have a lot of things in common, and there's just this connection there. It's hard to explain.

Kelly: Okay. I get that.

Kelly: But have you considered polyamory?

Bobbie: I don't think either of them would go for it.

Kelly: You're totally thinking about it, aren't you?

Kelly: You've already got your hand down your pants, don't you?

Bobbie: No.

Kelly: Liar.

Bobbie: Okay, I can admit that it's a nice mental image, but Rescue Girl isn't the only issue.

Kelly: Go on.

Bobbie: There's the fact that she just broke up with her boyfriend.

Kelly: Who was in the explosion. Right.

Bobbie: Yep. That whole thing is messing with her head.

Kelly: And you're worried about taking advantage.

Bobbie: Yeah.

Bobbie: And I'm angry. I mean, she's known how I feel for years, and she pulls this shit now?

Kelly: Girl, I don't mean to pry, but I feel like there's more to this than you're telling me.

Maggie leaned back and stared at the screen. Kelly was right, of course. There was more going on than Maggie was telling her, which was why it hurt so much, and why she was so angry.

Maggie stared at the chat box for a minute. She'd only known Kelly a few months, but they had hit it off in a big way, and she'd told her things she'd never told anyone. Things she'd never even told Sierra. Kelly had listened, and she'd never judged, but Kelly had always been a safe outlet, because Maggie had kept most of her details private. Kelly knew where she worked, but that was about the only detail. Maggie had gone out of her way to keep Digilife and real life separate. If she told Kelly who she really was, that protection went away. It was a scary thought, but she needed someone she could talk to about all of this.

Bobbie: Do you have a Facebook account?

There was a long delay before Kelly answered.

Kelly: Yes.

Bobbie: My real name is Maggie Bennett.

Maggie hit send, then tabbed out of Digilife and pulled up Facebook. It only took a couple of minutes before a friend request popped up for Chance Woodward. Maggie clicked accept, and an instant message popped up.

Chance: Hey there.

Maggie: Hey. Just a second.

Chance: Waiting, but not patiently.

Maggie laughed as she created a new photo album and set it up so that Chance was the only one who could view it. Then she opened the folder on her computer that held her medical records and dropped a handful of pictures into the album. Ones taken by her plastic surgeon. She double and triple checked the security settings on the album, then posted the photos.

Chance: You okay, Maggie? You're awful quiet.

Maggie responded with the link to the pictures. The ones of her in nothing but a bra and a pair of panties that were taken when she had been applying for an experimental form of reconstructive surgery a year earlier. The ones that showed her scars in all their glory.

Chance: You know, love, I'm not normally one to complain when I get random underwear pics from a hot girl, but whoever took these should be shot. The poses are terrible and the less said about the lighting the better.

Maggie thought she was going to laugh, but it came out as a sob. She wished Chance were there, because she wanted to hug her as hard as she could.

Maggie: Thank you for saying that.

Chance: It's true. I doubt the pictures show it to your best effect, but you are beautiful. Scars and all.

Maggie: You really mean that?

Chance: I do. And if I weren't already in a committed relationship, and five hundred miles away, I'd be tempted to show you how much I mean it.

Maggie felt heat rising in her cheeks. Chance had complimented her before, but it had always been her avatar, or her sense of humor, or her dirty mind. Knowing Chance had seen her the way she used to be and hadn't been repulsed, that she actually found her desirable, made Maggie feel exposed in a way she hadn't before. What she was planning next wouldn't help with that.

Maggie took a deep breath, and made her clothes disappear, leaving her sitting in her chair in a much sexier bra and panties than were in the photos she'd sent Chance. A purple velvet bra and boy shorts set with a floral burnt out pattern. She reached up and adjusted the webcam she used for video conferences, then clicked the video chat icon.

There was a long delay, but a moment later, the image of a woman about Maggie's age appeared on the screen. She had silver hair and brown eyes, and a cute little nose. She looked a lot younger than her avatar. She was wearing a thin white t-shirt over a black bra that showed through and was wearing silver lipstick that matched her hair.

"Oh, wow," Chance said, and Maggie might have swooned, because her voice was deep and husky.

"Hey," Maggie said.

"Old pictures, I take it," Chance said.

"Yeah," Maggie said. "A year ago. I was applying for a clinical trial for an experimental reconstructive surgery process that used nanites to rebuild the body. Apparently, there was a problem with one of the patients in the trial, and it got shut down."

"Oh," Chance said. "Um...I'm sorry."

"Not your fault," Maggie said. "But..." she gestured to her face, "This happened last Saturday."

"How?" Chance asked. "Skin grafts can do a lot, but girl, you're flawless."

"It's a long story, and the non-disclosure form is pretty strict," Maggie said.

"Okay," Chance said. Maggie could tell she wasn't happy about that, but she didn't push. Maggie saw the moment Chance connected the dots.

"Your friend decided to kiss you *after* you got rid of the scars," Chance said.

"Yes," Maggie said.

"Your friend is an asshole," Chance said. "She doesn't deserve you.

Give me her address. I have friends in Sun City. I'm going to send them over to punch her in the face."

"You're doing wonderful things for my ego," Maggie said.

"Well deserved things," Chance said. "You know, you make so much more sense to me now."

"What do you mean?" Maggie asked.

"You kept telling me how shy you were in real life, but it never made sense. You always seemed so confident and sure of yourself when we talked, and you never seemed to have any trouble approaching people in Digilife."

"Yeah. They couldn't see me there," Maggie said.

"Exactly," Chance said. "You actually remind me of C Cup in a lot of ways."

"Oh?"

"Yeah," Chance said. "She's trans. Before she had her surgeries, she... Well, she did what you did. She spent a lot of time in Digilife, kind of hiding from the real world."

"Not anymore?"

"No," Chance said. "She gave it up before her surgeries."

"But not you?"

"No," Chance said. "I...I don't...it's complicated. It's not that I don't want to tell you. It's just...complicated."

"That's okay," Maggie said.

"You know, a lot of people have issues with their self-image after a scarring injury."

"That's what all of my therapists have told me."

"Sorry," Chance said. "I'm not good at this. I just, I meant what I said. You were beautiful, even before all of this."

Maggie blushed and looked down. "Thank you."

"You should call Rescue Girl, invite her over, and let her peel you out of that bra and panty set."

"I'm considering it," Maggie said. "God, she's really hot."

"You like her that much?"

"I do," Maggie said. "Which is part of why I'm pissed at Sierra for fucking with my head."

"Sierra's stupidhead?"

"Yeah," Maggie said. "I don't know. I think this thing with Rescue Girl could really be something, but she knows how close Sierra and I are, and I'm afraid that if she finds out that Sierra is sniffing around, she'll run for the hills."

"That sucks," Chance said. "I'm not kidding about having friends in Sun City, though."

"I appreciate the offer, but I don't want Sierra punched. I just want..."

Maggie stopped when the earbud she'd forgotten she was wearing beeped.

"Hold on," she said. She paused the video chat and tapped the earbud.

"Maggie here," she said.

"Hey, Maggie," Nomi said. "Sorry to bother you. I know I said you'd have the whole day to decide, but I need you to come in if you can."

Maggie could hear the regret in her tone, but also the urgency, and knew right away that she would go.

"I'll be there in five," Maggie said.

"Thanks," Nomi said. "We're in Fractal's lab."

Maggie restarted the video chat.

"Everything okay?" Chance asked.

"Not sure," Maggie said. "New boss just called. I've got to go to the office."

"New boss?"

"Yeah. The school fired me, but I got two job offers today. I decided to take one. Bit of a career change, but I think it's going to work out."

"Okay. Take care."

"You too," Maggie said. She blew Chance a kiss, then ended the video chat, shut down her computer, conjured her clothes back into existence, and teleported back to her room at the Shiro.

Chapter Twenty-Two

MAGGIE ARRIVED IN FRACTAL'S lab, expecting an emergency. Instead, she found Nomi, Fractal, Sierra, and Junichi all standing in the middle of a room that looked like the love child of a LAN party and a server farm, staring at a monitor that could serve as the flat top of an aircraft carrier in a pinch.

"What's going on?" Maggie asked. The four of them turned around, and Maggie got three different reactions. Fractal and Junichi were both fairly neutral. About what Maggie would expect from people when a coworker arrived to help with a problem. Nomi gave her an apologetic smile and a small shrug as she gestured towards the screen. Sierra was blushing furiously and trying to avoid looking Maggie in the eye.

"Warrant came back on Fairchild's residence," Nomi said. "We've got her laptop here, and there's something we can't figure out. Sierra thought you might be able to help make sense of it."

"Sure," Maggie said. "I'll take a look." She walked over and looked at the screen, which was bigger than the wall in her bedroom and covered in math. "What am I looking at?"

"We were hoping you could tell us," Nomi said. "I'm good with differential equations and passable with quantum mechanics, but I don't even recognize half the notion here."

"There's a lot of linear algebra in there too," Fractal said. "But it doesn't make any sense. It looks like someone is trying to plot a course, but the vectors have too many dimensions."

"You're wrong," Maggie said, as what was seeing suddenly clicked into place. "You're just not wrong where you think you're wrong. The matrix is an attempt to plot a course through a volume with four Euclidian dimensions."

"I...no. I don't see it," Sierra said.

"Me either," Fractal said. "There are too many vectors."

"Nomi does," Maggie said. She could see it on her face.

"Both objects are in motion," Nomi said. "It's like trying to plot a course between two airplanes flying in different directions."

"Exactly," Maggie said.

"I still don't see it," Fractal said.

"That's because you've never seen Beth's work before," Maggie said. "There are multiple rotating reference frames involved. The problem is, Beth always sucked at plotting courses. The math is a god damned disaster. If I'm reading this right, she just randomly gains a couple of orders of magnitude somewhere along the way and overshoots the target by an astronomical unit or five."

"Any idea where she was trying to plot a course to?" Nomi asked.

"Well, my guess would be that the point of origin is somewhere on Earth. That would explain at least one of the rotating reference frames. I'm pretty sure the target is in a rotating reference frame inside a rotating reference frame. The transformations are a complete mess. I'd have to sit down and work the equations forwards and backwards to figure out where her errors are before I could say for sure. Given all of those caveats, based on the magnitudes, it's almost got to be the moon."

"The moon?" Nomi asked.

"Got to be," Maggie said. "Unless you can think of something else that's roughly 400,000 kilometers away."

"No," Nomi said. "Not off the top of my head. It's just...Focus and Scatter were sent to investigate a disturbance on the moon last night. One that happened around the same time as the incident at SCSU."

"Fuck," Maggie said. "Do you know what they found?"

"No, but give me a minute and I'll see if I can get ahold of them."

Nomi walked over into a corner of the room, away from everyone else, then tapped her earbud and started talking. Maggie turned back to the monitor and took another look at the math, which made her shake her head in frustration.

"Why the fuck...nope. You know what, never mind. Trying to figure that out will just make me want to punch her in the face."

Sierra snorted. "You always want to punch Beth in the face."

Maggie sighed and turned to look at Sierra. "That is base slander. Sometimes I want to punch her in the throat."

"My mistake," Sierra said.

Maggie turned back to the screen and glared. "The woman refuses to convert to polar coordinates. Ever. Ever! Do you know how much harder that makes the math?"

Sierra nodded. "I do, actually. You know why? Because you once spent four hours ranting about it."

"I did not," Maggie said.

"You did," Sierra said.

"Did I?"

"Yes."

"Oh."

Maggie turned back to the screen.

"Why the hell would she be plotting a course to the moon?"

"That's a good question," Nomi said as she came back over. "Focus and Scatter are dealing with an issue in the Bahamas at the moment. Deputy Marshal Perez said she would send them our way when they were done. It will probably be a couple of hours, though. If you have something you want to do, I can call you when they get here."

"I took care of everything I needed to," Maggie said. "We could talk, if you have a few minutes."

"Sure," Nomi said. "Follow me."

Maggie ignored the inquiring look Sierra gave her and followed Nomi out of the lab and down the hall to the same workshop where they'd spoken before. This time, though, she led Maggie into an office off the side of the main work area. Nomi dropped into a comfortable looking desk chair and pointed Maggie to some that were the same design but had obviously seen a lot less use. She sat down and faced Nomi.

"Yes," Maggie said.

"You're in?" Nomi said.

"I'm in," Maggie said.

Relief was clearly visible on Nomi's face. She looked like someone had taken a huge weight off her shoulders, and as Maggie watched, she leaned back and let out a breath.

"You have no idea how happy I am to hear that."

"I'm glad I could give you the answer you're looking for."

"Do you want to go over the business end of it? The salary is good. Better than what the DMA offers the publicly funded MERT Teams. The merchandising rights work a bit differently, but you still get a good chunk."

"I'll trust you on that," Maggie said. "I'm pretty sure whatever you offer is going to be better than what I was making. I wasn't hurting for money, but I wasn't exactly flush, either."

"I think we can do a bit better than a post-doc salary, yeah. I'm honestly surprised you decided so quickly."

"So am I, but I probably shouldn't be. I went to talk to my grandfather. He's always been good at helping me get my head on straight."

"My mom was like that," Nomi said. "Always knew when I was overthinking stuff and would give me an ever so gentle verbal slap to make me snap out of it."

"Well, Grandpa was a little gentler than that," Maggie said. "But he told me what I needed to hear."

"Good. Come with me," Nomi said as she stood up.

"Where we headed?" Maggie asked.

"Shopping," Nomi said.

* * * *

Shopping, as it turned out, meant going down to the conference room where Ashley was meeting with three people named Vera, Tracy, and Alan. Vera was a fashion designer who specialized in designing superhero costumes. She mostly worked for the various Champions teams all over the country, designing outfits for the various heroes that were both functional and looked good on the Champions line of action figures. Tracy was Vera's partner, who took Vera's designs and added important features like armor inserts, ballistic fabric underlayers, and insulation, so the costumes actually survived the things supervillains threw at them and protected the less resilient metas on the Tier One and Two teams. Alan was the head of the High Guard's marketing team.

"Here she is," Vera said as they walked into the room. "And even more lovely that you said." She turned to Ashley. "No fair, holding out on us."

Ashley just waited until Vera turned back to Maggie, then rolled her eyes. Maggie tried not to laugh as she and Nomi took their seats.

"Hey, Vera," Nomi said.

"Hello, Nomi," Vera said. "Please tell me you're going to let me have a crack at updating the look of your armor."

"I like my armor," Nomi said.

"Yes, I know, and it's got a very 20s aesthetic dear. Unfortunately, it's the 1920s and not the 2020s. We could do so much better if you'd just let me bring the aesthetic into this century."

"Leave the girl alone," Alan said. "She likes what she likes, and it's not her fault you're allergic to retro looks."

"I'm not," Vera said. "I've put quite a few people in retro designs. I've even thrown together a few retro futurist looks, but she flies around in power armor. That's not something you want to go retro with."

"You've done retro futurist?" Alan asked. "When?"

"Oh, just last year, I did one for a lovely hero named Steampunk out in Seattle. It was quite challenging, figuring out a way to get a top hat to stay in place with all the running around superheroes do, but I figured it out," Vera said.

"It really is a good design," Tracy said. "Though it took me forever to figure out a way to keep all the brass from tarnishing every time she uses her powers."

"And you both did a wonderful job," Nomi said. "But we're not here to deal with my aesthetic choices, or Steampunk's. We need a costume and an identity for Maggie here."

"I've been thinking about that," Maggie said.

"Oh, dear," Alan said. "Please, leave the branding and designs to us. Otherwise, you'll end up like that shape-shifter up in Atlanta with a circuit diagram on her chest."

Ashley turned to Alan.

"Transistor's my friend, Alan," Ashley said.

"Your friend has bad taste," Alan said. "Basing her name on a pun about her gender identity isn't doing her any favors."

"It's a good name," Ashley said. "It fits her powers, she likes it, and the transphobes would hate her no matter what her name is."

Alan looked like he wanted to argue, but the glare Ashley was giving him made him shut up. Ashley turned back to Maggie.

"What were you thinking?" Ashley asked.

"Well...I was thinking Aether," Maggie said.

"Really?" Ashley asked, clearly a little surprised.

"Yeah," Maggie said.

"I'm surprised you didn't go for something more scientific sounding."

"Like what?" Maggie asked. "Cosmic foam sounds like something they'd call a latte at a Star Trek themed coffee shop. Cognitive Quantum Field doesn't exactly roll off the tongue when you're talking on the radio. Quantum Ghost sounds like the title of a bad sci-fi horror movie. Besides, I'm self-aware enough to know that scientists shouldn't be allowed to name shit."

Nomi laughed at that, which made Maggie smile.

"It's true. Seriously, actual scientists named six of the fundamental particles in the universe Up, Down, Strangeness, Charm, Truth, and Beauty. They also named asteroids Larry, Curly, and Moe. I could go on, but really, scientists are shit at naming things."

"Okay. As long as you remember that you said it, not me," Ashley said.

"I will," Maggie said. "Besides, I've been changing my mind a lot the last few days, and Aether is a much easier way to describe the place I go. Maybe a bit poetic, but I've been using it in my head for a while."

Ashley looked over at Alan.

"Does that meet with your approval?"

"Yeah," Alan said. "I can work with it. We'll need some kind of symbol, though."

"We've had good luck with classic alchemical symbols on the team," Ashley said. She looked at Maggie. "My emblem is the alchemical symbol for the philosopher's stone with a slipper inside it. Element's is just the alchemical symbols for the four classical elements arranged around the symbol for the elements as a whole."

"And there's that one that Hannah wears," Alan said.

"That's the Tree of Life," Ashley said. "It's from Kabbalah, not alchemy."

"Right," Alan said. "I knew that."

Ashley looked over at Nomi, who shrugged. Ashley shook her head and tapped the surface of the table, bringing the touch screen to life. She typed in a couple of quick google searches and pulled up two symbols. One was a triangle with a second, inverted triangle laid over top of it. Together, the two triangles formed a six-pointed star. It wasn't quite the Star of David where all six lines were showing. In this symbol, the triangle in front partially obscured the triangle in back. The second symbol looked kind of like a lowercase 'q.' It was a circle with a line coming out of the bottom, going down and a bit to the left. At the lower end of the line, a sine wave like curve branched off, moving to the right.

"The star symbol is the classic alchemical symbol for Aether. The one that looks like a 'q' is the symbol for quintessence," Ashley said. She opened both images in Photoshop, and did a quick drag and drop, putting the quintessence symbol inside of the Aether symbol. "There. Simple. Easy to remember."

"Copyrightable," Alan said, which made Ashley smile.

"That too," she said.

"I like it," Vera said. "Of course, the costume will have to be purple to match her hair. We can do the symbol in white. White gloves and boots, and belt. Give me a moment."

She picked up her tablet, and Maggie watched as she worked for a minute, using a stylus every now and then, but mostly just poking at the tablet with her finger. After about five minutes, she tapped the conference table and hit a couple of buttons, then made a swiping motion on the tablet, and a costume appeared on screen. It was clear that Vera was working off a template of sorts, but the image on the screen was a surprisingly detailed 3D model of a woman with purple hair, a purple domino mask with white trim, a skintight purple suit with white gloves, white boots, a white utility belt, and the symbol Ashley had come up with done in white on the chest.

"It's a first pass, of course," Vera said. "We'll do things like incorporate a climbing harness, back support, armor plates, and so on. Ashley says you're tough, but all our suits come with basic armor. Bullet proofing and an anti-stab layer, along with thermal and electrical insulation. We'll also give you the true speedster package on the boots and a low friction coating. Consider it future proofing. Then we'll do the variations. Hazmat, diving suit, spacesuit, the usual."

"I usually just conjure my clothes," Maggie said.

"I know," Vera said. "Which is going to save Nomi here a fortune in replacements. Why, Ashley alone has been through ten costumes this year, and they aren't cheap, but you still need the templates to work from, and for the variations, you will need things like rebreathers and comm systems and the like. Ashley says you haven't got the knack for conjuring electronics and such, so we'll leave out the sensors and other technology we usually build in, and you can wear that separately. Things like your body cam and such."

"How quickly can you have it?" Nomi asked.

"Since most of this is going to be stock parts, I'd say between forty-eight and seventy-two hours," Tracy said. "My team can start on the underlays while Vera finalizes the aesthetic layer. A lot of it will depend on what the 3D print queues look like. We're doing a big replacement order for a team in California."

"That should be fine," Nomi said. She turned to Maggie. "What do you think?"

Maggie looked back up at the screen and took a moment to picture herself in the costume, standing beside Varsha the way she had when they'd first arrived at Sun City State the night before. She expected to have some mixed feelings about the idea, but instead, all she felt was eagerness, like the afternoon had washed away any hesitation.

"I like it," she said. She turned to Nomi. "Let's do it."

Chapter Twenty-Three

MAGGIE FOLLOWED VARSHA THROUGH the door as Sierra and the team piled into the same briefing room the day had started in, only this time, when they got there, two people were waiting for them. The first was a tall woman with long blonde hair in a red, white, and blue costume with a ray diagram inside of a circle on her chest. The second woman was shorter, with dark hair that was just long enough to cover her neck. She wore a navy-blue costume with red trim and had a circle with a Feynman diagram superimposed over a red S on her chest. Maggie would have recognized them anywhere. Before the invasion, she'd had a poster of the two of them locked in a kiss up on her wall, right next to the one of Airheart lounging on Ice Dragon's coils in nothing but a bomber jacket.

Maggie took a seat next to Varsha and tried not to frown when Sierra took the seat on her opposite side. It was normal for them. They always sat together. She knew that, and any other time, she wouldn't have given it any thought, but after what had happened that afternoon, she found herself wanting a bit of space. She was still confused, angry, and hurt, and the fact that Sierra had been so good at playing normal while they were working together in Fractal's lab earlier wasn't helping.

"Focus, Scatter," Nomi said by way of greeting. "This is Doctor Sierra Gomez. She's working with us as a consultant on this case, and this is Maggie Bennett. She's the newest member of the High Guard. Call sign Aether."

"Nice to meet you both," Scatter said.

"It's a pleasure," Focus said.

"Normally, I'd love to spend a few minutes chatting," Nomi said, "but given current events, I think we need to get down to business."

"Of course," Focus said. "You said this had something to do with our trip to the moon last night?"

"Yes," Nomi said. "We've identified three suspects involved in the explosions at Sun City State University. Doctor Alister Hastings, the Assistant Chair of the Physics Department, and two of his graduate students, Garrett Whitehall and Elizabeth Fairchild. When we did a search of Ms. Fairchild's computers, we found what we believe to be an attempt to plot a course from Earth to the moon for a space-fold device."

Focus looked over at Scatter for a moment, and the two of them shared a look that let Maggie know that she wasn't going to like what they were about to say. Focus turned to Nomi.

"That could line up with what we found," Focus said. She reached down and opened one of the compartments on her belt, took out a flash drive, and tossed it to Nomi. Nomi plugged the drive into the table, and the screen on the far wall from her came to life as a video began to play. It showed a short, gorgeous woman with full lips, sun kissed skin, and thick brown hair, who looked like she should be a supermodel rather than wearing tactical gear. The woman pointed at the camera.

"You bring my partner back in one piece, you hear me?" the woman said. "I get her back with so much as a scuff, I'll get my girlfriend's mom to eat your superhero ass."

"Rachel would never eat her ass," Scatter said. The video shifted so that Scatter came into frame, wearing a spacesuit that was modeled on her costume. "Cecile would get jealous."

The woman flipped Scatter the bird, which only made her laugh. She turned to the camera.

"Ready?" Scatter asked.

"Ready," Focus said.

Scatter reached up and closed her helmet. She took a moment to lock the face mask, then pulled down a second mask, this one bright gold instead of clear. She gave a quick thumbs up, then there was a moment of static on the video, and the room they were in was replaced by a lunar landscape.

"You know," Scatter said, "when I said we should try going somewhere new, I was thinking of that sushi bar that Kipengele mentioned down in South Shore."

"I was planning on saving that one for your birthday," Focus said.

"Really?" Scatter asked.

"Yeah," Focus said. "But we can go sooner if you like."

"I just thought it might be a nice change," Scatter said.

"You're getting tired of Thai food, aren't you?"

"No," Scatter said.

"It's okay if you are."

"I'm not," Scatter said. "Now, which way to the target?"

"That way."

The camera started moving across the lunar landscape.

"It's okay if you are," Focus said. "I know I can be a bit obsessive when it comes to the peanut butter thing."

"I'm not tired of Thai food," Scatter said, sounding a bit

exasperated. "I'm tired of that waitress flirting with you right in front of me."

"You know, we can probably fast forward a bit," the Scatter at the table said.

"She's not flirting," Focus said. "She's just friendly."

"To your cleavage," the Scatter on the video muttered.

Maggie bit her lip to keep from laughing. She looked around and saw Ashley pressing a fist to her mouth, and a strained look on Hannah's face as her shoulders shook slightly. Elisa looked like Christmas had come early. Nomi had a hand over her eyes and was just shaking her head slightly. Garnell and Fractal were both laughing and not even trying to hide it. Kevin and Juan were both smiling, while Junichi looked like he wanted to sink right through the floor. Sierra had her 'I'm a serious teacher' face on. The one she used when she thought she shouldn't laugh at something a student said. Focus and Scatter were both blushing a bit.

It was the look on Varsha's face that really caught Maggie's attention, though. There was a softness there, but also a bit of longing. She thought she understood it. The desire for a relationship, to be so comfortable with someone that a minor squabble was just something that happened and was funny the next day. She wanted to reach out and take Varsha's hand, but she didn't. She needed to settle things with Sierra first. The problem was, she had no idea how to do that without also setting their friendship on fire.

Nomi scrubbed the video forward to a point where Focus and Scatter started up the side of a small crater, presumably skipping the rest of their argument about the flirty waitress. When the audio came back on, all Maggie heard was the sound of Focus breathing as the two of them climbed up dirt that was much darker than the dirt they'd initially appeared on. It only took Maggie a moment to realize the crater they were climbing was new.

The two of them crested the rim of the crater and looked down into it. The whole thing was maybe fifty yards across. In the middle of the crater there was a single object.

"Is that...?" Scatter asked. "No, it couldn't be."

"What?" Focus asked.

Maggie stared at the object and understood Scatter's confusion. It was an object that pretty much anyone who had gone to school in the last century or so would recognize. A big steel tanker desk.

"What?" Focus asked.

"It looks like a desk," Scatter said.

"We should get a closer look."

Focus and Scatter both lifted off and flew down to the floor of the crater, and sure enough, the object turned out to be a steel tanker desk. The same kind that had sat at the front of school classrooms in the US for the last seventy years. Three drawers on each side, with a laminate top for a writing surface.

"It's definitely a desk," Focus said.

"But where did it come from?" Scatter asked.

"Only one way to find out," Focus said. She grabbed the handle of one of the drawers and pulled it open. There was a calculus textbook inside, along with a bunch of dry erase markers. She flipped the book open, but there was no name or school stamp, so she dropped it back in the drawer and opened the next one, and then the one after that. In the end, they found a couple dozen dry erase markers, three boxes of chalk, the calculus textbook, a battered copy of Atlas Shrugged by Ayn Rand, and a couple of melted candy bars.

"Why are the candy bars melted?" Junichi asked. "Radiation?"

"Yeah," Maggie said, "but not like you're thinking. The light from the sun isn't spread out by the atmosphere, and that desk is in full daylight. It's got to be running about 120 degrees Celsius. Hot enough to melt the chocolate, but not quite enough to melt the plastic in the markers or damage the paper."

"Nothing," Focus said as she finished looking through the last drawer.

"There's no property tag on the desk," Scatter said.

"Should we take it back?" Focus asked.

"Probably, but where should we take it?" Scatter asked. "Lunar dust is some nasty shit. We do not want to spread it around at headquarters."

"Good point," Focus said. "The DMA has an NBC decon chamber at their headquarters in DC. We can teleport back there and get our suits cleaned, then debrief and head home."

"Sounds like a plan. Grab the other end," Scatter said as she grabbed one end of the desk. Focus walked over and grabbed the other end, then there was another brief moment of static, before the two of them reappeared in a bare white room.

Nomi stopped the video at that point.

"Anything else you can tell us?" she asked.

"No," Focus said. "There was nothing to identify where the desk came from. The calculus textbook was thirty years old, so even if it had a school stamp, I'm not sure I'd trust it."

"The desk is old, too," Scatter said. "It had a steel tag with a maker name and a model number. I looked it up. That model was discontinued in 1973."

"So, the question is, how did a fifty-year-old desk end up in a crater on the moon?" Elisa said.

"That was definitely what we wanted to know," Scatter said.

"We have a good idea," Nomi said. "What I'm about to tell you is classified and compartmentalized, but I have permission to read the two of you and Doctor Gomez in, given that you're the closest assets we have that are capable of traveling to the moon. We believe the three people involved are trying to reverse engineer a Gacrux space-fold device left behind in the invasion. It's possible they used the desk as a test object to see if the device worked."

"But why the moon?" Focus asked. "There's not really anything up there."

"It's possible that's the point," Maggie said. "There's nothing up there. Not yet, but the US is going to start landing on the moon in a couple of years, and there are already plans to build a base. There's also talk of an orbiting space station. It's possible that the people involved think that if they can develop the fold technology, they could sell it to a private corporation, or another government so they could beat the US government to the moon and claim territorial rights."

"What?" Nomi asked. "Where did you get that from?"

Maggie shrugged as she looked over at Nomi.

"I was thinking about possible motives while we were discussing my suit design and code name," Maggie said.

"Seriously?" Nomi asked.

"Yeah," Maggie said. "I mean, the suit is cool, but when they started arguing over what shade of black to use, I kind of zoned out."

"Okay, yeah," Nomi said. "I can't really argue with that."

"It wouldn't hold up," Junichi said. "There are already treaties in place regarding territorial claims in space."

"Yeah, but like the saying goes, possession is nine tenths of the law," Maggie said.

"All of that makes sense, but how is that connected to what happened at SCSU last night?" Scatter asked.

"Their machine doesn't really work," Maggie said. "It opens a fold, but some of the particles decay after they cross through. Partial matter to energy conversion. The energy is released as gamma photons, or possibly a mix of gamma photons and neutrinos. We've only been able to record the gamma emissions, but that's not surprising. There are only about two dozen neutrino detectors on Earth."

"Maggie," Sierra said.

"Yes?"

"No tangent on neutrino detectors," Sierra said.

"Sorry," Maggie said. She turned back to Focus and Scatter. "I get carried away when I science, and I've been thinking about this for hours."

Focus and Scatter both smiled.

"That's okay," Scatter said. "We have a friend that does the same thing sometimes."

"Really?" Maggie asked.

"Yeah," Scatter said. "Chance is a bit of an odd duck, but if you're going to be on the team, you'll meet them sooner or later. They never go too long without visiting Ashley or Eurion."

"Did you say Chance?" Maggie asked.

"Yeah," Scatter said. "Why?"

"Nothing. Just an odd coincidence," Maggie said. "I have a friend named Chance."

"Not the same person." Scatter said. "I promise."

"I didn't think it was," Maggie said. "Just, like I said, an odd coincidence."

"You have a friend named Chance?" Sierra asked.

"What, you think you know all my secrets?" Maggie asked.

"I thought I did," Sierra said, and Maggie couldn't help but notice she sounded a little hurt. Something Maggie didn't really want to deal with in the middle of a meeting. She turned back to Nomi.

"So, I'm guessing they fixed Beth's math," Maggie said. "Not sure if that's good news or bad news,"

"Well, there's no way I'm lucky enough for them to just accidentally overshoot their target by a couple of AU and solve the problem for us," Nomi said. "But your theory aside, we still need to find out why they want to go to the moon, where they are, and who they're working for. Because something like this, they're either developing the tech to sell, or they're looking for something that can only be accessed by the tech. Either way, there's going to be a buyer."

"Haven't there been a few supervillains who operated out of lairs on the moon?" Elisa asked. "Maybe they're looking for one of those bases."

"Not likely," Focus said. "I've been up there seven times in the last thirty years to clear out supervillain lairs. I always strip them bare, then collapse any tunnels around them."

"Could you have missed something? A hidden supply cache away from the main lair?" Ashley asked.

"Maybe," Focus said. "But it would have to be pretty far from the lair. I swept out to a radius of ten miles when I destroyed the lairs."

"There's also the question of how they would know about it," Junichi said. "The supervillains we know of who were operating on the moon were all ones who had powers that let them get there and back easily, and the four that are still alive are monitored around the clock."

"Are any of them telepaths?" Hannah asked.

"I'd have to check," Junichi said.

"Might be worth looking into," Nomi said.

"Do you want us to bring you the desk?" Scatter asked.

"Maggie, what do you think?" Nomi asked.

"No," Maggie said. "It would probably be more trouble than it's worth. There's no way to link it to SCSU without an asset tag, and I doubt we'd be able to pull fingerprints after it sat on the moon for that long. The skin oils would have boiled off into the vacuum."

"Well, if you change your mind, just let us know," Scatter said. She turned to Nomi. "You need us for anything else?"

"Not now," Nomi said.

"Okay," Scatter said. She turned to Ashley. "Brunch will have to wait a week. Airheart and Ice Dragon have a new assignment that starts tomorrow. They wouldn't say what it was, so..."

"That sounds more like Ice Dragon than Airheart," Ashley said. "But I already knew about the assignment. I let Eurion know, and I talked to Naomi, Chance, and Anika. Naomi is going to let Elena know, as long as you let Cecile, Rachel, Ruth, and Lori know, I think we're good."Scatter shook her head and turned to Focus.

"Remember when brunch was just six people?" she asked.

"That was thirty years ago, love. You've got to let it go." Focus said.

Ashley snorted, and then started laughing softly as she shook her head. Maggie had the sneaking suspicion that she was missing some inside joke, but the sour look on Hannah's face kept her from asking. Focus turned to Nomi.

"We'll head out," she said. "If you need us, just shout."

"Thanks," Nomi said. "I have a feeling it might come to that." She looked around the table. "Unless anyone else has anything, I think we're done."

Everyone stood up, and Maggie waited as they all headed for the door except Varsha and Sierra. Maggie glanced at them both, and could feel the awkward coming, even before everyone else was out of the room. When it was just them, the awkward got thick, fast, though she wasn't quite sure if they were feeling it as intensely as she was.

"Um...are you busy?" Varsha asked.

"I was hoping to talk to her," Sierra said.

"Ah," Varsha said. "Well, I'll uh...I'll leave you to it."

"Wait," Maggie said. "Just give us a bit. Maybe stop by my room later?"

"Uh..." Varsha looked back and forth between Maggie and Sierra. Maggie could practically see disappointment written on her face, and she hated it. "Maybe some other time," she said, before she turned and headed for the door, leaving Maggie and Sierra standing in the now empty conference room.

"What was that about?" Sierra asked.

Maggie sighed. She didn't believe for a second that Sierra didn't know what she'd just done, but calling her out on it would start a conversation she didn't want to have until she'd settled things with her.

"Come on," Maggie said. "I'm guessing this is a conversation we should have in private."

"Yeah," Sierra said. "Probably."

Maggie gave Sierra one last look before she headed for the door, hoping that when all of this was over, they would still be friends.

Chapter Twenty-Four

MAGGIE LED THE WAY into her room. She heard the door close behind her as she walked over and took a seat at the table. She turned and watched as Sierra approached and felt dread fill her. This wasn't going to be a pleasant or easy conversation. She wished she knew how to deal with stuff like this, but she was never very good at social situations. Not when she was being herself, anyway.

She'd like to say that was the result of spending the last eleven years doing everything she could to hide away from the world because of the shame she felt from her scars and her disability, but that wasn't true. She'd never been very good at dealing with people. She'd always been the smart girl or the gifted kid. It had been isolating, even before the invasion. She wasn't sure why it was so much easier for her to connect to people online as Bobbie, but she'd never felt any of the social awkwardness there that she felt in real life. Until Sierra had come along, Digilife had been Maggie's primary social outlet.

After Sierra, that had changed, but only because of the connection she had with Sierra. A connection that worked so well because they'd both had the same experience growing up. Sierra had been the smart, gifted kid just like Maggie. The difference was, Sierra had learned to make friends and build a social circle by sheer force of will, while Maggie had spent her life waiting for people to come to her and drag her out of her shell. Up until she'd started at APL at NASA, Sierra had been the only person who bothered after the invasion. Ashley and Varsha had both tried over the last week, and Maggie was really grateful they had, especially in Varsha's case, but the thought of losing her connection to Sierra terrified her.

Sierra sat down across from her, and Maggie could already feel the awkward filling the room, but before either of them could speak, Maxine jumped up on the table, and looked at Maggie.

"Scratches," Maxine said.

"Demanding much?" Maggie asked as she reached up and scratched Maxine's head.

"I'm a cat," Maxine said, giving the same answer she had that morning.

"She's already got you wrapped around her little finger, doesn't she?" Sierra asked.

"I don't have fingers," Maxine said. "I have her wrapped around my paw."

Maggie laughed.

"She's got a point," Maggie said. "But yeah. She's a kitten. It's what they do."

Sierra reached out to pet her, only for Maxine to take a swipe at her with her claws.

"Hey!" Sierra said. "Rude!"

"Maxine!" Maggie said.

"You upset Maggie," Maxine said.

"What?" Sierra asked.

"She's unhappy and afraid of you," Maxine said. "I can smell it."

"Afraid of me?" Sierra asked. She looked up at Maggie.

"I'm not afraid of you," Maggie said. "I'm afraid of how this conversation is going to go." She looked down at Maxine. "And me being unhappy is no reason for you to take a swipe at her."

"Humans don't make sense," Maxine said. "If something makes you unhappy, you hit it."

"We're going to have to have a long talk about what is acceptable, and what will land you in the DMA's kennel for dangerous superpowered animals," Maggie said.

"They have one of those?" Sierra asked.

"They do," Maggie said.

"Humans are stupid," Maxine said.

Maggie leaned forward and kissed Maxine on the head.

"Thank you for trying to protect me, but next time, use words. I'll tell you when you can use claws."

"Fine," Maxine said before curling up into a ball and glaring at Sierra. Maggie kept petting her and looked up at Sierra.

"So..." Maggie said.

"So, I tried to kiss you."

"Yeah."

"And you ran away."

"I did. I did in fact do that."

"Want to tell me why?" Sierra asked. "I thought that was what you wanted."

"It was," Maggie said. "Once."

"Once?"

"Yeah," Maggie said. "I mean..." She stopped and sighed heavily. "How honest do you want me to be here?"

"What kind of question is that?" Sierra asked.

"Look, you know I love you, right?"

"I thought you did."

"That's...that's not what I mean. I mean, you're my best friend. You've been there for me through some of the worst shit in my life. I love you, and that's never going to change, but sometimes you can get a little...defensive."

"I see."

"Like now," Maggie said. "I just said something you didn't like, and now you've got your back up."

"I don't!"

Maggie just sat there, staring at Sierra and not saying anything. Sierra leaned back and crossed her arms, pouting. It wasn't what Maggie thought of as her cute pout, either. The cute pout was the one that she used when trying to talk Maggie into some ill-advised shenanigans that Maggie knew she was going to give into sooner or later anyway. This was the ugly pout. The one that meant Sierra had gotten offended because she's heard an uncomfortable truth she didn't want to admit to.

It almost always showed up right before an argument, and Maggie was usually glad she wasn't the one who put it there, but after years of friendship, Maggie had a strategy for this. She just scooped Maxine up in her arms and petted her while she waited, refusing to say anything that would trigger a blow up.

"Are you just going to sit there?" Sierra asked.

"Until you calm down, yeah," Maggie said.

"I am calm."

Maggie looked up at her.

"Okay, fine," Sierra said. "Be completely honest."

"You sure?" Maggie asked.

"Yes."

"Okay, but you asked," Maggie said. "I moved on."

"You moved on? That's it?"

"No," Maggie said. "But that's the core of it. I met you. I fell in love with you. I told you how I felt in a weak moment. You told me you didn't feel the same way. I got over it. I dated Sandra for almost a year. I started something with a girl I really, really like who seems to like me back. Then, you just drop it on me that you dumped your boyfriend for me. How am I supposed to react to that? Just walk away from a girl I really like? Just drop everything because you've finally decided I'm worth your time?"

"You've always been worth my time," Sierra said.

"Not romantically," Maggie said. "You made that very clear when I told you how I felt."

"I wasn't ready to deal with how I felt," Sierra said. "I thought I was straight."

"I know," Maggie said. "But that doesn't mean I should have put my entire life on hold while you figured yourself out."

"That's not what I meant!"

"That's what you're acting like," Maggie said. "You rejected me. I told you how I felt, and you rejected me. You told me to move on. So, I did."

"And now, what? You're with Varsha?"

"I don't know," Maggie said. "I'd like to be."

"You've known her a week," Sierra said. "You're seriously going to turn me down for someone you've known for a week?"

"No," Maggie said. "I'm going to turn you down because of someone I'm interested in. I'm going to turn you down because I spent a year with Sandra and figured out that there are people out there who will love me despite my scars."

"Varsha's never seen your scars," Sierra said.

"And you never showed any interest in me until they were gone," Maggie said.

"That's not true! I dumped Garrett before any of this had happened."

"And if you had said anything before the accident, my answer might have been different," Maggie said.

"So, what? Now that you're a superhero, I'm not good enough for you?"

"Don't you dare," Maggie snapped. "You know me better than that."

"I don't know how well I know you, if you think I only care about you because you're beautiful now."

Maggie felt the words like a slap. Maxine looked up at Sierra and hissed, which made Sierra stop and think about what she'd just said. Maggie saw the exact moment she realized what she'd just said. The color drained from her face and Maggie could see the regret, knew she was about to stammer out some apology that would only make things worse. An apology Maggie didn't want to hear.

"Don't say it," Maggie said. Maxine picked that moment to jump out of her arms and run for the door, which rippled like water as Maxine ran through it.

"Maggie, I didn't—"

"I don't need you to apologize," Maggie said. "I know you didn't mean it the way it sounded. You're angry, and you said something stupid. Which is exactly why I didn't want to have this conversation when you were upset. Or at all, if I'm honest."

"But—"

"No!" Maggie said. "I love you. I always will. I might even still have a bit of a crush on you if I'm being completely honest, but that doesn't mean that I'm available just because you finally decided you wanted to be with me. A week ago, my answer might have been different, but a lot of things were different for me a week ago. A week ago, I hadn't met Varsha. A week ago, I was a different person, with a different future ahead of them. I..."

Maggie stopped at the sound of a knock at the door. She looked over and expanded her senses, and somehow, wasn't surprised to find Varsha on the other side of the door, holding Maxine.

"Just a second," she said to Sierra. She got up and opened the door.

"Hey," she said.

"Hey," Varsha said. "Your little friend here said you needed my help."

"My little friend is a busybody," Maggie said. "But come on in. I *am* glad to see you."

Varsha looked over her shoulder at Sierra.

"Are you sure?" she asked.

"Yeah," Maggie said. She turned around and headed back into the room, to find Sierra looking at her with confusion.

"Take some time," Maggie said. "Calm down. We can talk some more later when you're in a better head space."

Sierra looked like she wanted to argue, but Maggie knew her well enough to know that she wouldn't do it in front of Varsha, which was half the reason Maggie invited her in. It wasn't exactly fair, but it was the only way she could think of to give Sierra a chance to calm down before they didn't have a friendship left to salvage.

"Okay," Sierra said. She stood up. "Just, don't do anything stupid until we finish talking." She gave Varsha a pointed look before she headed for the door. Maggie watched her go, then turned back to Varsha, who was standing in the middle of the room.

"Well, that was awkward," Varsha said.

"I know," Maggie said. "And I'm sorry you got dragged into it."

"I take it Sierra doesn't approve of me?"

Maggie sat down on the bed and patted the spot beside her. Varsha sat down, and Maxine hopped down onto the floor and curled up in the cat bed in the corner.

"It's complicated," Maggie said. "She um...she tried to kiss me earlier."

"Oh," Varsha said. "I didn't realize the two of you were a thing."

"We're not," Maggie said. "That's the complicated part. Until this afternoon, I thought she was straight."

"Because she was dating Whitehall?"

"That, and because she told me she was straight," Maggie said. "I want to be completely honest here, because I really, really like you, and I don't want to fuck this up."

Varsha smiled at that.

"That's good to hear," she said. "Because I really like you, too."

"I had a thing for Sierra. Maybe still do, sort of. It's..."

"Complicated," Varsha said. "I live in a castle with four other lesbians and a gay man with a swishy husband. Everything is complicated."

Maggie laughed at that, which made Varsha smile even wider. She reached out and took Varsha's hand in hers.

"I got hurt when I was sixteen. I missed a couple of years of school, and I just I took the GED, and I enrolled in SCSU because they have a good physics program, and they're a state school. They take people with GEDs. The thing is, when you're sixteen, and you have scars all over your body, you develop a lot of body image issues. It didn't help that I needed a lot of reconstructive work I couldn't get until I was an adult. I spent years afraid to talk to people because of the way I looked. Then I started grad school, and Sierra just...decided to be my friend. It didn't matter how grumpy I was, or how much I tried to chase her away, she was just there, refusing to leave me alone until I gave up and decided to be her friend."

"Except she's beautiful, and you're gay," Varsha said.

"Yeah," Maggie said. "She's beautiful, and I am so very, very gay. I think it might have taken me a month to fall in love with her."

"Well, if you're in love with her, why are you here with me?"

"Because I fell in love with her six years ago," Maggie said. "And then, I broke my hip. Normally, when I have surgery —and I've had a lot of surgeries—my grandparents are there. That time, it was emergency surgery, and when I woke up, Sierra was the only one with me. I don't know what I was thinking, but I was three bags of Dilaudid in when I told her I was in love with her. When I came down off the Dilaudid, I tried to take it back, but she gave me this very earnest speech about how she only saw me as a friend, and how she was straight. The usual stuff you get when you accidently admit to a straight girl that you're in love with them."

"Ouch," Varsha said.

"Yeah," Maggie said. "I mean, she had a boyfriend, so I knew she wasn't going to throw herself into my arms, but I'm not going to pretend it didn't still sting a little. She refused to let me pull away, and we got past it, and I...I don't know. The crush just sort of became emotional background noise, you know? Always sort of there, but just sort of this pleasant background hum that I didn't even notice half the time. Then Sandra came along."

"Sandra was the girlfriend you mentioned, right?"

"Yeah," Maggie said. "And I knew going into it that relationship would have an expiration date. It was just supposed to be two people who cared about each other having fun while they could. No real strings. I loved Sandra, but I think maybe part of that was because I knew things were going to end at a certain point. There wasn't a lot of risk there, so it was easier to open up to her, if that makes sense."

"Kind of," Varsha said. "I don't know if I could do that, but it sounds like it made you happy."

"At the time, it did," Maggie said. "But Sandra changed the rules. She asked me to move to California with her when her time at the APL was up."

"And you didn't want to?" Varsha asked.

"No, I did. I wanted to a lot, but I made a bad choice. I told her no."

"Why?"

"Because I was afraid. Because I didn't really trust it. Because when it was just a temporary thing, I could enjoy it, but suddenly it got very, very real, and all of my insecurities came crawling out of the woodwork. All the voices telling me I was too ugly to love, that I was just a charity case, a pity fuck. I think I might have dealt with her leaving a lot better if she hadn't asked me to go with her, but she did ask, and I listened to all of those voices in my head, and I said no, and she left without me.

"After she left, I was in a bad place for a while. I think Sierra might have mentioned that one day at breakfast, but the thing is, even if I couldn't accept it at the time, what happened with Sandra helped me realize that I wasn't some unlovable monster, just because I had some scars. I mean, she didn't magically erase my body image issues, or any of the self-loathing that came with them, but she did give me some rather enthusiastic proof that someone could find me desirable and sexy, despite my scars."

"Good," Varsha said. "I'm glad she did that for you."

"She was definitely good for me, but it took me a while to get to that point. I actually met someone online who helped a lot. A girl named Chance. And before you ask, there's nothing romantic there. She's in a poly relationship. She just spends a lot of time online because she has insomnia, so she needs something to do while her girlfriends are asleep."

"Okay."

"I, um...I spent a lot of time in Digilife. Do you know what that is?"

"Some kind of game or something," Varsha said. "I've heard Ashley mention it once."

"It's more of a virtual world than a game. There are games in the world, but there are also cities, clubs, resorts, horse farms. Pretty much anything you can imagine. You just build yourself an avatar, and you can do whatever you want."

"Sounds fun."

"It can be," Maggie said. "It can also be unhealthy. It gets easier to be in Digilife than the real world sometimes. In there, you can be whatever you want to be. You don't have to worry about a bad hip or burn scars or anything else. You can look like whatever you want. It's intoxicating, having that kind of power."

"You have that power in real life now."

"Yeah," Maggie said. "It's funny. I actually look a lot like my Digilife avatar now."

"Is that where the purple hair came from?"

"Yeah," Maggie said. "When I started with Digilife, I created this sort of idealized version of myself, and when I rebuilt my body last week, I did the same thing. Not intentionally. I just...wanted a body, and gave myself the body I wanted, I guess."

"Makes sense," Varsha said.

"Yeah."

"So, Sierra tried to kiss you," Varsha said.

"Yeah, I guess I wandered a bit from the point," Maggie said. "Not as far as you probably think though. It's just...a week ago, I probably would have been ecstatic if she kissed me."

"But not now?"

"No," Maggie said. "Now I'm hurt, angry, insulted."

"Why?"

"Because...I mean..." Maggie sighed. "Because she knew how I felt, but she wasn't interested until I didn't have my scars anymore. Because she just assumed I would be waiting when she finally decided she wanted me. Because she told me she didn't want me and now she's upset because I moved on."

"Did you?" Varsha asked. "You said a week ago, you would have been ecstatic."

"A week ago, I wouldn't have been wondering if the only reason she was interested is because half my face doesn't look like a deep-fried Barbie doll anymore."

"Do you really believe that?"

"No," Maggie said. "Yes. Maybe. I don't fucking know. She claims she dumped Garrett because she realized she wanted to be with me. I knew she'd dumped him, but at the time, she didn't say it was because of me."

"Maybe she wanted to take a little time before she approached you," Varsha said. "Maybe she didn't want you to think you were just her rebound girl."

"Maybe," Maggie said. "But it feels like I wasn't good enough for her until..."

"Until you looked like a supermodel," Varsha said.

Maggie felt herself blush. She looked up at Varsha, who was still smiling, but it was a sad smile.

"There's also you," she said.

"Me?"

"A week ago, I hadn't met you."

"That's sweet," Varsha said. "But if you want to be with Sierra, you should be."

"That's the thing," Maggie said. "I don't. I mean, I care about her, and I'm always going to love her a little bit, but I don't want to be with her. Not anymore."

"Are you sure?" Varsha said. "I know last night was...well, I hoped last night was going somewhere before the alarm sounded, but you didn't make any commitment. If you want—"

Maggie leaned in, cutting Varsha off with a kiss. It took a moment before Varsha responded, but when she did, Maggie knew she'd made the right choice, because Varsha could really, really kiss. Maggie didn't have a lot of basis for comparison, a few girls in high school, and then Sandra, but Varsha made her toes curl and her head swim, and that was before she reached out and rested her hands on Maggie's hips. Maggie pulled back from the kiss. She didn't really want to, but she wanted to say something, and she couldn't while they were kissing.

"I told you last night. I want you."

Varsha smiled the same breathtaking smile she'd had when Maggie had asked her to dance the night before as she leaned in for another kiss.

Chapter Twenty-Five

MAGGIE COULDN'T REMEMBER THE last time she woke up feeling so happy. She was naked and pressed up against Varsha's side. She could feel all the places she was touching Varsha's impossibly soft skin, from the shoulder where her head rested, to the strong thighs wrapped around her right leg. She could also feel Maxine curled up into a little ball just above her head, and hear her little kitten snores with each rise and fall of her chest. It was the perfect way to wake up, and it made her feel more alive than she had in a long time. She smiled as she pressed a kiss to the swell of Varsha's breast, and rubbed slow, gentle circles low on her tummy as she snuggled in closer. Varsha seemed to move in her sleep, tightening her hold on Maggie and humming happily.

"Mm...that's a nice way to wake up," Varsha said.

"I didn't mean to wake you," Maggie said.

"I'm glad you did," Varsha said as she opened her eyes. She turned to look at Maggie. "It's been a long time since I woke up like this."

"Really?" Maggie said.

"Yeah," Varsha said. "Since before I got my powers."

"What about Tux? I thought you said you and her had a thing."

"It's...different," Varsha said. "Things with Tux were always just one offs, you know? Sure, you wake up next to her, but it always just feels transitory, because you know she won't be there the next day, but this...this feels like something I could get used to."

Maggie smiled and rested her head back on Varsha's shoulder.

"Good," she said. "I was afraid you'd be worried about me and Sierra."

"The thought had crossed my mind," Varsha said. "I worried a little that you were just using me to get at her, but I don't want to believe that. I don't want to believe you would do something like that, so I decided if you were going to be here with me, I would just trust it."

"Just like that?" Maggie asked.

"Just like that," Varsha said. "Trust is a choice. Sometimes, it's an informed choice, but at the end of the day, it's always a choice. So I made the choice that would make me happy. I trusted you, so I get to be here today, and hopefully, I get to be here tomorrow, and the day after."

"Maybe even the day after that," Maggie said.

"As long as you want," Varsha said. "Though I'll be honest, if this is going to be a regular thing, we should move it to my room. This bed sucks."

Maggie laughed, and Maxine let out a grumpy noise in protest.

"Oh, someone's upset," Varsha said.

"I'm trying to sleep," Maxine said. "You're too noisy."

"Deal with it, kiddo," Maggie said. "You're the one who went and got her last night."

"Sierra was being a jerk," Maxine said.

"Hey," Maggie said. "That's not nice."

"Neither is keeping me awake when it's nap time," Maxine said as she stood up. She hopped down off the bed, and Maggie watched as she walked over to her bed in the corner and curled up into a ball, throwing a paw over eyes in the process.

Maggie turned back over and buried her face in Varsha's neck, trying her best not to laugh. She could feel Varsha silently laughing next to her, which was enough to crack her control and make her start laughing out loud.

"Rude," Maxine said, which set both of them off again. When they finally managed to stop laughing, Maggie turned her head so it wasn't buried in Varsha's neck.

"What time is it, anyway?" she asked. Varsha turned to look at the clock on the nightstand.

"About six."

"So we can stay here for a while."

"Yeah," Varsha said. "A couple of hours."

"Good," Maggie said. "I like it here."

"Me too," Varsha said. "But can I ask something without spoiling the mood?"

"Sure," Maggie said.

"You said last night one of the reasons you were upset with Sierra was that she didn't want you when you had your scars," Varsha said. "Does it bother you that we didn't...well...shit, I don't know how to ask this."

"It's okay," Maggie said. "But the answer is no. You didn't know me then. You didn't reject me when I had the scars, then decide you wanted me after they were gone."

"But you said she dumped her boyfriend before the explosion."

"Yeah," Maggie said. "But...it's complicated. Just trust me when I say I'm where I want to be, okay?"

"I do," Varsha said, before she leaned in and kissed Maggie on the forehead.

"Good," Maggie said. "Now, what are we going to do with the time we've got?"

"Oh, I can think of a few things," Varsha said.

"Show me," Maggie said.

"My pleasure."

"Hopefully mine too."

"I think that can be arranged."

* * * *

Maggie couldn't keep the smile off her face as the two of them walked towards the cafeteria. They were holding hands the whole way, which would have been enough to make her smile, but she was replaying memories of that morning in her head. Not just what they'd done in bed, but also of the shower they'd shared. She'd never made love in the shower before. She and Sandra had made love in a bath a couple of times, but given Maggie's bad hip and fragile pelvis, her usual approach to showering was to get in and out as quickly as possible before she slipped and broke something. The idea of getting down on her knees in her old body was about as far-fetched as the idea of her running a marathon. In the new body, not only had she done it, but she'd found she really liked it there. Part of it was the thrill she got from the way Varsha had responded, but part of it was just that she could, that the limits she'd come to take for granted were gone.

There was a tiny part of her that wondered if she was wrong for feeling that way, for resenting the body she had for all the things it wouldn't let her do, but she couldn't really bring herself to care if it was wrong. The relief and the freedom she felt was a little intoxicating, and left her torn. On the one hand, she wanted to spend the day in bed with Varsha. On the other hand, she was excited for training in a way she hadn't been the last few days. The reminder of how much more her body was capable of that morning had made her wonder how far she could push things.

"You still with me?" Varsha asked, shaking Maggie out of her thoughts.

"Yeah," Maggie said. "Just thinking about training."

"Honestly, if the combat training team wasn't coming, I'd be tempted to suggest playing hooky," Varsha said.

"So you can get some more nookie?"

Varsha laughed, but she also turned a little bit red. It was so cute,

Maggie had to lean in and kiss her cheek.

"That was terrible," Varsha said.

"I know," Maggie said, "but also true."

"Yeah."

They reached the cafeteria at that point, and Maggie looked around. She spotted Sierra at the usual table, along with Hannah, Ashley, Garnell, Fractal, and much to her surprise, Eurion.

"Oh, crap," Varsha said.

"What?" Maggie asked, turning to Varsha.

"Hannah is going to be in a mood all day," Varsha said.

Maggie turned back to the table. She couldn't see Hannah's face from this angle, but she could see Sierra's.

"I have a feeling she isn't going to be the only one," Maggie said. "Go grab a snack. I'll see you at the table."

Varsha nodded and headed over to the buffet that was kept stocked for her, while Maggie headed over and took a seat at the table.

"Ah, here she is. The lady of the hour," Eurion said, only for Ashley to elbow her in the ribs.

"Don't flirt," Ashley said.

"I wasn't!" Eurion said.

"You always flirt," Ashley said, before turning to Maggie. "If she offers you any gold, say no."

"You are a horrible person, Ashley," Eurion said. "Determined to see me die of loneliness."

Ashley rolled her eyes and turned to Maggie.

"This is Eurion," she said.

"We've met," Maggie said as Varsha sat down next to her.

"Eurion stopped by our table at Cape Town the night before last," Varsha said. "And she was a perfect gentlewoman. Didn't offer to buy Maggie once."

"Buy?" Sierra asked.

Eurion blew a puff of smoke in Varsha's face, making Ashley, Fractal, Garnell, and Maggie laugh. Eurion turned towards Sierra while Varsha waved the smoke out of her face.

"My dear, I would never offer to buy another human being," Eurion said. "But we dragons are creatures of tradition, and of honor. Well, at least most of us are, but we are also intensely territorial creatures. So much so that often we find ourselves unable to even tolerate a mate who is a dragon within our territory. We've been taking human brides for almost as long as there have been humans, but contrary to legend, dragons always pay for what they take. The rumors of us stealing treasures and carrying away virgin sacrifices were started by those jealous of our wealth, or of the fact that often the brides we took chose our company over some self-important human. Humans were the ones who started the tradition of the bride price, and in many parts of the world, a bride price is still commonly offered. We have stuck to the tradition largely because we don't wish to be accused of being thieves, or of carrying off the unwilling, though these days, the bride price is more often given to the bride herself than to her family. Ashley just likes to tease me because I'm honestly a bit awkward when it comes to modern human courting rituals."

"You tried to convince a couple to marry you in the middle of their first date," Ashley said.

"That's not an accurate description of events," Eurion said.

"Well, I suppose we can find out, since Naomi, Anika, and Chance will be here shortly," Ashley said.

"They will?" Eurion said. "I thought it was just Airheart, Ice Dragon, and Blink."

"That was the plan, but the roster got expanded at the last minute. Ice Dragon is bringing them," Ashley said.

"Wait, Airheart and Ice Dragon are coming here?" Maggie asked.

"Yeah," Ashley said.

"And I get to meet them?" Maggie asked.

"Yes," Ashley said, before turning to Eurion. "Why is it always like this?"

"It's the poster," Eurion said.

"Focus and Scatter have a poster," Ashley said.

"Yes, but they kept their clothes on in the poster," Eurion said. "And honestly, you should have seen Scatter the night she met Airheart. It was hilarious."

"Big gay meltdown?"

"Huge," Eurion said. "Right in front of Focus and Ice Dragon."

"Everyone has a big gay meltdown when they meet Airheart," Varsha said.

"Not me," Garnell said.

"You don't count," Fractal said. "You're a guy. But I'm more excited about Naomi, Anika, and Chance. I've been wanting to meet them ever since Ashley got back from that first mission."

"Who are Naomi, Anika, and Chance?" Maggie asked.

"Naomi is Transistor. Anika is Igeza. Chance is...Chance. I don't know any other way to describe them," Ashley said.

"Trouble," Eurion said. "Chance is definitely trouble."

"I can't argue with that," Ashley said. "Fun trouble, but definitely trouble."

Before Maggie could ask what they meant, Rob the waiter showed up and took her and Varsha's orders. Maggie got steak and eggs, while Varsha got her usual order. Once Rob had left, Ashley turned towards Maggie and Varsha.

"So, I couldn't help but notice that you two arrived together this morning," she said.

Maggie glanced over at Varsha, who shrugged.

"Can't keep a secret in this place anyway," Varsha said.

Maggie turned back to Ashley.

"Yeah," she said, doing her best to ignore the fact that Sierra looked like she wanted to scratch Varsha's eyes out, the same way everyone in the table seemed to be intent on ignoring the death glare Hannah was giving Eurion. She turned back to Fractal.

"Why do you want to meet them?"

"Chance is an emergent sentience," Fractal said. "They're a gestalt mind composed of trillions of nanites filtered through an artificial neural network that's modeled after Naomi's brain. They share a body with Naomi."

"Kind of like you and Kesha," Eurion said.

"No," Fractal said. "Kesha and I are the same person. Naomi and Chance are different people."

"Wait, what?" Maggie asked.

"Oh, you haven't heard the story, have you?" Fractal asked.

"No," Maggie said.

"Kesha's autistic, and she has severe social anxiety. She's what most people would call 'high functioning,' meaning she's capable of talking to people and communicating, but she's not really comfortable with doing it face to face. Especially with the social anxiety. She has trouble picking up on social cues. The thing is, she's a technopath. Her metahuman abilities allow her to connect to a computer the same way Hannah can connect to another human.

"She created me as a sort of social prosthetic. I started out as a series of machine learning algorithms designed to analyze social interactions, decode social cues, and help generate appropriate responses. The longer she worked on me, the more advanced I got, until I had developed something close to what most people would consider a personality, but unlike Chance, I never developed true sentience. I'm just a really sophisticated data set tied into a series of challenge and response algorithms.

"What makes me special is Kesha's technopathic abilities. When she first created me, she carried me around in a small portable computer about the size of a hardback book. Then a paperback, then a smartphone. Then, she developed an implant and wired me directly into her brain. I'm a part of her now, but I'm still just a prosthetic. The memories, the emotions, they're all Kesha's. We're still one person. It's just two different interfaces. Kesha's command line, and I'm the Graphic User Interface."

"That sounds like Dissociative Identity Disorder," Sierra said.

"No," Fractal said. "Well, yes, but no. DID is a trauma response, and it can cause a lot of problems for people who have it. We chose this because it helps alleviate Kesha's suffering. If I'm running the social interactions, Kesha isn't having panic attacks, or getting confused and embarrassed because she doesn't understand something. I can run social scripts, interpret social cues, and generally do all the stuff that gives her problems, leaving her free to do what she's good at. Abstract, high-level thinking. We share all the same feelings and emotions, but I'm a filter that keeps them from overwhelming and hurting her.

"It's a coping strategy that a lot of autistic people use. They create a persona that runs off memorized social scripts and behaves in ways allistic people understand, even if they don't understand why those social scripts work the way they do. The difference is just the level of sophistication involved. I, Fractal, the public facing persona, am a monolithic AI. I was created from the top down as a single suite of software for a specific set of tasks. The fact that I'm wired directly into Kesha's brain and her technopathic abilities allows me to be a lot more versatile than I would be otherwise, but I'm nowhere near what Chance is."

"If you and Kesha are the same person, why do you talk about yourself as if you're two different people?" Maggie asked.

"Habit, mostly," Fractal said. "Other people seem to be more comfortable thinking about Kesha and Fractal as separate people, and it's not usually worth the effort to correct them, but honestly, I find it kind of annoying."

"I apologize, then," Eurion said. "I meant no offense. My mistake was made entirely out of ignorance, and not a lack of care."

"Apology accepted," Fractal said, then turned back to Maggie.

"Chance, from what I understand, is an emergent AI, a single sentient mind that arises from the interaction of trillions of smaller programs. They are a separate person from Naomi, even though the two of them share a body."

"I can see why you'd want to meet them."

"I haven't been this excited about something since the first time Garnell asked me out on a date."

"I'm trying not to be jealous," Garnell said.

Fractal smiled as she turned to Garnell.

"Chance has two girlfriends," Fractal said. "I don't think she'd have time for me, even if I were interested."

"Two girlfriends?" Maggie asked.

"Yeah," Ashley said. "It's a bit weird, but Naomi, Anika, and Chance are all kind of an item."

"But...Chance has two girlfriends?" Maggie asked.

"Yeah," Ashley said.

"Let me guess. One of them is a really good-looking nurse, and the other one has C-cups."

Ashley tilted her head and looked at Eurion.

"As a matter of fact, yes," Eurion said.

"Son of a bitch!" Maggie said.

"I feel like I'm missing something here," Varsha said.

"You remember me mentioning I have a friend named Chance?" Maggie asked.

"Yeah," Varsha said.

"Well, my friend has two girlfriends, who she calls Nurse Hotness and C Cup."

"Oh, that's definitely our Chance," Eurion said.

"What are the odds?" Ashley asked.

"That would depend entirely on the circumstances of their meeting," Fractal said.

Everyone at the table turned to look at Maggie, who thought about exactly what she'd been doing when she met Chance, and promptly shook her head.

"Nope," she said, shaking her head. "Not for all the tea in China."

Chapter Twenty-Six

"HEY, MAGGIE," SIERRA SAID. Maggie, Ashley, Varsha, Eurion, and Fractal all stopped in the hall just outside of the cafeteria and turned towards her. "Can we talk for a minute?"

Maggie had to fight to keep from sighing. She'd been expecting this, but she'd hoped to put it off for a while. Unfortunately, it looked like she was going to have to deal with it before that day's training session. That might be better because she was relaxed and well rested, and hadn't spent a day getting frustrated at trying some new skill Ashley wanted her to work on, but better didn't mean it would be pleasant. She turned to the group that was walking with her.

"Go on," she said. "I'll be there in a few minutes." Most of the group nodded, and headed for the training room, but Varsha stayed.

"You sure?" Varsha asked.

"Yeah," Maggie said. "Go on. I'll be fine."

"Ok." She leaned in and kissed Maggie's cheek. "See you soon," she said, before she turned and jogged a bit to catch up with the rest of the group. Maggie turned back to Sierra and waited.

"What the hell?" Sierra asked.

"I'm sorry?"

"I tell you how I feel, so you go jump into bed with Vee?"

"First, her name is Varsha. Second, where did you sleep the night I told you how I felt?"

"That's different!"

"If you say so," Maggie said.

"Okay, I get it. This is revenge, right? You're getting back at me?"

"No. And I'm not sure now's a good time to have this conversation. I think you need some time to calm down, so you don't say something you can't take back."

"You think I need to calm down?"

"Yes," Maggie said. "I told you last night, I moved on. That I'd started something with Varsha. The fact that you suddenly decided you want to date me doesn't change the fact that I'm involved with someone else. It doesn't mean I'm obligated to put my relationship on hold while you sort out your sexuality and figure out what you want."

"I already know what I want," Sierra said. "I want you."

"I'm sorry," Maggie said. "I really am. There was a time when I would have given anything to hear you say those words, but you told me it was never going to happen. You told me I needed to move on. And I did. I dated Sandra for a year, and she left, and that was months ago. If she made you realize you wanted to be with me, you had plenty of time between then and now to speak up. You didn't."

"I was going to!"

"I know," Maggie said. "Breaking up with Garrett because you realized you want to date me is exactly the kind of thing you would do. The longer I sit with the idea, the more I'm convinced that you're telling the truth. It just doesn't change anything."

"But I love you," Sierra said.

"And I love you," Maggie said. "But that doesn't change anything either. Two people can love each other so much it hurts, and still not be right for each other."

"And you don't think we're right for each other?"

"No," Maggie said.

"But last night, you said your answer would have been different a week ago."

"I was a different person a week ago," Maggie said.

"But what's changed?" Sierra said.

"Everything," Maggie said. "My life, my future, all of it's different now."

"And you think that makes Varsha a better choice?"

"Maybe," Maggie said. "I know it might not work out."

"Then why her? Why pick her over me?"

Maggie thought about it for a minute. About the way Sierra had, however unintentionally, hurt her with the timing of her confession. She thought about the fact that she was going to be out in the street helping people at all hours, while Sierra would probably have a nice, cushy lab job for the rest of her life. And of course she thought about the big one. The fact that Sierra was going to grow old and die, while all signs pointed to Maggie just going on and on, and how that meant that any future she shared with Sierra would be short lived, while she might have centuries with Varsha. They were all good, solid reasons to make the choice she was making, but at the end of the day, they were all just nice little bonuses that went along with the real reason.

Varsha had given her a choice. When everyone else had just expected her to do what they wanted, Varsha had been there reminding her that she had the right to make a choice. There'd been no demands, no jealous tantrums, just Varsha sitting there, reminding Maggie that it was okay for her to choose what she wanted, instead of what everyone else wanted. Varsha was the only one, in all of this, that had put Maggie first. That was why she picked Varsha.

"She lets me be selfish," Maggie said.

"What?" Sierra asked.

"I've got to go," Maggie said as she turned and started towards the training room. "People are waiting for me."

* * * *

As it turned out, one person was waiting for her. Ashley was standing by the door to the training room, leaning against the wall.

"Something wrong?" Maggie asked.

"You tell me," Ashley said.

"Nothing on my end," Maggie said.

"You sure?" Ashley asked. "That didn't look like it was going to be a pleasant conversation."

"It wasn't," Maggie said. "I love Sierra, but sometimes, she's not good at listening, and absolutely terrible at reading the room."

"Are you okay?" Ashley asked.

"Yeah," Maggie said. "I mean, for now, yeah. If she decides she never wants to speak to me again, not so much."

"That bad, huh?"

"I don't know," Maggie said. "I...I just don't know. She tried to kiss me, and there was a time when I would have given anything for that to happen, but that was before...all of this. Before my life got turned upside down, before I had powers, before I knew I was going to join a MERT team, and before I met Varsha."

"I get it," Ashley said. "I'm going through something similar."

"Hannah?" Maggie asked.

"Yeah."

"Maybe you should just tell her what's going on," Maggie said.

"It's not that easy," Ashley said.

"It kind of is," Maggie said.

Ashley frowned and shook her head.

"We should go in," she said. Maggie waved towards the door.

"Oh, um, just so you know, Chance prefers they/them pronouns and refers to themselves as we/us," Ashley said. "They're a little shy about telling people that sometimes, but she/her and I/me makes them uncomfortable."

"Thanks for the heads up," Maggie said.

Ashley opened it and led the way into the room with Maggie right behind her. There was a large group already inside. Maggie spotted Varsha, Fractal, Eurion, Airheart, Ice Dragon, and Chance right away. There was another woman who looked a lot like Chance, but with brown hair and no silver lipstick, a light skinned black woman, and a Latino man in a black jumpsuit. As they got closer, Maggie noticed something floating above Chance's head as they talked to Fractal.

"Is this our new baby superhero?" Ice Dragon asked. Everyone turned towards Maggie.

"This is Maggie," Ashley said. "Call sign Aether."

Ice Dragon turned to Eurion.

"Why do you get all the pretty ones?" she asked.

"I don't," Eurion said. "Rachel snatched Cecile right out from under me, and she might as well have Scatter and Focus too."

"But you do have this one," Ice Dragon said. "And you have Ashley, Naomi, Anika, and Chance."

"And you have a wife," Airheart said. "Or have you forgotten?"

"Of course not, my dear, but you know how much we dragons love to collect pretty things."

"And people say I have no manners," Eurion grumbled.

"You tried to buy our girlfriends the day we met you," Chance said.

"I did not try to buy them," Eurion said. "I simply proposed marriage. The two things are completely different."

Ashley leaned over towards Maggie.

"This argument will take about twenty minutes," she said in a stage whisper loud enough for everyone to hear.

"We're not arguing!" Chance, Eurion, and Ice Dragon all said at the same time.

"They're definitely arguing," the woman who looked like Chance said. Maggie assumed she was Naomi. The black woman, Anika, sighed and shook her head.

"Now you've done it," Anika said. "Chance is going to pout for the rest of the day."

"We do not pout!" Chance said with a pout and a little stamp of their foot. Anika smiled.

"Yes, you do, love, but you're very cute when you do it," Anika said.

Chance's whole face changed. The pout went away and was replaced with a smile so bright it hurt to look at. Naomi smiled too and shook her head a little.

"You know, you dragged us five hundred miles from home to see your friend. You could at least say hi."

“Oh!” Chance said, turning towards Maggie. “Sorry. We get distracted any time Anika makes eyes at us.”

“I can see why,” Maggie said. “I mean, you told me your girlfriends were hot, but damn.”

Chance bounced on the balls of their feet and smiled smugly as they looked over at Anika and Naomi.

“So, which one is C Cup, and which one is Nurse Hotness?” Maggie asked. Chance’s face immediately fell, the smug expression replaced with a look like a puppy that knew it was about to get scolded. She glanced over at Anika, who just raised an eyebrow and crossed her arms. Ice Dragon looked absolutely delighted.

“Um...this is Naomi,” Chance said. “She’s an artist. She used to do book covers and illustrations, along with commissioned pieces. And that’s Anika. She’s a trauma nurse.”

“Nice to meet you both,” Maggie said. “Chance has told me good things.”

“Hopefully things other than my bra size,” Naomi said.

“What? It’s my bra size too,” Chance said.

“Chance does have a point,” Anika said.

“Is that so, Nurse Hotness?” Naomi asked.

“Is this where I point out that Chance’s brain is modeled on yours?” Anika asked. “Because right now, I’m pretty sure that means you’ve called me that in your head at least once.”

“She totally has,” Chance said. “Though, honestly, Amethyst came up with the name.”

“Snitch,” Naomi said.

“That does sound like something Amethyst would come up with,” Anika said.

“As fun as all of this is, we should probably get started,” Ashley said.

“Always the spoilsport,” Ice Dragon said.

“Behave, love,” Airheart said.

Ice Dragon rolled her eyes.

“So bossy,” she said. “I don’t know why I put up with you.”

“Because no one else will have you,” Airheart said.

Ashley cleared her throat, rather pointedly.

“If you two are done...introductions. Everyone, this is Maggie Bennett. She is currently a MERT trainee attached to the Sun City High Guard. Her powers include teleportation, shapeshifting, temporary matter creation, and the ability to make really big booms. How big, we're not entirely sure yet.

"Maggie, this is Emilia Rose, codename Airheart. Her powers include Invulnerability, super strength, super speed, enhanced senses, and flight. Hua Jia Li, codename Ice Dragon. She's an Asian blue dragon. Her powers include shapeshifting, being a great honking dragon, flying, breathing ice and fire, having exceptionally sharp claws, and being a world class troublemaker."

"Flatterer," Jia Li said. Ashley ignored her and gestured to the Latino man Maggie didn't recognize.

"Diego Varela, codename Blink. Like Airheart and Ice Dragon, he's a member of the Boston Irregulars. Powers include teleportation, increased toughness, and extrasensory perception. Eurion you know. Her powers include shapeshifting, being an even bigger dragon, flying, breathing fire, having huge freaking wings, sharp claws, and knowing how to fight with any weapon you put in her hand. Naomi Woodward, codename Transistor. Powers include shapeshifting, a touch of divine magic, regeneration and superhuman endurance, enhanced reflexes, and skill with sword, shield, and spear. Anika Tamru, codename Igeza. Powers include flight, healing, supernatural endurance, enhanced reflexes, and regeneration. Chance, codename Ex Machina. Powers include being an AI, being one of the most skilled hackers on the planet, and having the sense of humor of a five-year-old. Varsha Patel, who you already know, but for the new arrivals, codename Delta V. Powers include super speed, enhanced senses, extrasensory perception, superhuman endurance, and enhanced strength. Fractal, who shares her body with Kesha Jones, codename Fractal. Powers include technopathy, hacking, enhanced speed, and reflexes. Lastly, myself. Ashley Churchill, codename Cinderella. Powers include magic, astral projection, alchemy, and the ability to punch stuff.

"For the next few days, this will be your training team. We're going to start with Blink. He'll teach you everything he knows about how to use your teleportation abilities tactically, how to control the battle space through mobility, and how to avoid getting hit by the enemy. We'll also have Eurion and Naomi teach you how to fight with melee weapons. Sword, shield, spear, anything else they can think of. Varsha will teach you how to use your speed, and when all of that is done, Airheart, Ice Dragon, and I will be your final exam. We will kick your ass up one side of this room and down another, until we decide you know what you're doing."

"Right," Maggie said. "Sounds fun."

"Good," Ashley said. "Let's get to it."

Chapter Twenty-Seven

MAGGIE DROPPED DOWN INTO her chair in the cafeteria, panting and relieved to be off her feet. She hadn't really thought the new body could get tired, and if she was honest, she still wasn't sure if the body was actually tired, or if it just felt tired because she believed it should be. Either way, she wanted to curl up in bed with Varsha and sleep for a week. The rest of her training team all gave her amused looks as she picked up her water glass and emptied the whole thing in one go.

"Wow," Chance said. "We didn't think you'd get that thirsty until Rescue Girl got to the table."

Maggie glared at them.

"Rescue Girl?" Naomi asked.

"Varsha," Maggie said. "When we were talking the other day, I didn't want to use her name, so Chance here dubbed her Rescue Girl."

"I suppose it's better than C Cup," Naomi said.

"Don't listen to her," Chance said. "She's pretty fond of those C-cups."

"Chance," Anika said in a warning tone, at which point Chance at least had the decency to look chagrined.

"Sorry," Chance said. They turned back to Maggie. "Sometimes, when you share a body, it's kind of hard to remember where the line is."

Maggie frowned and looked back and forth between Chance and Naomi, who were sitting on either side of Anika. Ashley was on Naomi's other side, then Eurion, Jia Li, Emilia, then finally Diego, with an empty seat between Diego and Maggie left for Varsha.

"You know, I keep hearing people tell me you two share a body, but..." She gestured to where Chance was sitting. Chance looked at her for a moment, then pointed up at the small disk floating above her head.

"Hologram projector," they said. As if to prove their point, they swung their hand down, and it passed right through the table.

"Wow," Maggie said as Varsha sat down next to her. "I've never seen one that small. What's the power source?"

"We have no idea," Chance said. "Focus gave it to us on the condition that we don't ever let anyone try to open it or take it apart. Honestly, the curiosity is killing us, but anti-grav tech and mobile tankless hologram projectors don't exactly grow on trees, so we can live with it until the DMA gets their act together regarding our legal status."

"What do you mean?" Maggie asked.

"There's no legal distinction between artificial intelligence and artificial sentience," Chance said. "Under current US and international law, we have the same rights as a copy of Linux. Which means the DMA seized our entire stock portfolio and stuck it in a blind trust until our legal status gets sorted out. We get paid, but the money goes into a trust fund I can't access."

"That sucks," Maggie said.

"Yes, it does," Chance said. "How are we supposed to build an android body when we don't have money for parts?"

"We've offered to buy the parts for you," Anika said, which only made Chance frown.

"You shouldn't have to," they said.

"You're right," Anika said. "But I just wanted to remind you that we don't mind."

"We know," Chance said. "But until the legal stuff is sorted out, we couldn't own the body, even if we did build it."

Maggie winced, because she could see Chance's point. That did suck. Chance turned back to Maggie.

"We considered just taking a small tissue sample from Naomi and growing ourself a body, but we don't really know what we'd do with a biological body when we weren't using it."

"When you weren't using it?" Maggie asked. As soon as the words were out of her mouth, she knew she'd said something wrong. Chance's face fell, and she turned to Anika. Then something weird happened. The hologram of Chance shifted to one of Naomi, and Naomi's body shifted slightly, her hair and lips turning silver and a circuitry pattern appearing in her skin. She immediately leaned towards Anika, who wrapped an arm around her.

"Why does everyone always just assume we want a body so we can move out of Naomi's head?" she asked.

Anika slipped an arm around Chance's shoulders, then leaned in and kissed Chance's temple.

"She didn't mean anything by it," Anika said.

"Yeah, I didn't. I just don't understand," Maggie said.

"It gets lonely," Chance said. "We love being with Naomi and Anika all the time when they're awake, but humans sleep so much, and it's so quiet without them. That's why we spend so much time in Digilife and doing other stuff. Most nights, we've got Digilife open, we've got a couple of characters in Black Sky going, two or three Netflix streams, a couple of novels and a couple of fanfics open, and we're writing, but it's still so quiet. We're less than a year old, and we've written two thousand novels, done hundreds of digital paintings, learned physics, biology, chemistry, mathematics, engineering, robotics, computer science, artificial intelligence, information technology, theology, mythology, and literature in forty different languages all beyond the PhD levels. We've read Project Gutenberg. All of it. We've read a large percentage of the Library of Congress.

"All of that, and it still gets so quiet at night. We think the android would help. Give us more input to process, more ways to keep our mind busy. Let us do things with our hands and our body instead of just digitally."

"Okay," Maggie said. "That, I understand."

"We're sorry," Chance said. "But we don't think you can."

"But I do," Maggie said. "After I...well, died, it was only a fraction of a second between the time Varsha cut the power to the Quantum Imager and I learned how to create a new body. The thing is, without my body, without something to anchor me in a normal time frame, time moves a lot faster for me. I call it Planck scale time, because I can feel the ticking of the universe. Each quantized unit of time just slipping by like the clicking of the second hand on a particularly loud gear driven clock. It's not a big deal now, because I can return to normal time whenever I want, but that first time, that first fraction of a second for the rest of the world, felt like months, or years passing with me just floating there, alone, the world around me frozen in time. It was like...I don't know, a foretaste of hell, maybe. I thought for a long time it was hell. So yeah, I get it. The way the quiet creeps in on you, gnaws at you, starts to drive you mad. I'm sorry you have to go through it."

Maggie felt a leather covered hand slip into hers and squeeze. She glanced down to see the blue of Varsha's suit, then looked up at her face to see a horrified look there.

"I'm sorry," she said.

"Don't be," Maggie said. "You did what had to be done, and if you hadn't, if you guys had found some way to move the imager without turning it off, I'd still be trapped in it. It was bad, but I came out the other end better for it."

"Well, this is certainly an unexpected conversation," Jia Li said.

"Jia," Emilia said.

"We're sorry," Chance said, sounding miserable.

"Darling, you've done nothing wrong. I had no idea that nights were so troublesome for you," Jia Li said, before turning to Maggie. "And for you to have survived such a thing with your mind intact speaks of great mental strength, but I think perhaps both of you should spend more time with either myself or Eurion. We dragons often spend years of time alone, in silence. We can teach you both ways to quiet the mind."

"She means she's going to teach you both how to brood over giant piles of gold," Emilia said, which earned her a glare from Jia Li.

"I still don't know why I put up with your abuse," Jia Li said.

"Because I'm cute, and you love me," Emilia said, which made Jia Li roll her eyes, but a smile spread across her face.

"I admit, I feel ashamed of myself for not picking up on your distress earlier, my dear," Eurion said. "I would gladly teach you the meditation techniques Jia Li mentioned."

"Do you think they would work for us?" Chance asked.

"I don't honestly know. I believe it would depend on how closely your mind approximates a human one. Most of our kind learn them very young, but I've taught them to several of my wives over the centuries, so they're definitely something a human mind can learn."

"It's worth a try," Anika said.

"I wouldn't mind coming down whenever you need to," Naomi said.

"Thank you," Chance said.

Eurion turned to Maggie. "And you? Would you like to learn as well?"

"Yes," Maggie said. "Very much. I have a feeling I may need it."

Chance sat up, pulling away from Anika, and shifted back into Naomi as the Naomi hologram shifted back to Chance.

"What just happened?" Maggie asked.

"Food's coming," Chance said, nodding toward the kitchen. "Naomi's better at the whole food thing than I am."

"Better at eating?" Maggie asked.

"No," Naomi said. "Just better at stopping. I let Chance drive once when we went to brunch, and she got a little enthusiastic."

"She means I ate twenty waffles," Chance said.

"No, I mean you ate twenty peanut butter waffles," Naomi said.

"To be fair, you should probably blame that on Focus and her peanut butter obsession," Emilia said.

"Oh, I do," Naomi said. "The same way I blame her for the peanut butter bagels and the popcorn balls."

"But those are so good!" Chance whined.

"You know what else is good?" Naomi asked. "My ass actually fitting in my costume."

Chance rolled their eyes.

"As if I would actually let you gain any weight," Chance said. "I'd never hear the end of the whining."

Naomi flipped Chance off as the waiters started handing out plates. Chance responded by sticking out their tongue.

"Knock it off, both of you," Anika said. She looked over at Maggie. "I'd tell you they don't normally act like a pair of sugared up five-year-olds, but everyone at the table would call me out for lying."

Maggie laughed.

"It's okay," she said. "It's nice."

A waiter set a plate down in front of her, surprising her. She hadn't ordered yet.

"I took the liberty of ordering for you and Varsha," Eurion said. "I thought you wouldn't want to wait for your food. I hope you don't mind."

"No," Maggie said. "Thank you."

"You're welcome," Eurion said. "Though I do hope you like lamb. I'm fond myself, but I've been eating it for two thousand years."

"I love it," Maggie said. "I can't usually afford it though."

"Thank you, Eurion," Varsha said.

"Of course, my dear."

"I doubt you'll have much trouble affording anything going forward," Jia Li said. "As much power as you have, the DMA will pay quite a bit for your services."

"It's true," Emilia said. "If you didn't have reasons to stay here, I suspect Secretary Banks would try to get you to move to Pontian."

"Why Pontian?"

"She's been trying to build a Tier Three team around Focus and Scatter ever since Scatter showed back up," Emilia said.

"Why?" Maggie asked.

"Tony Ragusa," Eurion said. "I do wish Scatter had let me roast that man alive when I had the chance."

"I'm sure she wishes the same, most days," Ashley said.

"The head of the Ragusa crime family?" Maggie asked.

"That's the one," Eurion said."They operate primarily out of Pontian. Focus, Scatter, Jia Li, and I had a bit of a dust up with Tony's father back in '92, and Focus and Scatter put Tony and his sister in jail. His sister was operating as a supervillain called Null at the time. No one is sure what happened to her. She just disappeared out of lock up one day, but Tony took over after Scatter killed his dad."

"The worst part is, everyone thinks Ragusa has ties to the Unitarium," Emilia said.

Maggie froze for a moment, and the whole time, she could practically feel the gears turning in her head. She looked up at Emilia.

"The Unitarium," Maggie said.

"I know," Emilia said. "It's supposed to be a myth, but it's not. It's very real."

"No, I know it's real, it's just the second time it's come up in as many days. I knew Nomi had some issues with them a while back, but I didn't realize they had a permanent presence in the area."

"We're not sure they do," Ashley said. "There are rumors, but there are always rumors. Sorting rumors from the truth is always a pain in the ass."

"But they would be extremely well funded, right?" Maggie asked.

"Yeah," Ashley said. "They're a mafia made entirely of metahumans. They've got to be rolling in money."

"And we're looking for someone who would bankroll Dr. Hastings," Maggie said.

"Oh, shit," Ashley and Varsha both said at the same time.

"Yeah," Maggie said.

"But what would a mobster want from the moon?" Ashley asked.

"The moon?" Emilia asked. "What does the moon have to do with any of this?"

Maggie turned to Emilia to explain, but stopped, remembering how tight the security was around all of this. She reached up and tapped her earbud.

"Nomi, can you come to the cafeteria and bring a tablet with those equations from Fairchild's computer?"

"Why? What's up?" Nomi asked.

"I think we might have an idea of who is bankrolling Hastings, but we're still lost on why. I might need to explain all of this to our guests."

"Give me a minute," Nomi said. "I'll call Banks, then I'll be right down."

"Okay," Maggie said. She looked over at Chance. "You mentioned you taught yourself math and physics, right?"

"Yeah," Chance said.

"How are you with classical mechanics?" Maggie asked.

"Pretty good," Chance said. "Why do you ask?"

* * * *

"This is literally the worst math we've ever seen," Chance said.

"I know," Maggie said. "She's the worst."

"No, you don't understand," Chance said. "It's not just that her work is terrible. She's missing the fucking moon. How the fuck do you miss a whole ass fucking moon?"

"She's an idiot," Maggie suggested.

"She's leading it way too much. Here, have a look," Chance said, as she gestured towards the screen in the briefing room. It was a different room than the one the team usually used. A much larger one with a stage at one end and a DMA emblem on the wall, along with the High Guard's crest. It was large enough to fit the entire High Guard, Sierra, and the training team, which was why everyone was piling into the room for this. A diagram of Earth and the moon appeared on the screen, with a flashing red dot near the line indicating the orbit of the moon, but about sixty degrees ahead of the moon in its orbital path.

"That's a pretty big miss," Maggie said.

"Yeah, and it gets worse," Chance said. "Watch what happens when you change the time index."

Maggie watched as Chance advanced the time index on the model they'd created. The flashing red dot began to move in an irregular path, drawing out a shape like a kidney bean. It was around the Earth/moon Lagrange four point. A pocket of gravitational stability that existed due to the combined gravitational effects of the Earth and moon. It took Maggie a moment to realize what she was looking at, but she wasn't the only one.

"Motherfucker," Emilia said.

"Oh shit," Chance said.

"Son of a bitch," Maggie said.

Maggie looked over at Emilia, who had gone white as a sheet.

"Is it possible?" Maggie asked.

Emilia turned and looked at her.

"I don't know," Emilia said. "I don't know any reason it wouldn't be. That's part of the reason it was declared off limits."

"Um, guys, you want to share with the class?" Sierra asked. Maggie shrugged and gave Emilia a questioning look.

"It's your case," Emilia said.

"Right," Maggie said. She turned back to the diagram on the screen. "They aren't aiming for the moon. They're aiming for the Olympus."

Everyone in the room went deathly silent as the horrifying implications set in. The Olympus was one of those things people preferred not to think about, because if you thought about it too much, you'd probably go a little bit mad. Most people believed that metahumans had existed for the whole of human history. Legends of Gilgamesh, Hercules, Beowulf, and others had been considered myths for hundreds of years, but all of that had changed after the Tunguska blast of 1908 and the proliferation of metahumans that followed. The common belief was that prior to Tunguska, metahumans existed, but they manifested powers only very rarely. After an alien spaceship had exploded in the skies over Tunguska, the number of metahumans exhibiting powers began to increase rapidly over the following decades.

Then, in the mid-90s, an astronomer spotted the Olympus. A spaceship that was shaped like an old space capsule but was nearly ten miles tall. Once they realized the ship was going to settle into orbit at one of the Lagrange points around the moon, the various governments of the world had worked together to build a spaceship that could go out and meet it. Six astronauts had been chosen. Emilia Rose from the US, Douglas Chambers from Great Britain, Karina Yurievna from Russia, Jean-Claude Arsenault from France, Cai Jing from China, and Yasuda Higashi from Japan. They were packed into the rather hastily built United Nations spaceship Argo and fired at the Earth/moon L4 point.

It took them nearly three weeks of careful maneuvering to match orbits with the Olympus, and what they found inside was the stuff of horror movies. Everything was in perfect working order. All the gear was put away. The ship was absolutely spotless without so much as a speck of dust anywhere onboard. Only three things were missing. There were no food stores aboard. There were very obvious spaces, but they had been cleared out. Whether by the crew, or by whatever system kept the ship clean, no one knew. The second was a single ship from the docking bay. There were more than a hundred auxiliary craft of various sizes and purposes onboard, but a single docking cradle sat empty, next to a group of ships that, near as anyone could tell, were of the same make as the one that had exploded over Tunguska in 1908. The last thing missing, of course, was the crew. There was easily space for tens of thousands of people onboard. The Olympus was massive in a way most people couldn't comprehend, but in all the time the six astronauts were onboard, they didn't find a single, solitary soul.

The best guess, both by the astronauts and by people who examined their data later, was that the ship had been drifting for centuries. Possibly even millennia. It was a guess based entirely on the amount of dust accumulated on the outside of the hull, because aside from the single missing auxiliary craft, there was nothing to indicate anyone had ever set foot aboard the Olympus.

The astronauts had been onboard the Olympus, exploring for almost three months when one day, they just didn't report back to the Argo. Three days passed without a word from them, before they radioed in. They'd spent the whole time unconscious, knocked out by something deep inside the ship, and when they'd woken up, all six of them had superpowers. The same superpowers. Near total invulnerability, super strength, super speed, super senses, flight. There was a measurable difference in how strong they were, but all of them were insanely strong. Emilia was the strongest, followed closely by Douglas.

NASA had ordered them to come home as quickly as possible. They'd had to wait a day to be in the right place in the Olympus's orbit of the L4 point, but six days after the incident, the Argo's escape capsules had splashed down in the Atlantic Ocean and been picked up by a ship with a skeleton crew. The astronauts, and the crew of the ship that picked them up, had spent the next six months in quarantine, and over the next few months after that, all six of them had become superheroes. Emilia became Airheart. Douglas Chambers became Red Coat, Karina became Firebird, Jean-Claude became Cavalier, Cai Jing became White Tiger, and Yasuda became Hachiman. Collectively, they'd become known as the Olympus Six.

The UN had declared the Olympus off limits so it could never happen again. Maggie wasn't sure she blamed them. The idea of a device that could give anyone who got close to it the kind of power the Olympus Six had was insanely dangerous.

"They want to sell the ability to mint metas to the Unitarium," Maggie said.

"And not just any metas," Emilia said. "Olympus level metas."

Maggie looked over at Emilia.

"I think we might need to put my training on hold for a few days and focus on finding Whitehall, Hastings, and Fairbanks," she said.

"I think you might be right," Emilia said, before turning to Jia Li. "We need to go see Lynn, right now."

For once, Jia Li didn't make a joke. She just stood up and faced the far wall and let out a roar that seemed to shake the building, and for just a moment, whatever happened kicked Maggie out of her physical form. She watched as the fabric of space and time folded in on itself, watched as the spot where Jia Li's roar was focused pushed out through higher dimensions and bridged the gap between where they were and somewhere else.

She watched as Jia Li folded space, and finally, after all the time that had passed since the accident that transformed her into something not entirely human anymore, Maggie understood everything that had happened that day.

Chapter Twenty-Eight

"MS. BENNETT," SECRETARY BANKS said.

"Don't bother," Sierra said. "She's in full on math zombie mode."

Maggie shook her head, trying to brush aside the voices around her as she worked, desperate to get the math down. The scent of white board markers and the soft squeak of the marker on the board helped her focus as she laid out equation after equation.

"How long has she been like this?" Banks asked.

"Since Jia Li opened the portal to your office," Eurion said. "When Jia Li roared, she disappeared for a couple of seconds, and when she came back, she rushed over to the white board and started writing."

Maggie reached the end of the space on the whiteboard and stepped aside.

"Chance," she said.

"Got it," Chance replied. "Scanned and uploaded."

Maggie waved her hand, and the whiteboard was wiped clean. She walked over to the other end and started writing again. More equations, trying to keep up the flow of the work.

"What just happened?" Banks asked.

"We scanned and digitized her work," Chance said. "We're dumping everything into a LaTeX document for her."

"I don't know what that means," Banks said.

"LaTeX is a document formatting package used in academic writing," Chance said. "Especially math and sciences. We're also uploading everything into Matlab, which is a math package."

"Do you understand all of this?" Banks asked.

"We're having to learn a lot of physics on the fly," Chance said. "One of the advantages of having an artificial neural network, we process information really quickly. We've read every textbook ever published on cosmology, quantum mechanics, and nth dimensional spacetime, and gone through about thirty years of physics journals in the last twenty minutes."

"But do you understand it?" Banks asked.

"We *think* so," Chance said. "If we're right about what we're seeing, there are at least three Nobel prizes and a Fields Medal in here, but to be honest, she's inventing an entirely new branch of physics."

"You're going to have to wait until she's finished," Sierra said. "She'll explain it then, but when she gets into math zombie mode, interrupting her is a bad idea."

"How bad of an idea?" Banks asked.

"She's a little feral," Sierra said. "She actually threw a dry erase marker at a professor's head once, and that was before she could make things explode on a whim, but that's not even the worst part."

"What is the worst part?" Banks asked.

"She might lose her train of thought," Sierra said. "The last time that happened, it took her weeks of work to figure things out again. And if this is really as important as we think it is..."

"Point taken," Banks said.

"Maggie, is H sub zero there the Hubble Constant?" Chance asked.

"Yes," Maggie said.

"Well, that's fucking terrifying," Chance said.

"I am aware," Maggie said.

"What?" Banks asked. "What does that mean?"

"If we're understanding the math right, it means that this Hastings fellow is a fucking moron who forgot to account for the expansion of the universe when writing his targeting software for his space-fold device."

"Okay, but why is that terrifying?" Banks asked.

"Because...we're not entirely sure how to explain it," Chance said.

Maggie stopped writing and stepped aside.

"Chance," she said.

"Got it," Chance said.

Maggie turned and looked at all the people who were watching her.

"Chance is right," Maggie said. "Hastings forgot to account for the expansion of the universe in his targeting algorithm. It didn't even occur to me until I saw Jia Li's dragon portal fold space, but when she did, the ripples in the quantum membrane knocked me out of my physical body, and I felt the whole thing. I understood exactly how it worked, and because I understood how it worked, I understood exactly what went wrong during the explosion where Maggie and Garrett died."

"Wait, what do you mean, where Maggie and Garrett died?" Banks asked. "You're both still alive."

"No," Maggie said. "I'm alive, but I'm...a copy. An image. The original Maggie Bennett died on the table. I'm the image of her that was created by the quantum field imager. I'm an afterimage, stamped into the quantum membrane."

"You seem to be taking that pretty well," Banks said.

"I already suspected that was the case," Maggie said. "Functionally, it doesn't matter. I'm an exact copy. If you believe in souls, you'd have to ask a theologian if I'm still the same soul, but it doesn't really matter to me, other than from a purely academic standpoint. It's just important to make the distinction because in situations like this, details matter, and Hastings forgot a big one."

"Okay, but what does the expansion of the universe have to do with why there are explosions every time Hastings and Whitehall try to use their machine?" Nomi asked.

"Time," Maggie said. "Or more specifically, red shift. Does anyone here not understand the expanding universe theory?"

Maggie watched as a bunch of hands went up.

"Okay. Right. Not a group of physicists. I keep forgetting. So, the universe is a collection of discrete points. There's here, and there is there, and there are a lot of theres between here and there, but none of them are actually connected to each other. They're all separated by a distance. The thing is, that distance is constantly getting bigger. Now, normally, we don't notice. The value of the Hubble Constant, the speed at which any two given points are moving away from each other, is really small. It's measured in kilometers per second per megaparsec. In other words, if you have two points which are 3.26 million light years apart, they're moving away from each other at about seventy kilometers per second. That's something like 21.45 millimeters per second per light year.

"The expansion is inconceivably small over short distances, like, say, across a basement lab in a college. Inconceivably small, but still there. Under normal circumstances, it wouldn't matter, but it's like gravity, time dilation, and GPS. When you're calculating your position based on GPS signals, you have to take into account that due to time dilation caused by gravity, time moves slower on the surface of the earth than it does for GPS satellites in orbit. You have to adjust the time codes from the satellites in order to calculate your position correctly. Speed affects time the same way gravity affects time. When you fold space, you have to account for the fact that the place you're folding to is moving at a different speed due to the expansion of the universe. Otherwise, time on the other side of the fold moves more slowly. Slower time means more gravity. More gravity means that particles on one side of the fold will be pulled to the other side of the fold. What happens when the time frames aren't in sync on both sides is that you get something like an accretion disk around the fold. Like water going down the drain, only it's air or dust or other loose particles, but because time always is moving slower on the other side, the moment the particles are through, the gravity reverses, and the particles are pulled back the other way. They start to oscillate and get trapped in the fold."

"Wait, you lost me. It sounds like you're saying time is moving slower on the opposite end of the fold, no matter which side you're on," Banks said.

"Yes," Maggie said. "Exactly that. It doesn't matter which side of the fold you're on. If you don't account for expansion when you create the fold, then time will always move slower on the other side."

"How is that possible?" Banks asked.

"Relativity," Maggie said. "The area on your side of the fold is in a fixed position, relative to you. The area on the other side of the fold is moving, relative to you. The movement might be tiny, the time difference might be undetectable at human time scales, but it's enough to create a cloud of particles that are oscillating across the fold. They essentially get stuck in the doorway, and when the doorway tries to close, the particles get ripped apart and decay into gamma radiation."

"And this doesn't happen with dragon portals because...?" Banks asked.

"Because whatever process the dragons use to create their portals accounts for expansion. Time on both sides of the portal moves at the same rate. No time differential, no oscillating particles caught in the fold when it closes, no boom."

"Do you think Hastings and Whitehall will be able to fix the problem with their machine?" Banks asked.

"Yes," Maggie said. "He already knows how to fix it."

"How do you know?"

"Math," Maggie said.

"Math? Really?" Banks asked.

"It's all math," Maggie said. "From the first Planck second after the Big Bang until the heat death of the universe, it's all math. Math is the language the universe is written in." Maggie turned around and pointed at the whiteboard. "Physics is just poetry if you know how to read it. It's all right here, in the equations. The color of the evening sky, the smell of the ocean breeze, the sound of the waves crashing on the beach, the gravity holding it all together, the ticking of quantized time moving from one moment to the next. It's math, all of it. And the math says that Hastings knows exactly what the problem with the fold machine is."

"How?"

"There were three events that night," Maggie said. "We assumed the destruction of Tindal Hall was caused by the first event, because it happened first, but that was before we knew that time across the fold was asynchronous. Tindal Hall was caused by the last event. The parking structure was the second event. The stadium was the first."

"You're saying the events moved backwards in time?"

"Yes. No. Sort of. Kind of. Fuck. It's math. I don't know how to translate. Give me a minute. Okay. The longer the distance you're folding, the larger the temporal differential. Um...fuck. English. The longer the fold, the slower time is moving on the other end. We know they tested sending an object to the moon. That was the space-fold that destroyed the stadium. The second hit was tighter, more focused. That was the parking deck explosion. That was an attempt to deliberately repeat the Science Annex explosion but target the blast. My guess would be a fold target in geostationary orbit. The third one was close by. A fold somewhere in the city. That was Hastings and Whitehall escaping before the booms. The reason the first event hit the stadium and not Tindal Hall was the difference in relative positions caused by the difference in relative time."

"Shouldn't the blast happen where the fold was located?"

"It did. Sort of. Kind of. If you account for the time differential, it did. Basically, what happened was the fold closed from one end, the Tindal Hall end, but then it got blown back open from the other end. From the moon, from orbit, from wherever Hastings and Whitehall went when they left Tindal Hall."

"And that first day?"

"The Science Annex?"

"Yes."

"From the other end. Wherever Whitehall went when he did the first fold."

"Where's that?"

"Well, that's obvious," Maggie said. "Wherever the third fold machine is."

"Third?" Banks asked.

"Yeah. We know there was one in the Science Annex, and we know there was one in Tindal Hall. There has to be one somewhere else," Maggie said.

"How do you know that?" Banks asked.

"Because if there wasn't, they never would have risked using the one in Tindal Hall for the moon test," Maggie said. "The one in Tindal Hall was disposable. In fact, they *needed* to get rid of it before we found it. Hastings knew he had too many eyes on him to try moving it, so he used the one in Tindal Hall to do a range check and see if the machines could actually reach their target. They used the moon for the range check because it's the same distance, and dropping a piece of junk on the moon doesn't risk damaging what they're after. Then, he sets up a feedback event deliberately to destroy any evidence that might be left in One Park Place. Then, he and Garrett fold across town. That's how I know he understands the problem with the machines. He couldn't have engineered the blast that destroyed One Park Place unless he understood what had caused the gamma bursts in the first place."

"So, he could go to the Olympus at any time," Banks said.

"No. Yes. Maybe. It depends." Maggie said.

"On what?"

"Understanding the problem and being able to use the problem to your advantage is not the same as being able to solve the problem, and he can't solve the problem without one very specific piece of information."

"What's that?"

"The value of the Hubble Constant," Maggie said.

"You said it was...um..."

"I said it's *about* seventy kilometers per second per megaparsec. He needs the exact value to a high degree of precision, and there is only one place I know of where that information exists."

"Where's that?" Banks asked.

"The G-Four Source Technology Repository in the Project G data archive," Maggie said.

"But he has that," Banks said.

"Yes, he does," Maggie said. "But G-Four was a low priority archive, because research on the fold technology was banned. I'm not even sure if all the data was translated. If it is, he'll be able to find what he's looking for relatively easily. If not, it could take him weeks to translate the information. And he's had the repository for months at this point. It's possible, even if the data wasn't translated when he got it, that he's had time to translate it."

"Right," Banks said. "So we need a team to go to the Olympus."

"I'm in," Maggie said.

"No," Banks said. "I appreciate the enthusiasm, but you haven't finished your training yet."

"You have to let me go," Maggie said.

"Why?"

Maggie turned and held out her hand, making a twisting motion. As she did, space and time folded in on itself and a doorway formed, leading right into the docking bay of the Olympus. She turned back to Banks.

"Because I'm the only one who can get a team there before Hastings," Maggie said.

Chapter Twenty-Nine

MAGGIE DROPPED DOWN ONTO her bed and let out a sigh as she stared at the spacesuit hanging in front of her. Twenty-four hours had passed since everything had clicked together. The problems with Hastings's fold machine, the likely connection to the Unitarium and the Ragusa crime family. During that time, there had been arguments about who would go and who would stay.

Maggie hadn't shouted. She hadn't raised her voice. She'd just stood there as Jia Li and Eurion both confirmed that they couldn't open a portal to Olympus. Jia Li had explained that, as far as she knew, only moon dragons and sun dragons could open portals that reached outside of the Earth's ambient magic field, and that none of the dragons of either breed would be likely to offer their help.

Banks had suggested sending Focus and Scatter up to the Olympus. Emilia had pointed out that neither of them had ever been there before. That at least one of the Olympus six needed to go with whatever team was sent, because only the Olympus six were familiar with the ship. Since Red Coat was dead, and the other members of the six were all back in their home countries, if Banks wanted to keep this a DMA operation, Emilia had to be on the team.

After that, Banks had suggested getting Focus and Scatter to carry a crew up to the Argo and using that to make the crossing. Emilia had pointed out that while the Argo was still technically space worthy, it had been docked with the international space station for more than two decades, and large parts of the station were built around it. No one was even sure if they could open the docking clamps to separate the two, or if the pivots on some of the modules would work to move them out of the way so Argo could move away from the station without knocking entire modules off it. She also pointed out that if they did, the ISS would lose its ability to maintain orbit, and more than half of its livable space, along with three quarters of its oxygen supply, batteries, and its escape capsules. Worse, it would take nearly a month to get the Argo to the Olympus, unless Focus and Scatter physically dragged the ship there, which would probably tear the ship apart.

Maggie was sure it was that last bit that convinced Banks that Maggie was the only way to get a team to the Olympus in time to do any good. The fact that she could just wave a hand and open a portal meant she was both the best and only option.

Banks had finally conceded that Maggie and Emilia would have to be part of the team, which left the question of who else to send. Jia Li and Eurion both wanted to go, but Emilia had vetoed that right away, pointing out that without the ability to use their natural forms, they wouldn't be nearly the kind of heavy hitters they were used to being. Varsha had volunteered, and Maggie had to bite her tongue. She didn't want Varsha to go, because the thought that something might happen to her terrified Maggie. She did bite her tongue, because it wasn't her decision to make. Varsha was an adult, and she'd been doing this for years. The fact that she and Maggie were in a relationship didn't give Maggie the right to take that decision away from her. Besides, she could imagine what it would feel like to watch Varsha go without her, and she couldn't do that to anyone she cared about.

That brought the count up to three. Ashley, Hannah, Nomi, Elisa, Naomi, Anika, Chance, Garnell, and Diego all volunteered. Elisa was rejected because most of her powers would be useless. She couldn't reshape earth if she was locked in a giant metal can. There wouldn't be any large pools of water to manipulate. Even the amount of wind she could summon would be limited by the close confines of the ship. She argued that she would still have fire and lightning to work with, but Emilia pointed out that throwing around fire and lightning inside of what was essentially a giant bomb that could possibly be powerful enough to destroy the whole solar system probably wasn't in anyone's best interest. Diego was rejected because his teleportation abilities overlapped with Maggie's. Garnell, Naomi, Anika, and Chance were all rejected for space. Emilia didn't want to take more than six people.

The final team ended up being Emilia, Maggie, Varsha, Ashley, Hannah, and Nomi. Emilia because she was a member of the Olympus Six, and the commander of the original Olympus expedition. Maggie because she was their ride. Varsha because speedsters were always useful. Ashley because the Unitarium had been known to employ magic users. Hannah because her telepathic abilities were a backup for comms if something happened to the comms in their suits, and Nomi because she had a suit of industry armor designed to work in vacuum.

A couple of quick calls, and the production of Maggie's superhero outfits had been bumped up the queue. While everyone else got ready, Maggie had gone back and spent the night in the training room with Diego, Elisa, Naomi, Chance, Anika, Jia Li, and Eurion, working her ass off to learn everything they could teach her in the few hours she had. She'd finally taken a break around breakfast time, grabbed a quick nap, and slept until her suits had been delivered, which left her where she was. Sitting on her bed, wearing her superhero costume, staring at the spacesuit she'd never expected to get to wear.

As a kid, she'd dreamed of this. Of going into space, exploring the Olympus, being like Emilia and the other astronauts who came before her. After the invasion, that dream had been lost, but now, here she was, getting ready to do what she always dreamed of.

She should be excited. She should be thrilled. Instead, she felt numb, and she didn't know why.

"You're sad," Maxine said as she jumped into her lap.

"Not really," Maggie said as she reached up and started petting Maxine. "I'm confused."

"Why?" Maxine asked. "Scratch behind my ear." Maggie smiled and vanished her glove so she could give Maxine a good and proper scritch.

"I don't know," Maggie said. "I'm going to space. Something I've always wanted to do. I'm going to see the Olympus, which I used to dream of."

"And you're going after the people who hurt Henry," Maxine said.

"That too," Maggie said.

"Are you sad because you're fighting with Sierra?"

"Yes," Maggie said. "But I don't know if that's why I feel like this."

"You should tell her to stop being mean," Maxine said. Maggie laughed.

"I wish it were that easy, sweetheart."

"It is. Just tell her."

"I don't know if she'll listen," Maggie said. Maxine huffed.

"Humans are stupid," she said, and jumped down. Before Maggie could do anything, Maxine walked through the wall and disappeared.

"Well, cats are rude," Maggie said to the empty room, before dropping back on the bed and staring up at the ceiling. She glanced at the clock. She still had a little bit of time before the habitat module they were taking with them would be ready. A bit of time to try to get her head on straight. She wasn't sure it was enough.

She closed her eyes, thinking maybe a little more sleep would help, but before she could drift off, there was a knock at the door. She reached out with her enhanced senses, and somehow, she wasn't surprised at all to find Sierra standing at the door, holding Maxine.

"Come in," Maggie said. She watched as Sierra reached out and opened the door, then drew her senses back to normal human levels, listening to Sierra walking into the room and stopping beside the bed.

"Hey," Sierra said.

"Hey," Maggie said.

"Can I sit down?"

"Yeah," Maggie said. She felt Sierra sit down, then fall back on the bed next to her. A moment later, Maxine jumped onto her chest, curled up into a little ball, and started making biscuits on Maggie's left breast. She reached up and scratched the top of Maxine's head. Sierra let out a deep sigh.

"I can't remember the last time we did this," Sierra said. "Just lay on the bed and talked."

"I can," Maggie said.

"When was it?" Sierra asked.

"The night before my first date with Sandra," Maggie said.

"Really?" Sierra asked. "It's been that long?"

"Yeah," Maggie said.

"I guess...I guess we haven't really been okay in a while, have we?"

"I'm not sure we were ever okay," Maggie said.

"What do you mean?" Sierra asked. "We used to be great."

"Did we?" Maggie asked. "Or did we just want to be so much that we pretended not to notice how not okay we were?"

"I...I don't know," Sierra said. "I know that from the moment I met you, the thought of spending time with you made me happy. I know that for a long time, you've been the most important person in my life. I know that the thought of living without you is killing me."

"You're not alone," Maggie said. "I felt all of those things. Maybe not from the moment we met. I honestly thought you were kind of annoying at first."

"Really?" Sierra asked. "How long did that last?"

"I don't know. A week, maybe. After that, I was pretty much head over heels in love with you."

"But not now?" Sierra asked.

"No, not now," Maggie said. "I still love you, but..."

"But not romantically," Sierra said.

"I'm not sure I would say that," Maggie said. "You were my first real love. I don't know if I'll ever get over you completely."

"I'm confused," Sierra said.

"I don't blame you," Maggie said. "It's confusing."

Sierra laughed and turned on her side. Maggie turned her head so she could see Sierra's face.

"I'm sorry," Sierra said.

"For what?" Maggie asked.

"For everything," Sierra said. "For bad timing. For dragging you to the Science Annex that day. For getting you involved in all of this. For not...I guess for not being brave enough to be the person you needed me to be when you still needed me."

"I still need you," Maggie said. "I don't think I'll ever stop needing you. You're my best friend."

"Still?" Sierra asked.

"Still," Maggie said.

"I can't believe you're going into outer space," Sierra said.

"I can't believe it either," Maggie said.

"You could have at least asked to take me along."

"Is this where I point out that you get airsick?" Maggie asked.

"You're not flying, though," Sierra said.

"Yeah, I'm not taking my chances on how you'd react if the gravity on the Olympus fails."

"Yeah, I don't think I'd come out of that looking pretty," Sierra said. She sighed and rolled onto her back. "I hate that I'm a coward."

"You're not!" Maggie said.

"Yes, I am," Sierra said. "I spent years being afraid of how I felt about you. I was so afraid of it I missed my chance to actually be with you. Now, you're going off to fight Garrett and Hastings and God only knows who else, and I'm too afraid to even ask if I can go with you."

"Well, the answer is no, you can't," Maggie said. "But I think you can find your courage."

"You think so?" Sierra asked.

"Yeah," Maggie said. "I did."

"You were never scared of anything," Sierra said.

"Do you even know me?" Maggie asked. "I'm scared all the time."

"No one would ever know it by the way you act," Sierra said.

"Blame my mom for that," Maggie said. "She always told me, if I wanted to be an astronaut, I had to be fearless. I wasn't, but I wanted to be an astronaut so bad, I got good at pretending."

"Is that what you're doing now?" Sierra asked. "Pretending?"

"I don't know," Maggie said. "I don't really feel anything. I haven't since yesterday afternoon."

"Why not?" Sierra asked. "Is it...?"

"Is it what?"

"Is it because of what you said?"

"What I...oh. You mean about Maggie."

"Yeah," Sierra said.

Maggie looked up at the ceiling, turning the thought over in her head. The idea that Maggie Bennett, the real Maggie Bennett, was dead, and she was just a copy. Something created by accident. Something that had all of Maggie's memories but wasn't really her.

"I don't believe it," Sierra said.

"What?" Maggie asked.

"That you're not her," Sierra said. "I don't believe it."

"I can show you the math."

"I'm sure you can, but math has always been your blind spot, Mags. You believe it always tells the truth."

"It does."

"Within its limits," Sierra said. "Math is a language, and like any language, there are some nuances that it can't express. Do you know how many concepts there are that you can't express in English without borrowing words from other languages?"

"Not really. I know there are some, but I never tried to count."

"And it never even occurred to you that math is the same," Sierra said. "Math is a wonderful language for describing the physical, the statistical, the systematic. It allows you to say things about science and engineering that can't be said in any other language. It's a gift for problem solving, but it doesn't do well at all when dealing with metaphysics, with philosophy, with emotions or spirituality."

"Well, then, enlighten me," Maggie said. "Explain exactly how math is letting me down."

"Because math has no words for a distinction without a difference," Sierra said. "You might be the version of Maggie that was built by the quantum imager, but in the end, that doesn't matter. The fields were entangled, identical, and up until the moment the machine was turned off, they functioned as one unit. It doesn't matter which one collapsed when the quantum imager shut down, because the waves were in superposition, and two identical waves in superposition is really one wave of twice the magnitude. When you were in the machine, there weren't two Maggies. There was just one Maggie who was twice as big, and when the machine cut off, you went back to being regular sized Maggie."

"I definitely did not go back to being regular sized Maggie," Maggie said.

"What?"

"I actually have an ass now," Maggie said. "OG Maggie's ass was flat as a board."

Sierra laughed and shook her head.

"Leave it to you to focus on that," Sierra said.

"What? A girl can have ambitions," Maggie said.

"I'm not sure 'having an ass shaped like a peach' counts as an ambition."

"Hey, I told you that in confidence!"

"You told me that because we were both drunk off our asses," Sierra said. "Though, I will admit, you had a shorter distance to go."

"Bitch," Maggie said.

"The truth hurts," Sierra said.

Before Maggie could respond, there was a knock on the door.

"Come in," Maggie said. The door opened and Varsha walked in.

"Hey," Varsha said.

Maggie sat up, earning a small grumble of protest from Maxine before she jumped down and curled up on one of the pillows. Sierra sat up too.

"Is it time?" Maggie asked.

"Almost," Varsha said. "I just wanted to make sure you were okay."

"I will be," Maggie said.

"I'll let you two have a minute," Sierra said. "Maxine."

"What?" Maxine grumbled.

"Time to go," Sierra said.

Maxine stood up and marched huffily over to Sierra, who scooped her up before standing and facing Varsha.

"You take care of her for me," Sierra said.

"I will," Varsha said. "You have my word."

"Good," Sierra said. She turned back to Maggie. "And you. Don't be stupid out there."

"I won't."

Sierra nodded and headed for the door. Varsha waited until it was closed, then turned back to Maggie.

"You okay?"

"I don't know," Maggie said. "But I think I might be getting there."

"That's good to hear," Varsha said.

Maggie stood up and took a step towards the spacesuit.

"Show me how to put this thing on."

Chapter Thirty

"WHAT ARE YOU SMILING about?" Varsha asked.

"Just thinking about when we get back to Earth," Maggie said.

Since the team didn't know how long they would be waiting for Hastings and his people to show up, they had brought along a prototype Martian habitat module. It was about the size of an RV, complete with the slide out sections, designed to house eight people on Mars for eighteen months. The DMA had borrowed it from NASA, and Emilia had just picked it up and carried it through the fold once Maggie had opened it. They were on day four, and Maggie and Varsha were curled up on Maggie's bunk while Emilia and Nomi were on watch.

"Oh?" Varsha said. "And what are you looking forward to when we get back?"

Maggie gave Varsha a lopsided grin.

"Lots of things," Maggie said. "But I was smiling because I realized I get to tell Sierra she's wrong."

"Wrong about what?" Varsha asked.

"In our last conversation, she was talking about how math didn't have a way to express the concept of a distinction without a difference. I just realized it does."

"Oh?"

"Yeah. Point nine bar equals one," Maggie said.

"I'm not familiar with that one," Varsha said.

"I'm not surprised," Maggie said. "This is what I get for dating a college dropout."

Varsha poked Maggie in the ribs, making her yelp and try to pull away.

"I may be a dropout, but I will trounce your physicist ass in statistics any day of the week."

"I'll take that bet," Maggie said. "I'll probably lose, but I'll take it."

"Damn right you'll lose. Now, tell me."

"Okay, so point nine bar is another way of saying zero point nine repeating. Zero point nine followed by nine repeating an infinite number of times. And mathematically, it's exactly equal to one, which drives a lot of people nuts, because they think it should be less than one, or approximately one, but there's a whole proof that it is exactly equal to one. So, one and zero point nine bar are the same. A distinction without a difference. And Sierra was wrong."

"You really get a kick out of that last bit, don't you?" Varsha asked.

"I can't help it. I'm an academic. We're all petty little shits. Every single one of us love to tell our colleagues how wrong they are."

Varsha laughed and leaned in, kissing Maggie on the cheek.

"Can I tell you a secret?" Varsha asked.

"Of course," Maggie said.

"The math zombie thing...very sexy."

"Really?"

"Really," Varsha said. "The first time you did it, I wanted to throw you on the table and have my way with you right there in the briefing room."

"Well, that might have been a bit awkward," Maggie said.

"Only because I'd have had to fight off Elisa," Varsha said.

"Elisa? But her and Nomi..."

"Yeah. Elisa's totally head over heels for Nomi, but she's got a weak spot for smart girls. She was practically drooling."

"Next you'll tell me Nomi was into it too," Maggie said.

"Nah. Nomi's a morosexual. She likes 'em beefy and dumb."

Maggie snorted. "Did you just call Elisa dumb?"

"Yeah," Varsha said. "She's not, really. She's actually pretty smart when she stops to think. It's just, her first instinct is always to hit it with a rock. Which isn't a bad instinct to have in this line of work, but it can be frustrating sometimes."

"I can imagine," Maggie said.

"So..."

"Yes?"

"What was a distinction without a difference?" Varsha asked.

"Oh," Maggie said. "She um...she asked me about what I said, about not being Maggie Bennett. Or at least, not being the original Maggie Bennet. She said that it was a distinction without a difference. That when the machine created the duplicate quantum field, that there weren't two separate Maggie's, there was just twice as much of the first Maggie. That since we were both Maggie, it didn't matter which one survived, just that one of us did."

"Well, that is something Sierra and I can agree on, but I'll let you in on a secret."

"What's that?"

"I don't care if you're the original."

"You don't?" Maggie asked.

"No," Varsha said. "You're the person I met in your apartment.

You're the one I shared kulfi with. You're the one I spent those nights talking to. You're the one who picked me over that cape chaser that night in Cape Town. You're the one who picked me over Sierra. So, original, or new and improved, I don't care. I just know I'm really glad I found you."

"I admit, I'm pretty glad you found me too," Maggie said.

"I know you two are still in the honeymoon phase, but I swear to God, if you start making out, I will throw my shoes at you," Ashley called from the couch where she was sitting about ten feet away.

Varsha sat up and looked at Ashley.

"Don't be a hater, Ashley," Varsha said.

"I'm not hating," Ashley said. "I'm trying to do Sudoku, but you two are being all tooth rottenly sweet in front of my puzzle."

"Will all of you shut the fuck up and let me sleep?" Hannah said.

Varsha lay back down next to Maggie, resting her head on Maggie's shoulder.

"Well, someone needs to get laid," Varsha said. "Ashley, why don't you take care of that?"

"Fuck off," Ashley said, glaring at Varsha.

"I'd love to, if I could get some privacy," Varsha said.

"Enough," Maggie said. She reached up and grabbed the privacy screen and pulled it closed. She hadn't done it before because the space inside it was designed for one person, and as much as she liked Varsha, it got uncomfortably close inside the sleeping compartment with the screen closed. Honestly, it got uncomfortably close inside without Varsha, but that was less of an issue, because without Varsha, she didn't really feel the need for privacy so much.

"Sorry," Varsha whispered.

"It's okay," Maggie said. "We're all getting on each other's nerves a bit."

"Even me?" Varsha asked.

"No," Maggie said. "Well, except when you tease Ashley about Hannah. You know that's just going to make things awkward."

"I know, but I'm honestly getting sick of them dancing around each other. They're either going to fuck each other or kill each other, and I wish they'd pick which one and get on with it."

"I get it," Maggie said. "But whatever is holding Ashley back, it seems like it's serious."

"I figured," Varsha said. "I'm just tired of the drama. I really like Eurion, but every time she comes to the Shiro, Hannah gets her back up.

Same if they run into each other at Cape Town. It's a bit too close to home."

"What do you mean?"

"I have two older sisters. Meera is the oldest. Sita is next. Sita had a huge crush on a boy named Kavish, but our parents arranged a marriage between Meera and Kavish. Sita pouted a bit, but got over it, but for years, any time Sita said so much as a word to Kavish, there was drama. It made their visits unbearable until Sita got married."

"Yikes," Maggie said. "Why did your parents do that?"

"They thought it was a good match," Varsha said. "They didn't know about Sita's crush. Neither did Kavish."

"Oh," Maggie said. "Is Kavish the dick brother-in-law that used to give you a hard time about being gay?"

"The one and same," Varsha said. "Sita dodged a bullet. Her husband Rajiv is one of the sweetest people I've ever met."

"You mentioned you have a brother," Maggie said.

"Vimal," Varsha said. "The spoiled little baby of the family. He's a bit of a brat, but in an endearing way. He was the first person in the family to tell me it was okay that I was gay."

"Sounds like a great guy," Maggie said.

"You could meet him if you like," Varsha said.

"Introducing me to the family already?" Maggie asked.

"Too soon?" Varsha asked.

"No," Maggie said. "I was going to ask if you wanted to go with me to Atlanta to meet my grandparents."

"I'd love to," Varsha said. "When did you—"

The world slowed down as Maggie was knocked out of her body by a ripple in the fabric of spacetime. She'd thought after it had happened with Jia Li's dragon portal that she'd be able to ride out the ripples if she ever felt them again. She'd been able to create her own portals without issue. But this was different. There was more power involved. The fold wasn't an elegant twisting of the fabric of spacetime; it was more like rough hands snatching carelessly and bunching the sides together. A coarse, crude, brute force approach.

Maggie had to fight back into her body, and even once time returned to normal, she could feel the ripples around her.

"What is it?" Varsha asked.

"They're here," Maggie said. "Hastings and his people are on the Olympus."

* * * *

"You're sure?" Emilia asked over comms as Maggie and Varsha waited for Hannah and Ashley to finish suiting up.

"I'm sure," Maggie said. "It felt just like when Ice Dragon opened her portal, only...I don't know. Less elegant. More of a brute force approach."

"Is the portal still open?" Emilia asked.

"No," Maggie said. "But it was open for nearly a minute. That's enough time to get a lot of people through."

"Yeah," Emilia said. "Industry and I are headed your way. Once we're there, all of us will make for the Artifact as a group."

"Be careful," Maggie said. "I don't think they're in the hanger, but they're close. I don't think I would have felt the fold otherwise."

"Understood," Emilia said. "We'll be careful. Airheart out."

"Aether out."

Maggie glanced over to see Ashley putting on her helmet. Hannah and Varsha both already had theirs on, so Maggie picked up her own and pulled it over her head. She took a second to fasten the helmet to the neck seal, then pressed the button on her wrist console to start the air flow. The moment she did, she felt a cool breeze hit her face. A built-in option she'd found helped immensely with the claustrophobic nature of the suit.

She checked to see that Ashley had her helmet on, then stepped into the airlock and waited as Varsha, Ashley, and Hannah piled in behind her. Hannah closed the inner door, and Maggie cycled the airlock, pumping the air they'd brought with them back into tanks, then filling the lock with air from the Olympus. The air outside was theoretically breathable, but even after the initial Olympus mission samples were tested and found clean, Banks had insisted on full precautions.

Maggie looked around, using her expanded senses to search as much of the docking bay as she could, and not finding anyone. Sure that they weren't in immediate danger, she led the way down the steps from the habitat module to the docking bay floor, and then towards the hatch that accessed the rest of the ship.

Once there, they waited for Emilia and Nomi to get back. Something which took a lot longer than Maggie would have liked. She was worried Hastings would beat them to the Artifact. That would be catastrophic. The Olympus Six had been running from the Artifact when it did to them whatever it was it did. Emilia had been at the back of the line, making her the closest person to the Artifact. She'd ended up being the strongest, and the power level of the Olympus Six lined up perfectly with their distance from the Artifact when it activated. If Hastings knew that, and he would have to, then he and anyone who he brought with him could end up more powerful than Emilia just by standing next to the Artifact when it activated. Or, God forbid, touching it.

The hatch to the hanger bay finally opened, and Emilia and Nomi slipped inside. Maggie breathed a sigh of relief as soon as she saw them.

"Any sign of them?" Maggie asked.

"No," Emilia said. "You ready for this?"

"Yeah," Maggie said, before stepping into the Aether.

* * * *

In the four days they had been on the Olympus, they had mostly patrolled the area between the hanger bay and the Artifact chamber. Well, that's what official reports called it. Emilia was pretty much convinced the Artifact was the engine core. She was also convinced there were a number of smaller Artifacts. One in each of the shuttles on the ship. She believed that the shuttle that blew up over Tunguska and triggered the climb in metahuman manifestations had spread millions of tiny little pieces of one of the smaller Artifacts across the planet, and that they bathed the entire planet in a low level version of the energy which had given the Olympus Six their powers. Not strong enough to actually trigger power development, but strong enough to make power development much more likely.

It was as good a theory as any, and probably more informed than most, but it had left Maggie frustrated. She'd wanted to learn the entire ship, but Emilia had been so focused on where she thought the danger lay, she hadn't let them stray too far from it.

Now, Maggie had the freedom to roam. Time was at a standstill while she was in the Aether. She could scout as much as she needed too. She slipped through the hatch, moving the same way she had the day she had worked with Stutter in Planck scale time. She started with the familiar route from the hanger to the Artifact chamber, checking the side tunnels, passing though doors like they weren't there to check chambers along the way. She moved quickly and efficiently, or at least, it felt that way. Even though she could literally feel the ticking of the quantized universe, it was strangely hard to judge the passage of time when the world stood completely still. Quick and efficient or not, once she'd finished searching the routes she knew through the ship, she went back to the hanger bay hatch and started a methodical search of that part of the ship, stretching her senses as far as they would go as she walked the corridors, until finally, she found them.

Thirteen of them. Professor Hastings, Garrett, and Elizabeth Fairchild she recognized immediately. Hastings was a short man, balding on top, with curly gray hair around the sides of his head, and a little bit of a pot belly. He was dressed in jeans and a long sleeve denim button up, with a wide brown leather belt and a pair of Dickey's work boots. It was something of a uniform for him. Enough that students wondered if he owned more than one set of casual clothes and two suits. Garrett looked like himself, and Maggie was filled with a burning urge to smack him in the face with her cane. Nothing new. She'd felt that way since the day she met him. Fairchild was there. A young blonde that might have been attractive, if she didn't constantly look like she wanted to hold her nose lest she smell poor people. It wasn't any wonder that these three had ended up together. A group of entitled people who had risen beyond their merits and would do anything to hold on to places they didn't deserve.

Maggie turned away from them to look at what she could only assume were members of the Unitarium. There were three Japanese men in black suits and thin ties. Probably Yakuza, based on the briefing. A Chinese man. Likely a member of the Triad. Three men who, if pressed, Maggie would guess were Italian. All smartly dressed in expensive suits. A man in jeans and a t-shirt with Cyrillic tattoos down his arm that pretty much had to be Bratva. A big guy with a red face and a crooked nose that was probably part of the Irish mob. The last man was a Latino man. He was harder to place. From the briefing, Maggie knew the Unitarium had members pulled from the Mexican cartels and Latino gangs across several major US cities, but she was a rich white girl from Florida. She didn't know enough to distinguish the two.

She left the group and looked around the area, checking for any stragglers or scouts she might have missed. If even one member of the Unitarium got to the Artifact, it would be a disaster. She searched almost a quarter mile in every direction and found their arrival site. There was a large radio with a power pack, clearly meant to call for their retrieval. She wanted to go ahead and wreck it, but she had promised Emilia she wouldn't drop back into real time on her scouting trip.

She went back to the group of Unitarium gangsters, and examined them with her expanded senses, finding every weapon they had and cataloging them. She saved Hastings, Garrett, and Fairchild for last.

Hastings had what looked like an old-fashioned police revolver in one pocket. Fairchild was unarmed. Then Maggie came to Garrett. She let her senses check him over, assuring herself that he was unarmed, but as she did, something happened. Garrett stayed perfectly still, because it was Planck time, so of course he did, but he also turned his head in confusion, looking right at her. He didn't seem to see her, but there was this weird look of two Garretts, superimposed over each other, that made Maggie jump away, and wish herself back to the hanger.

She popped back into real time in the exact spot she left. Even though the search had felt like it had taken hours for her, it was barely a fraction of a second for the rest of them, and they all stood there, looking at her as if waiting for her to disappear.

She turned to Emilia.

"We have a problem."

Chapter Thirty-One

"I DO NOT LIKE the sound of that," Emilia said.

"I didn't like the reality of it," Maggie said. "There are thirteen of them. Hastings, Whitehall, Fairchild, three Yakuza, three Mafia, a Triad, a Bratva, an Irish mobster, and a Latino guy. Maybe the cartels, maybe the gangs. Hard to tell."

"Thirteen is a lot, but nothing we can't handle easily," Emilia said.

"Normally, I'd agree, but while I was checking them over in Planck time, Garrett Whitehall turned his head and looked at me."

"What?" Emilia asked.

"He turned his head and looked right at me. It was like there were two of him. One stayed perfectly still, but the other turned and looked right at me. It was like one was superimposed over the other. When it happened, I teleported the fuck out of there, and came back here, because chances are, they know we're here, and they know we're coming."

"Well, that's just fucking great," Emilia said. She took a breath, then shrugged. "We knew there might be metas. Let's just hope Whitehall is the only one."

Maggie had a feeling Emilia didn't expect that to be the case any more than she did.

"They're two decks up. Looks like they came in through a cargo bay close to the airlock where the Argo docked," Maggie said.

"Makes sense," Emilia said. "It's more visible than the hanger door. Easier to spot from the outside."

"Easier to plot a course to," Maggie said.

"Something doesn't make sense, though," Nomi said. "We know that the Unitarium has connections to a lot of the various branches of organized crime. The ones who came after my family were mostly Yakuza. The ones causing problems in Pontian and Sun City come from the Ragusa family. Triad, Irish mob, Bratva, the cartels, and street gangs. It makes sense to send a rep from each of the feeder organizations, but why three Yakuza, and why three Ragusa?"

"That's a good question," Ashley said. "Maybe...maybe two of the Yakuza and two of the Ragusa are already metas. They're here to protect the other six until they get their powers, or blast through any resistance."

"I hate that idea," Varsha said. "I agree with it, but I still hate it."

"It would make sense," Emilia said.

"Maybe Airheart and I should take a run at them," Maggie said. "See what they've got."

"Might be a good idea," Emilia said. "Aether and I are the toughest of the group."

"I also hate that idea," Varsha said. "Unfortunately, I can't argue with it."

"Then it's settled," Emilia said. "Aether and I will make a run at the group and test their defenses. Delta V and Industry will hold back as a reserve. Nexus will hold back and run the telepathic link. Cinderella will hold back unless there is magic in play."

Everyone nodded, and Maggie felt the faint touch of Nexus's mind as she set up the telepathic link. From there on out, it would be their only means of communication, so the radios in their suits couldn't give them away.

"Let's go," Emilia said.

* * * *

Emilia's idea of making a run at the group was simple. They placed themselves in the middle of a corridor and waited for the Unitarium group to come around the corner. Honestly, it was Maggie's kind of plan. Simple, elegant, and probably a disaster waiting to happen.

Maggie tracked the approaching goons with her extended senses. She suspected Emilia was tracking them with her super hearing as well. She kept telling herself not to worry, that it would be fine. It didn't help much, so she switched tactics.

When she and Sierra were raiding in Black Sky, Maggie would always just picture the fight in her head while everyone prepped for the boss pull. Everyone else's avatars would be sitting and eating, or drinking buff potions, or using repair bots to fix broken gear, but Maggie would just sit there, picturing the moment Sierra would start the fight. She'd run through her assigned role for the battle. Sometimes that would be doing as much damage as possible. Sometimes it would mean rounding up smaller monsters and leading them away from the rest of the party. Sometimes it would be laying traps and other crowd control measures. It changed from battle to battle. Each fight was a dance, and in order to win, you just had to learn the steps.

She did the same thing now, holding the picture of the Unitarium goons in her head, and picturing different scenarios in her head. It was harder than it was in the game because there was no script for the fight.

She couldn't go on YouTube and watch the fight ahead of time. Instead, she had to run different possibilities in her head, like running a differential equation with different starting parameters.

Surprisingly, it helped. Even without knowing the other side's power sets, it gave her something to focus on other than just standing there and worrying. In fact, it was so effective, she almost didn't notice when the first of the Unitarium goons rounded the corner.

One of the Yakuza appeared first, with one of the Ragusa coming up beside him a moment later. They glanced and each other and smiled as they turned back towards Maggie and Emilia. There was no delay, no back and forth. Maggie felt a sudden shift in the flow of energy in the space that reminded her of the way it felt when Ashley used her powers and knew what was coming. Sure enough, the Ragusa raised his hands, and a glowing pentacle appeared in front of him, etched with runes. Maggie nicknamed him Magic Guy in her head. The Yakuza started to glow, a bit like a lightbulb on a dimmer switch turned down low. His physical body disappeared into the glowing form that was left behind, and Maggie decided to call him Glow Stick.

"Magic," Maggie said.

"I see it," Emilia said.

Magic Guy slapped his palm against the pentagram, sending it racing forward, shooting right at Maggie, while Glow Stick thrust his hands out, and shot a beam of plasma at Emilia. It was the wrong choice in both cases. Maggie just stepped into the Aether and moved to the side, while the spell or sigil or whatever it was passed through the spot where she used to be. Emilia, on the other hand, just stood there, letting the plasma hit her and wash over her. Once it was gone, Emilia stood there looking smug, neither her nor her spacesuit looking any worse for wear.

Maggie shot forward, dropping out of the Aether right in front of Magic Guy, and drove a palm strike into his temple. He dropped like a sack of flour. Glow Stick started to turn towards her, but she popped back into the Aether, and reappeared next to Emilia just as another blast of plasma washed over her.

"Any thoughts on how to handle Glow Stick?" she asked.

"Glow Stick, huh? I like it. And no, not off the top of my head."

"Then let's get out of here," Maggie said. Emilia nodded, and took off at superspeed, while Maggie dropped into the Aether and followed. They stopped a few corridors ahead, where the rest of the team was waiting. Maggie dropped out of the Aether as Emilia came to a stop.

"So, they have one magic user and one energy projector who can transform into an energy state," Emilia said.

"I could take a shot at a telepathic assault on the energy projector," Hannah said.

"Okay," Emilia said. "When the time comes, we'll get Delta V to deliver you into range, but right now, we need to probe again. We only got a look at two of the metas' power sets. Aether put the magic user down, but I'm not sure how long that will last."

"Take a run from behind?" Maggie asked.

"Can you find a route?" Emilia asked.

"Yeah," Maggie said. She dropped back into the Aether for a moment and expanded her senses as far as she could and found the Unitarium group. They were a bit further into the corridor where she and Emilia had fought them. Glow Stick was trying to rouse Magic Guy. Maggie worried for a moment that she'd hit him too hard and killed him, but she felt his heartbeat and relaxed, then shifted her focus to finding a set of corridors that would put them behind the Unitarium group. She also looked in the other direction, for a rendezvous point closer to the Artifact chamber. Once she had both firmly fixed in her head, she dropped back out of the Aether.

"Got it," Maggie said. "A way around them, and a new rendezvous." She gave Varsha, Nomi, Hannah, and Ashley directions to the rendezvous, then turned to Emilia.

"Try to keep up," she said, then slowed time down as much as possible without dropping out of her body and took off at a run. She wasn't sure how fast she was going. She knew she'd clocked in at twenty times faster than her baseline when she'd been training with Stutter, but that was almost a week earlier, and she'd been practicing ever since. However fast it was, Emilia kept pace without breaking a sweat. The two of them moved down the corridors, circling around the Unitarium group, and came up behind them, dropping out of super speed maybe ten yards back.

"Hey, assholes!" Emilia said.

The whole group turned, and for a moment, Maggie saw Garrett, Hastings, and Fairchild before her attention was drawn to the two at the back of the group. Another Yakuza member, and another member of the Ragusa family. The guy from the Ragusa family raised a hand and a bunch of small metal disks floated up and rushed towards them, while the Yakuza just charged forward. Maggie stepped into the Aether, bypassing the disks, and reappearing in front of the Yakuza. She drove a palm strike into his solar plexus. It should have laid him out, but instead, she felt the bones in her arm give with a sickening crunch.

She dropped back into the Aether just as the pain hit, cutting it short, and reappeared behind him, arm whole again, only this time, when she squeezed that place inside her that put her body together, she squeezed harder than normal. Much harder. When her body formed, she could feel the strength in it, the power and resilience. She lashed out and drove a knife hand strike into his spine, just below the shoulder blades. The blow would have snapped the spine of a normal person, but the Yakuza just grunted and spun around.

"Got a brick," Maggie said as she dodged a fist thrown at her face.

"Roger that," Emilia said. "We'll call these two Tough Guy and Discus."

Before Maggie could answer, Tough Guy tried to drive a fist through her stomach. Maggie saw it coming and squeezed reality just a little harder. Tough Guy's fist rang like a bell when it hit her. He staggered back, and took a swing at her head, so she teleported behind him and shoved him into Discus. Discus screamed at the impact and dropped to the ground, holding a visibly dislocated shoulder. Tough Guy looked down at Discus, then turned towards Maggie, fury written on his face, but Maggie caught movement through her expanded senses. The Latino man raised his hands, holding them like a kid playing cowboy, index and middle finger pointed forward, ring and pinky tucked back, thumb pointed up. He pointed his hands at Emilia, and they started to glow, then each one shot a burst of light at her, his hands rocking up slightly as if from recoil before he aimed and fired again.

The bolts slammed into Emilia, and the spacesuit that had so easily shrugged off the plasma blasts from Glow Stick shredded under Finger Guns' assault. Emilia grunted each time she was hit. Maggie, a little panicked, turned and kicked Finger Guns in the side. The corridor filled with the sound of snapping bone as he screamed, but Maggie ignored it, and teleported to Emilia's side.

"You okay?" Maggie asked.

"Fine," Emilia said. "Just pissed."

Maggie felt a small pull from the direction of the Unitarium goons, one she'd felt before the day she'd trained with Stutter. She felt time start to slow down and turned towards the source. Bratva was a time stall speedster.

Maggie reached out and grabbed Emilia, letting her expanded sense take in every detail. She forced herself not to panic the way she did the night SCSU had been destroyed. She was calm, she was cool, and she was collected as she dragged Emilia into the Aether with her. She rushed through the ship to the new rendezvous point and dropped out of the Aether with Emilia standing beside her. Varsha, Hannah, Ashley, and Nomi jumped a little at Maggie and Emilia's sudden appearance. Nomi looked at Emilia's shredded suit and turned to Maggie.

"What happened?"

"Latino guy is a meta. Some sort of energy projector that got past her suit's defenses. I think they're all metas. We got a read on four more, though." She turned to Hannah and sent mental images as she walked through the list. "Yakuza one is the energy projector. Call him Glow Stick. Yakuza two is a brick. Call him Tough Guy. Ragusa one is a magic user. Call him Magic Guy. Ragusa two is a telekinetic. Uses sharpened metal disks. Call him Discus. Bratva is a time stall speedster. Call him Fast Russian. Latino guy is another energy projector. Call him Finger Guns."

"Great," Nomi said.

Ashley stepped forward and waved her hands, muttering something under her breath as she did so, and Emilia's suit quickly knitted itself back together.

"You'll still want to replace the suit when we get home, but this will hold for now," Ashley said.

"Thanks," Emilia said. She turned to Maggie. "I thought you couldn't take people through a teleport."

"It's not that I couldn't," Maggie said. "It's just, the one time I did take something living through the teleport with me, I turned an ordinary kitten into a kitten with human level intelligence, the ability to speak English, and the ability to walk through walls."

Emilia's eyes got big.

"I was more careful this time," Maggie said. "You should be fine, but let me know if you need a saucer of milk."

"That's not funny," Emilia said.

"It's a little funny," Ashley said.

Emilia glared.

"Do we need to move?" Varsha asked.

Maggie opened her senses up, reaching out towards the Unitarium group. They'd moved into a compartment off the corridor, and had Discus, Magic Guy, and Finger Guns laid out on the floor, while Glow Stick and Fast Russian covered the door. The Triad member was kneeing down next to them, writing Chinese characters in the air in fire using the tip of his finger. As he worked, Maggie could feel Finger Guns' ribs knitting back together. She pushed the image through the telepathic link.

"Ashley, does that look like magic to you?" she asked.

"Yeah. Fire mage?" Ashley asked.

"Not terribly original, but after Magic Guy and Finger Guns, I don't have a lot of room to talk," Maggie said.

"Maybe we should hit them while they're holed up in that compartment," Nomi said. "Only one way in or out. We could toss in a couple of flashbangs, then rush them."

"I'm liking it, but without knowing all of their powers, I'm not ready to risk it," Emilia said. "Tough Guy might not be affected by the flash bangs, and God knows what the last three are packing."

"And Garrett," Maggie said. "We still haven't seen his power set."

"I'm not sure if I'm more, or less worried about him," Emilia said. "Without training, who knows if he can control his powers."

"He probably has training," Maggie said.

"What?" Emilia asked.

"Look, Garrett is a bottle washer. I've said that before, and I'll say it again, but it isn't from a lack of intelligence or due to an inability to learn. He picks up information and skills fast enough. The issue he has is an inability to extrapolate and generalize."

"What do you mean?" Nomi asked.

"I mean, he only knows what he's been taught or read in a book or something. Figuring things out for himself isn't his strong suit. Like, say he wasn't familiar with the concept of gravity. If you showed him a rock dropping, he wouldn't assume that everything would drop if you let go of it. He wouldn't even assume that all rocks would drop of you let go of them. He would only assume that that particular rock would drop if you let go of it. At least until you'd demonstrated with a lot more objects. It's just the way his brain works. He can't ever seem to make that jump from the specific case to the general case. That's why I wasn't worried about him having powers when we talked to Banks after SCSU. Alone, on his own, it would take him months or maybe even years to figure out how to use them, but if he's been working with the Unitarium, and they've been training him, that's a whole different story."

"So you're saying he could be a real threat?" Emilia asked.

"Yeah," Maggie said. "I hate to admit it. I hate to admit the little fucker is competent enough to tie his shoes, but yeah. I think we have to consider him at least as dangerous as the other metas. Maybe more so if he figures out who I am because he fucking hates me."

"Great," Emilia said.

"I'm not sure we can afford to wait and find out what all of their power sets are," Nomi said. "We have to stop them before they reach the Artifact, and there's only so much space between where they are and the Artifact chamber."

"I don't like going in without intel," Emilia said.

"I think Nomi's right," Ashley said. "They have a healer with them, which means we can't just disable them in ones or twos. We're either going to have to hit them all at once, or...well, there's the other option."

Maggie looked around the group, watching all their faces harden.

"I don't want to kill anyone today," Varsha said.

"Neither do I," Nomi said.

"I'm not thrilled with the idea either," Emilia said. "But one of the problems with having the kind of power I do is what happens to the people I use it on. Unless they have a lot of power of their own, it doesn't end well for them. That's why they hold people like me back on the Tier Three teams."

"No one wants to kill them, but we may not have a choice." Ashley said. "As long as they have a healer, we can't whittle them down. As long as they have a speedster, they can match one of our main advantages. We don't have any way to contain anyone we disable—"

"What if we did?" Maggie asked.

"What do you mean?" Ashley said, and Maggie smiled.

"Let's send them to Godzilla's room," Maggie said.

Ashley smiled. "That might just work."

Emilia looked back and forth between them like they'd both lost their minds.

"One of you want to explain what the fuck you're talking about?" she asked.

"Yeah," Maggie said. "Listen up. This is what we're going to do."

Chapter Thirty-Two

FAST RUSSIAN HAD TO go first. There was never any question about that. Speedsters were, hands down, the most dangerous type of meta in existence because they could kill you before you had a chance to realize you were in danger. But there were speedsters, and then there were speedsters.

Fast Russian was what was commonly called a Time Stall Speedster. His power allowed him to speed up time in a small bubble around himself, so to everyone outside the bubble, it looked like he was moving really, really fast, which of course made him really, really dangerous.

On the other hand, Varsha and Emilia were true speedsters, which meant they could *actually* move really, really fast. That carried with it certain benefits. First, their minds had to be able to process information fast enough to control bodies that could move that fast. Secondly, their bodies had to be tough enough to endure the stresses that being a speedster put on them, which often meant enduring hundreds of Gs of acceleration. Third, their metabolisms had to keep up with all of that, which meant that they healed insanely fast.

A fight between a Time Stall and a True Speedster, if the two were anywhere close to the same speed range, was a foregone conclusion. A fight between two true speedsters and a time stall was no fight at all.

Glow Stick was chosen for their second target, because once he was in his energy state, he'd be much, much harder to deal with. It was possible that Hannah would be able to contain him with her telekinesis, but there was no guarantee of that, so Emilia made the decision to grab him on the first run.

Once the targets were selected, Maggie waited and watched through her expanded senses as the Unitarium moved out of their hidey hole and started heading towards the Artifact again. As soon as they did, she gave Varsha and Emilia a small nod and raised her hand, opening a portal to Godzilla's guest room, also known as Explosive Ordinance Disposal Facility Nine. The facility where Maggie had first trained carrying objects through the teleport with her just in case they exploded. The same facility that was designed to shrug off a fifty-megaton nuke. The same facility that was currently filled with sleeping gas and pumped down to an atmospheric pressure two hundred millibars below the Olympus, so any airflow through the fold would be from the ship to the EOD facility, thanks to a quick call to the DMA office that controlled the facility.

At her nod, Varsha and Emilia ran, shooting through the corridors at speeds that would reduce a normal human to something resembling chunky tomato sauce before very briefly coming to a stop next to Glow Stick and Fast Russian. Varsha grabbed Glow Stick, and Emilia grabbed Fast Russian, and they shot back to where Maggie's portal was waiting and tossed them through.

As soon as they were through, Maggie closed the portal, locking them away on Earth and letting the sleeping gas do its job.

Maggie watched as the Unitarium reacted to the sudden disappearance of two of their members. Magic Guy and Fire Mage both readied spells. Finger Guns lit up his fingers. Tough Guy took a fighting stance. Discus floated a small cloud of his metal disks. Irish pulled out a pair of small sticks, which grew into a pair of blackwood staves, each about thirty inches long.

Hastings and Fairchild both looked ready to panic, while Garrett just looked bored.

"You said you could handle anything we ran into," Hastings said.

"Shut up, old man," Magic Guy said. "If you idiots hadn't turned this into a spectacle, they never would have known we were here."

"They're arguing over whose fault this is," Maggie said, which made everyone else smile. Maggie didn't. She didn't like how calm Garrett was at all. Usually when things weren't going his way, he was the one who threw a fit.

"Magic Guy and Fire Mage next?" Emilia asked.

"Sounds good," Varsha said. "Give us the go, then count to two."

"Okay," Maggie said. "Three, two, one, then go."

"Got it," Emilia said.

"Three. Two. One. Go!" Maggie said. "One, two." Maggie threw her hand out and opened another portal just as Emilia and Varsha dropped out of superspeed and hurled Magic Guy and Fire Mage through it. She dropped the portal again.

"Okay, who's next?" Varsha asked.

"Finger Guns should be in the next batch," Maggie said. "We know he can slow Airheart down, so getting him off board is a priority."

"Discus," Emilia said. "Near as I can tell, he's the only ranged fighter they have left."

"Right," Maggie said. "Airheart takes Finger Guns, Delta V takes Discus. You ready?"

Emilia and Varsha both nodded.

"Three, two, one, go!" Maggie said. "One, two." She opened the portal again, just in time for Emilia and Varsha to toss Discus and Finger Guns through.

"That leaves Tough Guy, Irish, the two unknowns and the three Civies," Emilia said.

"Let's call Irish Shillelagh," Maggie said.

"Works," Emilia said. "So, who next, the UnSubs, or Tough Guy and Shillelagh?"

"I'd say the UnSubs," Maggie said. "Without knowing their power set, they're the biggest potential threat."

"I agree," Nomi said. "UnSubs first, then the melee fighters."

"Right. Aether, on your mark."

"Three, two, one, go!" Maggie said. "One, two." She opened the portal again, and Emilia and Varsha tossed the last of the Yakuza and Ragusa crime family members through the portal before Maggie closed it.

Maggie's attention was pulled back to the Unitarium.

"I can't believe this," Hastings said. "You people are supposed to be competent."

"Shut up," Tough Guy said.

"They're out here swatting you like flies," Hastings said.

"Shut your mouth," Shillelagh said, before turning to Tough Guy. "We need to get out of this corridor."

"No shit," Tough Guy said.

"They're going to move," Maggie said.

"Then let's do this," Emilia said.

"Three, two, one, go!" Maggie said. She gave a quick two count, then opened the portal. Emilia and Varsha tossed Tough Guy and Shillelagh through.

"Hastings and Fairchild next. Three, two, one, go!" Maggie said before anyone could argue. She knew the others might want to go for Garrett first, but after what she'd seen earlier, she wasn't sure Emilia and Varsha could handle Garrett. If he could really move in Planck time, it might come down to her against him. She opened the portal after a two count, and Hastings and Fairchild went through. Maggie closed the portal.

"That just leaves Whitehall," Emilia said.

"Yeah," Maggie said. "I'll get this one."

"Okay," Emilia said. "But I'll go with you."

"I've got it," Maggie said.

"Maybe," Emilia said, "but you haven't finished your training yet, and I'm in command, so I'll go with you."

"Okay," Maggie said. "But we don't know his power set, other than that he's fast. Be careful."

"I will be," Emilia said. "You open the door, I'll walk him through."

"Right," Maggie said. "Let's finish this."

Maggie and Emilia both took off down the corridor. Emilia was faster than Maggie was with a body, so she stepped into the Aether to keep up. As they rounded the last corner and came face to face with Garrett, Maggie dropped out of the Aether and conjured the fold portal as Emilia rushed down the corridor to knock Garrett through.

For a moment, Maggie thought it would work. She thought this would all be over, and they could go home, but then Emilia reached Garrett and slowed down to grab him so the sudden acceleration didn't turn him into a cloud of chunky Garrett soup. Maggie watched in horror as Garrett split into two identical copies of himself, one appearing on Emilia's right, and one on her left. They both turned and punched her, catching her helmet between their fists. The helmet shattered like an egg thrown at a concrete wall, and Garrett's fists slammed into the side of her head. Emilia stopped for a moment, then stumbled back a few steps.

"Ow," she said, before her legs buckled.

Maggie teleported across the distance between them, scooped her up, then teleported back to where the others were.

"Airheart's down," she said as she laid Emilia on the deck. Varsha dropped down next to her.

"What happened?" Varsha asked.

"Two impacts, one from each side of the head. Crushed her helmet. She stumbled, said ow, then passed out," Maggie said.

"Fuck," Varsha said. "How the fuck...she's fucking Airheart."

"I don't know," Maggie said. "What do you need?"

"A fucking MRI," Varsha said as she checked Emilia's vitals. "Head injuries are bad. Especially on metas. She could have a brain bleed, and there's nothing we could do to stop it."

Maggie knelt and expanded her senses, focusing on Emilia's head, on every detail. She pictured it, the skull, the brain, the blood vessels, and the reality came into focus.

"I'm not sensing any brain bleeds," Maggie said. "Multiple skull fractures though."

"Fuck," Nomi said. "How the fuck do you fracture the skull of someone who once knocked a Kaiju out by headbutting it?"

"I don't know," Maggie said.

"We need to get her to Igeza," Ashley said. "She can heal her."

"Okay," Maggie said. She opened the fold portal again and activated her comm. "DMA command. I need a current location on Igeza and Transistor!"

"One moment," a voice said. "I have them at the Fulton Country Georgia US Marshals' station."

"Thanks. Tell them they have injured inbound. Then tell Secretary Banks that Task Force Omicron has asked for the Phi Sigma contingency," Maggie said. "Aether out."

"Roger. DMA command out."

Maggie dropped the portal, and waved her hand, opening a new portal.

"Varsha, go," Maggie said. Varsha didn't wait. She scooped Emilia up and rushed through the portal. Maggie turned to Nomi.

"The rest of you, too," she said.

"No," Nomi said. "You need backup."

"Backup is on the way," Maggie said. "Focus and Scatter will be here in ten minutes. I know Garrett. I can stall him for that long," Maggie said. "Go. I've got this."

Nomi stared at her for a couple of seconds before nodding.

"Cinderella, Nexus, through the portal."

Ashley and Hannah didn't argue. Nomi lingered for a moment, but then turned and walked through as well. Maggie closed the portal, then took a deep breath and teleported to the habitat module. Once she was there, she teleported again, this time, leaving behind her spacesuit and reappearing next to it in her normal superhero costume without the mask. She walked down the length of the habitat to the bathroom, looked in the mirror, and made another change. Her scars reappeared, covering the side of her face. She wasn't sure what she was about to do was a good idea, but if Garrett was powerful enough to take down Airheart, then she needed every edge she could get.

She stepped into the Aether again and rushed back to the corridor where they had fought the Unitarium. Garrett was gone, but she opened her senses up, stretching them out until she found him a few corridors away in the direction of the Artifact. She dropped out of the Aether in front of him.

"Hey, Garrett," she said.

"You!"

"In the flesh."

"You're supposed to be in a coma."

"Turns out your little science experiment had unexpected consequences for both of us."

"You don't know what the fuck you're talking about."

"Sure I do," Maggie said. "You were running the space fold experiment for Hastings. Except, he fucked up. He forgot to account for the expansion of the universe. Tell me, did he blame you for his fuck up?"

"Of course he did," Garrett said. "And the fucking High Guard figured out it was me in the lab somehow, so I couldn't just go back to my life. Everyone thought I was dead."

"You could have come forward," Maggie said.

"And what?" Garrett asked. "Admitted I'd been experimenting with stolen alien technology? Spent the rest of my life in prison?"

"The DMA would have offered you a deal if you flipped on the Unitarium."

"Are you insane?" Garrett asked. "The Unitarium would kill me."

"The DMA could protect you."

"Bullshit," Garrett said. "The Unitarium has people inside the DMA. They have people inside the MERTs. They have people inside the Marshals. They're fucking everywhere."

"If the Unitarium had that kind of reach, I wouldn't be here. The DMA sent us to stop you."

"God, you're an idiot," Garrett said. "Always have been."

"Yeah," Maggie said. "Maybe I am. But you don't want to be a supervillain. Come with me. Talk to the DMA. They can help you."

"Help me what?" Garrett asked. "My life is over. I'll never get my degree. Sierra will never speak to me again. Everything I ever wanted is gone."

"So, what?" Maggie asked. "You're just going to give up?"

"What do you know about it?"

"A hell of lot more than you," Maggie said. "I was on track to be an astronaut when the invasion happened. One minute, I had everything I wanted. The next minute, my parents and my brother were dead, I was crippled and burned, and any hope I ever had of being an astronaut was gone. You know what I did? I picked myself up, I got a degree, I went to work designing engines for NASA. My life was over, so I built a new one."

"Yeah, and you spent all your time feeling sorry for yourself."

"I never said it was easy," Maggie said. "And I never said I didn't feel sorry for myself. I had bad days, I had bad weeks, but so does everyone. I got through it, and you can too. There are people who will help you."

"I don't want their help. I don't want to be a fucking charity case like you."

Maggie stared at Garrett for a moment, thinking back to that day before the accident when he'd come to her office. The day his resentment had finally boiled over and he'd almost attacked her. She played it over in her mind and realized that she was the wrong person to help him. That he would never accept help if it came from her.

He couldn't because he'd pushed all his insecurities onto her. Maggie had spent so long being hurt because Sierra didn't love her that she never noticed that Garrett felt like he was the charity case. All the things he'd called her, a cripple, a diversity hire, a charity case, it was because he felt like a fraud, and he'd pushed that on to her because he resented her for having the closeness with Sierra he'd never quite managed, for having the knack for science and the intuition he lacked.

He was jealous of her.

If it wasn't so sad, she would have laughed at the irony of it. She considered waiting for Focus and Scatter, but as soon as they showed up, she would lose any chance to get him off the ship, so she decided to make one last attempt to avoid what was about to happen.

"I don't want to fight you, Garrett. This is over. The Unitarium members are in DMA custody. Hastings and Fairchild are with them. They *will* give you up to save their own asses. Save yourself. Surrender. Cooperate. Let Hastings be the one who gets fucked over for a change."

"You, fight me?" Garrett asked. "I just put down Airheart, for fuck's sake. You think I can't kick your crippled ass?"

Maggie blinked into the Aether for a split second, and when she returned, her scars were gone.

"Not crippled anymore," she said. "You know the kind of power you got from the accident. You really want to see what kind I got?"

Garrett smiled.

"Yeah," he said. "Yeah, I think I do."

"Fine," Maggie said. "But not here."

"Why not?"

"Because this ship is a giant bomb hanging over the whole fucking planet," Maggie said. "You want to fight me? Fine. You want to give me the ass kicking you've been dying to give me since Sierra dumped your pathetic ass, fine."

Maggie waved her hand, opening a portal back to Earth.

"There," she said. "A nice, abandoned strip of land in Wyoming where no one will bother us."

"All right," Garrett said. He turned and walked through the portal. Maggie followed. Once she stepped through, she dropped the portal and took a deep breath.

"You ready?" Garrett asked.

"Do you care?" Maggie asked.

"Not really," Garrett said, and suddenly there were two of him, one racing at her from each side. Maggie stepped into the Aether and watched as both Garretts came to a stop and looked around, trying to find her. After a couple of seconds, the two of them snapped back together, like there was a limit on how long they could stay apart. Maggie filed that little tidbit away and dropped out of the Aether behind him.

"Is that the best you can do?" she asked.

He spun and tried to punch her, but Maggie just teleported behind him again.

"Well, this is off to about as good a start as you tanking a dungeon," Maggie said.

Garrett spun and lunged at her, and she teleported ten feet to his left.

"Jesus fuck, Garrett. You can't land a single punch on a poor little crippled girl. How pathetic is that?" she asked.

He screamed, and this time, four copies appeared and rushed her. Instead of teleporting away, she slowed her personal time down, watching as they came at her in slow motion as she squeezed the place that held her body together as tight as she could. She waited until the last second and ducked, driving a punch into the gut of each of the four Garretts as hard as she could, sending all of them sailing back through the air away from her.

She teleported thirty feet to the side, and watched as the Garretts fell, but before they could hit the ground, they all snapped back together, and he landed in the spot she'd been occupying and spat out a mouth full of blood.

"Is that the only trick you've got?" she asked. Garrett looked up at her as blood dribbled down his chin.

"No," he said. He raised his hands and thrust them out. Maggie felt time slow down space time rippled around her and Garrett folded space. It wasn't a strong enough fold to knock her out of her body, but she could feel the out of sync times on both sides of the fold. It collapsed almost as quickly as it opened, and a beam of gamma shot out from the collapsing fold. Time seemed to snap back to normal as a blast of searing heat slammed into her.

Maggie staggered back, looking down at the burns spread across her arms and chest. Horrific, bloody burns. Lethal burns, if she had still needed her body to survive. She looked up at Garrett, who was staring at her with a look of vicious satisfaction on his face.

"Die, you bitch," he snarled.

Any sympathy, any pity she might have left for him vanished along with her body as she stepped into the Aether. She came out next to him, squeezing as hard as she could, with her personal time bubble sped up as fast as it would go as she drove a fist into his face. She expected the sound of cracking bone, but instead, he split into three duplicates of himself, each tumbling across the prairie before the three of them snapped back into one. She didn't give him a chance to regroup, though. She teleported next to him and drove a palm strike into his chest, knocking a duplicate out of his back, then she teleported again and hit the duplicate so hard it knocked another one out to the side.

She teleported again and again, hitting him each time, and each time she did, he split into more and more duplicates, until there were twenty Garretts. She had her arm pulled back to make number twenty-one, when whatever time limit there was expired, and all of them snapped back together with so much force a sound like a sonic boom rang out across the prairie. Garrett, whole once again, fell to the ground, covered in cuts and bruises.

Maggie walked over to him.

"Surrender," she said. Garrett looked up at her, glaring out of bloodshot eyes.

"Fuck you," he said.

Maggie expanded her senses, letting herself take in everything about him. Everything. She went down past the cellular level, past the atomic, all the way down to every single quantum mechanical detail. Time slowed to a stop as, for the first time ever, the world slipped into Planck scale time without her leaving her body. She examined him for what seemed like hours, or days of relative time, until she found what she was looking for. The thing inside him that had changed. The place where his connection to the quantum membrane was different than that of a normal human.

She studied it, learned everything about it until she understood exactly how it worked. Then, she let time start again so she could reach down, grab him, and pull him into the Aether with her. She carried him with her across the country as she returned to the Shiro with just a thought, arriving in the medical area. Then she reached inside of him, took hold of the thing that had changed him, that had given him his powers, and she tore it loose, letting it vanish into nothing as the Aether itself absorbed it, before she slowly and meticulously put him back together.

The two of them dropped out of the Aether, Garrett on a gurney, broken and beaten and barely able to move, and Maggie standing next to him, her hand on his chest. She let go of him and stepped back as Doctor Sanchez rushed forward to tend to his wounds. Then she turned and walked away, leaving him there, powerless, to face the consequences of the choices he'd made.

Chapter Thirty-Three

MAGGIE SMILED TO HERSELF as she lay on Varsha's bed and watched Varsha playing with Maxine. Varsha was pulling a catnip mouse on a string across the bed, and Maxine kept trying to pounce on it, only for Varsha to pull it away at the last moment. It was one of those fleeting moments that was so perfect, so peaceful and wonderful that you wished it could last forever. Especially after the last couple of days.

It had been forty-eight hours since the fight on the Olympus. In that time, the DMA had made almost fifty arrests. Hastings, predictably, had folded like a cheap suit the moment he woke up in custody. He'd given up everyone he knew who was involved in the plot, along with the location of the last Space-Fold Generator. The UN was working with the DMA to set up permanent security and research teams aboard the Olympus. The former because no one could be sure the Unitarium didn't have the plans for the Space-Fold Generator, the latter because now that they had easy access to the Olympus, there was no reason not to.

Well, aside from the possibility of accidentally creating a bunch of insanely powerful metahumans.

Anika had been able to put Emilia's injury right with her healing abilities. Banks had made a few grumpy noises about them breaking quarantine, but in the end, had admitted they'd done the right thing, given the circumstances.

That should have been the end of it, but Maggie couldn't help but feel like more trouble was coming. The Unitarium had come out in a big way with all of this, and she doubted they would just skulk back into the shadows. Still, that was a problem for another day. The people who had destroyed her and Sierra's lives and killed so many people would never see the outside of a jail again, and she and Sierra, along with everyone else who's world had been turned upside down, were free to make a new start.

Varsha looked up at the sound of a knock on the door, which was enough of a distraction for Maxine to finally sink her claws and fangs into the catnip mouse.

"Who could that be?" Varsha asked. Maggie had her suspicions. She could only think of one person who would knock instead of just calling on the comms. She extended her senses, and sure enough, Sierra was standing at the door.

"It's Sierra," she said.

"Oh," Varsha said.

"I'll be back," Maggie said as she got up. She headed out to the living room and opened the door.

"Hey," she said.

"Hey," Sierra said. "Can we talk?"

"Of course," Maggie said. She stepped back, making room for Sierra to come in. Sierra stepped into the apartment and Maggie closed the door, then led her over to the living room and dropped down on the sofa. Sierra sat next to her.

"What's up?"

"I had a long talk with Nomi today about my future," Sierra said. "I thought maybe I should let you know what we decided."

"I don't think I like the sound of that," Maggie said.

"I don't think you will either," Sierra said. "But I've been doing a lot of thinking about what you said, about how maybe we don't have the healthiest of relationships. I think maybe you're right."

"Sierra—"

"No, let me finish," Sierra said.

Maggie nodded.

"I know you're with Varsha, and I want to be happy for you, I really do, but I'm not, and seeing the two of you together every day hurts. You can understand that, right?"

"Yeah," Maggie said. Of course she could. She'd lived it for six years.

"Nomi said that Hashimoto Enterprises had written SCSU a hefty donation check to go towards the rebuilding effort in exchange for all rights to my Quantum Field Imaging research and hardware. She was going to set me up with a lab here in the Shiro so I could keep working on it, but I asked if she could set me up in the Hashimoto Research Park instead."

"Oh," Maggie said as she thought about what that would mean. The Hashimoto Research Park was on the other side of town, nearly sixteen miles from the Shiro. That meant no more lunches together, no more popping into each other's offices to bounce ideas off each other. No more seeing each other every day. It was an idea that left a hollow pit in Maggie's stomach.

"I don't want you to think I don't want to be your friend anymore, because I do. You mean the world to me, Mags. I just...I need some space to get over you. You get that, right?"

"Yeah," Maggie said. "Yeah, absolutely, I get that."

"Good," Sierra said. "That's good."

"Just don't be a stranger, okay?"

"I won't," Sierra said. "I promise. I was thinking maybe...well, you know how Focus and Scatter have their brunch group, right?"

"Yeah."

"I was thinking maybe we could do that. You and me. Brunch every other week or something."

"I'd like that," Maggie said.

"Good," Sierra said. "And it's not right away, either. I still have to finish the tear down and rebuild of the imager as part of the investigation, so I'll be here another five or six weeks, but after that..."

"Yeah," Maggie said.

Sierra didn't seem to know what to say after that, and for her part, neither did Maggie, so silence filled the room, becoming awkward, then oppressive, until finally, Sierra couldn't take it anymore.

"I should go," she said.

"No," Maggie said. "I..."

"Maggie, I should go," Sierra said. She stood up, and Maggie did the same.

"Can I have a hug before you go?" Maggie asked.

"Of course," she said. Sierra held out her arms, and Maggie pulled her into a hug and held on for dear life, until tears threatened to spill down her cheeks.

"This isn't goodbye," Sierra said. "I just...I need to figure myself out. Who I am on my own. Then, maybe I can figure out this whole sexuality thing."

"Well, when you do start looking, I happen to know a very eligible dragon," Maggie said, which made Sierra laugh.

"Let me figure out if I'm gay or bi first," Sierra said. "I'm not quite ready to jump the species barrier."

"Okay," Maggie said. She turned and pressed a kiss to Sierra's temple. "I love you."

"I love you, too," Sierra said before she let go. "Now, see me out, then go back to that girlfriend of yours."

* * * *

Maggie dropped back onto Varsha's bed with a heavy sigh.

"That bad, huh?" Varsha asked.

"Sierra asked Nomi to set her up with a lab across town," Maggie said. “Something about needing space to find herself.”

Varsha shifted so she was lying next to Maggie and rested her head on Maggie’s shoulder.

“I can’t say I blame her,” Varsha said. “But I’m sorry. I know it’s going to hurt you.”

“I’ll live,” Maggie said.

“You better,” Varsha said. “I have plans for you.”

“Good plans?” Maggie said.

“Very good plans,” Varsha said. Maggie slipped an arm around her.

“Tell me,” Maggie said.

“I’d rather show—”

“Oof!” Maggie said, cutting Varsha off as Maxine landed on her chest, clutching a catnip mouse that was nearly as big as she was in her mouth. She dropped it on Maggie’s face.

“I killed it!” she announced. Maggie reached out and grabbed the mouse off her face.

“It’s a toy,” she grumbled. Maxine walked up her chest and glared down at her.

“I. Killed. It.”

“Someone is stoned,” Varsha said. Maxine looked over at her for a moment, then turned back to Maggie.

“Pet me!”

“Yes, your highness,” Maggie said as she reached up and started petting her.

“Well, there go my plans for the evening,” Varsha said.

“Nah,” Maggie said. “She’ll be asleep in ten minutes.”

“You think so?”

“I know so,” Maggie said, scratching behind Maxine’s ear as she lay down on Maggie’s chest. “You know, I never did thank you.”

“For what?”

“For giving me a choice,” Maggie said. “No...that’s not quite right. For...for making me really look at the choices I had in front of me. I spent a long time making bad choices for a lot of reasons, but you were the first person in a long time to make me stop and consider my options before I decided. I don’t think things would have turned out as well as they did if you hadn’t.”

“I’m glad I could help,” Varsha said.

“You did. You helped a lot. I just hope I can live up to the choices I made,” Maggie said.

“I think you will,” Varsha said. “But remember, you don’t have to do it alone. I'm here to help, and so is the rest of the team."

"You know, that's going to take a lot of getting used to," Maggie said.

"What?"

"Being a superhero, with a whole team."

Varsha smiled.

"Yeah," she said. "Yeah, it does."

Maxine chose that moment to let out a snore.

"Oh," Varsha said. "Someone's asleep."

Maggie smiled as she very carefully picked Maxine up and set her in the heated cat bed that had taken up permanent residence on Varsha's nightstand. Then she turned back to Varsha.

"I believe you said something about having plans for me."

"Yes, I did," Varsha said. "Yes, I did."

The End

About Molly J. Bragg

Molly Bragg is an autistic trans woman with a degree in Astrophysics and a love of storytelling. She loves science fiction, superheroes, and giant robots. Her hobbies include collecting Transformers, watching way too many crafting videos on YouTube, playing Dungeons & Dragons, and complaining bitterly about the way a certain comic book company treats her favorite superhero.

Connect with Molly

Email mollyjbragg@gmail.com

Website http://www.themollyjay.com

Facebook https://www.facebook.com/themollyjay

Twitter https://twitter.com/themollyjay

Tumbler https://www.tumblr.com/blog/themollyjay

Note to Readers:

Thank you for reading a book from Desert Palm Press. We appreciate you as a reader and want to ensure you enjoy the reading process. We would like you to consider posting a review on your preferred media sites and/or your blog or website.

For more information on upcoming releases, author interviews, contests, giveaways and more, please sign up for our newsletter and visit us at Desert Palm Press: www.desertpalmpress.com and "Like" us on Facebook: Desert Palm Press.

Bright Blessings

Made in the USA
Columbia, SC
19 September 2023